"Why would you ca

Copyright

To You Whose Reading This...
As I grow older, I realize that everyone goes through something.
It's how we get through it...
It's how we keep on despite the bullshit.
From my heart to yours,
Enjoy.
With Love, Nako

If you're interested in listening to Nako's thoughts on Is She The
Reason, check out The Passport podcast.

Introduction

"We in this together," Kadeem reassured the love of his life.

She now seemed unsure of this "ride or die" thing, but it was too late.

"Ten years will fly by," he said, more so to himself than her.

"I know, baby, I know," she tried to convince herself.

It was all fun and games until the FEDS came in and took everything they worked hard for. Contrary to popular belief, hustling wasn't easy. It required sacrifices, a lot of sacrifices.

Kadeem and Yara had been joined by the hip since high school. Love was an understatement when it came to their union. She was it for him, and in return, he felt the same way. When you saw Kadeem, you better believe you saw his bitch too. She was never far away. They did dirt together, traveled, stole, robbed, and hustled. He was more of the muscle, and she was the pretty face, but together they got shit done. And now their empire had crumbled, but still, they remained solid.

His mother promised to see about their three children, promising that she would do her best to raise them in their parents' absence.

Yara was a mother first before that street shit, and she wasn't prepared to spend time away from her kids, *let alone ten years*. But they had done the crime and now had to do the time. Ten years. Ten mother fucking years.

Money was funny right now. Everything they owned had been taken, and their accounts were on snow. Thankfully, they had a few stocks they could cash out.

Kadeem encouraged his mother to choose her priorities carefully and to spend wisely when it came to getting shit done for the kids. The children would finish up their last year at the expensive private school they attended, and next year would start public school. They were smart and humble kids but were oblivious to real life.

Kadeem and Yara hid them from a lot, but the news had exposed them. The kids had questions, and they tried their best explaining to the kids why mommy and daddy did what they did.

"Did you give Yanise her bear? She has to have the bear to fall asleep, especially when she knows we are out of town," Yara remembered as she turned around and asked her mother-in-law.

Kadeem's mother shook her head. "Baby, y'all will be out of town for a very long time." She hated to say it in such a harsh tone, but her daughter-in-law was in denial, at least that's how it seemed.

"Ma!" He knew that Yara's feelings were hurt by the revelation.

"No, she's right. Well, I want my babies to remain babies for as long as they can, and she likes her bear. Can you please make sure that she has it?" That's all she was asking of her mother-in-law. It wasn't much.

He looked at his mother, wishing she would stop giving Yara a hard time and just give her the damn bear to pacify Yara and give her peace. He loved his kids, but his wife had a special connection to their children. For goodness sake, she carried them in her womb for nine months. Her children were her world.

"Give us a second," he told his peoples, who had all rode along to drop her off at her new home. His lawyer told him that nine times out of ten she would be transferred in six months, and he had yet to share that tidbit of information with her. His wife was a rider, but she often panicked at news she wasn't expecting. Yara was a true Libra; she needed to know what was going to happen beforehand. Spur of the moment shit caused her to act out.

Her eyes danced across his face, trying to read him while all he wanted to do was savor this last moment. This moment right here had to last them for ten more years.

"It's going to fly by, baby," he promised her again.

She shook her head, not wanting to hear that bullshit. "It's really not, but okay."

"Give me a kiss, show me some love." He didn't have to turn himself in until tomorrow and was thankful that she didn't have to watch him walk through the gates. He could handle the separation; his head was already mentally in jail. Kadeem would stay focused and knock that shit out like a champ. As long as his kids were straight, he could do the time.

Yara loosened up and let the attitude go. "If we could run away, I damn sure would have got the hell on," she kept it one hundred with him as he held her close and planted a big kiss on her lips.

He laughed, "Your ass knows that you love shopping too much to be hiding out somewhere."

For the sake of her kids and freedom, she would have gladly given it all up. "Ten years," she said again.

He nodded his head. "It's going to fly by," he repeated.

Yara didn't want to hear that. She wasn't built for jail but could hold her own, plus Kadeem had already sent word to a few folks, and she was guaranteed to have protection.

"Do you think the kids will hate us?" That's what bothered her the most, her kids forgetting their beloved parents.

Kadeem didn't think that way. "How could they? We're going to be calling and shit. Stop thinking negative." He wouldn't have her in a doozy over nothing.

"What else can I think?"

He felt her blood pressure rising again. "We not about to do this. Not right now, okay? We can't…" He rubbed her shoulders, attempting to peace her.

"Let me get in there." She checked the time on her diamond watch.

His best friend wasn't in their conversation or anything, but he did peep in and say, "Homes, might as well take that now cus they damn sure not gon' have it for her when she's released."

Kadeem picked up her wrist and then took a glance at her ears, wondering what the fuck she was thinking. He motioned to the almost two-carat diamond earrings in her ears. "Take them off too."

Yara removed her jewels and handed them over. "I love you."

He kissed her again. "I love you so much more, baby."

She would hold on to that last declaration forever. They shared that kiss for what seemed like infinity until his mother nudged him. "Let her go." The time had passed for her to turn herself in to the authorities.

Yara held onto him, refusing to do this. She couldn't. "Let's take the kids and-"

Kadeem shook his head. "Stop that shit. We talked about this. Toughen up." He wouldn't have her lose it in front of everyone.

"I can't. Kadeem, I can't go to jail!" she cried. Tears, boogers and snot covered her face.

The sight was heartbreaking to watch, and his mother turned around and headed for the car. She had warned him when they met many moons ago that she was too slow for him, that he would break her heart. And what did the nigga do? Marry her and drag her into his hell. Yara wasn't from the streets, but for him, she would do whatever, and look where it landed her.

"Yara!" he shouted her name.

"Ma'am." The officer came outside with two more guards in tow.

Yara shook her head and walked in the other direction of the jail. "No, no, no, please, please!" She wasn't prepared for this day.

"Yo, let them take her, bro. You gon' have to," his brother told him, although he knew he didn't want to hear that.

The hardest thing he ever did in life was to turn his back on the woman he promised to never walk away from. He had vowed his loyalty and his life to her. Her piercing screams and tears broke him into a million pieces. Yara was tazed for her failure to cooperate, and Kadeem cried in the back of his best friend's Escalade the entire way back to the city. He would have done four consecutive life sentences if that meant she could be free, but shit didn't work that way in the courts. The judge and jury were determined to prove a point with their case. And what a point they fucking proved. The only thing he told himself when it was his turn to get dropped off was, *"It's ten years. Knock the ten years out and get back home to wifey and kids."*

However, in some weird way, the stars ended up aligning in his favor… and not Yara's. Kadeem's planned ten-year sentence was barely 365 days before he was released for a discrepancy in the case. When asked about his wife, a star witness was the nail in her coffin. The lawyer asked Kadeem did he want to break the news to her or should he handle it. It would kill her to know he was free, so he made the decision to tell her; one day. And that fucking day never came.

Three years turned into five, and five turned into seven, and before he knew it, everything had changed. And nothing was the same.

Chapter One

"Don't you be afraid, I'ma guard you with my life." - Future

"Are you nervous?" her sister, Kamile asked her. She was uneasy, and this wasn't even her situation to be worried about.

Kamala twirled her engagement ring. It was loose, and she had been complaining to her fiancé for quite some time now. He wouldn't hear her until he looked at her finger and the damn thing was missing.

"Hello, earth to..."

She heard her. She could comprehend but wished her sister would stop talking. Her mind was racing... today was the day.

"What's wrong?"

The questions. Her sister was all over the place with the fucking questions this morning. She couldn't catch a break. She needed to think.

"I need a second!" she screamed and then stepped back from the latte that her sister made her. Tears flooded her eyes. How in the hell did this day come so fast? She wasn't expecting him to tell her so casually, *"Yara gets out next week, catch you later,"* with a quick kiss on the cheek before he was out of her bed and out the door. That's not how their relationship went, but on that day, she felt cheaper than a quick weave.

Her younger sister, who she had practically raised, didn't give her the second she requested. Instead, she moved closer to her and wrapped her arms around her lean frame.

"He loves you, that's not going to change," she promised her. Kadeem was like her big brother, and the past four years had been blissful because of him. He came in like a superhero and put the biggest smile ever on her sister's face that she had ever seen. Surely, he wouldn't give up that love for his wife, the convict.

"They have kids together, she has his last name…"

Her sister held her left hand up. "And what do you have?" The rock leaned towards the right. It was so damn big and gaudy. When he first proposed, she hated the ring. It was way too flashy and caused so much attention, but now she loved it. She had worn it proudly for the last nine months.

"I think I need to throw up." She moved her sister out the way and bent over in the kitchen sink and hurled up the chicken quiche she had for breakfast.

"Girl, get it together." Her sister rolled her eyes. Kamala was dramatic as hell if you asked her. Kadeem or the kids barely spoke about this woman, so why was her sister so worked up?

"Babe, you okay?" He appeared in the kitchen, dressed like the millionaire he was. "What's wrong with her?" Kadeem turned and asked Kamile.

Kamile shrugged her shoulders. "Uh, your wife comes home today," she said sarcastically.

He was the one nervous. What the fuck was she throwing up for? "Kamala," he called her name. Today wasn't the day. He had no time or patience to deal with her insecurities. "Why are you acting like this?" he asked her. She was now wiping her face with a kitchen towel, droplets of vomit were speckled on her white blouse.

"Are you going to take her back?" There was so much fear and worry in her eyes.

Take her back? She had the story wrong. "I can't take her back. It's not like that. Look, I gotta go, can't miss this flight."

"I thought you were picking her up from the airport?"

"I'm flying there and then we are flying back, then we going to my mom's house so she can see the kids."

"So, when will I meet her?" she wanted to know.

In his head he thought, *no time soon*, but instead he told her, "Let me get through today first." Kadeem didn't want to leave her in distress, but he really had to go. "I'll call you when I land. Watch her." He made sure her sister knew to take care of her today.

He grabbed his phones and headed out to the garage where his cars were parked. Kadeem smoked a blunt on the way to the airport. His heart was beating out of control, and the one person he knew would give him sound advice was now calling.

"You know your son," was how he greeted his father.

KK chuckled, "Good morning. You there yet?" Everyone knew what today was.

"Headed to the airport now." He took a deep breath as he got on the highway.

KK wasn't in favor of him not holding his wife down while she took a charge on his behalf and over the years, he and his son had several heated arguments on his wrongs. Now, he kept his opinion to himself and served as a listening ear for him.

"What do you think is about to happen?" Kadeem asked his father.

"Oh, you don't wanna know," KK chuckled.

Kadeem didn't know what to expect. There were so many lies being told. Yara was a calm soul, a firecracker if she needed to be, so he was unsure of how things would go.

"I do," he told his father.

KK sat up on the couch and lit a cigarette. "You lied to your wife. She's under the impression that you just got out of jail, not even a few days before her, when in fact you've been free for ten years."

"Nine," he corrected him.

"It doesn't compare to what she's been through, and not only are you a free man, but you're engaged!" It was a disaster waiting to happen. "She was crazy over you before she went in there, I can only imagine how that girl feels now."

"Yara is grown now, she's damn near forty."

His son was in denial. "Kadeem, what does age have to do with being in love and betrayed?" His dad had a way with harsh words.

"Why you gotta use the word betrayed?"

"If the tables were turned, what would you call it?"

η

Love was their glue, that and loyalty. He fucked with her on some real shit. He married her at twenty-one, and she had carried three angels for him. And not only did she carry his daughters, but them birds as well. Yara was the glue to his operation; they were a team. Everyone knew she was the one. She was the thinker, and Kadeem was a hothead.

He didn't think before he made decisions. Well, the young him didn't. He was chilling now, sitting on old money and investing his investments into more investments. He did a few things under the radar, but for the most part, the streets were behind him. He never wanted to see prison again. And the fact that she did ten years earned her the purple heart in his eyes.

Life moved slowly without her, and him meeting Kamala wasn't even in the plans. She was a breath of fresh air. They would wed soon after he divorced Yara.

He had to end things with her. It wouldn't be today, but once she was settled and back on her feet, he would tell her that he loved her and always would.

This is what he told himself in the car on the way to the airport as he went through security and was buckled on the plane. He attempted to convince himself that what he did was acceptable; like lying to his wife, making the kids lie to her as well, moving on, falling in love and dreaming and planning to have more kids with another woman. This was okay because she was in jail, and he was free. He told himself that he deserved new love.

Kadeem and Yara had the normal problems, nothing out of the ordinary. She was his Queen. He worshipped her and vice versa, there was nothing he did without her. Yara was his best friend. He wondered what she expected to happen, and if she assumed that things would return to normal. Kadeem called his mom on the way to the prison.

"Ma," he said her name slowly.

"Yes, Kadeem." Charlie sounded irritated. He knew she was angry with him, but he was a grown man.

"I don't need the attitude today."

"Did you get her yet, Kadeem?"

"On the way there, I just got in the rental. What the kids doing?" His three daughters, Yanise, Ayanna and Amina, who they called Meme, were now fourteen, eighteen and twenty-one, and they lived with their grandmother. They'd been living with her since their parents' arrest.

When Kadeem was freed from prison, he stayed at his mom's house for a brief period of two weeks and then got his own place, promising the girls every other day that he would get a house soon for all of them.

One month turned into three, and then a year later he moved into a three-story townhouse and still, the girls remained with their grandmother. As they got older, they stopped asking and caring if they lived with him. The girls wanted for nothing, so they let it go.

"Kids? These grown ass women need to move out, especially Meme." She wanted her house back and hoped that Yara came home and got on her feet quickly. Charlie was ready to live her life. She had one son and couldn't believe she had raised three more kids.

"They ain't going nowhere," he chuckled. His daughters were still babies in his eyes, no matter how grown they thought they were.

She swore up and down that she was ready to do her own thing. He wasn't hearing shit she was saying, Charlie loved her grandbabies.

"I can't believe it's been ten years already," she admitted.

"Time flew by." He wished he had more time to figure out what to do and how to say it, but there was no more time, the day was here.

"It's so easy for us to say that when we were on the outside while she was in there…" His mom was a realist much like his father, which is why they were still somewhat connected.

However, his mom's advice often fell on deaf ears. "We both did the crime," he had to remind her.

"She did that because she loved you." Charlie openly blamed him for Yara's arrest. Comparing him to his father over the years didn't make it easier for him to accept his wife's fate.

"Ma, not today." He couldn't hear the truth today.

"I ain't gon' sugar coat it for you. Yara deserves to know everything. Don't lie to her no more, Kadeem."

He hung up in her face. The GPS had taken him the long way, which wasn't a good thing because it gave him more time to think, and he didn't need or want more quiet time with his thoughts.

He stopped and picked her up a bouquet of roses. She loved fresh flowers, and he knew it had been a while since she had smelled some. Kadeem planned on giving her a few racks to get on her feet, and he wanted the girls to take her shopping and get their mommy back fly how she used to be. This could be a smooth process if God were on his side.

Everyone was on eggshells waiting to see how it went. His older daughter called. "You got her yet?" She was the one that remembered their mom the most and often kept in contact with her as much as she could.

She felt guilty about the lack of communication and visits with Yara, and he blamed himself for keeping her at bay, due to the fear of her slipping up and telling Yara that he was free and had been free for nine years.

"I just got here. She should be coming out in an hour or so."

"What Kamala saying?" she asked nosily.

"Threw up this morning, being dramatic."

Meme was too tickled by her father's *fiancée*. "She gon' have a heart attack when she sees how pretty mommy is."

And that was a fact. Kamala was cute, but Yara was breathtaking. "Your mama probably fat," he teased.

She shook her head on the facetime call. "I saw her last year. I told you she still fine, I put a hundred on that," she said with confidence.

"Take that hundred and pay your phone bill then."

Meme was in school but didn't want to be. She wanted to be a stylist, and he told her to finish school then they could talk about a hustler's ambition. He wanted his kids to have everything he never had, so school wasn't an option, it was mandatory.

"Do you think she will hate us?" Meme and her sisters were sat down about four years ago and told the truth. He couldn't hold it in anymore, and he told them that Yara wasn't to know that he was home because she would be mad, which was kind of the truth.

"No, baby, y'all are her kids. It will be me that she'll want to kill."

"Do you regret not telling her?"

Damn, why was everyone full of questions today? "She wouldn't have been able to handle it, I know her."

"Well, Charlie got food and stuff together, so text me when y'all get on the plane." She had shit to do today.

He hated that his mama refused to be called "grama." "You got your mom something to wear, right?" Yesterday, he gave her money to cop her some toiletries and one outfit for her welcome home party, which was tonight.

"Yeah, I got a shirt from Zara and three pairs of jeans cus I couldn't remember what size she was, ma got them hips, and some Gucci sneakers. She gon' be cute."

"What about her hair and stuff?" He knew the hood was coming to show love and wanted her to look her best.

"I got all of that." Meme couldn't wait to wash her mother's hair and give her a fresh wrap.

"All right, love you." He made sure he told his daughters that every time he spoke to him.

"Love you too, Daddy." Meme hung the phone up and said a prayer for her parents.

Kadeem sounded all cool, calm and collected, and she hoped that her mother didn't kill him. Meme would if she were Yara. Not only did her mom do a bid on his behalf, but she was coming home thinking that her man had been in jail as well. That was strike one. Strike two; he was now engaged to the intern assigned to their case, who was now a lawyer. If her mother were still the same Yara, she would know exactly who Kamala was. Strike three was; her dad was trifling as fuck. The whole situation was sticky, and she had already started smoking to prepare her mind for tonight.

Kadeem ended the call with his oldest daughter and leaned his head back and closed his eyes. How did this day come so fast? It seemed as if the FEDS had just busted into their home and snatched them out of bed.

Yara didn't cry until the day she was to turn herself in. Before then, she remained quiet and trusted him to handle the situation. He would never forget what she told him in the first letter his mom slid into a letter that she wrote him. For a while, that was how they communicated. Yara would mail letters to the girls with one for him, and Charlie would mail it to him.

She told him in the first letter that she would do it again, that she had loved him since she was old enough to know what love was. He was all she ever knew. And as long as she had him, foolishly, she could make it through her sentence.

Guilt hadn't bothered him until a few months ago when she called the kids and told them that she would be home soon and wanted to take a trip with them and daddy.

Charlie called him fussing saying that Yara was full of dreams, saying they had to get in the gym and get back right for the kids while the girls held the phone listening to her go on and on about everything she wanted to do as a family. When the whole time, Kadeem had been home. They didn't speak to him for two weeks. He was the bad guy.

Meme was the most affected. He had to apologize to her first, and she would get her sisters together.

"God, I'm sorry," he apologized out loud, hoping that He heard him. He didn't want any discord or beef. They could still successfully raise their children and co-parent.

Yanise was the youngest, but probably the fastest. He was sure of it with her smart-ass mouth. And she swore she didn't remember her mom at all, and Kadeem told her every time she said that, "Your mama loves you, girl. You were her baby."

Yanise didn't want to hear it and would roll her eyes behind her father's back. In her eyes, they both were deadbeats, in jail or not. Kadeem wasn't stunting them, and he used dollar bills to buy Meme and Ayanna's love, but hers couldn't be copped in the form of Gucci. Yara was coming home at the right time because she secretly wanted and needed her mama.

His phone vibrated. It was Kamala, and she had sent the longest text message in history. He scanned through it, looking for keywords, and there were none of importance. She was attempting to be supportive, but he didn't need her support right now, what he needed was space.

Yara had been gone for ten years, and there was a lot to be discussed. He needed his fiancé to understand that for a few days.

"Love you, call you tomorrow." He knew that him saying tomorrow would make her mad, but he knew that she wouldn't see or hear from him anymore today.

A knock at the window petrified the hell out of him, that's how he knew he wasn't living right. Out of habit, he reached for his gun but remembered that he was in a rental car in a desert city without his piece.

It was her. It was his wife.

Yara stared at him with a weak smile on her face. "I been out here for thirty minutes and something said, he's in that truck," she explained.

Kadeem got out of the car and came around to greet her. She looked at him with big, hopeful teary eyes.

"Damn, baby." And in two seconds, every single feeling that he didn't know still existed flushed like a tornado.

In the clothes that she was arrested in, she stood before him. "You look good, Kadeem." It had been ten long years. She had made it though. It wasn't easy, and on some nights, she thought of taking her own life but couldn't find the courage to do so. Yara was ready to put prison behind her and start life over with her family. Her kids and her husband is what kept her alive on the dark days.

"Me? You."

She didn't feel that way though. "My hair, my nails…" That was the one thing she was looking forward to doing; a wax, manicure, pedicure and a massage, oh, and a facial. Yara couldn't wait to be pampered.

"Are you going to hug me or something?" she asked him nervously. She missed her husband.

Kadeem walked toward her with his arms open. He didn't expect to feel this way upon seeing his wife.

"Missed you," he whispered in the crook of her neck as they shared a moment of intimacy. He could feel her heated tears on the side of his face.

"We're back together again, I dreamed of this day," she told him happily.

Chapter Two
"Show these disloyal niggas how to ball." – Tee Grizzley

The ride was silent. Yara was so grateful to be in air conditioning that didn't have a funky scent to it, she was soaking up everything.

"Hungry?" he asked her. They had a few minutes to spare before they headed to the airport.

She shook her head. "Not really." She reached over and grabbed his hand. Back in the day, they used to hold hands and ride through the hood, talking about all their plans and dreams.

Kadeem tensed up, and she felt it but swept the movement under the rug. Ten years was a long time to be away from the love of your life. She knew that things would take some adjusting to.

"Did you get a chance to talk to the lawyer?"

"About what?"

She didn't want to be on probation or house arrest. She felt as if she had served all her time and should be a free woman. "I don't want an ankle monitor or probation."

"Oh yeah, no house arrest, but the probation is mandatory. I'm on probation too." He almost slipped up and said he had been on probation for years. He sat up in the truck, breaking free of her hand and turned the radio up. "You smoked yet?"

All her questions were around jail and things that people do when they first got out. However, he wasn't in the same boat as she was. Kadeem barely got comfortable in that ma'fucka.

"Yeah, lil bit."

His phone rang. It was his father. "KK calling," he told her and handed his cell to Yara, who lit up when she saw Pops.

"What kind of phone is this?" It was light and sleek, nothing like she remembered phones to be before she went in.

"Answer the phone."

She rolled her eyes at him and pressed the green moving phone icon. "Is this the best father in the world?" she giggled into the phone.

His parents loved her like a daughter, especially KK. Yara was family, and Kadeem knew that him being with Kamala wouldn't affect how his family interacted with her.

"How are you, sweetheart? Hungry? I'll be up there next week to lay eyes on you."

Her smile was wide, and she kept pushing her hair behind her ears. It was way longer than he remembered.

"I'm fine, no complaints. Allah has given me another chance," she told KK. Kadeem almost swerved into another lane, and she eyed him. "Are you okay?"

"Allah? You're Muslim?" He was in shock. Not saying that they were perfect Christians, but they prayed to one God and one God only.

She ignored him and finished her conversation with KK. "Hold on, someone else probably calling Kadeem phone to talk to me." She knew the news had spread fast.

Yara was low-key famous in the hood. Not only was her beauty intriguing, but her personality was unmatched. Once you had a conversation with Yara, your life would change. That was the effect she had on people.

His heart thumped erratically when she asked him, "Who is K?" She answered his phone like she used to do back in the day. "Hello."

Kadeem could have shit on himself.

"Can I speak to Kadeem?" Kamala asked.

Yara looked at him. She wasn't dumb. "No, his wife is home now, you can't speak to him," she told the bitch and hung up, forgetting KK was on the other line.

"Damn, baby, you ain't even been out a week, you couldn't wait until I got home?" She was hurt, he heard it all in her voice. And the sad thing was, there was more, so much more hurt to come.

η

She didn't say two words to him, so the flight was awkward. The drive from the airport to the hair salon where Meme worked as an assistant was quiet as well.

When they pulled up to the curb of the salon, he put his truck in park, and Yara asked him, "Did John get you this?" She thought they went to jail dead broke since they used the little money the

FEDS didn't take on legal fees. So, when they landed and hopped in a new Escalade, she was confused.

He shook his head. "Nah, I came up on some money," he lied a tad.

She pursed her lips together and then told him, "I'm not going back, so you on your own out here."

"Yara, we need to talk."

Before she could give him her full attention so he could tell her who he fucked and why he fucked her, her door was jerked open. Instead of her reacting to her old hair-stylist, she screamed and held her arm up. She was caught off guard.

"It's me, girl," the woman apologized.

Kadeem was alarmed as well. "Why your ass ain't wait until she got out?" He was pissed because she interrupted their conversation.

"We saw y'all pull up. I'll be in there when you ready, girl." She closed the door, and it took Yara a while to calm her heartbeat.

"I don't do well with folks walking up on me." She was still in defense mode.

"What was it like in there?" he questioned, out of concern and curiosity.

"I'm sure you had it worse," she exhaled.

Kamala was calling again, and Yara saw the "K" on his phone and got out, slamming the door behind her. She was nervous about being back in the hood. She was convinced that someone had snitched on them.

Before they got knocked, they were all over the world with their kids in tow. She had been to every continent there was. The young couple was getting so much money that it was hard to keep up with. She had even stopped coming to the hood to get her hair done because the last time she did, which was almost thirteen years ago, someone shot through the window, and she knew they were gunning for her. So, she took a deep breath before she opened the door to the salon, and was surprised to see wine, fruit and a "Welcome Home" banner across the stations.

She used to be expressive, but prison had hardened her. To show her gratitude, she smiled and said, "Now y'all didn't have to do this."

There were only a few faces she didn't recognize. For the most part, she knew everyone and made sure to hug and thank everyone individually.

"Where is Meme?" she asked her stylist, Andrea.

"Back there hiding."

Yara wondered why. She walked toward the back and peeked in the break room, and there her oldest baby was.

Meme smiled and wiped her tears. "Mommy!" She got up, and they hugged for what seemed like an eternity.

"You are thick, girl. Oh my, turn around." She twirled her and was so amazed at what she and Kadeem had created.

"I'm so thankful you're here," Meme told her.

"Where are your sisters?"

"You'll see them later, daddy wanted you to get dolled up first." She escorted her to the wash bowls and told her, "I'm going to put a deep condition on your hair, I know you need it." Her mother's hair was always fine and long, and now it seemed longer, so she definitely needed a trim. She could see her brittle ends from the slicked-back ponytail she wore.

"I want some color too. You see those greys."

Meme shook her head. "Ma, you can barely see them lil' hairs."

It felt so good to feel hot water and not lukewarm temperature water on her scalp. Meme's stiletto nails scratched the dandruff and filth from her hair, and after the second wash, the sink was full and dirty.

"Okay, Mama, sit up. I'ma put you under the dryer so this leave-in conditioner can sit," she told her as she massaged the tea tree solution in her scalp and it tingled.

"Girl, what's that?"

"Some new stuff, you gon' love it."

Yara looked down at her bare fingernails, and her daughter noticed. "I got you, Ma, don't worry."

She wanted to cry but remained strong. For three hours, she caught up on the hood's gossip and was surprised that so many people had died or were locked up. All the lil mamas were now grandmothers, and Yara really enjoyed herself.

The first glass of wine was the only one she had. She didn't want to be tipsy when she saw her babies.

"Okay. Look, Ma." Meme had the pleasure of doing her mother's hair after she received a manicure and pedicure, and the make-up girl in the shop hooked her already thick eyebrows up and gave her a light, natural application of makeup.

Yara heard Meme whisper to the girl, "My daddy don't like makeup, so don't add too much. Keep her natural and pretty." She looked at her mother in the mirror and beamed with joy.

She was her mother's twin. Her whole life she had heard that she was the spitting image of Yara when she was her age, and now she could see it clear as day. Thankfully, prison didn't harden her mother's looks, nor did she age a million years.

At about five-feet, five inches, she was considered short to be thirty-nine, especially when she stood before her husband, who towered over her by ten inches above her head. Yara was mixed. Her mother was of Japanese, Spanish and Dominican descent, and her father an African American male with Native American heritage. She excused herself from the family many years ago and clung to Kadeem as if he were all she had. Yara stuck out like a green thumb in the hood with her slanted eyes, thin lips and full cheeks paired perfectly with her structured jawline that rarely needed concealer or highlighter when she was getting dolled up to go out.

His favorite feature of hers was her smile and the tiny gap she had between her teeth. You couldn't see it if you weren't all in her face since she smiled with her lips pursed together. Yara's hair was long and wavy when wet. Her breasts weren't big or small, they were a perfect helping in a man's hands when he squeezed them.

Her hips… she had hips that could make you seasick when she swayed them, coming and going, a blind man could see those thick ass hips. In jeans, a robe, a skirt… it didn't matter. She was heavy on the bottom which is how Kadeem preferred his women.

Yara mainly wore gold jewelry, and she was ready to put her shit back on. The wedding ring would be the last to slip on her finger, depending on what her husband was up to. Kadeem was on her shit list right now.

"Memeeee!" She held her hands to her mouth. She hadn't felt pretty in such a long time.

The salon grew quiet, and then Andrea said, *"Yara is back!"* She was happy that she made it home in one piece and couldn't wait to hear how she took the news of finding out about Kadeem.

Meme told everyone not to mention her dad. Everyone thought that shit was fucked up on his part, but that wasn't their business.

Yara moved her neck, and her hair swung down past her shoulders. Even with Meme giving her a trim, her hair was still long as hell. It was pressed bone straight with a middle part. For her to be turning forty soon, no one could put her past twenty-one. She looked divine.

"Okay, Ma, we gotta go, you can stare later," Meme said as she took her cape off.

"You called your father?" she asked her once they stepped outside of the salon.

Meme shook her head. "No, I drive," she chuckled.

Yara saw the lights on a white BMW coupe come on across the street and asked, "That's your car?"

Meme nodded her head. "Yeah, Ma, come on. We late."

Kadeem had a brand-new ride, and her daughter was driving a BMW. Did he have some money hidden in the ground that she didn't know about? She thought they were broke.

"When did you get this?" The wheels in her brain started turning. Something was off.

"It's old. I got it when graduated high school."

Yara remained silent as they headed to their destination. Meme's phone rang the entire ride, her daughter was popular.

"Do you have a boyfriend?"

"No, I wish I did though, but I don't have no room on my schedule for a dude. I work at the shop and go to school full-time," she somewhat told the truth.

She smiled at her daughter. At her age, she was already a mom and wife. "Stay focused, baby." Her children were better than her, that made her feel warm inside.

"I'm supposed to wrap this around your eyes," she told her once they pulled up to Charlie's house.

"For what?" She didn't do well with her eyes being covered and unaware of her surroundings.

"It's a surprise, Ma. Come on, be a good sport."

She wanted to protest but didn't. They got out of the car, and Meme came around and covered her eyes with two bandanas. "Okay, we about to go up some steps so be careful… I got you, Ma, step up," she instructed.

She heard whispers behind and in front of her. "Is that Riq I hear?" she asked of Kadeem's lil shooter, Riqardo, but known as "Lil Riq" who was basically her baby when he was younger.

Riq snickered, "Nope," lying through his teeth.

Yara was ready to take this shit off. "Okay, where we going?"

"All right, all right!" They snatched the scarves off, and everyone yelled, *"Welcome home, Yaraaaaa!"*

Charlie's home was filled with their old crew and family and friends; all Kadeem's because she had no family outside of his.

She looked around. Finally, the tears came once she laid eyes on her daughters, Ayanna and Yanise. She had seen Meme but not those two since she turned herself in. Tears spilled down her face as she went toward them and hugged them tightly.

"I missed y'all so much!" she sobbed terribly. Being a mother was an honor and one that she never took for granted.

Ayanna wept silently, but Yanise never shed a tear. Her mother was a stranger. She didn't know her at all.

Charlie couldn't take it anymore and went into the kitchen to pull some more plates out. They had a house full, and she didn't think she made enough food. Meme and Kadeem followed her, and he closed the door behind her.

"Why didn't you speak to her?" he asked his mother. It wasn't the time to be rude. His mother could be so unpredictable at times.

"That girl ain't aged at all," she said, ignoring her son's question.

"Ma look good and thick," Meme commented, happily. She was thankful her family was back together. Even if her daddy had a new boo, she had her mother again.

Kadeem stood near the wall with his arms crossed. He was conflicted, and his mind was racing on how things would play out tonight. He had to go home once the party ended. Kamala would slit her wrists if he stayed out, especially now that she knew Yara was home.

"She asked about my car. She seemed really confused."

He looked at his daughter. "And what you say?"

"That it was a high school graduation gift." Which was a lie because her car was brand new.

"Good."

Charlie shook her head. "Ridiculous," she mumbled under her breath. He had his kids lying for him.

"Is the party in here?" Yara asked as she slowly opened the door and stuck her head in.

Charlie smiled. "Come on in, baby, of course not. We trying to make sure we got enough food for you."

They always had a love-hate relationship, and it was more pity than hate.

Kadeem was too rough for Yara, and she had been telling her that since she was a young girl wanting to be up under him. She never listened to Charlie. Her only response would be, "I love him so much, Ms. Charlie."

"I want a hug," she told her mother-in-law.

They hugged, and Charlie kissed her cheek then eyed her son. She was sick of his ass and wished they would address the elephant in the room.

Yara rubbed her stomach. "I'm hungry now."

"Eat then, I'm about to go smoke," Kadeem said and left the kitchen.

The three women looked at each other, but no one said anything. Charlie fixed Yara a big plate of her favorite foods and gave her a glass of wine.

"Who is K?" she asked her mother-in-law.

"Huh, baby?" Charlie prayed over her food before she scooped up a helping of rice and peas.

"Some girl keeps calling his phone, he got her saved under K." She wanted to know who the girl was.

"Grama, Yanise said the music is too low," Meme hurriedly invaded the conversation.

Charlie knew. Yara could tell. And why was this *her* welcome home party and not *their* welcome home party? She told herself she was being dramatic, but really, something wasn't right. Everyone seemed so familiar with Kadeem, as if he had been home. This is what she observed an hour into being around her peoples. They all looked at her with the same pitiful eyes. What was she missing?

"I need a stronger drink and something else," she mumbled under her breath and walked off from a small group of people who were talking to her. She went back into the kitchen and poured a small glass of Hennessy. She used to love margaritas topped with some brown before she was arrested. At the window, she watched Kadeem and his people in the backyard, passing blunts and chopping it up. *Who was K?*

"Oh, my bad," Yanise apologized as she bust in the kitchen and saw her mother staring out the window.

Yara wiped her face of the tears that fell as she thought about her husband fucking around on her.

"No baby, you're good, come here. How have you been?" She wanted her near.

Yanise was her *boo-boo baby bear.* She couldn't believe she was almost fifteen-years-old. Yara felt old as hell.

She was uncomfortable around her mother but tried her best not to show it.

"Good, I guess."

"I'm excited to be home. Are you involved in anything at school? Meme hogged the conversations when I called, and you rarely came to the phone." She didn't want to harbor on the past though. "Anyway, I'm home now. What are you involved in these days? Cheerleading, track?"

Yanise shook her head. "Nothing, I just come home," she said.

"Oh, baby, we gotta change that. You have to stay active. What do you like to do?" She was desperate to build a connection and relationship with her youngest daughter. She wasn't too worried about Ayanna and Meme, they remembered her. Yanise didn't, and she could tell that she was uneasy.

Her daughter shrugged her shoulders. "I don't know, Ma."

"We can figure it out together. Your dad and I will get on it so we can get a house and be a family again," she told her with a smile.

Yanise looked behind her mother's shoulder. "He already got a house," she mumbled before walking out of the kitchen.

Yara heard her loud and clear but didn't ask her to clarify what she meant. After finishing her drink, she took the back door and steps into the backyard.

The whole crew cheered, "Look at you!" They were ecstatic that she was home.

"Riq, pass me that, you too young to be smoking anyway." She was still shocked that he was grown now.

"I been smoking since I was twelve, Kadeem just kept it from you," he laughed, pulling up his sagging pants.

"What's the point of having on a $500 belt, and your pants still sag?" she asked him.

"Too much money." He grabbed a stack of bills through the Levi pants he wore and smiled at her, exposing a mouth full of gold teeth. Riq had changed.

"Let me hold something then," she teased.

With no hesitation, he pulled out the stack and peeled off a few hundred-dollar bills until her husband warned him, "Riq, don't disrespect me, she's good."

"Am I?" She looked at him, wondering had he changed. *Were they still on the same page?*

"What you out here for?" He didn't discuss his personal business in front of his friends, even if he did consider them family. She ignored him and took a deep toke of the blunt that Riq passed her. Kadeem didn't hang with many, believing that quality over quantity was the best way to be.

"It's *our* welcome home party, ain't it?" Her eyes studied his, and he never looked away.

"Yep, baby."

"Time to get some money." John rubbed his hands together like Birdman.

Yara wasn't doing that anymore, she was done with the streets. She took a few more pulls. It didn't take much for her to get high because it had been so long. She handed it to Kadeem and blew the smoke out of her mouth and into his face.

"Welcome home, baby," she smiled at him slyly and walked out the backyard and back into Charlie's house.

Once the coast was clear, Riq commented on what had just taken place. "Bra, she know."

Steeno, Kadeem's other best friend, nodded his head. "I think so too. She was in jail, but shit, they gossip more than we do out here."

Kadeem shook his head. "She ain't got no friends, no family. The only person she was talking to was Meme." He knew without a doubt that Yara didn't know, and he wanted to be the one to tell her.

Nigel, the newcomer in their circle said, "It's something about her eyes…"

Riq laughed, "Nigga, what about them?"

"I thought she was gon' kill Kadeem out here."

Everyone knew it was a matter of time before shit hit the fan, and they seemed to be more worried and nervous than the actual person who lit the moth to the flame.

Around midnight, Charlie started cleaning up which was everyone's sign to bid farewell. People kissed Yara and dapped Kadeem up, playing the part of wishing the couple happiness and success back in the free world. Yara was high, tipsy and sleepy but ready to wash her ass. She had been dreaming of the day she took a big bubble bath and relaxed. No more hard cots, no more being on other people's times or watching her back for the bullies. Ten years of that shit… and it was now over. Tomorrow would be a fresh start, and she was eager to repair her life.

"Are we staying here?" she turned to her husband and asked once the house was empty, and the only people remaining were the ones she assumed lived there. Charlie, her kids and him.

"Uh, yeah, where else would we go?"

She was thankful for the party, truly she was. However, half of her was expecting a hotel room to unwind with her husband since it had been so long since they were intimate.

"A room?" she went on and spoke her mind.

Charlie and the girls looked at him, wishing he would just tell her the truth.

"Damn, baby, I ain't think of that. I was ripping and running to make sure the flight was in order."

"It doesn't have to be anywhere fancy, we've done that a million times. I'm fine with the Holiday Inn…" she told him. The fact that she went from the bottom to the top with him, she didn't need bells and whistles. They were starting over and rebuilding together.

Yanise shook her head and walked off. Her dad was an idiot.

Ayanna told her grandmother, "I'll be back in the morning."

"Where are you going?" Kadeem asked his daughter.

"My friend outside, we going to the hookah lounge."

Her baby would be graduating high school in May. "You can get in a lounge?" was all she asked.

"Look, you been home not even twenty-four-"

Charlie interrupted her, "Slow your roll now before you don't get to go nowhere."

"Why is she even going anywhere? It's almost one in the morning."

"Bye, Yanna," Charlie told her. She left, ignoring her parents.

Charlie said to Kadeem more than his wife, "I raise them how I raised you. She knows right from wrong, and it's the weekend." That was all she would say before she blasted his ass.

Meme was tired and had an early day tomorrow. "Goodnight, y'all. Ma, you can sleep with me if you want," she told her before going to her room.

Yara wanted to sleep with her husband. "You sleep on the couch?" she asked him.

"Yeah, until I get on my feet."

"So, you bought a new car before buying a place? We can't live here forever," she said, forgetting what Yanise had told her a few hours ago. The mixture of weed and drinks had her mind cloudy.

"I'm working on it," he lied again.

"Yeah, we got a lot to work on," she said before going down the hallway so she could take a shower.

Prayer. Tipsy and all she needed to pray because things were in disarray. One daughter was focused, so that was one load off her shoulders, her other daughter was too young to be in the streets, and her other child obviously had no one. And Charlie was too old and too damn laid back to be raising three girls by herself. She was thankful for what she had done in their absence, but now it was time for her to step up to the plate and get her family on the right track.

In the bathroom was everything she needed to wash, and she hoped that no one needed to use the toilet because she planned on soaking in the tub for hours and then scrubbing her body for more hours.

Yara used the iPad and turned Lauryn Hill on as loud as it could go. She was optimistic about readjusting and was also thankful that she wasn't old and outdated, she still knew how to figure things out and use technology.

She hummed to the beat as she undressed and ran the bath water, adding whatever soap she saw under the cabinet to the tub. It felt so good to ease her body into the body of water. "Aaahh," she exhaled loudly.

Yara reclined her head and closed her eyes. *Peace enter this home,* she thought to herself as she meditated on good things and all she had to look forward to. Prison was behind her, and she made a vow as she soaked her body not to dwell on the past but to press toward the future.

She was disgusted by the amount of built-up dirt on her body as she scrubbed her skin with the washcloth. Even behind her butt cheeks, she almost threw up at the old tissue and clumps of shit that was on the washcloth.

She hadn't had a bath longer than five minutes in so long. It felt good to receive a manicure and pedicure today, and tomorrow she was getting a wax. The hairs on her pussy were long and matted, and it would be painful but worth it. However, she couldn't care less about the bush in between her legs, it had been ten years, and she was still craving and wanting her husband tonight.

Kadeem made love to her so good the night before she turned herself in and the morning of. It was that one memory she held on to the nights where she had to masturbate to fall asleep. Many nights, she had whispered his name deep into her pillow, missing him oh so much.

He didn't have the sparkle in his eyes today, but she knew that it had been ten years, and it would return real soon.

Yara was satisfied with her bath and shower. She dressed in the new pajamas that Meme had bought for her and then cleaned the tub that now had a ring around it.

"Where is Kadeem?" she asked Charlie after searching the house for him. She was in the kitchen having a mug of hot tea, which was her nightly ritual.

"He had to handle something. He told me to tell you don't wait up." She hated lying for him and made him promise that when he returned he would tell her the truth.

Kamala, his fiancé, was blowing his phone up, and he had to get home before he lost the new… love of his life.

"On our first night home, is he back in the streets already?" she questioned, worried.

Charlie wasn't telling more than one lie, so she shrugged her shoulders. "I don't know, want some tea? How was the bath? You been in there for two hours."

She smiled at her mother-in-law as she took a seat across from her at the breakfast table.

"Good and the water was hot, I know I burnt my skin," she giggled.

Yara was an angel, still pure and peaceful. "Yara, you can tell me, were you okay in there?" she grabbed her hand and asked. Charlie tossed many nights wishing that things were different. If it were KK, she knew that without hesitation he would have fought tooth and nail for it to be him in prison and not her. Kadeem didn't do that. He didn't try if you asked her. She wondered what kind of love was that? Not only for your "baby mama" but for your wife.

"No, but for my kids I maintained," she admitted to Charlie. For her children, she couldn't give up or give in. For her kids, she took those beatings. She did what she had to do to stay alive.

Prison was evil, and the guards failed at protecting the inmates. What she hated the most was that even though they were considered criminals, it was still the guard's responsibility to protect the well-being of the inmates. The prison system was fucked up.

Her heart broke when she saw girls not even twenty-five years old come in to serve ten to fifty-year sentences for the dumbest shit. At one point, she got angry and blamed Kadeem, but then quickly let the thought go because he didn't make her do anything.

She wanted to be by his side, be the Bonnie to his Clyde. The only thing now was that she prayed she didn't live to regret the decision.

Chapter Three

"Tell me if my words are getting through, so I can stop explaining." – DVSN

Kamala couldn't function during work and should have taken the day off. Once she made it home, that's when she started blowing his phone up, wanting to see him, talk to him, hold him, kiss him, anything. She had to lay eyes on her man to be assured that they were still on the same page and that everything was still in motion, mainly the wedding.

Kamala loved Kadeem more than she could ever put into words. From his dark skin, pearly whites, beautiful smile, long beard, charming ways and rugged, thuggish behavior all bottled into one man, he was everything to her. And her heart went out to Yara in court when they were found guilty, really it did, but that was ten years ago.

Her and Kadeem meeting and deciding to date wasn't a part of a plan she put together, they literally just clicked. And he was the perfect gentleman. Kadeem was witty, he took what he learned in the streets and built her a better model for her business, figuratively.

She often confided in him when making serious decisions for her life and her brand. Kamala was eager to start life with him and couldn't wait until he gave Yara the divorce papers so they could proceed with the plans they made.

When she heard the garage going up, God had surely answered her plans. She texted her sister and told her that he was home, and instantly she responded with the praise hands emojis. Her close friends all knew what today was, and everyone was optimistic except her.

She tried to roll over and act sleep, but she knew he would know she was faking so she said, "What the hell," and turned the television off and instead picked up the glass of wine and downed it.

After a few minutes, she realized he wasn't rushing up the steps to explain himself, so she went to speak to him. As an Alpha woman, it was hard for her to submit to him and his ways. She had to tell him early on that she made her own money and had her own dreams and shit. She was all for letting your man lead the way, but she had a voice and an opinion too.

Kamala knew that she and Yara were different women from how he treated her at the beginning of their relationship. Now they had a perfect balance, and he knew what lines not to cross and vice versa.

"Hello, stranger," she said as she tip-toed into the kitchen where her fiancé was rolling a blunt.

"What up." His voice was low and raspy. She could tell today was long and was eager to hear all about it.

"I'm listening." She hopped on the island where he stood and folded her legs.

On a regular day, seeing her exposed kitty would have his dick at attention, but not tonight. His mind was elsewhere... it was on his wife.

"She's home, the kids happy I guess. Everyone showed love."

"How do you feel?" She needed to know where his head was.

He didn't answer her question. Instead, he stuffed the backwood with more weed. His pants were slightly above his waist, his gun that he shouldn't be carrying because he was a felon, was on the island along with two phones and some loose bills.

"Kadeem, you have to tell her."

"She ain't been home a whole twenty-four, don't get on my nerves about this. I will tell her."

"And then you got her answering your phone? Like, what the fuck?"

He rolled the blunt and licked it with his lips to conceal it. "Why would you even call and you knew what today was? That's stupid." He had forgotten all about that shit and was glad she brought it up.

"She used the word *wife*, like-"

He cut her off, "Like what, Kamala?" She was tripping if she thought that Yara wouldn't come home and assume they were still married. She went to jail a wife and came home a wife. What else would she address herself as?

"You're lucky I didn't tell her myself!" she spat.

He ignored her again and lit his blunt. Being high would help him go to sleep, and tomorrow before he returned to Charlie's house, he would smoke again.

"So, where do she think you at now?" She wanted to know everything.

"I left when she got in the shower, she was trying to get a room." He was faithful to his fiancé but knew that sooner than later, Yara would hem his ass up and wonder why they hadn't had sex.

"Wow." She shook her head and hopped off the island. Her ass cheeks bounced as her feet hit the floor. His dick jumped for joy, but he didn't.

Their home was massive. Her name was on the lease although he paid the bills and the rent. Kamala handled the domestic duties, and she did a wonderful job decorating the townhouse they resided in Chelsea, New York, a suburban area not far from her job.

The townhome was more of her idea because he preferred land and no neighbors. Kamala often joked to her friends that she felt like a housewife of Orange County when she entertained because of how their kitchen was designed. It had stainless steel appliances, white countertops and grey cabinets with light hardwood floors and modern furniture. She loved their home and the memories they had made and were making. She wanted them to make more and hoped he wanted the same.

He watched her walk away as he puffed on his blunt. Kadeem wanted to say something but couldn't find the words.

An hour or so later, his eyes were growing heavy, so he set the alarm and joined her in bed, skipping out on washing his ass because he was too tired to do so.

"You need to wash," she complained as soon as he flipped the comforter back to get in bed.

He went to do as she asked and he ended up gathering his thoughts under the hot water. He planned on taking Yara out to breakfast tomorrow and telling her the truth and then giving her half the money he had put up specifically for her.

If she wanted to move, he would help her. Whatever he had to do to make the process easier he would do. Now wasn't the time to bring up the divorce, so that would be the next step in a few weeks after he delivered one blow to her.

Kamala was sitting up in bed when he entered their bedroom with only a towel over the bottom of his tall and dark body.

"Why are you still up?"

She held her hands up, feeling defeated and confused about what was going on between them. "How I am to sleep when I don't know if these are the last few days you'll be here," she cried.

"Yo, are you crying?" He had no time or patience for her drama.

She hated how blind he was acting to what could occur. "Kadeem, your *wife* is home, why are you acting like she's not free?" she yelled from the top of the lungs.

η

It was three in the afternoon when the smell of salmon cakes and grits woke Yara up the next day. Her stomach grumbled, and she sat up and rubbed her eyes. She had slept with Yanise and held her baby close all night, so excited to be home.

"You're up? Charlie cooked. We go to the fresh market on Saturdays, you wanna go?" she asked her as she looked over at her mother.

"What are you doing?"

Yanise had a sketch pad in her hands and headphones in her ear that she had pulled out to speak to her mama.

"Nothing. You was snoring. You always snore?" She looked at her as if she had never seen her before.

"Tired, and your bed is so comfortable. Yanise, you don't remember me at all?"

The teenager shook her head. She looked just like her father and had his stubborn personality. She was a little chubby in the face, and her smooth chocolate skin and beautiful smile made her look like one of those little girls on the Just For Me perm box from back in the day. She wore gold hoops in her ears and a name necklace around her neck. Thankfully, Charlie did a great job with keeping up with the girls' hair, and Yanise had her thick hair in box braids to the middle of her back, and it was all hers.

"Not really, are you mad?" Her eyes squinted when she spoke.

"Of course not. You were young, and we shouldn't have gone anyway."

"What did you do?"

She didn't expect her to ask that. "Everything you're taught not to do."

"Do you regret it?"

Damn, she had a lot of questions. "Not sure yet, but I missed my babies every single day I was away," she told her the truth. And then she got out of bed. "Have breakfast with me," she asked her daughter.

"Already ate."

Yara left her alone and went to wash up in the bathroom before putting on one of the robes hanging up behind the door. She wasn't sure what made her search the cabinets for Kadeem's toiletries. She counted the toothbrushes, and there was only three; for the girls and now hers. There was no Axe or male body wash, nothing that showed her he lived there.

Yara went back into her daughter's bedroom and asked, "Last night you said your dad had his own house, what did you mean by that?"

Yanise looked at her and said, "Exactly what I said." She then put her headphones back in and went back to sketching on her pad.

"Yeah, we gon' get that mouth together," she said to herself before closing her door and then going to the kitchen.

Last night, she and Charlie stayed up for a while catching up on KK, the girls and a few other things she was behind on.

"Girl, you needed that sleep, huh?" Charlie addressed Yara once she entered the kitchen.

"Definitely. You got coffee?" she yawned. To be frank, she could sleep for another few hours.

"Yep, you hungry?"

She nodded her head and picked up the paper and looked through it. "Who's the mayor now?" She used to love politics and current events when she was home. Charlie answered her question and then sat a plate of salmon croquettes, grits and eggs in front of her. "Eat up."

"I need to slow down with the eating. I plan on getting in the gym to tone up."

"For what?" Kadeem came into the kitchen and kissed his mother's cheek, but she rolled her eyes at him.

"When did you get back? I tried to wait up," she said to her husband.

"Grinding, baby. You already eating? I was going to take you out to eat," he told her.

She planned on eating and then going back to sleep. "I'm free for dinner." She winked her eye and dove into the plate.

Kadeem sat down and looked at her tear the food up. "Yara, we need to talk."

Charlie didn't want to be around for that conversation, so she excused herself from the kitchen.

"Don't rain on my parade. Whatever it is, save it," she told him.

He couldn't save it though. It wasn't that easy. "It's a lot that you need to know."

She got up, and he grabbed her arm. *"Yo!"* Yara tried to jerk away, but he had a firm grip on her. "Ten fucking years, Kadeem, so whatever you about to say to me you think about that shit then try again." She had tears in her eyes as she stared him down until he let her arm go, and she ran out of the kitchen.

Two seconds later, the front door slammed. She didn't have on any clothes or shoes, so she didn't go far.

Charlie was at the door when he walked through. "That girl gon' try to kill herself and your ass too when you tell her." She saw it clear as day.

"No, she's not, Ma. Yara ain't weak." He knew that for sure. No one knew her better than he did. "If anything, this gon' make her stronger."

"I'm a woman, and I been there before." He wasn't being realistic. They were sitting on the couch caught up in their own thoughts when she returned.

"You got money? Money that we made together?" she asked him, her arms crossed.

He looked at Charlie and back at his wife. "What made you ask me that?"

"I want my cut." She was dead ass serious. Kadeem had new cars and nice threads, and she was broke and wanted her half. Nah, she needed her half. Yara needed a day to herself, and that required money.

"What cut?" He had his chest out, not appreciating how she was stepping to him.

"Nigga, you owe me! You got some money, I can tell. I know you, Kadeem, give me my half!" she screamed at him.

He hopped off the couch and yoked her up, holding her jaws in his bare hands.

Charlie yelled, "Not in here you not!" She had seen them get down and dirty with each other before and hated it every time. She didn't know where he got his anger problem because her and his father were both peaceful beings.

"Mind yo' business," he said over his shoulder.

Yara was no punk, and she tried to scratch his damn eyes out.

"You got me fucked up," he told her.

"Fuck you!" Tears spilled from her eyes.

"Don't you ever say I owe you. I don't owe you shit. I'ma give you some damn money, but don't come at me like that." She had clearly forgotten who she was married to, and he had no problem reminding her.

"Give it to me then," she told him after he released her and pushed her back against the wall.

He pointed his finger in her face. "You better watch your damn mouth," he warned her. They had never argued about who did what. They were a team; they had always been a unit. *Where was this coming from?* she wondered.

"I don't even know you no more," she wept.

"Baby, I don't even know myself," was his reply, and that was the truth. He was lost and barely remaining afloat mentally. He carried the burden of holding that secret from her, and her acting out like this wasn't making it easier for him to spill his soul.

He turned on his heels and went to the back of the house where his things were.

She was blowing steam out of her mouth when he returned, and Yanise stood there looking on at the madness.

"Here." A duffel bag full of drug money from the last drop that Riq did on his behalf was now at her feet.

He planned on only giving her ten thousand to get her on her feet, but she could have it all. Kadeem had more money, this wouldn't put a dent in his pockets. She felt as if he "owed" her, well here it was, the last job they technically did as a couple.

"What else I owe you?" he asked her, his feelings hurt by the words she used against him.

She ignored him and picked the bag up and left them in the living room to do whatever they wanted. She closed and locked the door to Meme's room and counted the money. Yara wasn't about to be sitting around for much longer.

Yanise told her dad, "You could have told her right then."

Charlie agreed, but she remained silent.

"Stay in a child's place," he scolded her before walking out of the front door, slamming it behind him. He was heated.

Charlie lit a blunt. She was stressed her damn self and was thinking about going to Atlanta to get away for a few weeks. "I'm probably leaving in the morning, baby," she told her granddaughter.

Yanise couldn't care less. She mumbled under her breath, "Have fun, chile."

Two hours later, Yara was able to find something in Meme's closet that she could fit, and she had Charlie call Riq to come pick her up. She was standing outside looking like a teenager when he pulled into the driveway.

"Hell you got on?" he laughed.

"Shut up. You can either drive me around or let me borrow your car to run some errands." She wasn't in the mood to talk or laugh with him.

"Drop me off on the block." Riq put the car in the park. "Wait, do you remember how to drive?"

She rolled her eyes and told him, "Boy, I taught your ass to drive." This lil' nigga quickly forgot all she had done for him.

Yara dropped him off on 14th and Broadway. Her first stop was the DMV, who gave her a headache with the run around. She had to basically yell through the glass window, *I just got out of jail and need my license renewed!*" Her nerves were shot.

After leaving the DMV, she went to a dealership and bought a 2010 Honda Accord for six-thousand dollars. It had way too many miles on it, but she didn't care. She needed something to get from point A to point B, which would be a job and home.

She told the dealership she would be back before they closed to get the car.

Thankfully, it was a cash deal, so they didn't ask her any questions about income or where the money came from.

It had been so long since she paid a car note. She and Kadeem normally cashed out on cars, and that's what she did today.

After leaving the dealership in Riq's whip, she went to the mall and spent two-thousand dollars on clothes. She got enough to last her for a while, knowing it would take her more than two-thousand dollars to build her wardrobe again. And honestly, she planned on living a minimal lifestyle now that she was legit. Yara was over the whole Gucci, Prada and Versace phase. She had it all at one point but when you go to jail, they strip you of everything, mentality included. None of those things mattered to her.

She spent most of her budget in Zara and Victoria Secret, buying bras and panty sets. On her list now was to get a much-needed Brazilian wax. Because they lived in the suburbs, she went to the first wax place she passed.

"Damn, I need to get a cell phone," she remembered after she parked. That would be the next thing on her to-do list.

"Who do you want?"

"The best," she told the Dominican woman sitting at the front desk. Yara slid her a hundred-dollar bill and took a seat on the couch in the lobby. You couldn't be cheap when it came to maintenance.

Clearly, the best was in high-demand because she waited almost forty minutes for the young girl to come out and wave her back.

"Undress, and I'll knock before I enter."

Yara removed her clothes and folded them neatly in the blue chair in the corner of the small room. Today was long, and she had way more stuff to do before she felt accomplished with moving in the right direction.

She was scheduled to meet with her probation officer on Friday and wanted to be fully prepared. Yara wasn't depending on anyone else to make sure she was straight.

The woman knocked, and she jumped. "I'm ready." She laid on the bed and covered her private parts with the white towel. She knew her pussy was a hot mess, and it would take the girl forever to get it back in shape.

"Whoa," the technician said as she lifted the towel. "First time?"

Yara nodded her head. "No, I used to get them on the regular, before it became a trend. I've been in prison for ten years, and in there we don't-"

She sympathized with her, "My sister is serving twenty. It's okay, I will get you taken care of. Lay back, where were you at?"

"Everywhere. They moved me a few times. I finished my sentence in Louisiana," she said as she took a deep breath. Yara hated being so exposed, she had her legs in a butterfly pose and knew that her pussy was in terrible shape.

"This is going to hurt," the young girl winced, showing sympathy for what was about to take place. She pulled out a bottle of spray. "This will help a little, and then I'm going to trim the hairs because they're very, very long," she explained.

"Can we turn some music on?" Yana asked, nervously.

"Sure." She went out to the hallway and came back with a white portable Beats by Dre pill speaker.

"Okay, mama, let's get started."

About forty-minutes later, Yara was a new woman. Her vagina was smooth, bald and a little red from so much activity. She had screamed, yipped and groaned from the constant pulling of hair and Lord Jesus, the clit area caused her to curse so loud she knew the entire building had heard her.

"It looks great. I should have taken some before and after pictures." She was pleased with her work.

Yara giggled, "No ma'am, but you officially have a regular client. I'll see you in five weeks," which was how often she got them back in the day.

"Sounds good to me. I'm always booked, so I suggest making the appointment now before you leave," she told her as she removed the gloves and threw them in the trash.

Once she left the room so Yara could redress, she looked in the floor length mirror and smiled at her body. After jail, childbirth and a few lost fights, she was still a good-looking woman.

Once back in Riq's truck, she headed to AT&T to get a phone so she could call Riq, not wanting to take advantage of him doing a favor for her. She wasn't sure if credit went away when you went to jail or not, being that the woman was having a hard time pulling her information for her to get a phone.

"I… ummm, I just got out of prison, do I need to call my daughter and maybe she add me to her line?" she whispered across the counter.

"Oh no, ma'am, you're good, it's the computers. They're sometimes extremely slow," she apologized.

Yara felt so stupid, and she vowed to stop explaining herself every time she went somewhere too.

Another hour had passed, and the woman gave her a tutorial along with a phone case and screen protector.

"And I can press this button and then my kids will see me?" she asked, surprised as hell at how things had progressed since she'd been gone.

"Yep, if they pick up, of course."

Once back in the truck, she "Facetimed" Meme twice and on the third time, Meme finally answered, but with an attitude. "Who is this?" The other side of the camera was black.

"Girl, your mama, why can't I see your face?"

Meme laughed, "I don't answer numbers I don't know."

"Lock me in," she smiled at her.

"Wow, you look… different."

Yara was relieved to hear that, today had been full of adventure. "Getting back to me, baby girl."

Tomorrow, she would look for a job, open a bank account to put the rest of the money up and find an apartment. She planned on being out of Charlie's house by the end of the week.

She was so tired when she got back to Charlie's that she heated the remainders of the brunch that her mother-in-law cooked, showered and went straight to sleep in Meme's bed. None of the girls were home, not even Charlie and thankfully, some things hadn't changed. She still had a key under the flower pot in the back of the house by the trash can.

The next morning, she was up bright and early, ready to start her day and so was Charlie.

"You still wake up with the sun," she commented as she walked into the kitchen.

Charlie turned around and smiled. "You do too."

Charlie was a beautiful woman, and back in the day, she couldn't stand her. Kadeem was relatively close with his mom, and she seemed to always dish out her unwarranted advice and a lot of tough love. In Kadeem's face and behind his back, she would tell her to keep it moving. She would warn her that his life was dangerous, and that she was getting caught up in the wrong thing. And no, she didn't attempt to run off every woman her son met, but it was something about Yara that drew her to the young, lost girl.

However, her opinion fell on deaf ears, and before anyone knew it, Yara was pregnant, and then again, and again. Then they got deeper in the game; together.

They got rich, then became wealthy, and still Charlie warned them both to slow down, move out of the city or start over elsewhere and as always, they laughed her off and ignored her.

When they were arrested, she was saddened and worried, but she was not surprised. Yara's hands were as filthy as Kadeem's, and they had to deal with the repercussions of committing crimes.

"I bought a car," she told her mother-in-law.

Charlie nodded her head. "Saw it last night, good for you, baby." She was happy that it wasn't taking her long to get the ball rolling on getting back into the swing of life.

She sat down after washing her mug out and sighed. Yara always admired the simple things about Charlie. She was a beautiful woman and never had to do much to showcase her beauty because it was true and pure.

She was mocha colored, petite and her long dreads hung past the top of her butt cheeks. Back in the day, they were multi-colored, and now she wore them black with the speckles of grey at the corners of her roots. Charlie wore two nose rings, one gold and one silver, and always could be seen with lots of bangles and necklaces around her neck. She moved with the wind, and you could never predict what would come out of her mouth. Everyone said she resembled Lisa Bonet, but Charlie Franklin would say, "No baby, lil' Lisa resembles me," with a wink of the eye.

"Thank you for everything, for raising the girls, for being there for them, I don't know where they would be if it wasn't for you." She was sincere. She didn't know where she would be without them either.

"They are a handful and now that you're home they need you, they need that mother's touch. I could never be their mother, and I never tried." And that was her being honest.

Charlie didn't lay hands on them, raise her voice or govern them with restrictions. She was a free bird, and so were the girls. She didn't believe in beating them to get them to listen. They respected her, and that was all she ever asked of her granddaughters. In her eyes, they turned out pretty good.

"I'm back, my only concern is Yanise, she's so…"

"You," Charlie smiled at her with squinted eyes. "Reminds me of you so much, Yara."

She rolled her eyes. "Now if that's the truth, we got a lot to work on."

"Yeah, you got your work cut out for you. She's a firecracker but sweet as hell."

Loud music could be heard near the window, and Yara was now alarmed.

"That will be my son."

"He's just now coming home?" It was going on seven in the morning.

Charlie's face went still, and her smile disappeared. "I'm going to go prepare for the day." Charlie excused herself from the breakfast table, and that told Yara everything she needed to know.

Yara closed and opened her eyes, blinking back tears. How could he? She had so many questions for him and today, on this bright and sunny morning, Kadeem needed to answer every single one, or there was a slight possibility her ass may be going right back to jail for attempted murder.

When he walked into the house, he didn't expect to see her sitting at the table with her arms crossed and anger vividly etched across her face.

"Who pissed in your Cheerios?" he tried to get her to smile, knowing that she was probably still mad from their conversation yesterday.

"What do I need to know about you that everyone seems to know and I don't?" She had one question and one question only. It was time to lay the cards on the table and deal with it.

Chapter Four

"You could have told me a change was gon' come." – Destiny's
Child

Meme was about to walk into the kitchen to get something
to drink. Her alarm wasn't set to go off for another hour, but she
got up earlier so she could get her day started.

Charlie stopped her in her tracks. "Go back to your room."

Yanise and Ayanna were behind her because they had to
get ready for school.

"My head hurting," Yanise complained.

"What's wrong?" Meme was confused.

Before she could tell them, she heard Yara scream from the
top of her lungs, *"You did what!"*

Meme tried to go around her grandmother, but she pushed
her back. "That has nothing to do with you." Yara needed to hear it
all today. "You can't keep protecting him, do you hear her?"

Their mother's sobs were uncontrollable.

Yanise got mad and went back to her room and slammed
the door.

Meme wasn't going any damn where, she was grown. And
Ayanna was just plain nosey.

"Is he going to tell her about Kamala?" They had only met
the chick a few times, and she was a cool person. The fact that

their mom had been gone for most of their lives, Ayanna didn't really have any loyalty to her, so she was okay with her dad's new chick.

Meme, on the other hand, wasn't with it. She didn't understand how a woman could be with a man who didn't even have custody of his kids. And her father was still married, and Kamala was aware. It wasn't as if her mama were sentenced to life, she was only given ten years, and Kadeem couldn't even stick it out. She loved her daddy up until she heard her mother's cry. Things had now shifted in their family.

Charlie's heart was thumping, and she told Ayanna, "Call KK."

"What is he going to do all the way in Atlanta?" Meme asked her.

"Call Riq." John was Kadeem's best friend, but he was probably still sleeping.

"For what? You act like she's going to kill him or something. She's not that mad." Ayanna was always talking back.

"Do what I said, lil girl!" Charlie wasn't the one to play with.

The whole house went quiet. Meme looked at her grandmother, and her grandmother looked at her, they both went dashing for the kitchen.

Yara was still seated. Her body was shaking, and her face was beet red.

Tears flooded past her cheeks.

"Y'all knew? Meme, you knew about this? You visited me and listened to me talk about missing your father, and the whole time he was home?" She felt betrayed by everyone.

Yara didn't expect Charlie to say anything, that was her son. She rode for her but knew that at the end of the day she wouldn't defy him.

"I was a kid," Meme said in her defense.

"Oh, you're not an adult today?" she laughed, but nothing was funny. She shook her head. "I knew it! Something never sat right with me. My roommate would request my files, and my dumb ass, I didn't even think to look at the case myself. I trusted my husband!" she cried. This was some bullshit.

"Where is Kadeem?" Charlie asked.

Yara ignored her as the wheels in her brain turned. She was putting so many scenarios together, so many pieces of the puzzle.

"Yara, did you-"

Yara pointed to the door. "Fuck nigga left, I didn't even get out of my seat," she told her in a dry tone.

Charlie breathed a sigh of relief. She closed the back door and locked it. "How did he tell you?" Charlie wanted to know.

Yara had nothing to say to any of them. "I need to get out of here." Fresh air was needed.

"Ma, he made us promise. He begged me..."

Charlie's eyes bucked. *"Amina!"* She couldn't believe her.

"Oh, I'm not supposed to know that?" she asked her mother-in-law.

So many secrets and lies.

Meme was crying, "Please don't leave us again."

"I didn't want to leave the first time." Everything she did was for her family, mainly for him. When he first asked her to come on board with her pretty ass face, she obliged, and then he used those love-sick eyes and that monster between his legs to pursue her. Before she knew it, she was knee-deep in the game right beside him. And those charges, yeah, she cried and complained, but she never snitched when given the opportunity to do so. She didn't even think about turning on her man. And this is what he does? There was nothing he could ever say to her again to make her look at him in the same light. He preached loyalty to her and didn't know the first thing about it.

Charlie reached for the phone to call Kadeem. There was no way you drop a bomb like that and leave them to clean up the mess. "He needs to come back. Y'all got three kids together and twenty years of love, you don't walk out on that." She was pissed at him, and now she was about to cry.

"Charlie, you should have told him that when he called you and said he was coming home early." She wasn't about to sit here and let her play her. Not today.

"First of all-" She was about to give Yara a piece of her mind, but Yara stood up and stuffed her hands into her pockets.

"Save it, please. I don't believe nobody in this house, y'all are liars in my eyes." She walked out of the kitchen and grabbed everything she had to her name, which wasn't much.

Meme begged her to stay, "Ma, please don't take this out on us." It wasn't their fault. They were only kids at the time, but the fact that Meme came to visit her and listened to her sound so drunk in love is what kept replaying in her head.

She had combed her hair the best she could, considering that she had none of the products she preferred to use because her commissary was low and her roommate, Miko, was released a few months ago and had always looked out for her on pretty much any and everything.

When they escorted her to the table, her whole body tingled all over. Seeing her offspring made this shithole so worth it. The time was moving slow as hell, but she knew one day she would be free and back in the arms of the man she loved and with her kids.

"Ma!" Meme was happy to see her mother.

They couldn't have too much contact, so she settled for the forehead kiss that she planted on her head.

"I love you, I miss you, how are you?" Yara bombarded her with questions as if they didn't speak at least once a week or sometimes twice a month, depending on if they were home when she called. The percentage of answered calls compared to unanswered calls was disappointing.

"Good, we all good, staying focused," she nodded her head.

Yara couldn't stop staring at her angel. She was gorgeous. "I don't know if you look like me or your father, seeing you makes me think of him so much. I can't wait until we're home," she said with a smile, but her voice didn't match her facial expressions.

Meme was so uncomfortable. Her father was parked outside. "Soon, Mama, soon."

Thankfully, the conversation moved along. And it was like that every single time.

When Meme got in the car, she busted out in tears.

"What's wrong? What she say?" he asked her, turning the music down and needing the conversation he was having with someone.

"She talks about you every time. I can't keep visiting her, Daddy. It's too hard, I'm not a good liar." She shook her head as the tears continued to fall.

"You gotta visit, your mama ain't got no real friends or family."

"Where is auntie Kara and her friends who used to come to the house?"

"Fake ass hoes," he mumbled under his breath.

"Meme, your mother needs you," he tried to get her to understand.

She shook her head. "I can't."

And after that day, the visits went from every month to barely twice a year, and now Yara knew why.

"Who is K?" she asked her daughter.

Meme looked at her grandmother, and Yara said, "Another secret."

"Why did you scream so loud then? What did y'all talk about?" Charlie needed to know because she wasn't as mad as she should have been if you asked her. And Kadeem left so swiftly, half of her felt as if he wanted them to tell her the truth because he didn't have the balls to do it.

"He told me that he was released earlier than me because of a discrepancy in the case and was scared to tell me because he knew I wouldn't be able to handle it."

Meme shook her head and walked off mumbling, "I'm done."

Ayanna was stepping in the shower, she had a test today and couldn't be late.

Charlie was speechless. He hadn't told her much of anything. "Did he tell you when?"

"A year ago, I guess. I don't know." She was still leaving. She was pissed.

"Let me call Kadeem."

She didn't have time to sit around and wait for them to tell her more lies. She put her shopping bags from yesterday in the back seat along with the money on the floor covered with a jacket.

Once she got in the driver's seat, the tears poured out. How could this be? How could he lie to her? And, everyone knew. The welcome home party was bullshit.

A tap on the window startled her. It was Yanise, headed for the school bus, but she had something to say to her mom.

"I'm coming back, baby. I just need a day to gather my thoughts, I'm still in shock at your dad-"

She didn't want to hear it. Yanise interrupted her and said, "Daddy got out of jail almost ten years ago, and he's engaged, Ma. They're still lying for him. I ain't gon' lie to you," she told her and walked off with her MCM book bag on her back.

Yara saw red. Blood. Murder. Death. Nothing attempted either. She was a shooter, a sharp one at that. She had bodies on her hands, their eyeballs had been jiggled in her palms.

"Ten years? How in the hell was that even possible?" she asked herself. Ten years meant he never went to fucking jail at all. She needed facts. Yara had to see some proof, and she only trusted one person.

Before they even went to trial, no one wanted to be around her. They avoided her like the plague. She was once the chick with all the friends. As long as she was up, they were down, but as soon as she and Kadeem got busted, her "girls" were nowhere to be found. She didn't know what a support system was.

Thankfully, the first few years of her being in prison she had the same roommate, Miko. The wife of a famous rapper, Miko was also a member of The Underworld. Miko never understood her case, and Yara didn't know much to tell her about the damn case anyway.

She pulled out of the driveway on a mission. Yara needed her help to get to the bottom of what her daughter had just told her.

And if it was the truth, she had no idea on how she would handle the situation.

The devastating part is the engaged didn't affect her yet. All she heard was *"Got out of jail almost ten years ago."*

η

Charlie didn't come to the hood. And because she rarely got in her son's mix, she tended to stay on her "side of town."

Kadeem wasn't in the streets but still hung with the folks who were, so she knew where to find him, or so she thought. He wasn't in the normal spots he normally hung at.

She called Meme, who had an attitude, but she couldn't care less. She was just as bothered as she was about the situation. "Send me your dad's address," she said without even saying hello.

Meme hung the phone up, and before Charlie could call her back to check her, she had a text message with the address. Charlie would deal with her later, right now she needed to talk to her son.

Twenty minutes later, she was pulling up to a British-styled townhome and rolled her eyes. Her son was living lavish, and there was plenty room for his children.

She took a deep breath as she got out of her car and closed the door, not bothering to lock the doors. Nobody was breaking into houses over in this area.

She rang the doorbell and then knocked twice.

A woman answered the door with a confused look on her face. "Ms. Charlie, hi, oh my God, this is such a pleasant surprise. I was telling Kadeem we needed to formally-"

She wasn't here for her. When he first brought his "fiancé" to her house, she said two words to the girl and told him in front of Ms. Kamala that she didn't agree with them dating while his *wife* was behind bars. It wasn't right. She had suggested to him to write her since he couldn't visit because he was a felon, and to tell her the truth and then send her divorce papers if that's what he wanted to do. He told her no.

"Is Kadeem here? I've been calling his phone?" she asked.

Kamala could tell that something was wrong. "Are the girls okay?" She was genuinely concerned.

"If they weren't, would you care? I can recall several situations where they weren't okay, and you nor he came running. Is my son here, Kamala?" She didn't have time to play around.

"Yes, come in."

Charlie didn't like her. Kamala knew that, and Kadeem had confirmed it.

Their house was nice, but the fact that his kids didn't live here made her uncomfortable in the home. She stood in the foyer and waited for Kamala to get him. The girl was a lawyer, which explained the room on the left turned into a home office with books all over the place.

Kamala returned two minutes later. "He said... that he will call you later," she told her. Kadeem had left out early to go running and returned and went straight to sleep after they made love in the shower. So now that Charlie was here, arms crossed and visibly irritated, she knew that something had gone down.

"Where is he?" She had no to play with him.

Her curiosity was the only reason she led her to their bedroom. Charlie closed the door behind her. Actually, she slammed it. The room was decorated nice, royal blue and gold. The tufted bed cost a pretty penny along with the art behind the headboard.

"Wow, son, you're living good, real damn good," she clapped her hands as she walked around the room.

Their dresser was full of pictures of the couple at church, vacation, the park, the movies, concerts and all. And his children weren't in one picture, nor could she recall him coming to pick them up and take them either.

Kadeem got out of bed and stood to his feet. "This ain't got nothing to do with you."

Charlie turned and looked at him with disgust in her face. She placed her hands on her head and tried to calm down, but she couldn't. In one swift motion, everything on the dresser was knocked over.

Kamala came in the room. "Oh my God!" she squealed when she saw her perfume shattered on to the hardwood floors.

"Get out," Kadeem told her, but she didn't move. "What the hell is going on?"

Charlie pointed her finger at her son. *"You lied to that girl and dragged us into it. Do you know she's not talking to Meme?"* She was pissed.

"She's in her feelings right now. Yara loves her kids, Mama. You know that." He was hurt too.

"Why did you tell her you got out of jail last year, Kadeem?"

Kamala crossed her arms. She wanted to know as well.

"She asked me was it last year, and I never said yes or no. She assumed-"

"What is wrong with you? Me and your father did not raise you-"

"He ain't raise me at all!"

Charlie wanted to smack the fuck out of him. "Don't you dare do this today. You don't get to blame anyone for this bullshit but yourself!" She was angry. "I can't even look at you." She backed out of the bedroom, and he sat on the bed with his head in his hands. The world was on his shoulders right now.

"Did you tell her about me?" Kamala threw in.

He looked at her with tears in his eyes. "Are you fucking serious right now?"
He couldn't believe her.

Charlie wasn't surprised. Kamala may have been a nice girl, but she would never know because she didn't give her a chance. "And this is who you left your wife for?" She was done. "Come get your kids because I'm moving to Atlanta. I've done enough for you," was the last thing she told him before she walked out of his townhouse.

Charlie loved Yara, and she loved her son and her grandchildren too. For the last ten years, she had stepped up to the plate and now, she felt as if she had fulfilled her role. They both were home and needed to figure out what they were going to do with co-parenting Yanise and getting Ayanna across the stage for graduation.

She was getting older and couldn't let them stress her out and raise the risk of her having a heart attack. Stress was a silent killer, and the way her heart had been beating all day, she was taking this as a sign.

KK had been calling her phone all morning, and she was just getting some free time to call him back.

"I'm on the way there," she told him as soon as she answered.

"Do I need to come there? What's going on?"

She sighed into the phone, "Kadeem told Yara but left out every important detail."

"And now what? Shit, is he still alive?" he asked, seriously.

She looked back up at the window of his townhouse before she drove off. 'Yeah."

"Why do you sound so tired?"

Charlie hadn't cried in a long time. "I'm tired and mentally drained. I told him that he needs to come get the girls because I'm moving."

"Where are you going?"

KK, first name Kourtland Moreland, had her heart on lock, and he would probably never really know or hear that come from her mouth. She loved him once, she loved him twice, and he betrayed her trust. Years later, she never really moved on or dated anyone else. Somehow, he always made his way back to her, and she *always* let him in. Now that they were older and the drama was out of the way, she realized that life was short, and she was ready for her fairytale.

"Hello?" He thought that maybe the line disconnected, but she was still there, searching for the words.

"I'm here KK, I'm here…" her voice trailed as she got on the highway.

"Are you sure you okay?" He was worried about her.

Charlie needed to eat. She felt weak. Kadeem and his bullshit had her head hurting.

"Yeah, look, I'll be there soon," she told him, hurriedly.

He smiled as he closed the book he was reading. "I'll be waiting for you, dear."

Not one to be mushy, she hung up without saying goodbye.

η

Kadeem hadn't said two words to her since his mother stormed out. She watched him smoke his head off and drink himself back into a deep slumber and once he was up, she was right there with two Aleve and a bottle of water.

"We need to talk." She wasn't playing with his ass either, nor was she going to allow him to embarrass her.

He rolled over and stuffed his face into the pillow. "My head hurt, I don't feel like talking." He was hoping she went away.

"Kadeem, take these pills," her voice was firm. She didn't allow him to run over her or beat around the bush with her. Respect was shared in this relationship, and she deserved some answers.

Many people acted as if validation was a sign of insecurity in the relationship, but for her, it was not. She needed reassurance that he wasn't going anywhere.

Kamala had been patient and would remain that way if he told her that he was divorcing his wife and soon.

Slowly, he rolled back over and sat up in the bed. She handed him the medicine and then the water. He was gorgeous, and his chocolate skin was edible. If they didn't have to talk about where their relationship stood, she would have jumped in his lap and gave him the business.

The day was a productive one. She had completed her to-do list, folded laundry and cooked dinner and lunch for tomorrow.

"I didn't expect her to be so calm, and I froze and left," he shared with her.

"Does she know about us?" That was all she really cared about.

He shook his head. "No... not yet," he added before she could get to cursing and hollering.

"When?"

Kadeem looked at her with a confused expression on his face. "Do you not care what is happening to my family? I dropped one bomb on her, I'm not doing all of that right now. Let her process this shit first."

"Why? Give it to her at once so we can move on and get married." She didn't understand why he was trying to spoon feed her. Even during court, he stayed close to her, rubbing her back, attempting to speak for her while on the stand to the point where he was thrown out of court twice for disrupting the district attorney. It was no longer his responsibility to protect Yara. "She's a grown woman," Kamala added.

He didn't agree with her. "Who served ten years, came home and found out her husband didn't do the same. How would you take that news?" he wanted to know. He blamed only himself for the situation he was in. It was his selfish decisions that had his family at odds and his mother mad at him. He was disheartened.

She snaked her neck back and lifted her manicured finger, pointing it all in his face. "First of all, I wouldn't have gone to jail in the first place-"

She had worked way too hard to be where she was today. A man could never convince her to cop work, carry drugs, drive it across the bridge or none of that. Her mother taught her better than that. Kadeem would have been doing that time by his damn self.

That rubbed him the wrong way. "Word? You wouldn't?"

She wasn't taking it back either. "If you loved me, you wouldn't have put me in the position to be arrested or incriminated for a crime. You don't love her."

Loyalty didn't have to be measured by jail. That's not how she proved her love to him, nor would she ever, and if he thought that's what made a woman loyal, then she wasn't the one for him. Period.

The veins on the side of his forehead began to thump, and it wasn't because he had a headache. *"Watch your damn mouth!"*

"Why? Cus it's true?" she questioned.

He snatched her down to him, the grip on her neck was a firm one. She punched him with her left hand and stepped back from the bed. He had taken it too far.

"Don't ever put your damn hands on me again." She wasn't with the shits and would fight him even if he was bigger and stronger than her. No one put their hands on her and got away with it anymore, those days were long gone.

Kadeem had never seen this side of her before and wondered what else would she reveal over time. His hotshot lawyer fiancé had some hood in her.
She was a sweetheart, she wasn't even rough around the edges, or so he had assumed.

Kamala Crawford was a thirty-two-year-old woman who had her shit together. She wanted, didn't need, a man. And everything she had she got it on her own. She was the black girl in the club buying bottles along with her group of college-educated, jet-setting friends. From the slums to the hills, she got it out the mud. And the Harvard degree, Mercedes Benz and closet full of designer threads was the proof of her blood, sweat and tears.

Her family only consisted of her, her sister and her uncle, who had raised them until they were eighteen, so no, she didn't come from money and appreciated every red cent that she owned. Kamala had nice things, but they didn't make her who she was, and she understood hard work and sacrifice.

He loved her because of what she brought to the table, and the love she showed him. Thankfully, he didn't have to lie about his relationship with his wife because Kamala was actively involved in the case on the legal side, and when they ran into each other after his arrest, the meet up was innocent.

The heart can only control itself for so long and off the bat, Kadeem never saw himself with anyone other than his wife. He loved Yara with every bone in his body, but Kamala was a breath of fresh air he didn't know he needed. He didn't feel obligated or compelled to do anything other than show her a good time and make her smile. Being with her didn't come with baggage or promises and before they knew it, they were saying "I love you" and buying a home together.

"You hit me."

She was now looking at her neck in the mirror for any sign of a bruise. If there was one, she would be gone. "And you choked me," she mumbled.

Kadeem got out of bed, and she tensed up as he came her way and got right behind her.

He exhaled deeply, "Kamala, this is not us."

And he was correct. They had fun together. They laughed, giggled, danced, prayed and enjoyed life as a couple. There was hardly any discord between them, and he wanted it to stay that way. She didn't appreciate him yelling at her or putting his hands on her, and it had better not happen again, or there would be some problems.

"Ever since you knew she was coming home, things have changed." She wouldn't bite her tongue to hold onto the truth. Their relationship had been built on being honest, and it would remain that way.

She loved her fiancé and wanted a life with him, but he had some things to handle first, and it started with being honest with his wife, divorcing her, putting his foot down with his family and leaving the past behind him.

"It's all fucked up. My mama is mad, and I'm sure my dad has called-"

He cared about what everyone else thought, and she noticed that a long time ago. Even with his daughters, they seemed a tad bit spoiled and ungrateful. She had told him a few times that she didn't like how they spoke to him, but because they lived with his mom, he let a lot of their actions and words slide. And it shouldn't be that way.

Her parents didn't raise her at all, yet she still showed respect because if she didn't her teeth would be knocked out of her mouth. This new generation of kids was a different breed and when she became a mother, Kamala was raising her kids the old-school and right way.

Kamala turned around and faced him. "Kadeem, you are grown and so is Yara. Everyone else's opinions are void. Fix this, fix it this week. I'll draw up the divorce papers for you. Someone in my office can represent you."

There was nothing else to be said until he handled that. Kamala wasn't giving him a million days to divorce her. Now that Yara was free, she was sleeping with a married man, and it didn't feel good.

He didn't respond, but she knew he heard what she said. So, she patted his arm and stepped away from him and glided into the master bathroom. She needed a bubble bath to calm her nerves.

Being abused during her childhood made her the tough cookie she was today, and she didn't take lightly to being hit, whether he barely choked her or not. Kamala was now out of her element and needed to be brought back to peace.

Kadeem leaned against the dresser, stepping on the glass from one of the frames his mother angrily knocked over this morning.

"What am I going to do?" he asked himself.

Chapter Five
"Your vibe… I can feel it." – Joe Gifted

Riqardo knocked on the door and called her name softly, "Meme, let me in."

He woke up and saw blood in the sheets, already knowing what it was and what she was going through. He wanted to be there for her.

She blinked back tears as she held her mouth, attempting to silence her pain.

"Babe." He placed his head on the door, wishing she would let him in so they could get through this together. He was sure that she was more hurt than he was, but still, it took two to tango.

"I'm okay, Riq, go back to sleep," she lied.

He walked away from the door but only to get a knife so he could give himself access to the bathroom.

She was in the corner of the bathroom, as far away from the bloody toilet as possible. "Why does this keep happening to me?" she sobbed.

He went to her and picked her up, wrapping his arms around her and kissing her neck. "It's okay baby, I promise," he told her repeatedly.

The sad thing was that she didn't want children right now, but the fact that she couldn't even successfully hold a child for longer than a few weeks is what frazzled her mind.

"Every time!" she cried. This was her third miscarriage, and she swore her soul was chipping away every time she saw the blood. It would take her so long to come back to life and smile again.

"I need to get this up." His bathroom was a massacre. After calming her down and putting her in the shower, to most likely cry some more, he tossed bleach on the floor and scrubbed the sink, floors and toilet back to normal.

Meme now laid in bed, naked but wrapped in a towel with her eyes to the ceiling wishing God could deliver her a sign.

"Baby, you hungry?" He was patient and kind, nothing like the man he portrayed himself to be on the streets.

He wasn't supposed to be the love of her life, but he was, and she couldn't help that she had fallen head over heels in love with him. He was all she knew. He had taken her virginity at seventeen and four years later, she was still rocking with him.

Riq had fathered two children with two women that he had no kind of relationship with, and one of the kids' mamas he didn't even know her real name until he signed the birth certificate after the DNA test came back. He was a man that admitted to thinking with his dick and not his mind.

Riq took care of his kids, and to him, that's all that mattered. When the time came for him to settle down and take someone seriously, Meme was the one who would get his last name. Thankfully, she didn't put much pressure on what they had. They didn't use words like relationship and commitment. What they had was special and understood between them both, and that's all that mattered. She knew how to speak up when he was doing too much or she wasn't seeing enough of him and vice versa.

For now, she was extremely focused on college and building a career as a hairstylist. He was her downtime whenever her schedule freed up, and he was cool with that.

"No, if you got somewhere to be you can go," she dismissed him, wanting to be alone.

"I don't," he shot back. His trap phone had been ringing, but he wasn't going anywhere. For one, it wasn't enough money for him to run out of the house anyway. His shorty needed him.

Riq was fine as a mother fucker. He was short and cocky, and his raspy voice made her lady lips melt faster than an ice cream cone on a sizzling summer day on the block. She enjoyed being in his presence. He was a hard worker, and everything he had coming for him was deserving because he came from nothing. If it weren't for her parents, he would still be a nappy-headed kid straggling the streets.

Riq reminded Meme of her favorite rapper, Shy Glizzy, from the way he dressed, talked and walked. She was seriously smitten. And it was the lips, yeah. His style and shit made him fly, but his lips, that's what pulled her in. She could kiss and suck on his lips for hours without doing anything else. As long as he had his lips on her, she was good and turned on.

He got back in bed after he smoked and ate two bowls of Frosted Flakes. "Do you know that I think you're the prettiest girl in the world?"

Meme wanted to be discouraged but couldn't, him and his constant showering of affection always put a smile on her face. "You told me that before, so I guess it's true," she sheepishly responded.

He pulled her close and kissed her lips. "I know you don't wanna hear this, but if it keeps happening, God is trying to tell us something, and I'm going to stop going in you raw." He was serious about what he said. The fact that he was her first made his dick hard every time he thought about the love of his life.

"You're right." She nodded her head and laid her head on his chest.

"Can we stay like this forever?" He was so comfortable and at peace whenever she came to his crib.

"I wish." Meme closed her eyes and fell back to sleep.

She had been in the bathroom for hours before he woke up and realized she was no longer in bed with him. She planned to tell her parents that she was carrying, hoping they would put aside their bullshit and celebrate their future grandchild, but now she had to come up with another plan to get them in the same room again without her mom trying to kill her daddy. Kadeem seemed like he was doing better and told her to not worry about her mama, she just needed space.

She called Yara's phone for two days straight, and she never picked up. She prayed that her mom went to see her probation officer. Even if she wasn't talking to them right now, Meme didn't want to see her mom go back to jail.

η

"Thanks, girl," she told Miko again as she slid in her Maybach. The car was so nice. Yara thought that the desire of wanting nice shit was gone since she had spent ten years in jail for committing crimes to buy those same nice, expensive things. Before the FEDS ruined their lives, she was pushing a different whip every other day, but now she drove a Honda and was content. The way Miko's car weaved in and out of lanes made her want one.

"No problem," Miko told her.

When she got in touch with Miko, she realized that she needed more than one favor. Along with figuring out what happened in her case, she also needed to tell her probation officer that she found a job sooner than later. She wanted to find one on her own before he tried to stick her somewhere. Thankfully, Miko's husband had a few businesses, so they drew up some quick paperwork for her to show the probation officer.

"Did you see if I can have the job for real? The money he gave me is a lot, but I don't want to depend on that as my only source of income."

The last forty-eight hours had been busy. She didn't give herself a chance to stop and cry because there was so much for her to do.

Yara found a two-bedroom apartment. Although she wanted a three, the complex was in an okay neighborhood and only had two bedrooms available for immediate move-in.

She paid up the rent for six months and got everything she needed the first day. The apartment was fully furnished, TVs plastered and all, and she had groceries. She was thankful that she came home to some money because after Yanise told her what the real deal was, if she were broke she wouldn't have had a choice but to march back in Charlie's house and sit there, angry. Now, she had her own crib.

Yara put the rest of the money in the bank, and the debit card would be mailed to her new address in a few business days.

The second day had approached, and here she was, riding around with Miko looking like old money. Her hair was still straight and silky from when Meme did it a few days ago. She had on a pair of denim jeans and a denim top with the Gucci sneakers that Meme gave her the day she was released from prison. She wasn't feeling like herself yet, and this morning she thought, *Maybe that's a good thing.*

"Yeah, I got you, you'll start Monday. Before I drop you back off, remind me to give you the lady's email and number you'll be working under, she's cool," Miko told her.

She took a deep breath. "My probation officer was so mean. I'm like damn, what I do to you? It's my first day, and I already got a job." She didn't understand why people took their frustrations out on other people. If you don't like your job, then quit.

"Mine is the same way." Miko was still on papers as well. "We got here fast." They had made it to the lawyer's office in no time.

"It was only a few minutes away. Come on, they better not give us a hard time."

The two women got out of the car and headed into the building. "This is it," she remembered. They were here damn near every other day dropping off money to their high ass attorneys who promised them one thing and ended up doing another.

"Hello, how may I help you?" The receptionist was hanging up the phone when they entered.

"Is Mr. Arrington in, or Mr. Phillips?" she questioned.

The woman shook her head. "No, they're both in court. How may I help you?"

"They represented me about ten years ago, and I wanted to review the files if possible."

She wasn't here ten years ago. "Let me call one of the attorneys up front to see if they can help you out. I'm new here."

Yara didn't bother responding, she and Miko went to sit in the lobby and wait.

"Ms. Moreland, how may I help you?" one of the junior attorneys approached her.

She didn't even catch on that the woman knew her name or called her Ms. and not Mrs. Yara's mind was on the case.

"Hey, about ten years ago I was represented by this office and recently found out that my husband was released earlier because of a discrepancy in the case, am I able to review the files?" she questioned.

"No, not able, we *want* to review them," Miko added.

The woman nodded her head. "Well, I'm sure it's public record, so you can try and Google it. Have a good day."

The woman turned on the heels of her red bottoms, but Yara grabbed her arm, and the woman looked at her like she had a problem.

Yara held her hands up to show there was no issue. "My apologies, I really need to know about this case, ma'am. It's serious," she pleaded.

"Again, Google is your friend."

Yara held back her tears, and Miko told the woman, "We will be back."

Once they were outside of the office, Yara said, "That girl looks so familiar." She couldn't remember if she worked there or not. Ten years was a long time.

"I know some people that know some people, I will get you the information you need," Miko promised.

Miko dropped her back home after they grabbed lunch, but Yara's mind was so boggled with this "discrepancy" that she couldn't even eat or think about anything else. Charlie had called her twice, and Meme had texted and phoned her, but she needed a minute to herself. There was no need for apologies because she could forgive them, but would never forget.

She made a new email account and Googled her attorney's email and sent them both an email to please call her. After she did that, she showered and was out in less than five minutes.

Another day of pushing Yanise's other comment to the back of her mind was only adding fire to an already hot flame.

η

Kamala was on her second bottle of wine. She was drunk as shit when her man got home.

"Bae?" he called out as he came through the hallway that led into the kitchen from the garage.

She was still in her work clothes, sprawled on the love seat in their living room. Fuck the glass, her day was so long that she drank from the bottle. Her jewelry, except for her engagement ring, was on the coffee table, and her heels were on the floor.

"Why you in here listening to Mary?" He knew his lady well, she only jammed to Mary J. Blige when she had a long day at work, a case was driving her crazy, or she was spring cleaning.

She turned around, and he saw her red eyes and came closer. He needed to shower from going to the gym and working on one of his investments all day.

"She came to my job."

He wasn't sure who *she* was, at least he was hoping that *she* wasn't Yara.

"My wife?"

Kamala rolled her eyes. "Please don't fucking say that in here," her words slurred. She put the bottle to her mouth to take another sip, but he took it from her and sat it on the end table.

"What did she come up there for?" The girls or Charlie knew better than to lead her to Kamala's place of business.

"She was with some Asian girl. She wanted to review the case files."

Kadeem didn't expect her to do all of this. "I'm sorry, it wasn't a scene or anything?"

She shook her head and sat back on the couch. "No, I told her to Google the record if she wanted to know so bad."

He was confused. "Why didn't you just show her the files?"

"For what?"

"Because there is nothing to hide."

Kamala told him, "That wasn't my case, I was only an intern at the time. Vince needs to deal with her."

That was bullshit, but to avoid an argument, he let it slide. "And then what happened?"

"She grabbed my arm and then let it go, begging to see the files again, and then she left."

Yara was desperate to know something. He needed to talk to her. It wasn't fair to her. She wanted to understand why she had to serve ten years when he was the culprit. She was considered an accomplice.

"So why are you in here drunk and crying?" Kadeem asked her, wanting to know if he missed half of the story.

"She's beautiful!" Kamala cried again.

He rolled his eyes and got up.

"Where are you going?" She came behind him.

"To shower. Ain't shit wrong with you." He couldn't believe her. Kadeem thought that they had a showdown or a conversation. Kamala was fucking crying because his wife was bad? That was weird.

She stood at the island in the kitchen and watched him walk away, wondering was she really tripping? Even in her distress, Yara's beauty radiated. To be almost forty, she resembled a young college girl. She wondered when he saw her did old feelings arise again? She was drunk and thinking of everything under the sun, creating unnecessary issues.

Taking the steps one at a time because she didn't want to fall, she heard the water running and sped up her pace. Kamala undressed and joined her fiancé in the shower, kissing his back as soon as she saw his chocolate skin.

"You're drunk, carry your ass to the bed." He wasn't in the mood and hadn't really been in one since him and Yara talked.

"I want you," she moaned as she moved in front of him and bit his bottom lip.

"Ouch!"

She ignored his fake pain and discomfort and went for his neck, planting soft and tender kisses all over his collarbone, ear and chest. Kadeem dropped the soap, and that was her cue to move in like a Cheshire cat who had found her meal for the night.

"I love you," she mumbled as she fell to her knees, not caring that her hair was freshly done.

His dick was only slightly hard, and that was cool because she knew what to do to make him as stiff as his attitude was.

Kamala hawked a healthy amount of saliva on to the tip of his dick and used her lips to smear it in before taking the salty thing into her mouth. She knew that he only came when he was at the back of her throat, greeting her tonsils. She took all of him in like a big girl.

"Shit," he groaned.

Glancing up and seeing his head bobbing backward only made her suck and choke on his dick harder. He had a thing for reflex noises, so she made sure to sound like she was having a damn asthma attack.

Kadeem put his hands on her head and pushed her down a bit more, and she swore that if he made another move, she would probably sneeze one of his balls out. How deep did he want her to go? She pushed him away and coughed onto the shower floor.

"You make yourself try to do shit you know you can't do," he told her as he lifted her up and placed her back on the wall. He had one leg in the crook of his arm, and the other was her support not to fall.

Rarely, did he fuck her without protection. He didn't want any more children, and that was one conversation they hadn't gone too deep into, thank God.

"Hmmmm," she moaned as soon as he entered home. Their sex was probably at the top of the list of things that made her love him. He had a way of making her weak with his dick, which was something that no other man was successful at doing.

Kamala experienced multiple orgasms every time she made love to her fiancé, and he actually made love to her back, whereas most niggas expected you to ride there barely there dick all night. She hated a lazy lover.

They equally gave each other everything they had in them when they fucked. There was no such thing as mediocre with Kadeem Moreland. He was a beast in the bed and a monster between the sheets.

"I love you, stop acting like you don't know that shit!" he roared as he pulled out of her and nutted on the floor.

Her eyes sprang open. There was no way in hell they were done already. It hadn't even been two minutes.

"Really?"

"You know when you deep throat my dick I don't last long, and it's been like three days," was the excuse he gave her as he washed off.

Kamala told him before he stepped out of the shower, "You owe me another round before bed."

"I'll be back later, gotta go check on my kids," he said as he dried off and went into their closet to find something to wear.

She said nothing back because he could have seen them before he came home.

After showering, she applied a mask to her face and went downstairs to finish the bottle of wine and call her sister.

"I'm tired, what do you want?" her sister answered on the third ring, sounding exhausted.

"Long day?" Kamile was getting her Master's in Social Work and worked two jobs.

"Girl, hell yes. I'm looking for the weekend with a flashlight cus' I am not working." She couldn't wait to sleep in on Saturday morning.

"Sounds like I need to book us a spa day," Kamile suggested.

Now a massage and a facial was something she would get out of bed for. "Yes, your lil' sister needs it, honey," she told her, yawning into the phone.

"Sooo, guess who came in my office today?"

"My future husband," she joked, tired of being single.

Kamala laughed, "Not yet, sis. Yara came."

Her sister turned re-runs of *Grey's Anatomy* off. "Wait, what? Did y'all fight?" she questioned.

"Are you serious? Hell nah we didn't fight! I'm up for partner, do you think I would risk my career for her?"

"Shit, for Kadeem I don't know what you would do," she teased.

Kamala rolled her eyes. "Nobody is worth that law degree, baby girl, and that's a fact."

"All right. I know that, it was a joke. Spill the tea, hoe."

"It wasn't anything big. I'm still in shock that I saw her face to face. It's been ten years."

"Do you think she remembered you?"

Kamile was curious if Yara had a good memory. That's what she was thinking about on her way home. "I don't know, she should though. I was at their house a lot once the days got closer to the sentencing." She bit her bottom lip.

"Girl, when she finds out who you are she is going to lose it."

Yara didn't look or talk like the woman she remembered from ten years ago. The woman that came in the office today had bass in her voice. Ten years ago, Kamala pitied her and classified her as the young, dumb and submissive wife.

"Do you want something to eat? It's food, y'all have been here all night," Yara offered, *barely above a whisper.*

Kamala shook her head. "No, Mrs. Moreland. I'm fine, thank you."

Yara stood back, wanting to help, but didn't know what she could do.

Kadeem was the one they mainly addressed. In their eyes, she was the wife, nothing more or less.

"Baby, come here," he called out to her.

She damn near ran to him. "Yeah?"

He handed her a black and white photograph. "That trip to Denver, did I go with you? I can't remember." His mind was drawing a blank.

"I don't know, when did we go?" They took so many trips, how could she remember one state out of fifty?

He suggested, "Look at the flights, go do that." He moved her out of the way and went to the next thing on the list. They were trying to pin them at several locations and so far, only four of them stuck.

Yara felt dismissed, and everyone in the room heard the tone of his wrathful voice, except him.

He turned around. "You need something?"

She shook her head. "No, baby." Yara smiled at Kamala before walking out of the dining room they had turned into a meeting room for the attorneys and went to see if she was in Denver alone or not.

Kamala vowed never to be that kind of woman.

"Sis, you heard me?"

Her mind had drifted off. "Huh? My bad. Girl, I'm drunk. What you say?"

"Did she look old? Or beat up?"

"Not at all. If I didn't know the backstory, I wouldn't look at her and say, ooh she been locked up."

Her sister cackled in the phone, "Does anyone look like that?"

She would be surprised. That little time Kadeem did had definitely aged him.

"Well, you'll be seeing her a lot soon, so get ready."

"And why would I be seeing her?" she asked her.

"Uhhhh, they got three kids together, and you're about to marry Kadeem. Y'all are officially a blended family, sis," she said knowingly.

Kamala downed the wine and told her sister, "Let me call you back, I need to make a liquor store run," before hanging the phone up and grabbing her keys.

Blended family, co-parenting and joint holidays, none of those things had crossed her mind before her sister brought it up, and she wasn't trying to do any of that.

As soon as Kadeem made it home, she was going to talk with him.

When she made it to the garage and noticed her car was gone, she screamed. "I need more wine." He took her whip instead of his.

Kadeem knew her too well. As soon as he answered her call, he said, "You're drunk, your ass ain't going nowhere, drink some water. I'll be back in an hour."

"Bye, nigga."

He looked at his two daughters and apologized for interrupting Ayanna. "My bad, so ma gone?" he asked again.

"I think you stressed her out," Ayanna told him.

His mother needed a break. He wasn't tripping. "Y'all should come stay with me until she gets back," he suggested.

Yanise wasn't going over there with him and his girlfriend. "For what? We always stay here when she visits Papa." They had been taking care of themselves just fine.

"I know but-"

"We good, Daddy," they told him in unison.

He looked at his teenage daughters and asked, "Are y'all mad at me?"

Meme wasn't fucking with him right now.

The question really was, are they mad at her? Apparently, the cat wasn't out of the bag yet because her dad seemed relaxed. She didn't regret telling her mom the truth. In a way, she wanted to punish her father for being absent in their lives.

Yanise looked at her sister and shrugged her shoulders. "I got my own problems."

Kadeem and Ayanna laughed. "Girl, what problems you got? You're fourteen."

If only they knew, she thought to herself. "I'm going to bed, goodnight," Yanise excused herself from the conversation.

Ayanna looked at her phone and then at her father, wondering if the conversation was over. She needed to watch her shows before bed. Ayanna was a smart girl, and she had big plans after graduating. She loved to have a good time with her friends, but nothing stood in the way of her studies. In a few months, she would be graduating with honors and hopefully a full-ride to an Ivy League School.

"Are you mad at me?" Kadeem asked with grief-stricken eyes. All of this was stressing him out. He loved his daughters and knew that he needed to show them more with his actions and not only his words.

"No, I don't know, Daddy. Is it bad that I really don't care?" Ayanna asked him.

"You don't care about your mama and me?"

She shook her head. "Not really. I mean, I love y'all, but I'm not as invested as Meme. I remember mama, but it's not like I'm jumping for joy that she's home. I'm glad she's not in jail no more, I cried at the party… never mind, I can't explain it." She decided to be quiet and keep her thoughts to herself.

"No, talk to me." He wanted to know how she felt.

"It's like as long as I got my sisters and Charlie, I'm good. I don't feel like I need y'all."

That hurt. "Ayanna, who do you think takes care of you?" he questioned, because it surely wasn't Charlie, not on the financial end.

"I'm not talking about money, I mean for support. Okay, for example, with school and doing the college tours, Meme's been taking me, and with the doctor, Charlie takes me. I don't ask you for nothing because I don't need your help," she explained.

"But why not? I can go see the schools with you, and I'll take you to the doctor and dentist and shit, you never asked me," he said, defensively.

"That's the thing, Daddy. Why do I have to ask? Meme and Charlie do it without me asking."

He got up and went to sit right next to her. "Listen, I haven't been daddy of the year, and that's something I'm going to work on starting tonight. From now on, I'm there. I will be at all your stuff, baby girl. Number one cheerleader, that's officially daddy. I'm going to be at everything, every program, awards… whatever. I love you and your sisters, y'all are my heart," he told her the truth. He planned to show her rather than keep talking.

"Love you too, Daddy."

"You still a virgin, right?" The question was random, but he wanted to know.

She looked at him. "Uh, yes I am."

Ayanna liked boys. She went on a few movie dates here and there, but until she met the right one she wasn't giving her goodies up.

He wiped sweat from his forehead. "Whew, okay good. Let's keep it that way," he said and kissed her cheek.

"Have you talked to mama?" she asked him.

He shook his head. "I don't even know what to say to her or where to start."

"Do you feel bad for lying all these years?"

A deep breath came from his mouth, and he lifted his hands over his head. "I wish I wouldn't have let so much time go by without me reaching out to her. I kept saying in a month, then that month became another month, and now she's home… it was never the right window of opportunity."

"When she was here those few nights, she screamed a lot in her sleep." She wasn't going to say anything, but Ayanna believed that her mom went through hell in jail.

"Like nightmares?"

She looked at him and nodded her eyes. "Yeah, Charlie went in there one night, and I don't think mama knew that she helped her get back to sleep, but she woke the whole house up."

Kadeem could only imagine how her time was in there. He knew that she had requested to be moved several times. She was at Riker's Island starting off, and that shit was no joke. Prison wasn't a place for women like Yara, and he was filled with guilt all over again.

"I gotta go. Lock the door and set the alarm," he barely said to his daughter as he backpedaled out of the kitchen.

Ayanna saw his whole mood change and seriously didn't know who to feel bad for. Her mom and her dad were both going through the motions, and she wondered if her family would ever be back together. Sadly, she already knew the answer.

Chapter Six

"Even though we see the stars, we still wish." – Nipsey Hussle

Denial is the action of declaring something to be untrue, the refusal of something requested or desired and a statement that something is not true.

No one returned her calls or responded to her email, and that was three days ago. She couldn't dwell on it today because she was starting work, nor could she ponder over the fact that Kadeem was engaged.

Kadeem and that word in one sentence made her stomach hurt, and in the middle of the night, it came to her. She had jolted out of bed and ran to the bathroom and vomited. Had he found love? Well hell, ten years of being a free man, of course he had found love.

She was up before the sun and didn't get a wink of sleep, thinking of her husband wanting to marry someone else. Did he get on one knee? Was is fiancé aware that he was technically a married man, still? When would he call her or reach out to her to see if she were still alive?

Meme kept calling and calling to the point where she finally texted her and said, "I AM FINE."

Yara wasn't having a temper tantrum or being a brat. Her heart was broken, and her feelings torn into pieces. She didn't expect to stay away from her kids forever, that was already done while she was in prison. But for now, she needed a second to herself to recover mentally and to figure out what she was going to do next.

Work… Yara never had a job a day in her life, so today was new for her. She prayed she looked the part. The black, high-waist pants she wore paired with a red blouse and a pearl necklace and black patent leather flats that she found at Target on the clearance rack came right in handy because the parking garage was a little far from where she was instructed to go. Miko had texted her about thirty minutes ago and said she would swing by later to check on her, and she appreciated her going out of her way to help her.

Yara stayed home all weekend, drinking wine and smoking weed that Riq gave her. She didn't question him about Kadeem, and he was thankful because he loved them both and didn't want to get in the middle of their issues. Kadeem was like a father and had paved the way for him to be where he was at now, and Yara provided love and comfort, something his mother never did.

"Yara Moreland," she introduced herself as soon as she got to the front desk.

"Good morning! I'm Marsha. We've been talking back and forth over email." Th woman extended her hand.

Yara shook it firmly. "Pleasure to put a face to a name. How are you?" She was polite.

Marsha told her, "Good, come on, let me give you a quick tour, and then we will go over your position, starting salary and all that good stuff."

"Salary?" Again, she never had a job before, so she knew nothing about minimum wage, salary, promotion, insurance, or benefits. When she or the kids got sick, Kadeem paid cash. Nothing was ever given to her, she earned everything she ever had, and what they couldn't get, they took. Robbery. Yara had robbed banks, homes, jewelry stores and even charity galas. Sadly, whatever he asked of her, she did. Thankfully, those days were behind her.

"Yes. If I'm not mistaken, you're entry-level but interested in moving up?" Marsha was sure that's what Nash, her boss, told her when they spoke.

"Of course."

Marsha gave her a tour of the place where dreams were made and brands created. Miko's husband, Nash, was more than a rapper these days, he was like the new and younger, more innovative Diddy. Nash had his hand in everything, which was a good thing for Yara because with one phone call she had a job.

"And this is your office. If you don't like this color, we can have it painted something else."

It was hard for her to keep her cool because it wasn't too often people went out of their way to do nice things for her, if ever. She could see Miko's touch of class all over the office, from the glass desk to the shades of purple in the pillows on the small grey couch in the corner of the room.

"Does everyone's office look like this?" she asked Marsha.

Marsha nodded her head. "Pretty much. As far as size, yours is designed a little nicer, but being that we are a small department in the building, everyone has their own office and space. We meet once a week and sometimes more depending on what's on the schedule. If we have to meet more, you'll be notified through the app, which brings me to the next thing. Let me see your phone," she said and held her hand out.

Yara fished through her clutch and passed her cell.

"Okay, so now you have the work app. We use this app to communicate for shows, last minute changes on sets and stuff like that. You'll also get a ching sound like a register closing once your check is cleared in your account. Before you leave today, I'll get your banking and routing information. Checks are every two weeks and tons of bonuses. As you know, any travel for work is on the company." She began to talk fast, and Yara had to keep up as she dished very important information out.

"Also, we are a flexible, laid-back office, so wear what you want, business-appropriate of course, and you can work from home if you choose. You'll have your work cell by the end of the week as well, so make sure the app is on both phones, and I'll get you your ID. Uhhhh, what else?" She raked her brain to see if she forgot anything. Yara watched her tap her fingernails on the bottom of her chin.

"Oh! Do you have any kids? We work a lot of late nights in the studio, but if you have children, we can figure something out."

"Three, but they're big girls, fourteen, eighteen and twenty-one."

Marsha was in disbelief. "You do not have teenagers, let alone an adult. Girl, you my age!" She was so surprised.

That put a smile on Yara's face. "Yes, I'll be forty this year." She planned on getting in the gym to tone up her flab.

"Wow, me too." Marsha heard the front door chime which meant her appointment was here. "Okay, Yara, that's my nine o'clock. I think you're good to go."

Well, she didn't feel good to go yet. "One question. Miko never told me exactly what I'm doing, what does my job consist of?" she questioned.

η

"I knew this was a setup," Kadeem teased as he dapped his father up, who was chilling comfortably in the booth of Savoy, an upbeat brunch place located in the Bronx.

"Yeah, cus I been calling your knucklehead ass," he replied.

Kamala stood behind him, excited but nervous to be doing the family thing.

Charlie had her hand in KK's lap and when she spotted her son's 'fiancé', she gripped his thigh.

KK looked at her and smiled. He reached over to kiss her forehead and told her, "Be cool, baby."

She rolled her eyes at him and then blushed. He was the only person that could even fix their lips to tell her what to do. Her time in Atlanta was what she needed, a break away from the madness.

When it was time for her to head back up North, surprisingly, he came back with her. They still wanted to be up under each other, and she knew that once this little buzz left them, he would return home and the pattern would repeat itself.

"Son, are you going to introduce your father to your… fiancé?" The word stung her throat.

Kadeem looked at his mother with tight eyes. "Baby, come here. Why you behind me? This is my dad, Kourtland. We call him KK." He brought her to him and gently pushed her forward.

"Pleasure to meet you, sir. Good morning, Charlie," she smiled as they slid into the booth.

"Do you ever go to work?"

Kadeem knew this was going to be a long day. When his mom wanted to meet him for breakfast, he didn't expect Kamala to want to tag along, nor did he know his Pops was in town.

"Ma," he warned her.

"What do you do?" KK asked. He knew nothing about the girl.

"I'm an attorney, and yes ma'am, I do. I work a lot, actually."

Charlie picked up her mint tea and sipped it before moving the conversation to her son. "How have you been? You should take the girls to see their cousins. I know Yanise will love Giselle's place, they just remodeled the backyard. It's so big."

That was a good idea, especially since he was making an effort with his children. Whatever it took, he would do it.

"I think we may do that. Next weekend I'm going to call Kasim."

"Yep, and let them be out there on all that land, they stuck up asses need to go to the country," she laughed.

Kamala had something to do next weekend. "The gala is Saturday, did you forget?"

He actually did. "Oh yeah, you're right. We can go after that." He wasn't tripping on when they went.

KK picked up the menu. "What are we ordering? I'm starving."

"I think I want bacon and sausage, I'm starved." Kamala rubbed her stomach.

Kadeem could predict his mom's next statement.

"We don't eat meat, me or Kadeem's father, and the smell drives me insane." She was honest. She only cooked fish for the girls, but she could go without it all together.

"Veggie omelet it is." Kamala was trying her hardest to make things work with his mama, but she was a bitch.

Charlie wondered how this woman could accept a ring from him without meeting his family or having a real relationship with his daughters. It made her question this chick's intentions.

"Kamala, get what you want. Ma, chill out. Dad, please get her," he asked his Pops.

KK was tickled by the whole situation. "You got the real black mom," he laughed.

His fiancé agreed with him there. "Indeed."

"Where did you study?" He was curious to know more about her. If Kadeem proposed to her, he clearly had to like her, or even love her. So, why give her a hard time? He planned on talking to Charlie about that when they left.

"I went to Spelman and then studied Law at Harvard." She didn't want to sound boastful, that would give Charlie something else to complain about.

KK was thoroughly impressed, and even his mama raised an eyebrow. Kamala wanted to ask Kadeem did his parents know anything about her, this brunch was something that should have taken place when they first started dating. Were they moving too fast?

"Wowwww, black girl magic! That's amazing, congrats, and do you have any children?"

Kadeem shook his head. "No kids."

"Do you want children?" Charlie asked.

Kamala nodded. "I do, when the time is right."

Kadeem didn't react or respond, and Charlie made a mental note.

"I have two sons. My other son has a set of twins; a daughter and two sons, and Kadeem has three girls, so I'm all for more grandkids."

"Not me, them girls stress me out." Charlie took another sip of her tea.

Kamala spoke up, "It's just my sister and me. She doesn't have any children either. I think one or two is good for me, maybe boys since Kadeem doesn't have any."

There was a silent and uneasy feeling that fell over the table, and they all seemed to have mentally went somewhere else. Kamala could tell they were full of untold stories and hopefully, Kadeem would open up to her soon because she didn't want to marry a stranger.

η

Time flies when you're busy, and it felt good to keep her mind off the pain and heartbreak. Friday afternoon had finally arrived, and Yara was looking forward to cooking something yummy for dinner and winding down this weekend. She texted her daughter and asked if she could come to get her hair shampooed, and Meme told her just to pull up. She waved goodbye to Marsha before stepping into the elevator.

"Hey, so how was your first week?" Marsha asked her.

Yara smiled. "Better than expected, see you Monday."

Tomorrow, she planned on going shopping to get more business casual clothes. Everyone in the office wore cute dresses, denim and blouses, jean jackets and skirts with tall boots. She was wearing suits and shit. Yara knew exactly what she had in mind when it came to comfortable and casual work clothes.

In her car, a gospel song came on, and it was perfect timing because God had surely blessed her. Miko downplayed the job that she got her. She thought she would answer the phone and fax papers, but no, Yara had a real J-O-B.

She was the assistant to the account executive, who was Marsha, who quickly told her that they all did everything. On some days, she would be at the front desk all day, and on other days, she would schedule posts for the social media accounts. They were a team, and everyone had one goal in mind; to keep the artists satisfied.

This week she was able to do a little of everything. She called promoters back who wanted to book artists signed to Nash's label, she booked two venues for a Spring concert, sent thank you cards to sponsors for an album release last week and mailed orders.

Yara loved the hustle and bustle of her job and liked that she wasn't confined to the same task every day or stuck in one room. Maybe that's why Miko gave her this certain job because she knew how it felt to be in one room for twenty hours out of the day.

Yara wanted to see the sun and the light. She filled her tank up and headed to the hood to get her hair done. When she saw her daughter hopping out of Riq's truck, she was very surprised. She knew good and damn well they weren't fooling around. After she parked, she walked up to him and tapped the window.

He got out instead of winding it down and talking to her like she was a bird.

"What up, ma?" He hugged her, and she hugged him back but stayed focused on what she had to say.

"Meme is my baby. You know that, right?" Yara wasn't smiling or shooting the shit with him, she was serious.

He nodded his head. Riq was grown, no longer the little boy she had damn near raised.

"I love her." He knew that Meme would kill him if she were out here right now.

"Girlllll, I think yo' mama saw you get out of Riq's truck," one of the other shampoo assistants came and told Meme. She was in the locker room putting her things away.

"Swear to God!" She damn near broke her neck as she spun around to see if her friend was joking. Meme left the locker room to see what was going on and ran smack dab into her mother.

"Hey, you got here early," she tried to play it cool.

Yara looked at her, controlling her facial expressions. "It was no traffic. You ready?" she asked her.

Meme nodded her head and moved out of the way so she could walk to the bowls. Yara leaned back into the shampoo bowl, and Meme turned the sink on so she could get started.

"When I met your father, I was fifteen. Did you know that?"

Meme knew the story. She had heard the good and bad version of their fairytale.

"Ma, we not like that, we're cool. I'm focused on my school work and getting a chair in here," she explained.

"Is that what you tell yourself? It sounds so rehearsed."

Meme looked at her mother. "What did he tell you?" she wanted to know.

"He said he loved you. Do you love him?"

She was going to fucking kill him. "Ma-"

She was grown, so there was no need to lie. "Yes or no, baby."

Meme continued scratching her scalp. "Yeah, I do, but we good how we are. I don't need or want more from him."

"Riq is my baby, but you're my daughter, so if he hurts you I will kill him."
And Yara wasn't playing.

Her heart stopped beating. Did her mother approve? "You not mad?"

Yara shook her head. "Nope, I want my children to be joyful and to experience love. Love is beautiful when it's reciprocated the right way."

"Do you still believe in love?" Meme asked her.

Yara took a deep breath. "I don't think about it anymore." She was so focused on herself that love wasn't a factor in her life right now. "Meme?" Her eyes were now closed as her daughter rinsed the shampoo from her hair. "No matter how close y'all get and how the love grows, never stop loving yourself more than he loves you. You are the priority always." She wished someone would have told her that many moons ago. But they didn't, so it was her responsibility as a mother to make sure her daughters learned from her mistakes.

After her hair was blown out and pressed, Yara paid Andrea and tipped Meme. "I'm headed home," she told her daughter.

"Where is home, Ma?" No one knew where she had been staying.

"I got me a lil place around the way, dinner soon, you, me and your sisters," she smiled. Meme walked her to the car since it was dark. "You know I can hold my own, right? I used to be out here day and night with your daddy and sometimes on my own," she reminded her.

"Things have changed, Ma. It's twelve-year-olds out here with more balls than grown men. They robbing and killing without blinking an eye."

Yara had heard the horror stories. "Yanise told me that your father is engaged." She watched Meme closely as she spoke.

Meme's eyes lit up and then dimmed, and then her head dropped. "Why did she tell you?"

Yara shrugged her shoulders. "Not sure." She knew why she told her but kept that to herself.

"I think that's a conversation you and daddy should have." She wanted no parts in the madness.

"Have you met her?"

Meme nodded her head. "Maaaaaa," she whined.

She held her hands up. "One more question and then I'm gone."

Meme took a deep breath, knowing her mom wasn't going to ask any normal shit. "Yes, Mama?" She bounced from one foot to the other nervously. Yara had a way of not revealing much with her eyes or her face, so you could never predict what she would say.

"Is she a lawyer?"

η

"Baby?" She rolled over and laid her head on his chest. He wasn't a hard sleeper, and she wasn't either. Shit, the life they lived, how could they sleep hard when you never know if someone was coming back to seek revenge. Guns were under the mattress and behind the pillows, and a knife was in the second drawer on the nightstand. Not only was their house armored the fuck up, but the windows had burglar bars along with four pit bulls who were trained to kill.

Their children were their life, and home was to be a safe place for them, and as parents, it was their job to ensure that no hurt, harm or danger ever came their way.

"Yeah?" His eyes remained closed as he waited for her to say what she had to say before he dozed back off.

"Are you going to jack off in there?" She never used the word jail or prison. She was still in denial that in a few days they would be serving ten years.

He laughed, "I just dicked you down, and you still got sex on your mind?"

"No, I'm sore as hell. I'm saying, like what are we going to do for ten years? That's so long, I been having sex since I was fourteen."

Kadeem groaned, "Fast ass." He didn't want to think about them being away from each other.

"I'm for real! What are we supposed to do for ten years? And I can't get no wax, my pussy gon' be a mess." She began to think of all the other things she couldn't do once she was locked up.

"It's going to fly by, baby. Let's not focus on that right now, get some sleep. Tomorrow we are spending time with the kids, and we need sleep to deal with their bad asses."

"And more sex?" She was trying to get as much as she could before the day came for them to say goodbye to each other.

"Whatever you want, Yara," he told her as he drifted back off to la-la land.

She was wide awake. What if she got raped? What if they tried to turn him into their bitch in there? Yara was frightened. Then the way the hood was set up, she could see a project hoe trying to visit him and fuck him. Women were always trying to get him, but he knew better. Yara didn't play when it came to her husband.

"Baby?" she tapped him again.

"Yaraaaaaaaa!" Kadeem was sleepy, and she wanted to pillow talk.

"Last thing, I promise," she whined to her husband. He rubbed her back, hoping she would get sleepy. "That girl, Kamala. Do you think she was kind of snappy today?" The lil' intern started off so sweet, but these last few days she had been really short with Yara, and she didn't understand why. It wasn't as if she were boo-hoo crying and asking a million questions every other second. The few questions she did ask were because she didn't know how sentencing went.

"Go to bed, you worried about stupid stuff. They stressed out just like we are."

He saw the good in everyone, but Yara knew how to read through the bullshit. And the girl's patience was thin when it came to her, and for the life of her, she didn't get it. "I think she got a crush on you."

He rolled over on his side and fluffed his pillow up to the crook of his neck. "My ass is headed to jail, what can I do for her? Goodnight, baby. I love you," he added a few seconds later.

She didn't respond to him. If only she could turn back the hands of time, she would have attended college, got a job, became a soccer mom, and maybe Kadeem would have been a barber or a construction worker. Why did they turn to the streets for money?

She wished she had the balls to take her kids and leave but didn't, and she refused to be without Kadeem or her children, so if they all couldn't run, then she would stay.

Yara sighed. No one was as stressed out as she was, they weren't the ones about to turn themselves in.

Once she got home, she realized that it was still early, and this was her first weekend as a free woman. Last weekend was hectic with getting settled in her new place and preparing for a job on top of trying to get in touch with her lawyer. Everything had fallen into place, and Yara wanted to do something.

Before they got knocked, if they weren't hustling they were celebrating life.

Her and Kadeem used to be the most fly couple in the clubs whether they were in their city or out of town. People flocked to them and showed them love from all over the place. No matter where they were, all eyes were on them.

Kadeem would get the biggest section they had, and sometimes it would be just the two of them rapping and drinking out of the bottle, hugging and kissing each other. They would be dripped and draped in designer and diamonds from head to toe, and one would expect him to be a rapper and her a model but no, they were criminals, married criminals with three kids at home.

You couldn't look at Yara and see her as a hit man, robber, murderer, drug dealer, and a few other terrible things. She seemed so sweet, but Yara was sinful.

Kadeem was dangerous, and together they were a deadly couple with a thrill for living life in the fast lane. They were crazy in love, and for ten years those memories kept her sane and focused on getting out and back to the love of her life and her children.

Ten years had passed, and her kids had a life of their own, and her husband was engaged to another woman. And what about her? What would Yara do? What did she have going on?

As reality set in, she dropped a bottle of wine on the tan carpet in the living room of her apartment and cried as she fell to her knees, with her hands on her head.

He had moved on, had broken their vows. He was in love, but she was alone. On a Friday night, as a free woman, this isn't how it was supposed to be. She was supposed to come home to her family. They had a "Life After the FEDS Plan." It was all mapped out. Together, they had gone over the plan a million times. Come home, do probation, get some dumb ass jobs and once the kids were grown, they were moving to Jamaica and growing weed. It sounded stupid, but she had that plan in her head for ten years.

They were supposed to grow old together. She never saw herself without him.

Single? Yara had been with Kadeem her whole life, what the fuck did single mean?

It took a few days for her to come to the realization of him moving on, of him being out of jail for ten years and her not knowing. It was all real now; everything.

She couldn't run from the truth anymore. There was no work to do, emails to send, drug tests to take for the probation officer or organizing closets. There was nothing else to do other than deal with the actuality of her husband giving his love to another woman.

The clock read 3:46 a.m. That's what time she got up and climbed into bed. She only had one tattoo, and that was the "K" on her ring finger. Yara bit her finger until she drew blood. It was painful, and it made her feel good. That's what she needed right now, something to numb her heart.

Kadeem couldn't hide from her forever, and when she saw him, she didn't know what she would do or how she would react. He better be on his knees praying that the old her didn't act up on his ass because if so, he and his fiancé were in for a rude awakening.

Yara was a good girl when they met, but he turned her into a savage. He was the one who taught her to never let a nigga take anything from you. And in her eyes, that bitch took her man. Yara could kill her if she wanted to. She could do it with her eyes closed. If she didn't care about her children, her life, her freedom and what she possibly had to look forward to, she would choke her until she took her last breath.

See, half of her thought about filing for a divorce before he could try to have one up on her, and then the other half of her wanted to make him suffer. And then another part of her felt as if she were a catch and it was his loss, and then at the same time, she wanted him back.

Yara didn't even look at other men or think of them, nor did she want to be alone for the rest of her life. How do you even start over after being with one person your whole life and doing ten years for him? Her mind was boggled with what her next step would be. She decided not to do anything. The next move would be on him.

Yara pushed last night to the back of her mind and showered, preparing for a Saturday with herself. She thought about going to pick up Yanise, her youngest daughter, but didn't want to talk to Charlie or risk seeing Kadeem. She eventually had to go over there. She couldn't let him keep her from getting back in her daughter's life. And Yanise seemed to need her more than her other two girls anyway. She told on her dad for a reason, and Yara wanted to know why.

After she finished dressing, she went to get her car washed and then headed to the mall.

"I want a Lexus," she said at the red light when she pulled up next to one and admired the cherry-red exterior and dark interior. Thinking that she deserved one, she made a right instead of a left at the light and pulled right into the dealership. Four hours later, she drove out of the dealership in a used Lexus, cherry-red just like the one she saw and sold the Honda for much of nothing, but she didn't care.

Yara could afford a car note now that she had a job, and she deserved to ride in style with all the shit she had been through. On top of last night, a new car had her feeling like she was "that bitch" again.

Chapter Seven
"Saw the pain in yo' face and still you maintained a smirk." – Jay Z

"Yara, how does this look?" Marsha was working on a vision board for Nash's next album and needed some feedback.

Yara pulled the headphones out of her ears. "What you say?" All this week she had been in classic throwback Jay-Z mode, and you had to be feeling some type of way to listen to the *Blueprint* album. Many people didn't respect the craft of Jay-Z, but she loved him. He was arguably the best rapper alive, in her opinion.

"We're going for, expect the unexpected, with this new album," she explained.

Yara came from behind the table where everyone migrated after lunch and looked at the board. "Why not just do black and white then," she suggested.

Miko lifted her hands in the air after damn near snatching the blue Tiffany reading glasses from her face. *"Oh my God! Yes!"*

"So, all of this in black and white?" the designer asked to be sure.

Yara nodded her head. "Yep, it will be considered a classic. Simplicity is sometimes best." She sat back down and went right back to work as if she didn't just literally make a big ass decision.

Album work was serious these days. It was the first thing a person saw when they clicked the iTunes, Tidal, Pandora, Spotify and any other music host app. People spent months creating the perfect album cover, and it came to Yara in a matter of two seconds.

Marsha was impressed, but it had been that way since Yara started. She was always early, never late, nor was she rushing out the door. Although she was only paid for nine hours a day, she attended all the mandatory events. She brought lunch, coffee, extra materials and a smile. Yara was always in a good mood and ready to serve wherever she was needed.

"I love her, and I love this idea. Okay, let's do this right now. We meet with Nash tonight at eight before his session."

Miko was a wife and a mother, and she loved both roles. Working for the president early in her career and then the financial advisor and accountant for The Underworld, the most notorious criminal organization ever, had her mentally trained to handle business, and she did an excellent job at it. Money was her thing; she could do figures in her sleep. Marketing and shit wasn't her forte, but apparently, it was Yara's.

"Hey girl, you wanna roll over to this meeting at Atlantic with me?" Miko asked her friend.

Yara was doing inventory. "I need to finish this-"

"One of the interns can do it, come on," she told her while typing away on her phone, telling the driver to pull around so they could go. Miko didn't like to be late for meetings. She was a reflection of her husband.

Marsha was elated that Yara was going to see another side of the business.

"Have fun!" she told Yara.

"Girl, I don't know where I'm going. I wish I would have worn flats today."

Depending on her mood, she would dress up or down, and today she had on a fuchsia knee-length dress and leopard four-inch, pointed toe pumps. Her hair was in a low ponytail, and she wore a pair of diamond earrings and a Michael Kors watch. It wasn't a Rolex or a diamond cut Audemar like she was accustomed to, but the watch was cute, and it clashed well with her outfit.

She was humble and didn't even attempt to live above her means or her budget plus, the Lexus was her first and last splurge. Yara wasn't a millionaire anymore. She had a few dollars in the bank, but she wasn't dwindling through it because once it was gone, she had no one else to ask for more. She didn't depend on anyone but herself these days.

It had been three weeks since the incident at Charlie's house and still, no communication from Kadeem.

Meme picked up Yanise, and they spent time with their mom, so she didn't have to run into her mother-in-law or estranged husband. Every time she reached out to her middle child, she was told that she was busy, but Yara kept trying and wouldn't give up on getting their relationship back intact.

She noticed that the more she came around Yanise, the warmer she got, and she was confident that soon she would be moving in since that was why she got a two bedroom. Yara wanted her kids back.

Meme was grown, and Ayanna would be going to college soon, so although she was concerned about all her daughters, Yanise was at the top of the reconnection priority list.

"Where are we going again?" she asked her friend once they were in the back of a car being chauffeured to the city.

Miko was now checking on her kids. "Meeting with a new artist," she whispered.

Yara busied herself by texting in the group message that Meme created for them to keep in contact. "Taco night?" Hopefully, the girls were free. She loved spending time with them.

A minute later, Ayanna texted back and said, "Dad is making us spend time with Kamala, raincheck."

Meme sent the throwing up emojis, and Yanise responded with a thumbs down. "Ma, I'll come over if you come get me."

Yara wrote back, "No, have fun with your step-mom and dad. Will catch y'all another time." She knew they weren't the ones to be mad at but hell, she was human and now pissed.

As they got out of the truck and rode to the elevator, Miko sensed her mood shift. "What happened?"

Yara sighed, "Kadeem is getting the girls tonight, and they're hanging with the fiancé. I'm jealous," she admitted. She wanted to fucking cry. How was it even possible that he was living his life without clearing the waves with her? Did he not expect to ever talk to her again? She didn't understand his logic.

"I'm so happy y'all don't have babies. Shit could be so much worse. Your girls are old enough to think for themselves, and you're the mom, she can't replace you." Miko gave her a side hug, hoping she cheered her up.

Yara thought to herself, *Yeah, but I've been gone for ten years."*

The girls didn't go into detail about Kamala, whether she was around often, was a wedding in motion, did their dad really love her… nothing. They said nothing; ever. Yara didn't know what to do. Her feelings were incredibly hurt.

Her cell phone began to buzz repeatedly. She saw sad faces, crying faces and all kinds of other emojis of Meme and Yanise feeling bad for canceling on their mom. Ayanna, of course, never responded. They were being tugged between the two of them, and they needed to tell them both that they had their own lives to live.

Yara was trying to play catch up, and Kadeem shouldn't have to play the same game because he wasn't away for as long as she was.

She turned her phone on silent as they were escorted into a boardroom with a round table that had almost twenty chairs.

"Important meeting?" she asked Miko.

"Yeah, sort of, well it's a big deal. I just want you to see how things flow and if artist development interests you, let me know." She wanted Yara to be where she could grow and excel. And that would require her going to different meetings to get a feel for every department at the label.

She nodded her head and took a seat in the corner and pulled out her notebook.

"Girl, come sit by me!" Miko told her. Yara was always trying to fade out, and she wanted to pull Yara out of that.

Yara rolled her eyes. "Don't call me out in this meeting," she warned her.

And that clearly fell on deaf ears. Yara's eyes grew wide when Miko asked, "Yara, how do you feel about the EP?"

An EP was the project before or after an album. It was a marketing tool used by record labels to either hype a future release up that was already in the works while building a buzz around a few tracks that were leaked on purpose. Most EP's are four to six songs, something like a tease of what to expect from an artist.

This EP was coming from a young teenager that Nash believed in and had put millions into his project.

"I'm old school, don't ask me," she said, avoiding the truth.

"We all are older than thirty except for the artist," the lead A & R on the project said snidely.

Yara smiled, wishing Miko didn't put her on the spot.

"What did you think?" the artist asked her. He didn't know who she was and really didn't care, but the boss's wife was in here, and this had to be her peoples, so he waited for her feedback.

All eyes were on her.

"I didn't like it… at all." Her palms were sweaty, and she prayed that Miko didn't get mad at her honesty.

One of the older execs at the end of the table chimed in, "Me neither."

Miko quieted the chatter. "What needs to happen for this to drop by Friday?"

How in the hell was Yara was supposed to know? This wasn't her field. She didn't go to college for this. She listened to music while she was driving home and cleaning up, that was about it. She shrugged her shoulders.

Miko pushed her further, "Think, when you heard the tracks, what did you think?"

Yara didn't like being put on the spot, and she squinted her eyes at Miko. "I don't know," she said.

Miko got up and played the song again, turning it all the way up. "Let's all put our creative hats on."

An hour later, she had played the songs so long Yara had memorized the words. She raised her hand.

"Girl, you are not in school," Miko laughed.

"Shut up. Okay, so the first track, scratch completely. The second one, I think a Marvin Gaye sample at the end would be perfect. I like the song, it's missing something, and I think the *What's Going On* sample would make it pop. And the fourth song, what if Nash hopped on the chorus? Same chorus different voice, and the last song I would have a choir singing the introduction and then do the rest acappella."

Yara had read from the notes she jotted down, and when she pulled the book from her face, everyone was staring at her with their mouths wide open.

"Oh no, did I say something wrong?" She looked at her friend, apologetically.

Miko started clapping her hands. "Girl, where were you a few years ago when Nash was losing money on record sales?" She was so thankful that Yara found her when she got out.

"I need her in Cali on this St. Janine project."

"Nah, she needs to come hear Cardi album before we go to mastering."

"We just signed a kid group, do you mind taking this flash drive with you?"

Everyone started flooding her with questions.

"Hey, hey, hey, let's stay focused on the project at hand. We have to get all of this done ASAP. Yara, you got plans?" Miko asked her.

Her kids had canceled on her, so nope, she didn't. "No, I'm free."

"Let's grab food and head to the studio."

And that's where she was holed up at for the next two days while her kids played family on the Northside.

"More wine?" Kadeem eyed his eldest.

Meme smirked at him as she filled the goblet glass close to the brim. "Long day."

"What did you do today?" Kamala chimed in. She was excited that the girls agreed to come over for a mid-day dinner with her and their father. She didn't have time to cook because she was in court all day, so she ordered takeout.

"School, braided hair, worked my second job and now I'm here, sleepy and tipsy," she said in one breath.

"You can spend the night if you're not sure about driving, we have plenty of room," Kamala said with a smile.

Yanise mumbled, "I bet."

Kadeem told her, "Speak up, baby." He wasn't with her smart-ass mouth.

"Y'all got all of this room, but we live with Charlie, sharing a bathroom," she snapped.

Kamala got up to get another bottle of wine because she really wanted this to be a fun night.

"You want to stay here?" He already knew the answer to his question but asked anyway since she wanted to start shit.

She rolled her eyes and crossed her arms. "I shoulda went to mama house."

"You've been spending time with Yara?" He was shocked to hear this.

Meme said, "We all have. Well, not Yanna, but us two have."

"And why am I just now hearing about this?" he asked his girls.

They all shrugged their shoulders and resumed eating.

Kamala rejoined the table and said, "Eat up because I have *Dulce De Leche* cheesecake for dessert and then a game of Uno." She had the biggest smile on her face, and the girls just looked at her and rolled their eyes. *Would this have been easier if they were in elementary school?* she wondered. "Ayanna, what do you plan on studying in school?"

"Not sure yet, either Economics or International Business." She was still undecided.

"Wowww, tough choices, what are your top schools?"

Kadeem was thankful that she shifted the conversation because Ayanna had lightened up and didn't sound so dry anymore. Dinner continued without another glitch, *thank God.*

"UNO!" Meme slammed the cards on the table. They were on the third round and the final one.

Kamala had washed the dishes and told the girls, "Thank you so much for coming over, it meant so much to me." She was truly thankful.

"Girls, we want to try and do this like once a week if it's okay with y'all?" He pulled his lady into his lap as they moved the conversation to a more serious topic.

"I'll try," Meme said.

Ayanna was okay with that. Kamala was smart and cool.

Yanise said, "I'll let y'all know what days I'm free," as if she worked three jobs. She was only in the ninth grade.

"Let us know, Oprah," Kadeem joked with her.

"Well, we can try for once every two weeks. Kamala and I want to spend as much time with y'all as we can. Soon we will be married, and I want y'all to be in the wedding as her bridesmaids."

She didn't expect that to come from his mouth. This was her first time even hearing him discuss the wedding. For a while, she thought it would never happen.

Kamala looked at him and smiled. "Yes, yes, we do," she followed up.

"Is that why y'all invited us over?" Ayanna questioned.

Kadeem looked at her and shook his head. "Of course not."

Meme and Yanise didn't look so convinced. "It's getting late, we need to go." Meme stood up, and her sisters did the same.

"That wasn't my intention. I didn't even have an intention."

Yanise chuckled, "Bad timing then." She was so over him it was ridiculous.

Kamala saw her man's face go from terrific to hopeless in two seconds. He walked off and left them in the kitchen. She had to say something.

"Listen, I know it's not my place-"

"So, don't even go there," Meme told her before she could even try.

"Well, this is my house, so I can say what I want to say." She was a grown ass woman. Meme had the right one today. "It's like y'all don't even see his effort. He loves y'all more than anything in this world."

Ayanna looked at her like she was crazy. "Girl, since when?"

They weren't buying the soap opera. Yanise waved, "Night-night." And just like that, they let themselves out.

Kamala locked the door, turned the alarm on and headed to check on her fiancé. The smell of marijuana led her to the living room.

"Baby." She was hurting for him. They were hard, and she now understood what he had been trying to explain to her for the longest.

Lone tears fell from his face, and he didn't even try to wipe them away. "I don't know what else to do," he whispered.

Kamala sat down and rubbed his chest. "They love you, it's taking some adjusting to, but I can tell they adore you."

He didn't believe her, and she didn't believe it herself.

"I wish it were her that got out of jail first. I wish that shit every night," he admitted to Kamala.

And that broke her heart. If that were the case, they would have never met, fell in love or be engaged right now. She vowed to make things right with him and his children because if it remained this way, he would never have peace, which meant the divorce would never happen or the wedding or her perfect family. Kamala loved him too much to let him go or to let him beat himself up. She did the only other thing she knew how to do to get his mind off what just took place.

Dropping to her knees and pulling his shorts down with the trims of her fingers, she purred, "I'm sorry about tonight, let me make you feel good, daddy." The wine she'd been sipping on tonight had her hormones raging.

Kadeem pulled from the blunt and inhaled deeply. "Do you love me?" He needed someone to love him right now.

She nodded her head as she exposed his penis to her lips. "With everything in me," she confessed before taking the whole thing in her mouth.

η

Charlie and KK were nestled up on the couch when Meme dropped her sisters off, honked the horn and kept it moving.

"Where she headed?" she asked her grandchildren after they locked the door.

"Who knows, chile. You won't believe what daddy said to us." Yanise kissed her papa's cheek and then sat in the middle of them.

"What?"

Ayanna told the story, and her grandparents shared a look before Charlie said, "Go get ready for bed, no phones," she dismissed them without offering her feedback. Charlie wasn't about to gossip with kids.

KK asked, "Do you think he's going to marry her for real?"

She shrugged her shoulders. "Hell, I didn't think him and Yara would last as long as they did, he loves hard."

"Like his father," KK said and kissed her cheek.

"I can't keep interfering, he needs to fix this. That girl can't be speaking for him. He's a grown ass man."

"Now I know you not talking," he teased the love of his life. Charlie was a feisty woman, and the one thing she never played about was Kadeem. Only recently did she start telling him a piece of her mind. For years, she kept her opinion to herself. Charlie only got in the mix when she needed to.

"If anything, she needs to be trying to win them over, not sticking her neck out for Kadeem's ass. Them girls ain't easy to impress."

"The concern shouldn't be to impress them, she's not marrying his kids," he argued.

"Well, what's the concern then?" He always had a different logic than she did, and almost forty-something years later she didn't know if she loved or hated that about him.

"The well-being of the children. They're torn because they don't know what's going on between him and Yara. They are confused. I'm going to talk with him."

The next morning, they saw the girls off to school, and Charlie told him she had errands to run and would be back later in the afternoon.

After she left, KK got dressed and drove to his favorite coffee shop in New York.

Kadeem took his fitted cap off once he crossed over into the bookstore where his dad asked him to link.

"Kadeem!" he called out to him. After ordering a beer, Kadeem joined his Pops. "Drinking so early?" KK asked.

He didn't get much sleep last night, even after his fiancé rode him for hours.

Ignoring him, he asked, "What are you reading?" His dad was an avid reader and the wisest man he knew.

"Something you wouldn't read."

"My life is fucked up, and I don't know what to do," he blurted out.

KK closed the book and looked at his son. If he wasn't going through something, then his brother was. He couldn't wait until the day where they both got a grip on life. Lately, Kasim was seeing better days, and that's because he listened to him when he gave him advice.

"Are you back in the streets?" was his first question.

He shook his head. "No, sir."

"Kadeem, are you back in the fucking streets?" he asked him again.

He looked into his eyes this time. "No, I'm not."

When he got out of jail, he dug up some money that he hid and cashed in on a few owed favors along with the percentage of one last drop. Riq was a real one, and he could have said, "Fuck you, nigga" but didn't. He gave him what was owed to him and Yara.

Kadeem would probably never have the millions he once had, and that was cool with him. As long as he could keep a roof over his head and provide for his children, he was content.

"When do you plan on speaking to Yara?"

He exhaled loudly and then took a swig of the beer. "What am I supposed to say? I can't even look at her." He knew that he had fucked up, and to see her look at him like he wasn't shit would kill him.

"You tell her the truth, whether it will hurt her or not. You get that shit in the open, and she gotta accept it and move on."

He had been in this place before when he fathered another child. Charlie was devastated. She hated him and cursed his name, but he couldn't hide his child anymore to keep her merry.

"I still love her." Now that was something he never told anyone. Hell, it was his first time confessing it, even to himself.

KK wasn't surprised. "Did you expect what y'all had to disappear?"

"But I love Kamala too. She's who I want to be with. Shit is fucked up." He didn't know what to do. What he and Yara had was special, and something he would forever cherish. However, they had been through some shit together, and he respected her for bearing his children and being the only person in his corner on many occasions. Now, the love he had for her was different; it was on the same level as the love he had for his mom and grandmother, aunts and shit. It wasn't the "head over heels, you make me happy" kind of love. And was it the ten years that did it? He didn't know.

Did he feel this way before the arrest? Kadeem couldn't answer that. However, he didn't want to explain himself, and he knew that wasn't cool, but it is what it is.

"If we can bow out of this gracefully, with no drama and just be there for the girls, I'll be good and at peace," he added.

KK said, "So, after you tell her the truth, you say exactly what you told me, and I believe she'll agree."

"And if she doesn't?"

KK pushed the beer towards him and smiled. "Then you got a problem on your hands, and it's called baby mama drama."

η

"Yara, I owe you my first Grammy."

She smiled at the youngin. "No, you don't. I'm happy I could help," she told him.

The sun had set, rose and went away again, and they were finally done. She was damn near forty, so the studio life wasn't for her. She was tired and hungry, but rather sleep than eat.

Miko left after the second hour saying that her late night and early morning days were over. There were about eight people left in the studio when she pulled her charger out of the socket and stuffed it into her purse.

"How do I get back to my car?" she asked one of the A & Rs.

"Uber will be your best bet."

She didn't know how to work Uber, so Yara called Meme and thankfully, she was up and told her she would be there soon.

Yara sat outside to get some fresh air after being in that dark and smoky studio for two days straight.

"Who are you?" A man got out of a Mercedes Jeep and questioned her.

She looked at him and then back on her phone. That was not how you talked to her.

"You're at my studio, I think I can ask you who you are?"

"Yeah you could, if you had said it nicer," she shot back. *Who in the hell did he think he was?* she thought to herself.

He stepped back and greeted someone who had walked out of the studio. "You know this chick?"

One of his producers informed him, "She's the shit! Bye, Yara."

She waved goodbye and went back to her phone. The man wasn't done with her though. "Yara? I like that. You're African?"

Yara laughed. *Laughter.* It had been a long time since she did that.

"Yo, where are you from?" He was ignorant. "Shit, I'm used to meeting Tanya's, Michelle's and shit, your name ain't common."

"My father is Muslim," she explained. No one had ever asked her about her name, nor did she talk to her dad at all.

"Nice to meet you, Yara." He held his hand out, hoping she wasn't offended by his direct approach.

She didn't shake his hand, but she acknowledged his greeting with a head nod. "I would say nice to meet you too, but I don't feel that way." Honesty was her thing. She didn't beat around the bush with niggas.

"Why did he say you're the shit? I know you ain't no model." He was trying to figure her out.

Should she be offended? "What are you trying to say?"

He snickered, "Nah, I was saying you dressed nice, most of the video vixens that slide through the studio be naked," he cleared it up.

Meme pulled up, and Yara was thankful. "See ya." She got up and headed to her daughter's car.

He turned around and followed her with his eyes, and the view was breathtaking. Her face was gorgeous, and so was the backside. Mama was stacked too.

"He got his eyes on you. Who is that, Ma?"

She shook her head. "I don't know, and I don't care." She leaned back in the chair. Yara was tired as hell.

"What you been doing? What is this?"

"Girl, pull off," she told her. She was ready to get to her car so she could go home and get in the bed.

"I had to be here for my job."

"Is it a club or something?" Meme wasn't familiar with Manhattan.

"No, baby, a studio."

She could tell her mom wasn't in the mood to talk, so she turned the radio on and took her to her car.

"I'll call you tomorrow, I'm drained," she somewhat apologized for being so short.

"Love you." Meme wasn't tripping. She was glad that her mama was staying busy and keeping her mind off her trifling daddy.

After she dropped her mother off, she went to school. Meme had a long day ahead of her, books and building her brand were her priorities right now.

When he made time for her, she made time for him, and last night he told her that he was about to slow down in the streets and wanted her to be around when she made that move. Words never impressed her, so she would watch him closely and see what he did.

Once Yara got home, she undressed and threw the clothes in a hamper before taking a shower. She brushed her teeth and washed her face while her body air dried. No matter how cold it was in her house, she still had to sleep with the fan on and one foot sticking out under the covers. Plus, now she had to be bare. Sleeping naked was her new thing, the feeling of her skin against the sheets did something to her that she couldn't explain.

"Thank You, Lord." She had confidence that things were about to turn around for her. It was never too late for a person to discover their purpose and passion, and no one could ever tell her that she would have spent forty-eight hours in a studio, especially after three kids.

Yara was looking forward to whatever was about to fall on her horizon. She had a whole new outlook on life. And for all those dark and disappointing days she spent in prison crying and being miserable, God was preparing her for the sunshine and infinite blessings.

Chapter Eight
"I hope you do good my nigga." – Txs

"Yeah… huh?... what?" She was still sleeping and trying her hardest to hear what her daughter was saying, but her voice was muffled which made it difficult for her to follow the conversation.

"She passed out on the floor." Ayanna was afraid and didn't know what to do.

"Where are y'all?"

"Headed to the hospital, Charlie told me to call you," she cried.

Yara figured they were going to the hospital closest to where Charlie lived. "I'm on the way."

She hung up the phone, threw on something quick to wear, locked her apartment and headed to the hospital. She didn't know if something was wrong with Meme, Charlie or Yanise, but whoever it was, she had already started praying.

The thing with her and religion right now was confusing. In her spare time in prison, she spent a lot of hours at the library and researched on a few religions. For the most part, she could connect with Muslim the most, but had grown up believing that there was one God, and so she fell into the Christian category. But for the past four years, she'd been praying to Allah.

"Inshallah," she whispered as she parked her car. In His will, she knew that everything was already handled. Tragedy wouldn't dare strike as soon as she made it back home. It couldn't.

"I'm here for... uh…" She didn't have a name, and luckily one wasn't needed because Meme and Riq were right behind her. "Ma, they this way." She dragged her arm down the hallway.

Yara looked at Riq and gave him a half smile. For now, he was on her good side until he did something to piss Meme off, then she was gon' cut his neck.

"What happened?" she asked her eldest.

"I don't know, Charlie called and said Yanise fell out on the floor while she was fixing some cereal."

That sounded unusual. They made it to the lobby, and there was Kadeem, Charlie, a red-faced Ayanna and a woman, the lawyer. It was Kadeem's fiancé.

Yara looked like shit being that she was in a deep slumber. The grey jogger pants were baggy on her shape, and she had on a white cotton t-shirt and Nike slides. Her hair was in a bun on the top of her head and a jean jacket under her arm in case the lobby got chilly.

The woman was dressed in business casual, and Kadeem had on active wear.

"What happened?" Meme interrogated.

Riq saw the uncomfortable look on Yara's face, but then it quickly went away. Seeing her shift so quickly reminded him of the old days when they would be in the trenches. No one could turn that good girl-bad girl shit off quite like she could.

She remained by the vending machine, refusing to be buddy-buddy or cordial with Kadeem or any of them. She hadn't spoken to Charlie or Kadeem since the situation in her kitchen and wouldn't be the first to reach out. Call it petty or whatever, but she could still be in support of her child from afar.

KK came from across the way with two coffees in his hand. When he saw his daughter-in-law, his face lit up.

"Despite the circumstances, it is very good to see you, daughter." He smiled at her, and she gave him a faint expression back.

"Let me take these to Charlie," he told her after kissing her cheek and walking off.

Kamala saw the exchange and wondered if his parents would ever greet her that way. Yara seemed uncomfortable, and she expected that, but she wasn't leaving.

Kadeem tried to come to the hospital by himself, and she told him, "We are a family, I want to be there."

He knew that Yara would come. Why wouldn't she? Yanise was her daughter. And because he didn't know what state of mind his wife was in, he didn't think Kamala needed to be there. Yara wasn't *hood-hood*, but if stroked she could go gangsta.

KK made sure his lady was good, and he hugged Meme and shook hands with Riq before returning to Yara.

"How are you?"

She shrugged her shoulders. "Tired. I been up for two days, shouldn't we be focusing on Yanise though?" She wasn't trying to be rude.

KK took no offense. "Certainly, they're running some tests. We should know something soon. Do you want to take a seat?" he asked her.

She shook her head. "I'm fine right here, with my arms crossed, so I don't have to punch a bitch." There was no laughing, she was serious.

"Ole Yara," he said before walking off to join everyone else.

Yara stayed right where she was, staring straight ahead at a portrait of a boat in the middle of the water until she heard the doctor ask for the family of Yanise Moreland.

She stepped forward and stood behind her daughters as the doctor flipped through his notepad.

"You don't know off the top of your head?" Kadeem cross-examined, impatiently.

Charlie cleared her throat and looked at him, silencing him. She learned a long time ago that you didn't be rude or mean to the people caring for your loved ones. Some doctors would go above and beyond to fight and make sure your family lived, and some didn't care at all.

"Yes sir, my apologies I was trying to find her levels. So, your daughter is pregnant, thirteen weeks. She fell out because she was dehydrated, and the baby wasn't getting any vitamins or nutrients," the doctor explained.

All of them were quiet. No one had anything to say. Yanise was having sex? She was pregnant?

Tears ran down Charlie's face. No one was more hurt than she was. Yanise was in her care. She was her baby, she was the one she held close. How did this happen? How could she have missed this? Where was the time for her to even have sex? Sure enough, she was a little snappy, hell, they all were. All three of the girls had their father's personality. But she wasn't a grown or fast child, not at all.

"I can't believe this. Can you run the test again?" she requested as tears fell down her face.

"We ran it three times ma'am, to be sure."

Kadeem dropped his head, and Kamala rubbed his back. "It's okay, baby."

And that's when Charlie fucking snapped, "She's fourteen, it is not okay!"

"Well, she lived with you, so what was she doing? Who is the father?" Kamala questioned.

Meme stepped forward. "You better watch your mouth."

And her boo couldn't do much without blowing their "low-key" status of the relationship.

KK thanked the doctor, "Thank you, can we go see her?" he asked, wanting to see his granddaughter.

"Yeah sure, she can go home in a few hours with some prenatal vitamins and stuff for the baby. I would suggest making her an appointment with an OBGYN as soon as possible to explore her options."

Options. A fourteen-year-old child shouldn't have to be exploring any options other than what college she planned on going to and what color polish to get on her toes. They were all lost in their thoughts of why this happened.

Ayanna felt as if she should have been spending more time with her little sister.

Meme wondered did they ignore the signs of her being pregnant. She couldn't remember if her tummy was getting bigger or not. And then a flash of jealousy ran through her mind of her sister being able to carry a child, and she could barely get through six weeks. Something must be wrong with her, it had to be.

"So, what are we going to do?" Meme asked her folks.

Charlie was silent, and KK believed that this was up to Yanise and her parents.

"Kadeem, son, I know you're probably wondering what, why and who, and y'all will figure that out-"

He cut his father off, *"I'm going to kill whoever the fuck did this!"*

"Did what?" Kamala was lost. She prayed he wasn't one of those dads that acted as if their daughters did no wrong. And until they knew the whole situation, he shouldn't be trying to kill anyone.

"Fucked my daughter!" He was enraged.

"She fucked back, what is that going to do?" she grilled him. Kadeem sounded stupid and to throw his freedom away again sounded ridiculous.

Everyone looked at her, they were thinking it but wouldn't dare say it to him. She had a mouth on her.

Riq walked off to answer his phone; his baby mother was blowing up his line.

"What is he doing here?" Kadeem wanted to know. He loved Riq like a son, but this wasn't a hanging out type of event. He didn't even plan on telling anyone that his baby girl was pregnant.

Meme looked at her mother but she had nothing to say, so she lied and said, "He brought ma up here."

Kamala turned to Yara, and she cocked her head and stared back, wanting the bitch to say something.

"Y'all should go in there and talk to her, let her know that she is not in this alone," KK suggested to the parents. They needed her right now more than ever.

Kadeem couldn't do it though. His baby girl... was pregnant. This still didn't sound right. "Not right now, let mama go," he said. He couldn't lay his eyes on her now.

Charlie shook her head. "This is all my fault." She was too cool, too laid back, too chill with them. For a second, the thought ran through her mind of molestation. But the way Yanise's mouth was set up, she knew she would have spoken up if someone was messing with her, or would she? There were so many stories on the news about little girls being touched by uncles, coaches, teachers and sometimes, their own damn siblings. Never in a million years did she expect to be in this situation with her own grandchild. Pregnant at fourteen. Charlie was heartbroken. Honestly, she would have expected this from Ayanna or Meme, but Yanise? She was very shocked.

"Charlie, no it is not."

Yara chimed in, "Whose fault is it then?"

All she did was ask them to watch after her children, and this is what she comes home to? A pregnant fourteen-year-old, a daughter who is in love with a drug dealer who was raised to be like a brother to her, and another child who she still hadn't figured out yet. Together, they had all failed these damn kids. That's how Yara looked at it.

"Yo." Kadeem didn't play when it came to his mother, so she had better tread lightly.

Her eyes cut at him, and she couldn't even speak to him. Yara walked off, arms still crossed because on her children, if she even dropped them she probably would have knocked him clean the fuck out.

"Ma, where you going?" Ayanna asked. They had to figure out what they were going to do about Yanise. Right now, it wasn't about her and daddy.

"Home," she chunked the deuces up.

They all exchanged looks, but no one said anything until Kamala suggested, "How about we stay here with her until she's released and then meet at Charlie's house, give her time to talk and decide what's best for her and the baby?"

Ayanna and Meme wanted to say, "bitch mind your business" but her suggestion was a good one.

Charlie ran her hands through her dreads. "My heart is hurting," she complained, and she wasn't speaking figuratively.

"It's going to be okay, my love," KK whispered in her ear.

She didn't believe him. Nothing would be okay. Whatever Yanise did, whether keeping the child or getting rid of it, she would be scarred either way.

η

There was a knock on her door, and it had to be one of her kids because no one else knew where she stayed.

"All I want to do is sleep," she mumbled under her breath. She flipped the comforter back and got out of bed, sliding her feet into a pair of house shoes and moseying slowly into the living room where the front door was.

When she left the hospital, she stopped and got a coffee and cried, weeping silently for her daughter. She had failed her, and Yara wished she could reset. She didn't regret meeting Kadeem because he gave her God's greatest gifts, and those were her children. However, she had several chances to leave him and never did. She was foolish and blind for love.

If she would have left after Yanise, then she could guarantee her baby wouldn't be pregnant right now. And maybe, Meme would have moved after high school instead of still being in the hood, in love with a D-Boy.

Before she went home, Miko had texted her to slide through the office and look at the finalized images for Nash's album cover, and she ended up being there for three hours.

She had concluded that her job no longer had set office hours. It was a Sunday morning, and she was at work, and the office was in full swing. She didn't make it back home and in the bed until one in the morning, and she swore her eyes hadn't been closed more than twenty minutes before her door was being knocked on.

"Who is it?" Her ear was to the door.

"Me."

Kadeem? What the fuck did he want? "Yanise with you?" she questioned, thinking that was why he came over. If it had nothing to do with Yanise, he shouldn't be at her door.

"Nah."

Well, why was he at her house? And which one of her kids told him where she laid her head? Yara didn't trust him anymore, and he couldn't come in her house.

"Why are you here?" she asked. She was exhausted and wanted to go back to sleep.

"Yara, you know we need to talk. We can't keep avoiding each other."

Typical Kadeem, putting the blame on her as well. He wasn't man enough to carry the load by himself. "You've been avoiding me," she responded.

"Man, open the damn door." He knocked again, this time a little harder.
Patience wasn't his forte, and he came over here on a peaceful tip, and she was making him lose it.

She took a deep breath and unlocked the door. "You ain't got no business over here at no one in the morning," she said to him.

"We gotta come to some common ground, *tonight*. I'm not leaving until we do that." He was serious.

She rolled her eyes and closed the door behind him. A bulge was poking out from the back of his jeans, and she reached forward and grabbed his gun.

In five seconds, she had removed the clip and put the gun on safety. He spun around and said, *"What the fuck?"*

"You on papers, right? Or is that another lie you told me? You shouldn't be carrying a gun. And I'm a felon, I can't be around armed weapons," she said and winked at him.

"Give it back."

She shook her head. "Why? You scared I'm going to shoot your lying ass?"

He exhaled loudly. His eyes were bloodshot red, and his shoulders slumped. He seemed irritated and relaxed at the same time, which told her that he was high and possibly tipsy.

"Yara, give me my gun."

She walked around him and sat the gun on the small bar top, which separated her living room from the kitchen.

"What are we talking about? I don't need an apology," she tried to speed up the conversation, eager to return to bed.

He didn't know if he should sit down or not, her attitude was throwing him off.

"You don't need an apology, but I need to apologize for lying to you and keeping you in the dark about what happened. Yara, you gotta believe me. I wanted to tell you on so many occasions-"

"Why did you marry me? Because of the girls or because you needed me to help you get money?"

The past few weeks she had been busy with work and still had time to think about the why and what of what went wrong.

He looked at her, saddened by her question. "So now you think I don't love you or never loved you?" He couldn't believe her.

"I don't know you at all. Because the Kadeem Moreland that I once loved would have never done the shit you did, let alone get engaged while still married to me. How does that even work? And she's not even your type," she added.

He looked at her, knowing she didn't want the truth, nor could she handle it.
"Yara, things happen, and I'm here to admit my mistakes. We gotta get this shit together."

She shook her head. "It's so easy for you to say things happen. You weren't sitting in a cell for ten years. You didn't come home to children who didn't really care if you were here or not-"

"They're happy you're home," he interrupted her.

She wasn't stupid. "If I never came home they wouldn't have cared, let's keep it one hundred. I'm a big girl, I can handle it. You moved on, and they moved on. Everybody living their life. I'm the one trying to catch up." And that was the truth.

He wanted to make this better. "What do I have to do for you not to hate me?"

She leaned against the wall and closed her eyes, holding her tears at bay.

Kadeem finally sat down on her leather sectional and pulled a blunt from his ear and asked her for a lighter. She didn't have to respond, he peeped one on the end of the table. He sparked the blunt and took a few deep pulls on it.

After they picked Yanise up, of course, she had nothing to say. Every question he asked her came with a shaking of the head, and all she could do is fucking shrug her shoulders until he got fed up with her nonchalant behavior and slapped her.

Kamala yelled at him, and he got out of the car and walked off, trying to cool his head. He was so angry and embarrassed. Why was she even having sex? He couldn't understand any of this. Yanise didn't even react or respond when Kamala asked her was she okay.

When Kadeem got back in the car, he told his fiancé, "Drop her fast ass off."

Tears ran down her face, but she never said a word. No one understood what she was going through. They dropped her off and didn't even bother coming in.

Yanise walked into the house, bypassed her family, stormed into her room and slammed the door. She was done with all of them. No one cared about her for real.

Kamala preached to him non-stop until they made it home, and he was thankful that she got out and told him she had to do some work before bed.

As soon as she walked into the house, he pulled off. Getting drunk and high led him to Yara's house. And he sat in the car for two hours before he found the courage to knock on her door.

"Yara, you had my heart… and then you went away."

"Correction, baby. *We* went away. *We* were sentenced at the same mother fucking time. *We* were supposed to do those ten years together. *You* bailed out."

"That's not what the fuck happened!" he said. He blew out smoke through his nose. "Can we put that behind us and focus on Yanise please?"

"No, we can't put it behind us, Kadeem. Not only did you lie to me, but you also had my kids lying, and you are engaged. What the hell am I supposed to do with my life when you were my world?"

John was his best friend. They didn't talk every day, not even every week. John was still in the streets, so of course there wasn't much to chop it up about, but that was still his homie. At Kadeem's age, niggas really didn't pillow talk. However, he needed to talk to someone.

"We fucked. I fucked the shit out of her… nah, she fucked the shit out of me," he told him as soon as he sat down at the table where they agreed to meet for breakfast.

He hadn't even been home to take a shower. Kamala had called him three times, and he sent her a quick text saying he was talking to his father and then turned his phone off. Of course, he felt bad about cheating on her and at the same time, he was still a nigga, and Yara was his wife.

"Nigga, you wanted to fuck her when you scooped her up," he laughed. John wasn't surprised, he was always team Yara. They didn't make women like her anymore. She was definitely one of a kind.

Kadeem shook his head. "If I never fucked her again, I would have been all right. I love my lady. She caught me off guard with calling me her world and shit. Man, I don't know. It shouldn't have happened." It was a bad idea. A good, toe-curling experience, but it solved nothing.

"Now what?" John was curious as to what was next on his list to do since he knew all about his engagement.

He sat back in the booth and shrugged his shoulders. "When I woke up this morning, she was on her balcony praying or something. I don't know, she a lil' weird to me now too..."

"Did y'all talk?"

That was the thing, did they *really* talk or did she just say anything to get him out of her place.

"I asked her how she felt about last night, and she said she was relieved."

"Yara got the dust knocked off that pussy," John laughed and clapped his hands together.

He closed his eyes and his legs, thinking of how tight she was. The thought alone had his dick hard again.

"Yeah, she said she was relieved, and then I told her that I loved Kamala and she said, I know."

John's eyes got big. There was no way Kadeem really said that shit. *"Nigggaaa, and you still alive?"*

Kadeem dropped his head. "Yara be knowing shit, it's crazy how her mind works."

"She's always been that way though."

"I told her I wanted to marry Kamala, and she said okay, and then I left."

Kadeem left out the conversation they had about his daughter and her pregnancy.

"Do you think she will tell your girl?"

Kadeem shook his head. That wasn't how Yara rolled. "Nah, for what? It was one time, that shit ain't happening again."

John smirked, "Nigga, please." He still had a little hope for him and Yara. They belonged together, despite the bullshit.

"I'm for real, man. It was good, but for the sake of the kids, I can't be fucking they mama. I got a good woman in my corner."

"You keep saying fucking, nigga. That was your wife... still is! The kind of love that y'all had ain't wrapped up in one night."

His words had some truth to them, but the way she put it on him and vice versa was enough to make up for lost time and give them closure all in one night and into the wee hours of the morning.

Yara fucked him like she had a point to prove, and hopefully she didn't, because he meant what he said. He was sorry about what happened, but he couldn't take it back, and he also loved his lady and wanted a life with her.

Yara was short with him this morning, but he knew if she had more to say she would have. She didn't bite her tongue for no one.

"Damn," he mumbled under his breath.

John was now on the phone. "What?"

Kadeem shook his head. "Nothing…" He still couldn't believe that he and Yara had shared a bed.

"What you mean?" He was such an idiot and couldn't think of anything else to say.

Yara shook her head. "Get the fuck out." She wasn't about to let him play mind games with her.

"I already told you I'm not going nowhere until we talk."

"What is there to talk about? I'm over you, I don't care about you. Fuck you and the bitch you're about to marry," she snapped and rolled her neck with every 'fuck you' that fell from her lips. She was mad and hurt and lonely. Her job was cool, and she was thankful for the opportunity and after a long day, making dinner and taking a bubble bath was cool. However, she had no one to share the events of her day with.

"You're so little, why your ass ain't grow taller while you were away?" That question came out of nowhere. He was staring at her as she went off on him, and all he could think about was how cute she was. Yara was seriously a work of art. And she couldn't have done ten years. Her face bore no signs of jail time.

"Kadeem, if you really think you about to sit here and kick it with me like we are cool, you clearly don't remember how I will fuck you up in here. Now, I'm trying to be cool with you off the strength of not wanting to lose my freedom again-"

He cut her off, "You would kill me?"

He should have already known the answer to that question. Her eyes darkened, and she told him without hesitation, "If I could get away with it, I would." And that was the truth

Her wanting to kill him turned him on. He stood up, the blunt hanging in the corner of his mouth as he walked towards her. "You got my gun, shoot me," he taunted her.

"Kadeem, I'm barely in my right mind these days, don't play with me," she warned him.

He pushed her to the wall and pulled her arms up over her head. He took the blunt out of his mouth and blew the smoke in her face, and she turned to the side.

"Yara, I never meant to hurt you." He needed her to know that deep down in her soul. He never had ill intentions.

"FUCK YOU." She tried to knee him but didn't move fast enough because he dropped the blunt and grabbed her leg with his now free hand and pulled that up too.

Her heartbeat increased. "What are you doing?"

"I used to have you in all kinds of positions. Do you remember that?"

He was drunk. She was still angry. Their daughter was pregnant. There was too much going on right now.

Yara told him, "We can't do this." She refused to give him her body, not caring how horny she had been since she got out, and she had lost count of how many times she had played with her pussy, wishing someone would lick and suck on her clit.

"I don't want us beefing," he whispered.

She closed her eyes, feeling the temperature in the room go up and suddenly, her body got clammy. "You'll never be on my good side again."

Kadeem licked her neck and then bit into her bronze colored skin. "What I gotta do, Yara?" He would do anything for her not to hate him.

She whimpered as he planted kisses in every spot he bit. The pain and pleasure he was presenting to her had her mind all over the place. He dared not play with her. And in one motion, he had his hands in between her legs while he continued to kiss her neck.

"You're a cheater! You cheated on me-"

"Shut the hell up and let me make you cum."

And it went from there. He removed his clothes and then slipped off the shirt she was wearing and tossed it onto the floor. Kadeem picked up the blunt that was already out and placed it on the table. They were naked. She was nervous, and he was horny.

"Your body still... shit." He was anticipating what she would feel like and prayed he still had the green light to proceed.

Her chest heaved up and down. She was riddled with so many emotions. He had to make the first move because she didn't dare possess the strength to do so.

"Kadeem, I can't believe-"

She was about to start back up with what he did and didn't do, and he didn't want to hear it right now. His dick was rock hard. Kadeem rushed her and kissed her with ten years of backed up passion, and she melted in his arms.

As the tears ran down her face, she kissed him back, wanting him to feel what she had always felt for him, even when she was away, holding him down.

He pushed her legs apart and went right in without warning or foreplay. She was wet, she was already a tsunami, and he knew that didn't change. With every stroke, she got wetter.

Yara was moaning so damn loud he moved her from the wall to the bed and damn near drowned in her pussy. Her body was shaking, her legs vibrating and her honey pot was pouring out buckets of cum.

He fucked her in every single position he could, and she begged him not to stop. Yara felt liberated and on fire. He was the same man that she had loved since her younger days, and sadly, that damn dick was still spell-binding. When she came for the very last time, he joined her, nutting all in her pussy.

"Damnnnnnnn!" He was exhausted. Kadeem pulled out of her and fell straight to sleep.

Yara peeled from under him and showered. She never went to sleep, and when he found her on the balcony a few hours later, he told her that last night was good, but he still loved his new chick.

She had the sign she had been praying for.

Chapter Nine
"It's like a lot of games are being played right now." – Drake

"Shit," Yara moaned out in pleasure. He was taking her there, *nah*, he had already got her to her peak, and yet and still, her body never stopped pouring out its riches. She hadn't felt this way in ten damn years.

There wasn't a rabbit, butterfly, not even a gorilla dick that could do what her estranged husband was doing to her body. He didn't deserve her. He wasn't worthy of being granted access to hearing her scream. She never called his name. She refused. Kadeem wasn't her nigga no more.

"Why you acting like you getting sleepy?" he challenged her in a low husky tone.

She ignored him and mounted his dick, sliding down slowly, inch by inch. He opened her up like a flower blooming for the first time.

"Don't make me remind you of what I'm good at," she replied with attitude. She got hers and then allowed him to reach his climax before she rolled off him and caught her breath.

"Yara-"

She jumped in her seat, coffee now sprinkled all over her white button-down. *"Oh my God."* She didn't feel like going home to change, and she had a meeting today that she absolutely couldn't be late for.

"I'm so sorry," the woman apologized.

"It's fine. Can I help you?" She didn't recognize the woman and was now irritated that she had interrupted her dream of her wack ass husband, who she needed to stop thinking about but couldn't.

"I'm Heather. Miko sent me over. I do the paperwork," she said and smiled.

And still the question was, "And how can I help you?" Clearly, Yara didn't understand what she wanted. She wasn't rude about it at all.

"I need you to confirm that this is how you spell your name for the EP." She fished inside a tan Dange Dover laptop bag and handed her a manila folder. "I'm going to come back around and scoop it from you in an hour or so." She left the paperwork on her desk and walked out of her office.

Yara had no clue what she was talking about, and when she opened it and properly read every page, she was in disbelief and complete shock. Using the work phone on her desk, she called Miko who answered on the last ring.

"Hey, girl?" She sounded exhausted.

"Hey, were you sleep?" She never started a conversation without making sure it was a good time for the person on the other end of the line. Yara had always been a sympathetic person.

"Yeah girl, wasup?"

"Cool. So, some lady named Heather just dropped off some paperwork saying I needed to sign it, but I read it, and it says-"

Miko interrupted her, "That's right. You're the executive producer. You did the whole mixtape, girl. You are getting a check and your credit," she said, yawning loudly into the phone.

Yara wasn't expecting this. "I did that to help. All I did was listen and critique. I am not a producer." She didn't think she deserved the title or the money.

"You are a beast, embrace it, Yara." Before she could tell her no again, Miko told her, "Are you going to the pop-up show in Miami? You should have gotten the email."

Yara checked her email while they were still on the phone. "Tonight?" She had so much she needed to take care of with her family. They still hadn't reached a decision with Yanise and her pregnancy.

"Yep, see you then. I'm trying to catch up on some much-needed sleep," she said.

They ended the conversation, and she checked the calendar. Other than her meeting at two, she had time to run and get her eyebrows done and stop by Charlie's house.

"Hey, I'll be back. Can you tell Heather I signed the paperwork?" she told her new friend, Marsha.

"Sure thing, mamacita."

Yara hopped in her Lexus and headed downtown, remembering that she had no suitcase and was unsure if she could even leave the state. She had more to do than she realized and might not be able to swing by Charlie's before her meeting.

It hadn't even been a month since she was released from prison, and her life was already busy, busy, busy but she dared not to complain. Other than her child being pregnant, her husband in love with someone else and them randomly making love, she was thankful. There was more going for her than against her right now, and maybe that's why she still found the strength to smile and not complain.

η

"Why you looking at me like that?" Riq asked his boo.

Meme licked her lips and sat back on the bed, pushing her knees to her chest and shrugging her shoulders. "Would you judge me if I tell you that I'm getting turned on watching you lick that blunt?" She was horny, and it had been a minute since he blessed her in the bedroom.

Meme was feening for a touch and a release from her man.

He shook his head. "Nah, I know these lips do something to you." She was always kissing, licking and pulling on them whenever they were on that type of wave.

The late night, early morning, before and after work, in the shower, drunk after the club kind of wave. Her body reacted to him in a way that men only dreamed of. You wanted your girl to love you and fuck with you because you were real and because you made her happy. And he knew that they were in a great space, and that shit made him feel good on the inside, but he could never verbally tell her that.

"I miss you," she admitted to him. Lately, she had been in her feelings, and he could tell.

Riq laughed, "Where I been, bae? Where I'm going?" He was bare-chested, and his shirt was on the iron board for when it was time for him to get his day started.

She came over to kill time until her next class, and he had just woken up. "Hopefully nowhere."

Riq concealed the blunt. "I ain't, this right here is forever."

"Till death?" she raised her eyebrow, wanting to know.

He nodded his head. "Yep."

The way her dad handled the situation with her mom bothered her and had been weighing heavily on her mind since Yara had been released.

"Can I ask you something without you getting mad?"

He lit the blunt and sat back on the bed, coming in between her legs and laying his head on her breast. Riq propped one arm on her thigh and got comfortable.

"You know we talk about everything, speak your mind."

She took a deep breath. "When it all went down with my folks, how did you feel? Would you ever do that to me, Riq?" she had to ask.

She wanted to know because loyalty was rare. And, how much did he love her? On a serious note. Meme had her eggs in his basket whether she wanted to admit that or not. Riq was all she wanted.

For a while, he said nothing. He smoked while she waited for him to voice his opinion. "You know if it weren't for your parents, I wouldn't have shit or be the man I am-"

She knew all of that. "You don't have to tell me, I know how you feel about them, that's not what I'm asking you."

Meme didn't give him a chance to finish. "I was getting to the point of me loving them, and honestly, it was your Moms who looked out. She loved me, nurtured me like I came right out of her, and I was fucked up behind the case. They took all them charges for us. It was a lot of us that should have went down, but Yara and Kadeem ate them charges for the sake of everybody," he kept it real with her. "Your Dad has always been a cool nigga, and I respect him to the fullest, but if that was you and me, I wouldn't have been able to sleep knowing you in there while I'm out here."

"And he moved on, like could you ever do that to me?"

Riq shook his head and handed her the blunt. "I never even want you to ask me that shit cus what we got is different."

"Baby, how? We going down the same path they are."

He turned around and looked at her. "Don't you ever say that shit, we are nothing like them."

Riq knew that she didn't have a clue on the real story behind her parents and the crimes they committed. She knew bits and pieces, and even the little she did know was far-fetched.

"What the fuck does that mean?" she questioned. Should she be offended?

Riq laid back down and said again, "Nothing, baby. Don't say that shit no more. We got our own thing going on. Period."

He would never leave her in jail to rot while he was out getting money. As a man, Kadeem should have made a better decision or at least tried to fight to get her out. Maybe he did. He really wasn't sure, but on the outside looking in, it didn't seem that way.

His opinion hadn't changed about him because that was a personal situation. And thankfully, he handled all his own business now, delivery, transactions and customer interactions included. Riq made his own moves and no longer had to answer to Kadeem, so everything was peaches and cream. He wanted to tell him soon about his relationship with Meme, but the right time never presented itself.

"Get your mind off them. They grown, they'll figure it out," he told her. The room was so silent he could hear the wheels in her brain turning.

After another minute or so of silence, she exhaled, "I love you, baby."

He was happy to hear her say it, finally. He smiled to himself as he told her, "And that's all that matters."

Little did he know, she wanted to hear it back…

η

Today was a long day, and she knew she would be knocked out on the flight to Miami. Somehow, she managed to get her eyebrows waxed, purchase a small suitcase, go to the meeting for her job, clean her place up, do laundry and now she was at her mother-in-law's house sitting in the driveway, wishing things could be different.

She didn't like Charlie anymore and didn't think that they would ever recover from what had taken place. Charlie picked and chose when she wanted to be on her side or input her two cents, and she didn't appreciate that shit.

Kadeem wanted to talk, that's what he claimed, but she couldn't tell from how quick he fucked her. And don't get her wrong, it was astounding. He knew what he was doing in between the sheets, but the feeling of being damn near electrocuted didn't take place, and that's when she had to admit that no matter how much you love someone, ten years apart is still ten years apart. And it took them having sex for her to think about a few things.

The morning he woke up and found her sitting on her balcony, she had been heavily meditating on things she had pushed to the back of her mind to recreate a life she had always wanted with him. And sadly, before she went away, the love was still there. She loved him beyond measure but no longer was it how it was when they first met.

She had been reading a book called "The Love Languages" by Gary Chapman and discovering her love language, and they weren't on the same page. *Before or after prison.*

Yara couldn't put too much thought into the "what could have and what could it be" because the truth of the matter was that they were over. So, she closed her mind off and got out of the car and walked up the driveway to the woman who she had looked at as a mother and knocked on her front door.

Yanise answered, and she almost thought she saw a glimmer in her eyes but then it went away, and she rolled her eyes instead. "What are you doing here?" she questioned.

"Uh, I came to talk to you, lil girl. Is Charlie here?" Yara was giving her the same attitude she gave her.

She walked in and sat on the couch, putting both of her phones on vibrate.
Yanise locked the door and stood right by it. She was frightened. Maybe because no one had yelled at her yet, and she needed to hear someone raise their voice at her, then it would seem as if someone was concerned, or even cared about her for once.

"Come sit down. I'm not going to punch you… yet," she added that last part under her breath. Yanise had her phone in hand, and she couldn't believe that Charlie didn't take it. "Let me get that, lil girl. Ain't no phone. Who you texting?"
She pried into her "personal business."

"What am I supposed to do without a phone?" Her mama was tripping.

Yara shrugged her shoulders. "You'll be fine. I didn't have one for ten years. Read a book, learn something new," she suggested and put the phone in her purse.

There was no telling when she would get it back.

"This is ridiculous!"

Yara agreed with her there. "I feel the same way about you being pregnant, so let's get to the bottom of this. No attitude, no talking back and from now on it will be yes ma'am and no ma'am." She wasn't playing with her anymore. Yanise was damn near grown and acted like the world owed her something.

"What?" Yanise rolled her eyes.

"Roll them again, and I'm going to snatch them *out*."

Charlie and KK came giggling through the front door. She still wasn't fucking with Charlie, but it did please her to see them smiling and getting along. Back in the day, Charlie used to damn near tear KK's head off. They were now seeing better days, and that was a good thing.

"Heyyyy, Yara." KK came and kissed her forehead.

Charlie saw her car outside and had prepared herself before they walked in.

"Yara," she said in a dry and boring voice.

"Charlie." She didn't even look her way.

Yanise chimed in, "She took my phone."

KK told his granddaughter, "Well that's what moms do."

"She don't pay the bill."

Yara eyed her, and she sat back and shut up.

"What brings you by?" Charlie wondered.

"Checking on Yanise and trying to see what are we doing about the… baby." It was still so hard for her to say. No one talked about the baby; it was as if the whole thing never happened

"Uh, we don't know yet," she said slowly.

KK continued walking to the bedroom for a nap.

Yara sat up and crossed her legs. "Well I'm here, let's figure it out. Yanise, what do you want to do?" She would give her a chance to speak her mind. The girl was fourteen, she had no clue of what she wanted.

In her son's absence, Charlie said, "Kadeem isn't here."

Yara couldn't care less about him being there. "Fill him in."

"Have you told the baby's father? Are y'all a couple?" she interrogated her, knowing that any sort of "connection" at that young of an age was only lust and temporary satisfaction.

Yanise shook her head. "Nah, we ain't like that."

Charlie stayed by the wall with her hands at her side. "Well, what is it like then, Yanise?" She wanted to know, and Yara did too.

"I was bored I guess," she mumbled and shrugged her shoulders.

"Yanise, how long have you been having sex? Was it here? In my house?" She was relieved that Yara came over and started this conversation because she didn't have the strength to do so. Charlie was still blaming herself.

"Yeah, sometimes, and not long, Charlie." She wasn't interested in this conversation and felt like she was being put on the spot.

"Why didn't y'all use protection? Did you want to get pregnant?"

Yanise stood up. *"Look, y'all not about to keep asking me all these questions. It was a mistake!"*

Yara said, "Mistakes have to be paid for, and in your case, you'll be a mother by the end of the year, so what you gon' do?" she gave it to her straight, no chaser.

"I don't know. Charlie here, she can watch the baby-"

And that's where Charlie now had to hurt her feelings. "Oh no, ma'am." She walked further into the living room where they were all in a triangle of some sort. "My raising babies days are over, I can't do it." She was grave about that.

"I can't drop out of school." Tears flooded her eyes, and Yara thought to herself, *Oh, now you wanna cry.*

"You don't have to drop out. You'll be the pregnant girl with the big stomach and swollen ankles until the baby gets here, and then you'll take a few months off, put the baby in daycare, go to school, go to work."

She cut her off, *"Work?"*

"Uh, who gon' buy pampers and stuff for the baby?" Yara wanted to know.

She looked around the room. "You, Daddy and Charlie."

"Yanise, you are fourteen-years-old. You wanted to have sex and be grown, now you really about to be an adult." And that was the truth.

She began to cry harder. "I was just bored!"

Who gets bored and has sex? A child with no supervision. No one was worried about Yanise.

Yara had to go. "This is what we are going to do. You are going to get an abortion and get on birth control. You will come live with me and be under strict supervision. You can still do some things, but you are about to be in activities. I don't care if it's tennis or golf, you will be active after school. No more lashes, stiletto nails or cut off t-shirts, and we are dying that hair back black. You can get color when you are sixteen-"

"You got me so messed up!" Yanise clapped her hands together. She looked at Charlie to help her out but, her grandmother agreed with Yara.

"I think that's best, everything she said." It was time to slow Yanise down and get her on track.

"So, you don't want me no more?"

Charlie told her, "Don't even do that. I love you. I have had you since you were three years old, it's time for your mom to step in and be there for you."

"An abortion?" Yanise whispered.

Yara and Charlie both nodded their heads. "I'll take her tomorrow."

She was against all of it. "Give me my phone so I can call my daddy."

Now that was funny. "Girl, you think he about to be a grandfather, he's barely a father," she laughed.

Charlie warned her, "Yara, watch it now."

"I said what I said." And she meant that shit. She stood up. "We have a plan and should all come together to make it happen. I'll be back in two days."

Yanise rolled her eyes again and stomped to her room. They heard the door slam loudly right after.

Charlie faced Yara. "Do you think the abortion will scar her?" She was worried about Yanise's mental state of doing something so traumatic at such a young age.

"Having sex didn't, so no, she will be okay."

"Yara, we seriously need to talk," she said with sincere eyes.

She backed up and shook her head. "Ten years... I been calling your house phone for ten years. Charlie, we have had plenty of time to talk."

η

It wasn't her first time on a private plane. It had been quite a while since she had been on one though, so it felt good to enjoy a few hours of luxury. Between her daughter, husband and this new busy ass job, Miami was what she needed. If only for about seventy-two hours, Yara planned on enjoying the business getaway.

"Where are we staying?" she asked once she woke up and saw that the pilots were preparing for landing.

"Fontainebleau. The Viceroy closed down, and I am pissed," one of the other chicks on the flight told her.

"Haven't stayed there in years."

"You've been to the Fontainebleau before?" she questioned.

Miko saw the look on Yara's face and thought she was going to let her know of her once fabulous life, but instead, she nodded her head and said nothing. She was such a quiet and humble woman, that's probably why they clicked.

"Better do your research on Yara Moreland," Miko said and winked her eye at the girl.

Yara shook her head and added, "Or not." She didn't want anyone seeing her mug shot and all the terrible things she had done ten years ago. She wasn't that person anymore.

"Listen up, y'all. So, tonight we will hit a lounge that Fredo will be hosting, tomorrow we are going to a brunch that the company was invited to and then chill before the pop-up show after that, and the next day we are free until the radio event at the University of Florida then home. Keep your work phones charged, that's how we will communicate," the road manager explained.

All of this was so exciting for Yara. She never had a real job before, and it felt good to be a part of something positive and legal. The few times she had been to Miami was all for drug deals. And now, she didn't have to look over her shoulder or be worried about getting arrested, or worse, being shot up in a deal going bad. No one had a clue how your life could turn around for the better.

"I'm hungry," she told Miko as they walked down the steps of the plane where four Escalades were waiting on them.

"Me too, do you eat Cuban food?"

Yara ate everything. "Now you know I'm mixed with all kinds of shit, girl I eat it all," she laughed.

Miko was also a rare breed. Her mother was Korean, and her father was straight out of the gutter of New York City.

"We will take our own truck then."

Over dinner and drinks, Yara shared the current news with her friend. "You know, I had two abortions before my daughter, and no one could convince me that God had punished me," she told her.

"She's fourteen," Miko reminded her. Miko was a grown ass woman, so it was different. "I get where you're coming from, Yara. All I'm saying is, think about it a little more because it could mess her up in the long run."

She wasn't thinking about thirty-year-old Yanise. Her fourteen-year-old daughter was not ready to be a mother. "If your baby came home pregnant at fourteen, what would you do?"

Miko downed her drink. "After I knocked her teeth out of her mouth, I would cry and blame myself, and then we would figure it out. I wouldn't make her get an abortion though. Yara, that's so extreme." She wasn't saying it in a judgmental tone, she was voicing her opinion.

Yara wasn't offended. "I can't help her raise this baby, I just started a new job."

"That's not going anywhere," Miko let her know.

She shook her head. "It's not that… I like my job, I'm in freaking Miami on legal business for goodness sake. With all the drama in my life right now, I need to stay busy, and her dad… I'm sure that young girl wants kids before she's a step-grandmother."

"Do you care about what she wants?" Miko wanted to know, she was hoping that she wasn't concerned with what that bitch wanted.

"Hell no, I don't. I was only saying that around the table. This baby… it can't happen. She's not ready."

Miko could tell that her mind was made up, so she wouldn't keep presenting her case. "Another round, please," she said to the waitress.

She had a crazy buzz, so when she finally made it to the hotel and checked in the junior suite that the label had paid for, she was out of it and barely closed the door behind her.

She undressed and crashed on the bed, sleeping until the next day. When she woke up, she saw all the messages from the team about last night's event and hated that she missed it. She hurried into the shower and dressed for the brunch with only twenty minutes to spare. Everyone was meeting in the lobby at twelve.

Yara wore a nude dress with rose gold flowers at the hem of the garment which stopped right above her knee and pink platform pumps. She barely wore makeup and did a shade of brown on her lips with eyeliner, and a messy ponytail completed the day look she was going for.

"Where was you last night?" Fredo greeted her as she rounded the corner and saw everyone waiting for the truck to pull up.

"Tired as hell," she answered while she hugged him back. "You ready for today?" She was so proud of everything he had coming to him.

He nodded his head and put his headphones back on along with his shades. "Miko said she'll meet us there, so let's ride," the road manager announced.

She didn't know what kind of brunch they were attending and soon realized that it was a big deal being that there was a red carpet, flashing lights, cameras and a lot of action.

"Whose event is this?"

The same rude girl from yesterday said, "Are you for real right now? We're at Quentin Brooks' house."

Yara was out of the loop. She had no clue on who Quentin Brooks was, and the girl had one more time to come at her incorrect before she checked her ass.

"There was no agenda sent, thanks," she told her as she undid her seatbelt and got out of the car. She hated rude and nasty people, especially when there was no need to be that way. Yara was pleasant and expected that same energy in return.

Cameras were pushed in their faces, and she held her arm up as she followed the team alongside the red carpet.

Fredo hit the carpet by himself. He had to get used to all the attention, Yara didn't. While she didn't know all the fresh faces, she recognized the greats of Hip Hop and R & B. Yara was from New York, so she loved classical rap and was all smiles at some of her favorite rappers in the place today.

She went to the bar and ordered a mimosa. Since she seemed to be tagging along, she wasn't necessarily at work but would remain professional and not over drink. Three mimosas would be her limit.

The DJ was jamming with the throwback tunes, and she was bobbing her head and swaying her hips to the beat.

"Quentin! Right here, my man," she heard so many people calling the owner of the house's name.

She strained her neck to see what he looked like since apparently, he was a big deal. Although she now had a phone with Internet, it still didn't register to her to just Google the man's name.

"Well, damn," she mumbled to herself as two things happened. She remembered the man as the asshole at the studio who wanted to know her name and second, they made eye contact, and he didn't take his eyes off her, even when she turned her head to hopefully not be caught staring. And when she headed for the bar to get another drink, something stronger on the second round, she would bet her last dollar that his eyes were still on her. She felt them.

Quentin Brooks… *Hmph.* His name was nice, the house was big as hell, and he seemed to be well respected and connected. She would even admit that he was attractive, young and fine. However, that "bitch, I'm the man" attitude that he greeted her with on their first encounter was enough for her never to care if they spoke again. First impressions were lasting for Yara, and he wasn't her cup of tea.

Chapter Ten

"You have the right to feel that way, but I ain't trying to change you." – H.E.R.

Another hour had passed before she decided that the brunch was more about who you knew and who you were than networking. She took an Uber to the mall and did some shopping for her and the girls. Her stomach grumbled as soon as she made it back to her hotel room and instead of ordering room service, she got back on the elevator and took a walk, hunting for some good Miami grub since the weather was nice.

She found a sports bar that seemed suitable, so she grabbed a seat at the end of the bar and ordered wings and a margarita. As beautiful as Miami was, she couldn't stop thinking about Yanise and her pregnancy. Yara hadn't spoken to Kadeem since they had sex and when he answered the phone, she felt as if he were expecting her to call.

"An abortion, Yara?" He didn't know how to feel, but good wasn't one of the emotions.

"What is she or we going to do with a baby?" she asked him since he didn't agree.

He told whoever he was with that he was stepping outside for a second and responded a few seconds later. "We help her. Killing a baby isn't the answer for her. She will hate us for this when she gets older and realize what she did," he said with a lot of passion in his voice.

She rolled her eyes. "This can't be you talking. The same mother fucker-"
Her voice went up a few octaves, and other patrons dining at the bar looked her way, so she lowered her voice and said, "Do you know how many abortions I paid for on your behalf?" She hated to go there because it was so long ago, way before he settled down and married her.

Kadeem used to be ruthless, yet she stayed with her man. She loved him too much to leave. She didn't turn a blind eye to his foolish and trifling ways, she dealt with them bitches and ran them all off. No one could have Kadeem Moreland but her.

"Man, that shit so old, this ain't got nothing to do with my baby girl."

"Karma!" she called it how it was.

She was childish, that's how Kadeem felt about what she said. "What I did to you or in my past is not karma on Yanise, you sound crazy as hell."

"And you sound like your *fiancé* convinced you to make her keep that baby!" she spat.

"No, this is me talking, and she's too young to get an abortion."

Yara shot back, "And she's too young to be pregnant!" She was standing firm on her decision.

"It's not happening, she can come stay with me," he said to her.

She wouldn't argue with him, that's what he wanted her to do. "Cool, I'm at work. I'll holler at you later." The conversation was over then.

"Work? Where?" This was the first he heard of this.

"I'm in Miami right now, my cellmate from prison hooked me up with a job," she shared with him.

"Doing what?" His first thought was dancing, but he knew his wife wouldn't degrade herself.

"I work for Hard Knocks Records," she said casually.

Kadeem scoffed, "Girl, please, where you working at? And what are you *really* doing in Miami?" What was she playing around for?

Her margarita was placed in front of her with a sugar rim. She used her finger to scoop up the sweetness and licked it from her finger.

"Kadeem, I'm serious. I was locked up with Nash's wife, and she did me a huge favor."

"His wife? Miko from The Underworld?" He was super shocked right now.

Yara said, "Yep, that was my roomie."

"Wow, ain't that some shit. So, you her assistant?"

She wasn't even offended. "No, I am not. I work in marketing, but she got me moving around getting my feet wet in all the departments until I figure out exactly what my niche is."

She left out of the part about her receiving music credit for executive producing Fredo's upcoming EP.

"Proud of you, ma."

She knew he would call Meme to confirm what she said once they were done talking. And she also knew that he didn't think her job was as important as it was.

"Blessings."

"Don't be out there doing too much. Niggas in the industry are assholes." He tried to put her up on game, but she didn't need it. She hadn't been with many men, none that she could even remember or consider other than her husband. And even if she were ready to jump back in the dating pool, she wouldn't dare take advice from his ass. Yara knew how to trust her gut; she could tell a real nigga from a fake one.

"Not interested in no one at the time." And that was the truth.

"Yeah, for now. Soon you'll be dating and shit." He wanted her to be happy so he could clear his conscious.

"Kadeem, I will sign the divorce papers if you have them when I get back." She didn't need him beating around the bush with her, she wasn't stupid.

"What the fuck are you talking about, man?"

"You're not really interested in my dating life or if a nigga gon' play me or not, so stop insulting me. I'll sign them when I get back, and you and that girl can live happily ever after," she snapped and then hung up in his face.

Truthfully, divorce hadn't been mentioned by Kamala in a few days. Yara was tripping for no reason. He shook his head and walked back inside the barbershop. "Why are women so crazy?" He would never understand.

"Good dick," one of the old heads blurted out.

"It don't even be that no more," another person said.

Kadeem texted his oldest daughter and told her to call him when she was free. He and Yara could never conclude when they spoke, and he had to talk to her again when she returned to the city. He was standing firm on his decision, Yanise was not getting an abortion.

Yara enjoyed her food and then walked back to the hotel. With nothing else to do, she took a nap, and this time made sure to set the alarm so she wouldn't have to rush and get dressed for the pop-up show tonight.

Miko asked her if she wanted her makeup done, and she was thankful that she said a slow yes instead of a quick no. The venue where the pop-up show was held was jam-packed and for Fredo to still be considered an underground artist, he seemed to have a big following and a huge buzz.

She wore a razor-back tank with the record label's logo on it, black skinny jeans, a plaid t-shirt tied around her waist and a cap pulled to the back so you could see the beat on her made-up face. The artist gave her a smoky eye and a nude lip, and she took a million selfies, storing them in her phone to admire later.

The VIP lanyard she wore around her neck granted her access all over the building. Once they were escorted to where they would be seated, which gave them a great view of the stage and audience, she took herself on a tour of the building.

The stark white walls were filled with graffiti and art by local artists in Dade County. Before she was arrested, she had a secret interest in art. On the days where she had nothing to do, which was rare, you could find her at a museum all by her lonesome.

Yara touched the paintings after she studied them, wanting to feel the texture of what the artist was trying to convey.

"Good eye," someone said from behind her.

Because she would never forget the voice of an asshole, Yara didn't bother turning around. "Yeah, it's nice," she commented.

"Why did you leave the brunch early?" He was curious.

"And why would I have stayed?"

He stepped forward and stood beside her. "It was a lot of people there you needed to meet."

"Needed?" She didn't understand.

He looked at her, studying her eyes, energy connecting to hers. "Yeah, a lot of people are discussing you."

She raised an eyebrow. "Really? Shouldn't they be talking about the artist?" Miko told her that she would be a hot commodity soon. However, she wasn't interested in all the attention being on her. "The mixtape hasn't even dropped yet," she added.

"The people that need to hear it always get it first," he told her. She recorded the fact in her mental. "How old are you?"

Yara laughed, "That won't be disclosed. Enjoy your night, Mr. Brooks." His name was sophisticated, and she loved how the "S" rolled off her tongue.

However, he had already done his research, so when he responded with, "You too, Mrs. Moreland," she was surprised. That emphasis on *Mrs* told her that he knew. He most likely knew it all and had probably judged her.

Yara went back to her seat and ordered a drink. Miko asked her was she okay, and she nodded her head. "Yeah, give me the rundown on Quentin Brooks."

Miko smiled slyly at her. "He's crushing on you, honey."

Yara didn't return the gesture. "He knows more about me than I know about him." She didn't like that.

"Well, get to know him," she suggested. Quentin was a good guy and one of Nash's most trusted friends. She could actually see them together because they came from the same hustle and walk of life. However, she wouldn't put his business out there, just as she didn't put hers out there when he dug for the real scoop on her. Silently, she was rooting for them. Her husband told her to mind her business and if it would happen to let it be natural, so she was staying out of it.

Shaking her head, she said, "No time, no energy and damn sure no patience." Kadeem had stripped her of all three.

"We will see. The show is about to start, I'm going to pee before it does," Miko said before getting up and walking out of the section.

Yara pulled her hat down and took a deep breath. She wondered what all did he know and what was his reaction after he had conducted his research on her. She was a good person. Damn, why she did even care?

She shook the thoughts away and sat up in her seat as Fredo's DJ's loud voice came over the speakers asking the crowd were they ready for the show to start.

It was her first time seeing him perform, and the fact that he was doing the songs that she handpicked and placed her special touch on had her on the edge of her seat. By the second song, she was on her feet, hype as shit.

Yara enjoyed the performance and clapped louder than anyone at the venue.

From across the room, Quentin Brooks never took his eyes off her. She looked like an angel, despite what her past was filled with. It was something alluring about her that had him very intrigued.

Yara Moreland had his attention, and normally, his span was shorter than a midget, but because she had danced on the wild side, he wanted her. She had a glow that followed her around, and the cute thing was that she was oblivious to her beauty and aura.

The pop-up show was a success, and everyone packed up and headed to the club. Quentin had a long day and opted out on popping bottles and making it rain.

He wasn't big on the clubs anyway, home was his happy place.

And on the other side of the room, Yara was telling Miko the same thing. "I'm ready to get in the bed." She wasn't in the mood to be in the club.

She headed back to the hotel, and Quentin headed to the home he owned in Miami. He was on her mind, and she was on his.

η

Black Girl Magic was in full effect at Kamala's monthly "Girls Night In." She loved to entertain, and that was one reason why she loved their house so much; it was perfect for hosting and entertaining.

She was going around the dining room table pouring everyone a fresh glass of Malvasia wine. For dinner, she made several pasta dishes, a Caprese salad and had bottles of wine on deck. For the past three years, on the first Friday of every month, she and her girlfriends got together at her place and once a year took a week-long vacation. It was something they all had grown to look forward to.

Kadeem already knew that the first Friday was reserved for her girls, and he normally didn't come home until he knew they were winding down. Her Girls Night In were big deals to her.

Kamala's hair was freshly pressed, she had on a cute outfit and even had the house professionally cleaned for tonight's gathering.

"Kamala, sit your ass down and give us the tea," her very best friend said in a drunken voice.

"No more wine for you. How you getting home, cus you can't stay here?" she laughed. She was joking. If April needed to sleep the wine off, her doors were always open to all her girls. The room was full of black excellence. Her friends were college-educated, and the ones that didn't go to college were still doing the damn thing.

"I'm the host, do y'all need-" She knew she was stalling, trying to avoid the conversation they all were anxious to have.

"Girlll!" everyone said at once.

She drank straight from the bottle, bending her head back as she finished it off. "Whew, I needed that," she admitted as she took a seat at the head of the table.

"Girl, have I told you that I loved your ring? Honey, he did that," her friend Denise complimented her for the millionth time.

She nodded her head. "Thank you… again," she said and smiled. Kadeem did a good job, that was true.

"Soooo, was she ugly?" April questioned.

Kamila took a deep breath. "No, not at all, nowhere near it. No bruises, black eyes, chipped teeth, saggy breasts or nothing," she told them. Everyone had this image of Kadeem's wife in their head, and she knew that if her girls ever met her, they'd agree with her.

"Well fuck her, did he give her the papers yet?" another one of her girlfriends questioned.

"Not yet, it's been so much going on since she got out."
And that wasn't an excuse, it was a fact.

"Friend, don't let him play you," Denise wagged her finger.

"No, seriously… it's been a lot going on. The daughter is pregnant."

Everyone's mouth fell open and Kamala's friend, Sue inquired, "Not the one who I wrote the letter for?" She was speaking of Ayanna.

"Girl, no, she gon' go far in life. The youngest, the fourteen-year-old," she shared with them.

"What!" April was surprised.

Kamala got up to grab another wine out of the cooler. "Yeah, so it's been hectic round here, he's so stressed out. The mama wants her to get an abortion, and he thinks she should keep it."

"I'm with the mama. Hell, she too young."

Denise rolled her eyes at India, the most bourgeois of them all. "In case y'all forgot, I had Anthony at fifteen, and I love my son, and I'm doing very well, so kids don't stop shit," she said in defense.

And in Denise's case, she was correct. However, everyone wasn't ready to have children, and Yanise damn sure wasn't.

"You were also with and still are with your baby daddy. That shit don't happen every day, and your mama helped you," Sue reminded her.

April chimed in, "So you don't count," she said, rolling her eyes at Denise.

Kamala didn't know how to feel, she was just trying to support Kadeem with whatever decision he thought was best.

"If it were your child what would you do?" Denise needled.

She closed her eyes and shook her head. "Please don't take me back down memory lane," she begged the ladies.

When her sister Kamile was seventeen, she made her get an abortion. Kamile wasn't ready to be a mother.

"Look at Kamile now though, that's what I'm saying. For some, kids are setbacks."

"She should have thought about that before she laid down!" Denise shouted.

"I'll speak for myself, I'm not interested in having kids outside of marriage," Susan dropped her two cents.

"But you'll sleep with a married man? You kill me." Denise looked at her and rolled her eyes from here to Atlanta.

Everyone had had too much to drink. Kamala stood up. "Y'all, we will handle it, thanks for the concern though, next subject."

She didn't want them to stop arguing and leave because that also happened often. When you had so many strong-minded, opinionated black women in one room paired with alcohol, the conversations sometimes got heated. She was the peacemaker in the circle being that she was the reason everyone was friends today.

"Friend, do not let him prolong that divorce, you've been patient enough," April stressed to her.

"She is going to get her wedding," Kadeem said with a tight ass smile plastered across his face.

The ladies were talking so loud that they didn't hear the alarm chime or the garage door go up.

She could have turned a million different colors, but she tried to play it cool, and so did the ladies. "Hey, baby." She went over to him and kissed his cheek. He hugged her lazily, and Kamala smelled the weed on his gym clothes. "It's plenty of food, do you want me to make you a plate?"

Kadeem shook his head. "About to shower, bring me one up when your company leaves," he told her before going upstairs.

They all remained super quiet until they felt like the coast was clear.

Denise was busy in her seat. "BIHHHHHH, he fucking hate us!" He always heard the wrong part of their conversations.

Susan was drunk and tickled. "He probably thinks we're some miserable, hating ass hoes."

April told her, "Speak for yourself."

And Denise laughed, "April, you the main one."

Kamala sat back down and poured herself another glass of wine. "Now, where were we?" She wasn't ending the night because he came home early. And nothing they said was incorrect. He didn't need to prolong the divorce, she was ready to get married.

Two more hours went by of laughter, girl talk and of course, more wine. Denise was the last to leave, and she also had the most to-go plates. "You know if you need me to talk to her, I will." She was a therapist and a good listener.

Kamala hugged her. "I love you, let me know when you make it home."

She was washing the dishes and cleaning up while Sade blared through the speakers in the kitchen when her hunk of a man walked downstairs, in nothing but a pair of Burberry boxers. She almost got lightheaded at the sight of him. Kadeem was chocolate. He was delectable; he was a God. On their first date, she barely talked because she couldn't stop staring at his fine ass. From the way he spoke, how he prayed over his food before he ate, and the way he conducted business, he was handsome. She loved how he was rocking his haircut and trimmed beard these days, and yeah, he was aging, but like wine he was getting finer with time.

She smiled at him, and he gave her a half-hearted smile back. "Girls' night over?" He already knew the answer because the house was empty. She nodded her head, wondering should she speak on what he heard.

"Fix me a plate please, I'm starving." He took a seat at the bar and scrolled through his phone, doing whatever he did on the device.

She had already put his plate in the microwave, so she all had to do was press the time to heat up his food.

"How was your day?" She was interested in his day-to-day activities.

Kadeem placed his phone down and gave his fiancé all his attention. His dark brown eyes fell on hers, and she blushed.

"What you doing all that for?" he teased, knowing when she was feeling like a girl in the presence of her crush.

"You already know." She turned the sink off and got his plate out of the microwave, placing it before him with a napkin and fork. Kamala wiped the counters down while he ate and shared the happenings of his day.

"Whew, I'm tired," she told him after they had retreated into the living room and she was in his arms while he searched Netflix for something to watch.

"Food was good too. What kind of sauce was that?"

She had made three different kinds of pasta, and they were all scrumptious. "You probably talking about the vodka one," she assumed.

"Let's watch this, we gotta catch up before next season," he said before settling on "Queen of The South."

Kamala looked behind her and puckered her lips. She wanted some love from her man.

"I love you," he told her and then smooched her lips twice.

She smiled and turned back around. He wrapped his arms around her tighter and slid one of his hands into her leggings and left it at the top of her pussy.

"Bring the papers home Monday, I will give them to her," he told her minutes into the show.

Kamala said nothing. She just nodded her head so he could know that she heard him. He had a way of reassuring her without her having to worry about what direction they were going in, and for that she was thankful. She couldn't wait to build a life with him.

The next day, Yara had called a meeting at Charlie's house, and Kadeem's presence was requested. He could tell that she was fresh from her trip and when he asked her how it was, she ignored him and said, "Okay, so we are all here. I have something to say." She stood up and took the middle of the living room floor.

"Can I go first?" Charlie raised her hand.

Yara didn't have much patience, but this was her house, so she sat back down.

Charlie stood where Yara was and took a deep breath. "First, I want to apologize-"

Kadeem cut her off, "Mama, no." He wasn't about to let her do this. His father told him that she hadn't slept much and was beating herself up for Yanise being pregnant.

"Let me talk please." Her eyes were already teary, and everyone saw that she was heavily affected by the situation. "I want to apologize first to my son, and Yara, for letting you down. The only thing I was responsible for doing was raising my grandchildren, and I was lazy. I treated them how I treated

Kadeem. And they are girls, they should have been coming in at a certain hour, and I didn't even try to put my foot down."

Charlie wasn't an emotional person, and her granddaughters began to cry seeing how hurt she was.

Yanise hated herself for being the reason they were even having this family meeting.

"I love y'all so much, and I hope that y'all will find it in your hearts to forgive me one day. Yara, you know that I know how you were raised, and I know that this is the last thing you wanted for your child."

Kadeem looked at his wife, and tears had flooded her face. She never spoke of her childhood. He knew she had shared with his mom about some of the things she went through, but that was their thing, he was never included. Charlie used to tell him to leave her alone because she was fragile.

"Please let me back in your life. I hate this discord between us. It's not how we rock." Charlie was extremely vulnerable, and that wasn't her thing. Yara never responded, and so she nodded her head. "That's all," she said and took her seat.

Kadeem wanted to curse Yara the fuck out.

"Who's next?" Ayanna posed the question to the family.

Yara was silent. Meme wanted to tell them that she was moving in with Riq but was fearful of what her father might say.

Yanise raised her hand, and everyone looked at her. "This is nobody's fault but my own. Charlie, I was sneaking and doing it, you would have never found out because I was good at sneaking.

I'm sorry everyone is so sad and not talking to each other. I'm sorry for telling mama about Daddy and Kamala. I just wanted some attention. It's like everybody got their own thing going on, and I'm alone," she admitted and then bust out crying. Yanise's face turned beet red, and she sobbed uncontrollably.

Kadeem had no clue that's who told her.

Ayanna and Meme went to her side and held her in their arms. They had failed as her big sisters as well.

And she wasn't lying; everyone had their own thing going on. Who saw about Yanise? Charlie did the best she could.

Kadeem wiped a lone tear from his face. He had really fucked up as a father.

"I don't want the baby, am I a bad person?" she questioned.

Charlie couldn't take it anymore, so she got up and walked out of the living room. Yesterday, she drove her to a clinic in Jersey, and Yanise didn't say one word. She asked her was she okay, and she never even reacted to the process.
When they made it back home, she took a bath, took her meds and stayed in her room until the meeting.

"Ma," Kadeem called out to her, but KK got up to check on her.

He told his son, "You are the head of *your* family, get it together."

What was he supposed to do? There was so much damage to repair.

Yara hadn't moved. She was as still as an owl.

"Listen up, y'all." He prayed the words came to him because he had no idea of what the plan was for the Moreland family.

They looked at him, and he pulled on his beard, something he did when he was contemplating his next thought.

Yara stepped in and said barely above a whisper, "We will get through this together. Yanise, you are changing schools. You will pack your things today, and I'll come get you tomorrow. We can get everything you need. Ayanna, it's your senior year, you can stay with Charlie, but both of y'all will be on birth control."

"I'm a virgin," Ayanna said proudly.

"I'm talking, don't interrupt me," Yara cut her eyes at her. These kids had no damn respect. "Yanise, we already had our talk of what was changing. Y'all two are basically grown. All I can do is be there for you if you need me and be a listening ear."

Kadeem was rendered speechless as their three children nodded their heads in agreement.

"And I don't want anyone feeling bad about what happened between your dad and me. That's solely on him. He made that decision, not y'all. Don't worry about that no more. I'm home now, and that's all that matters," she said to them. She then stood up and kissed each of her kids on the forehead. "Yanise, I'll be back tomorrow," she said, concluding the meeting. She picked up her purse and headed for the door.

"Mama, you okay?" Meme was concerned about her.

"Yep," she lied.

Kadeem knew her well, their daughters didn't. He followed her outside and called out after her, "Yara!"

She kept walking, needing fresh air and a minute to herself.

"Aye, you gon' ignore me?" Kadeem jogged after her, and she turned around and slapped the hell out of him.

"Fuck you!" She hated him. He didn't even deserve to be this close to her.

"I never claimed to be perfect, Kadeem, never, not once. But there was nothing I ever did to even compare to what I put up with when it came to you," she let him know. "And you gon' leave me and put a ring on the next bitch, a bitch that worked on our case? How could I ever trust you again?" Yara never had a potty mouth, but she got pissed every time she closed her eyes and saw that woman in her house pretending to be working hard to make sure everything went well during trial. She even had the nerve to look sad and hopeless after the verdict was read, swearing that she was going to help her boss figure something out because surely, this wasn't supposed to happen. The only word that continuously came to mind was *bitch*, *bitch*, and *bitch*.

Yara didn't do nice-nasty. She didn't do fake, nor did she beat around the bush. She was real and genuine, and those character traits were hard to come by. She was a rare woman with a heart made of gold, and Kadeem had ruined that.

Kamala had nothing to do with him getting out early, but he knew she would never believe him. He held his bloody mouth.

"Don't say another word to me, go the other way when you see Yara," she said, pointing to herself. She knew that Kamala was a good woman, at Kadeem's feet she would bow gracefully if he asked her to. He didn't deserve her loyalty. "I want my name back, tell that bitch to file the divorce papers," she spat, and spit at his feet before walking further down the driveway and getting into her Lexus and peeling off.

He stood there, with tears in his eyes. The look she gave him was one he thought he would never see on her face again. He had only caused her to look at him like that one time during their time together, and that's when he had really fucked up. As a man, he had failed his wife, his friend, his everything. Yara didn't repeat herself, and she wasn't the one to play with. He knew that she was serious.

She wanted her sanity back, she wanted the divorce and for him to stay the hell away from her.

Chapter Eleven

"Don't know where my mind at, hoping you can help find that." –
Bryson Tiller

She wrote a song. The song was the shit. She didn't know what to do with the damn song.

After leaving the "family meeting," she went home and hummed. That was all she could do to keep from losing her mind and going back to Charlie's house to bust the windows out of his car. Before she knew it, a melody was created and then words, and she wrote it all out, then she rewrote it, then she took out this and added that, and then she said out loud, *"This is a hit!"*

Yara was so ready to return to work, she didn't know what to do. As soon as she got off the elevator, Marsha was waving at her. She was always in a good mood, and Yara appreciated the good energy she carried.

Some mornings, she would wake up extremely down and depressed, missing Kadeem and wishing things were different for their family, and then a bright smile from Marsha would be the sign she needed that things happen for a reason.

If she would have come home and nothing had changed, she would never have this cool job making her own money, not worrying about having to commit crimes or steal, kill and destroy so her kids could eat. Yara was going to start seeing the light in a dark situation. That was a promise she made to herself.

"Marsha! I haven't been to sleep!" she shrieked.

The woman laughed, "I can tell, darling. Let me get you some coffee. You have something on your desk from a secret admirer that I know nothing about," she winked her eye and walked off.

Her and Marsha were the same age. However, Marsha gave you "auntie" vibes. Since Yara started working at the label, they had caught up after hours and grabbed dinner and wine. They had little in common, and she was also learning that sometimes people entered your life from a totally different background to show you different things. So, never block your blessings because they look unfamiliar to you.

"Here," she said, handing Yara her mug with her name on it. "Three creams and five pumps of sugar." She knew how Yara enjoyed her coffee. "Okay, tell me." She was now all ears.

Yara filled her in on the drama with Kadeem and how she slapped him and spat at his feet and then she took a deep breath. "Yesterday was crazy. But anyway, girl I got home and was sad and down, and I wrote a song." She handed her the notebook.

No one could tell her that this song didn't give off old-school Mary J with new school vibes. Yara knew she had a hit on her hands, and she wanted to sell the song to the highest bidder. She couldn't sing at all but knew she was in the right place to get the song off her hands.

"Did you talk to Miko?"

She shook her head. "She's still sleeping, it's early." The time wasn't even seven-thirty, and no one would be in the office until about ten, her and Marsha were the early birds. They were also the first ones to arrive and the last to leave.

"Well, holler at her, she should be stopping by today anyway. Nash has a meeting on the calendar," she noted.

"Let me get to work, I'm behind." Yara had her headphones on working, being diligent and dedicated to her job.

Marsha knocked on her door, and she removed the pods from her ear. "Lunch?"

Yara scanned the time at the bottom of the laptop she was working on. "Is it really one o'clock already?" She was in the zone.

Fredo's pop-up show went viral, and she wanted to capitalize on the hype while it was still there.

"Yep, and Miko, Nash and Mr. Brooks just got here. He may be the person you should talk about your song."

Yara rolled her eyes. "Did he really come back to New York?" She had just seen him in Florida.

Little did she know, he was all over the place. Mr. Brooks had a house and a condo in every major city, but New York was where his heart was. Harlem was home.

Marsha laughed, "You got a chance to meet Mr. Brooks?" She wasn't aware.

"Yeah, with his annoying ass. You like him?"

She nodded her head. "I love him, he signs our checks," she told her.

She didn't know that. "Huh? I thought we worked for Nash?"

Marsha stepped into her office and closed the door. "Okay, here is a quick rundown of what's going on. Nash is rich, we all know that, but he didn't want a joint deal, so Mr. Brooks got him out of his contract, and they went into business together-"

"They co-own the label?"

"Yep, I heard it was more of Mr. Brooks money because he was trying to clean it up," she shared with her.

"Clean it up? He went to jail?" This was all news to her, Miko had to know this but didn't tell her.

"Girl, yes. I heard he was doing white collar crimes, and when he got out, he came home to a billion dollars, and then Nash had blown up by then so they linked back up."

"Wow." So, he didn't judge her. Hell, he couldn't.

"Let's go eat, and then you can talk to them when we get back."

That sounded like a good idea to her. She grabbed her phones and purse and powered her laptop down.

Over lunch, Marsha confided in Yara, "I think I want to get a divorce."

She finished chewing a sweet potato fry before asking, "Have you tried to make it work?" Yara didn't necessarily believe in divorce, but if you weren't satisfied in your marriage then by all means, let it go.

"It's not even that. I... I just want to be by myself. I've been married twice, and I'm done. The next man I meet, we will have to be life partners until death." She was done with vows and the whole idea of commitment and submitting to a man.

"I don't think I want to get married again either."

Marsha shook her head. "Don't." In her opinion, marriage was outdated. Many people connected marriage to religion, and then some married for financial gain and benefits. Is that why she married her husband? She wasn't sure, nor did she no longer care. She had to get away from him and soon. Marsha had no desire to walk down the aisle again. Marsha didn't want to go to the courthouse either.

"After this divorce... I don't know how I'm going to feel," Yara exhaled.
Yesterday, the words flew from her mouth, and she wasn't thinking, but she knew that once he filed, she might not be able to accept that their marriage was really over.

She had let Kadeem off the hook easily. He should have received the wrath of Yara, but something in her didn't even let her go there with him. Yara knew her worth, and she knew that she gave him all of her, and that she poured from an empty pitcher to fill him up.

Going forward, if she did decide to date and take someone seriously, she knew to be more reserved the second round of love.

The next man she met would have to knock her off her feet and then carry her through their relationship because she barely had anything left to give.

"Let's get back," Marsha said after they finished lunch. She covered the check, and Yara left a ten-dollar tip.

"My daughter is moving in with me today," she told her.

"You know my kids are around her age, we should get them together," she suggested.

Yara smiled. "I would love that, seriously. Let's do that sooner than later, she needs to be around some new people."

As soon as they got off the elevator, Miko was sitting on the yellow couch in the lobby playing with her dog.

"Hey, y'all ate without me. I'm starving," she pouted.

"How you know we ate?"

"Intern told me. Yara, girl, did Miami wear you out?"

She forgot that she didn't look her best today. The green dress she wore was wrinkled, and her hair was pulled into a bun. She had barely brushed the fly-aways down before walking out of the house.

"I haven't been to sleep but forget that, I wrote a song, a good ass song. Who can I get to read it?" She was eager to hear someone else's thoughts about this song that she had so much confidence in.

Miko pointed to the glass room ahead and smiled at her friend. "Quentin. Nash is focused on his album, so I know he won't give you the feedback you want."

Yara took a deep breath, she had to push her feelings aside. "Can you let him know? I'll be in my office."

η

Nash dapped his longtime friend, business partner and brother up. "Facts, I appreciate you, my mans." He had put his two cents in on the marketing plan and social media strategy for the album release, and Nash was feeling more confident about his rumored, final project.

He didn't like the word "retire" because he wasn't sure if this was it. He had been in the game for a long time and had more money than he could ever count, so at this point, he no longer rhymed for the dollars, it was still a sense of therapy and an outlet for him. And everything he dropped went double-platinum. He had a room in his house reserved for Grammy's only. He loved the art of music and was eager to see how his fans reacted to this new album.

"Love you, brother." Quentin hugged him and kissed Miko on the cheek.

"Be nice to my friend, she doesn't have a good impression of you," Miko whispered in his ear.

Nash pinched her back, and she yipped out loudly, "Ouch, baby!" He calmed her with his eyes, and she rolled hers at him. "He's so annoying. Facts, I'm serious… be nice to her."

Quentin laughed. Only the people he knew from way back when still called him Facts. He was now known as Quentin Brooks. He got the name Facts because the old heads would always come to him when they were trying to prove a point amongst each other. There wasn't much that Quentin didn't know, and if he didn't, he would research and learn. He was a smart kid growing up, probably the smartest in his hood.

Quentin went to a community college and trapped until he had enough money to transfer. With a 4.0-grade-point average, he graduated at the top of his class at Columbia University with a degree in International Business. He then landed a job through the Dean of his department from college and climbed the ladder to the top of Wall Street. The hood was behind him, and he now owned his office along with a penthouse and a few cars. He could have any woman he wanted, no matter the race or tax bracket. Life was good for him. Quentin was feeling himself, and it was something he now shared with younger men; the importance of staying humble and grounded. He became the man to know when you wanted to invest in real estate and stocks until greed became his downfall, and he became crooked.

Quentin served five years in the FEDS for white-collar crimes. He should have gotten more time, but his peoples knew people, who knew people, and he paid the Judge a pretty penny to lighten his sentence. In fact, Facts was who Nash called to get Miko out on early release, and he made it happen.

Now in present time, Quentin owned several businesses. His most lucrative was the record label, so that's where ninety percent of his time and energy went. He had an ear for music and discovering diamonds in the rough.

He walked past Marsha's desk and stopped to see where exactly was Ms. Yara's office. "Which way?"

"Down and to the left," Marsha directed him.

He followed the directions and knocked on the glass door and then walked in. Yara had headphones on and was jamming with her back to the door. The flowers that he sent sat in a corner, and he wondered if she ever opened the note card to see who her admirer was.

He took a second and got a good look at her office, and it was bright. She had sticky notes of affirmation words and quotes all over the wall. On the floor sat a pile of books and another pile of magazines and notebooks. It was obvious that she took her job title seriously. The books were all familiar being that he had read them as well when he first got into the music industry.

She was singing low, *"To make sure that you can trust me, and you know the reason why, I can loveeeee youuu…"* She was jamming too.

He crossed his arms and stood to the side of her desk and watched her.

"I can love you, I can love you, I can love you better than she cannnn..." She was feeling the throwback classic. And when she finally opened her eyes, she damn near jumped out of her seat. *"Oh my God! You scared me!"* She snatched the headphones out of her ears and held her heart.

"I feel like we should start over. Quentin… Quentin Brooks," he said and stuck his hand out for a shake.

She looked at it and shook it. "Yara," she told him. He already knew her last name, so there was no need in doing all of that.

Quentin stuffed his hands into the pockets of the navy Tom Ford suit that he wore. It was tailored to fit his body.

He was handsome. Yara hadn't noticed before how structured his jaw line and cheekbones were, but he could pass as a model. Quentin was the color of cinnamon and nutmeg on top of a cup of coffee, and he was of average height. They both were obviously from New York, but his accent held a hint of Jamaican, and you could only hear it when he pronounced certain words.

She told him, "You look like Big Sean." That came out of nowhere.

He smiled at her. "I'm older, so that nigga look like me," he responded, flashing her a smile he probably paid for.

He sat down in one of the chairs in her office. "Miko told me that you wrote a song, let me hear it."

The song wasn't recorded yet. "Uh, it's not on audio. I wrote it last night, randomly," she said nervously.

"Wow, okay. Let's go." He stood up. They had to keep it moving.

She had work to do. "Where are we going? I can't go with you."

"To record the song. Is it a hit?"

She didn't want to seem overly confident but... "I think it is," she said and nodded her head.

"You think, or you know?" He didn't have time to waste.

"I know," she cleared that up.

"Let's ride, Yara." This was the last time he was repeating himself.

She grabbed her things. "I have to pick up my daughter today, so I can't be in the studio all night." She thought it would be the same way it was with Fredo.

"My late nights are over, you won't be there long." He was texting on his phone to make sure someone was there to lay the track, they needed an engineer and producer.

"I'm sure you have a melody in your head?" he wanted to be sure.

"Yeah, I do."

They walked beside each other toward the elevator, and Yara motioned to Marsha that she would call her later. Yara was quiet as he made a few phone calls to set up the impromptu session.

On the car ride, he was on the phone the entire time, and she wasn't even mad. What did she possibly have to talk to him about? They weren't friends or anything. He was her boss though, he signed her checks.

When they made it to the studio, he didn't get out.

"You're not coming in?"

He shook his head. "No, they will email it to me when y'all are done, and then I'll be in touch."

"Okay, you're going to call me?" She wanted to be sure because it was her damn song.

Quentin nodded his head and smiled. "Yes, sweetheart." She was beautiful, and he knew he would stare at her the entire session, and he had to play things cool, so he planned on getting breakfast and running some errands before he peeped in on the session.

"All right then." She didn't need the sarcasm. Yara got out and closed the door. Hell, if that were the case, she would have driven herself.

Quentin waited until the engineer let her in before he pulled off.

η

Her sleeping schedule was out of whack. She either slept well for a few days straight or deprived herself of no sleep at all. Quentin clearly lied when he said she wouldn't be there all night, and the man he sent to lay the track wasn't connecting to the song at all, and she was getting extremely frustrated.

She had the producer cut the track. "Listen, have you ever been cheated on?"

The man shook his head. "I do the cheating," he smirked.

She was irritated at his ignorant ass answer, so she asked the engineer, "Are there any females we can use?"

He raked his brain. "Actually, there is. She doesn't get off work till eight though."

That was perfect for her. "I gotta go get my daughter, so let's meet here at nine." She was pissed that she wasted her entire day up here with this ignorant nigga that Quentin found to lay the track.

The engineer was nice enough to drop her off at her car, and she sped to Charlie's house. It would have been rude of her to honk the horn, and since Yanise didn't have her cell phone, she had to go inside the house to retrieve her daughter.

She rang the bell and then knocked. Yanise had all her things at the door. "Am I going to be able to visit?" she asked her mama.

"Of course. She's still your grandmother, she ain't going nowhere."

"Good, cus I love Charlie food. Do you know how to cook?" She wasn't sure since this would be her first time being without her grandmother's good cooking.

Charlie was in the living room reading but chimed in on the conversation, "I taught her, she can cook."

Yara smiled weakly at her. "Hello," she spoke, but stayed in the doorway, refusing to come inside the house. "This is everything?" She wanted to make sure she had everything she needed. Yanise nodded and picked up a few bags while Yara got the rest.

After they loaded her trunk, she told her to go kiss her grandmother and then come on because they had a few errands to run. Their first stop was Target. Yara had already purchased a bed and television from when she first moved into the apartment. Yanise could get whatever she wanted and needed.

"Do you have pads and stuff?" she asked.

"Yeah, but I can stock up." Yara got a few things she needed as well.
After their Target run, they went to the grocery store and then home to get her moved in.

"Whew, chile, I'm getting old." She was out of breath. All the trips to the car had her tired and sweating.

"Me too." Yanise was exhausted.

"Get unpacked, I'm going to make dinner and shower." Meme and Ayanna planned on coming over tonight to hang with their sister while Yara went to the studio. She was thankful that everyone was pitching in and that it was a group effort to get their little sister on the right track.

"When do I switch schools?"

"Dang. I knew I forgot something. I'll do that tomorrow. I'm going to ask my friend at work what I need to do." She was sure that things had changed since she was dealing with paperwork and school with her other two kids. "Have you spoken to your father?"

Yara was on the last few bites of the dinner she cooked. Tonight, she made something quick because she was pressed for time.

Yanise nodded her head. "Yep." Both of her parents were concerned now, and she appreciated the attention. He promised to

pick her up this weekend so she could spend some time with him…
and Kamala.

"Yes," Yara corrected her.

All of this yes and no shit would take some time to get used
to. "Yes, I did. He's still sad about the abortion."

Yara rolled her eyes. "He'll get over it. Do you like the
food?" She knew she could cook, and hopefully, Yanise thought it
was good.

She smiled at her mom. "Ma, I'm on my second plate."
Yanise wouldn't come out and say how excited she was to be
living somewhere new. She was ready to start over.

Yara got up and put her dish in the sink along with the
others and then kissed Yanise on the forehead. "Wash the dishes
and do your homework, your sisters are on the way."

"Wash the dishes?" She wasn't used to doing chores.
Charlie did everything.

"That's what I said." She left her in the kitchen and went to
shower and get dressed for the session tonight. She really hoped
that this chick the engineer knew was talented and sadly, that she
knew pain and real love because that was the only way this song
would come out perfect.

"Mama, why you dressed like you going to do a stick-up?"
Ayanna laughed at her own joke. Meme and Yanise joined in with
the giggles.

"I have a session. What else was I supposed to wear?" She wanted to be comfortable, so she wore a black jogging suit and white Adidas.

"Something cute and girly."

"Girl, I'm grown. And ain't nobody in there looking at me." She wasn't looking at them either.

"Ma, you gotta start dressing up more." Meme wanted her mom to be happy.

"Hmm-hmm. Don't be up all night," she told them before she left.

In the car ride headed to the studio, she was conflicted, wanting to pray but not knowing who to pray to. Yara was raised Christian, but when she experienced church hurt, she turned away from God. She read something the other day that convicted her so badly, she hadn't prayed since then. *"When you stop going to God because of church hurt, you were never with Him to begin with."*

And that was true, but she was a young girl. A confused girl at that, so she didn't understand how the things she was forced to experience and endure could happen to her while she was in the house of God.

Yara discovered Allah in prison, and much of the population was Muslim. She didn't technically convert, but she studied the religion and found out that she agreed with a lot of their practices and beliefs.

Instead of prayer, she spoke positively to herself. "What I expect I will receive, and what I believe I can achieve."

She took a long deep breath before getting out of the car and typing the code on the back door to gain access to the studio. She was appreciative that everyone was on time because black folks rarely showed up at the scheduled time.

"Hey, everyone," she waved to the people in the studio.

They got started a few minutes later, and she explained to the young girl who was the engineer's cousin and the producer what she wanted done. The girl could apparently relate because she blew the song out the water.

"Yesssss!" Yara pumped her up, "Sing, girlllll!" She felt every lyric.

Quentin walked in, and the producer stopped the track. "What up, Facts?"

"Keep going," Quentin told them, not wanting to interrupt the flow.

Yara glanced at him and then refocused on the girl signing her pain and her truth.

"Shit is *hot*," Quentin said a few minutes later.

She smiled. Thankfully, he couldn't see her. They went over the hook a few more times, and she got it right on the first time. This had been a breeze. Yara found peace in the studio.

After she was officially done, she came out and ran right into Yara's arms and hugged her and with tears in her eyes. "So many women will be able to relate."

Yara didn't expect that kind of reaction. Her cousin gave the young girl a few dollars, and she left the studio.

Yara inquired, being that she was a beginner, "What happens now?" She had no clue on how the process went.

"Facts will shop the song and whoever buys it, they definitely got a hit on their hands," the producer explained.

"We get our cut when the song is sold, and Grammy's and all of that, hopefully," Quentin told her.

"What about the girl that just left? She sang it perfectly." And she was pretty. Yara wondered why Quentin never signed her.

"She got four kids, shorty ain't trying to be a singer."

Quentin chimed in, "A song this good? I'm taking this straight to Beyoncé, Rihanna, one of them."

"For real?" She thought it was a bomb ass song, but Beyoncé? That was a big deal.

He nodded his head. "Yeah, you got a few gifts; producing, writing, what else can you do?"

"You forgot marketing," she said while batting her eyelashes.

She looked good in her athletic get-up, and he appreciated that she could do both. So far, he had seen her in sneakers and heels, and he was now officially crushing on lil' mama.

"Woman of many hats."

Something happened, and she didn't know what it was. Plus, it was going on two in the morning, and she needed to get home. "Keep me posted on the track, and thank you for the opportunity." Yara was grateful.

"Let me walk you to your car," he offered, being the perfect gentleman.

It was late and dark, so she wouldn't dare try to be a bad ass. She waved goodbye to the engineer and the producer.

"Have you written a song before?" he asked her.

She shook her head. "Everything I'm doing is new for me, never in a million years could I have predicted I'd be doing any of this."

"I felt the same way. God works in mysterious ways."

"You believe in God?" she asked him, surprised to hear him speak of a higher power. For some reason, she believed that there were more female believers than male.

He nodded his head. "Yes, I do. Do you?" For him, religion was a deal breaker.

"Raised in the church. I've strayed though," she was honest with him.

"It happens, especially when you're in the church at a young age." He had been there before but quickly found his way back to the source of his peace. "I wanna know what else you're good at though. Fredo is on his way to the top. I don't know if we need you in artist development or the studio, you're good at everything." He could see talent with his eyes closed, and Yara Moreland had many gifts.

She smiled. "Fredo is so talented and easy to work with."

"Warning, every artist won't be as nice as him." He knew from experience.

"Not worried about that, I know how to keep my game face on."

He opened the back door, and she walked out first. "Do you have your game face on now?"

She looked down and then back up at him. "What do you want with me?" She needed to know because she was not about to beat around the bush with this man.

Quentin appreciated her straight forwardness. "I don't know yet," he answered truthfully.

She could respect that. Yara nodded her head. "When you find out, holla at me." Quentin opened her car door for her, and she got in. "Thank you, Mr. Brooks."

"How soon do you need to know?" He was low-key trying to shoot his shot.

Yara blushed, his voice was turning her on. "There isn't a time limit."

"You don't rush greatness?" He raised an eyebrow.

"Oh, that's what we will be?" she laughed at him, although he was serious.

The fact that she was even considering him made him happy. The idea of a "we" made his night. "Yeah, in due time."

Quentin had everything he wanted and no one to share it with. Women loved him, flocked to him, but with ill intentions. He had dated and failed miserably at connecting to a genuine soul. Relationships at his age were so complicated, especially when you were rich and successful. For the past year, he stopped wasting his time with pointless women who lacked an idea of love and purpose. And then came Yara. Quentin knew without a doubt that everything she had recently been through was for a reason, this moment had already been ordained.

Chapter Twelve
"So, when you talk I can't help but listen." – Jones

Energy was real, and it wasn't hard to pick up on when you had the spirit of discernment. Yara noticed the disgruntled look on her daughter's face. It was masked behind the concealer, popping lip gloss and false eyelashes.

Meme was a beautiful girl and at her young age, she had it together, balancing school and work plus a relationship. Most girls her age wasn't on her level. She hung with a few chicks, and they were all older than her.

Yara's kids were mature for their age, especially Yanise and her old soul. She was hardworking, focused, charming and kind. Yara was thankful that she had her baby girl to count on. There wasn't one time that she called needing a favor or some help with readjusting to the new world, and Meme didn't stop what she was doing to see about her mother.

It was a regular day out the week, and the girls were over for dinner. Tomorrow, she would be flying to California for a week-long session. Her song was picked up by Jazmine Sullivan, a neo-soul artist who didn't get much of a buzz in the industry. The girl was so talented and was long overdue for a number one hit, she was confident that the song Yara wrote was the one. She also wanted

Yara to hear the other songs she had been working on as she prepares for her next album.

It felt good to double back to these places for business and not criminal activities.

For dinner, she prepared baked salmon, jasmine rice and a vegetable medley. She and Meme had wine while the younger girls sipped on Shirley Temples.

"Ma, can I wash the dishes tomorrow? I'm exhausted," Yanise begged.

So far, she seemed to be enjoying her new school, had even tried out for the majorette team and was chosen. Yara loved hearing her stories when she picked her up from practice. Her baby was now seeing better days. She was sure that the abortion wasn't completely off her mind because it wasn't off hers either.

"Girl, I'll do it," she told her, fanning her away.

Ayanna got up to shower and get ready for bed since she had to wake up a little early to drive to school. She chucked the deuces up and headed toward the bedroom. "I'll holla," she told her mother.

Yara slept on the couch whenever the girls spent the night, and she had no problem doing so. She had slept on a hard ass cot for ten years plus, her couch was comfy.

"Do you want to talk about it?" Yara turned and asked Meme.

Meme shook her head and poured another glass of wine. "Nope, I'm going to keep drinking until I feel better."

She remembered those days. "It won't make you feel good, baby." Yara wasn't one to probe, so she started gathering the dishes so she could clean the kitchen.

"How do you know when to walk away?" The question came almost ten minutes later.

Yara turned the sink off and looked at her daughter. She leaned against the counter top as she dried her hands. "Are you fed up? Are you being disrespected? Are you adored? Do you feel like you're settling? Can you do better? Are you tired of repeating yourself?"

The questions came back to back, and Meme didn't know which one to answer first. "I like him so much…"

"But what?" Because there was always a "but". No relationship was perfect.

"The baby mamas are on my last nerve. I can't do it, and I don't like how I feel when he's with his kids. Mama, I think I'm jealous." She closed her eyes and tried her hardest to hold her tears.

"Have you told him this?"

Meme shook her head. "No, I know I'll sound crazy, so I haven't said anything, and then I don't want him to think I'm nagging him-"

"It's not nagging. You are entitled to an opinion, and I'm sure he doesn't bite his tongue when it comes to you."

She loved Riq, she could see the rest of her life with him, but everything wasn't peaches and cream. "My heart hurts," she admitted.

Yara had been there before. And damn, she hated that her daughter had to go through this pain. In the end, it would make her stronger.

Yara took a seat beside her and lifted her head. "Every day ain't gon' be the red carpet. Now I'm not saying to act out, and I'm not saying to leave him, but I will tell you that you are a queen. And, baby, if he don't see that crown on top of your head, it's not your job to remind him that it's there," she schooled her the way she wished she had a mom school her.

"I don't want it to seem like I'm being dragged because I'm not, I just want more. More love, more time, more attention, and I want him to get it together with his baby mamas. Like, why does he have to go to her house to see his kids? Why can't they come to his?" she laid it all out.

Yara rolled her eyes. Dating a man with kids was so touchy because nine times out of ten, they were still fucking around with the mama. She knew this to be true. Kadeem ate the P out of her pussy and went right back home to his fiancé.
In some cases, parents could co-parent successfully and in other situations, one person still had feelings involved.

"You don't have to put up with nothing you don't want to. You have no ties with that man. No kids, no house, no businesses, no deeds, nothing." The only thing that kept her tied to Kadeem was their three kids. If she weren't a mother, she would have moved across the country to heal.

"I know, Mama."

Yara pulled her in for a hug. "I love you, baby, and I only want the best for you. And you have to want the best for yourself." She wouldn't preach to her all night.

After she cleaned the kitchen, Meme told her that she was about to head home.

"You can stay here if you want to," she offered.

When Yanise moved out, that was her green light to move in with Riq, and now she wondered if they had moved too fast. Living together was a whole different ball game than casual dating. Riq was in the streets, and he had children, so she was always questioning where he was this time of the day instead of when she was just stopping by and spending the night when he requested her presence.

The late nights and coming in before the sun rose wasn't what she was accustomed to. Excuses of the phone being on the charger or dead had grown old, and she had only been there for two weeks. Meme was already visibly annoyed and irritated.

"I'm going home. Do you need a ride to the airport in the morning?"

Yara shook her head and held up her iPhone. "Finally downloaded Uber," she said and winked her eye.

They joked around the studio that she was a granny, although she looked younger than most of the people she worked with. She told them that she was adjusting slowly but surely, and now had Uber and UberEats and loved the convenience of both apps on her cell phone.

"Thank God!" Meme lifted her hands in the air to signify worship. She had fixed Riq a plate to go. "Well, call me when you land. I'm going to put this in the microwave, I'm sure he's not there." She rolled her eyes.

"Everything will work out. You're not a dummy, trust your gut, baby."

To Meme's surprise, Riq was home when she got to his crib. She came in and was greeted by the faint smell of marijuana. The television was turned all the way up, and there he was fixing a large bowl of Frosted Flakes. His gun was on the counter, and his pants were barely being held up, even with the Gucci belt on she had copped him the other week.

"I bought you food," she told him and sat it on the counter.

Riq quickly put the cereal back in the box. "Good looking, a nigga is high and hungry."

"Munchies," she commented. After she closed the door, she removed her sneakers and sat her purse in the chair and looked at him. Gosh, she cared about this man so much, if only he knew how much she prayed for his safety and well-being while he was out in the streets.

"We need to talk." She didn't want to argue, yell or fuss. She wanted to get her thoughts out and hoped he listened and they came to some common ground and then made love. She didn't like the tension in their home, and he had to know she was feeling some type of way.

Normally, they linked up for lunch in the middle of the day, and she would send him selfies and funny messages to his inbox on Instagram. When they were doing great, she would check in with him throughout the day and vice versa. If they were beefing, communication was nonexistent.

"What up, Meme?" He heated the food up and waited for her to start the conversation.

She turned the television off and sat down at the table. Once he joined her, she took a deep breath. "Okay, please don't take what I say and run with it. I'm only telling you how I feel."

He nodded his head. "Gotcha." Riq was so laid back that sometimes it appeared nonchalant and cold.

"Are you still fucking your baby mama?" She didn't expect it come out the way it did. She planned on easing into that part of the conversation.

He looked at her, and she looked back, raising her eyebrow and then folding her arms across her breasts. "Is that a yes?" She took his silence as guilt.

He closed the top of the container. "I was… I'm not anymore."

"When did you stop?" Her heart was beating so loud, she knew he could hear her nervousness.

"Does that matter?" He didn't want her to leave him.

"Yeah, Riq, it does," she snapped her neck. Meme was dipping if he told her some bullshit.

They wouldn't last if he couldn't be honest. A relationship built on lies could never be solid. Their foundation would be weak. "When you moved in, and I saw that this shit was serious…"

She didn't allow him to finish. "Say less." She got up and tried her hardest to get the hell out of there as fast as she could, but he was on her heels.

"Mannnn, now you gon' leave?" He grabbed her arm, and she gave him a look that told him to take his mother fucking hands off her without parting her lips.

"Meme…" He wasn't about to let her go.

"You got me fucked up! Why did you ask me to move in with you, and you out here giving dick away? Dick that you claim is mine?" She was hurt.

"It is yours." He moved around and stood in front of her, but she turned her head, not wanting him to see her tears.

"I'm with you. I only want you, Amina." He only used her government when he was serious.

"You fucked up, Riq!" She was pissed.

"And watch me make it better. All I got is my word. I cut her off, I'm not fucking her no more."

"Are you still fucking the other one?"

He shook his head. "I ain't touched that broad since I found out she was pregnant. I begged her to get an abortion, she trapped me." It was a good thing he was sticking to that story because if not, she was going to slap the hell out of him.

"Riq, if I find out-"

He cut her off, "You not baby, you not. I promise to God." He swore that he was doing the right thing by her. She had his heart.

"Sleep on the couch," was the last thing she said before walking to the bedroom and locking the door. He would be in the dog house until he showed her some papers that his dick was clean. Meme wasn't risking her safety any more.

And she was still unsure if she was going to stay with him, it was hard to restore trust. Most times, once it was gone you couldn't get it back, so only time would tell.

η

Charlie asked the doctor to repeat himself because certainly, she didn't hear him correctly.

"I am referring you to a cardiologist."

And then she questioned him again, "For what? Nothing is wrong with me." She was in denial. Her doctor normally had a lot of patience, but he had been going through this with her for months.

"There is nothing else I can do. The heart isn't my specialty, you need extensive tests ran."

Charlie grabbed her purse and didn't bother grabbing the note that had the cardiologist's information on it.

"Have a good day," she mumbled under her breath. What was wrong with her heart? Yeah, it would get tight, and sometimes she thought she was having a heart attack, but the girls had moved out. Her and KK were no longer denying their feelings, and Kadeem and Yara were free. No more stress.

For the past few years, she couldn't live and think freely. Charlie had so much responsibility, and that put stress on her heart. She was okay now. Her doctor ignored all of that when she tried to explain to him and still, he was suggesting that she see a cardiologist.

Fuck that, she wasn't seeing anybody. She planned on stopping by the herb store and picking up some fresh herbs to make her a tea to calm her nerves.

In the parking lot of the doctor's office, she scanned Google to see what could be wrong, if there was something off with her heart. Her fingers trembled as she tried to click the screen. She was nervous.

Charlie didn't want to die, and when she thought of her heart, the only thing she automatically associated with the problems she was having was death. She didn't want a pacemaker or a new heart. Charlie didn't do surgery or medicine.

Every article she read said the same thing, *"Live a healthy lifestyle."* But damn it, she lived a healthy life. She ate right, got enough hours of sleep in the day, she was active, she did everything they were suggesting. Charlie continued to read, family history… smoking… stress… she was looking for something else to pop out to her. *One out of four women dies from heart disease.* Well, that didn't make her feel any better.

She tossed the phone to the floor of the passenger seat and started her car.
Today was supposed to be full of running around and errands, but now she wanted to climb into bed and start over tomorrow.

Ayanna called out to her, "Charlie, is that you?" when she walked in the house. She didn't have the strength to answer her granddaughter. "What's wrong?" Ayanna was worried. She was making a sandwich before she started her homework.

"Why are you home so early?" Ever since Yanise's abortion, she had been on Ayanna's ass like white on rice.

"Uh, I get out of school at twelve, remember?" She only had a few credits to finish up and had been dual enrollment since she was a junior.

"Hmm hmm… I'm going to lie down. Don't bother me."

Ayanna looked at her crazily. "Are you okay?" Charlie didn't do naps. Ever.

"Do it look like something is wrong with me?" she snapped.

She walked out of the kitchen, and Ayanna was curious as to what was going on for real with her grandmother. Their family was so full of secrets, she wouldn't be surprised if she were holding something from them.

She pulled her homework out and slid her headphones over her head. A few more months until she graduated and went to college. Ayanna wanted to go far away from the hood. She had big dreams, and they couldn't come true if she stayed here.

Meme was supposed to go down south for school but stayed because of her and Yanise. Ayanna wouldn't be making that sacrifice for her sisters. She was a little more selfish than them and made no apologies for it.

After finding the perfect playlist on Apple Music, she zoned out and got to work. The countdown to graduation was ticking, and she wanted to graduate at the top of her class with honors and hopefully, Valedictorian as well. She could see the title by her name already, the black girl magic was in full effect.

η

"Stop, stop, stop," she commanded the engineer to cut the beat.

It was late, and she was tired. Her back and feet were hurting, and she needed to lie down for a second. Literally, ten minutes would be enough time for her to refuel. She took the cap off her head and ran her hands over her face.

"Your eyes are bloodshot red," Jazmine's engineer told her. He was used to working late nights and apparently, this new chick they sent over wasn't.

Yara ignored him and went into the booth and stood before her. She moved the microphone out of her way so no one could hear what she was saying but the person who needed to receive the message.

"What does it feel like when you wake up and realize that he don't love you no more? Do you know how that feels? To see the man you gave your everything to, give that love to another bitch?" She hated to curse and get in her face. Homegirl had the vocals, but she wasn't tapping into the song.

"I'm going through something, I can't do this tonight," she gave her a poor excuse.

"You're not the only one, sweetheart. I got divorce papers waiting on my desk when I get back, so trust me, I'm going through it with you. Use that pain and pour into this song. This track right here could be the gateway to greatness." Yara touched her heart. "Close your eyes and sing," she asked her nicely.

When she closed the door to the booth, her eyes landed on Quentin. She wanted to ask when did he get here and what the hell was he doing in Los Angeles, but they weren't the only people in the studio. And unbeknownst to Yara, the microphones were high quality, and everyone heard what she said.

"She's ready, run it back."

It wasn't perfect, but it was damn sure better than what she had been doing, and everyone agreed to go home to get some rest. She didn't expect it to be this hard being that Fredo was so easy to work with. Her and Quentin stood back while everyone left.

"For future reference, am I allowed to sell the song and move on with my life?"

He laughed heartily, stuffing his hands into the pocket of his Givenchy track pants. "Not having fun?"

Yara was tired as hell. "No, not at all, so we can scratch this off the list."

"I think that if her mind were clear, it would have flowed. Y'all been in here for hours working on one song."

"Is that not normal?"

He shook his head. "A twelve-hour session, she should have at least been able to lay four tracks."

"Yeah, she must have really been going through something. Do you think anything is open? I'm starving."

He knew an after-hours spot that she would love. "Yeah, grab your stuff. I know the perfect place."

And he was right. Yara was stuffed after eating a double stack turkey burger with grilled mushrooms and swiss cheese, onion rings, and a milkshake with waffle crumbs. She chewed a stick of gum and then thanked him for treating her to the meal.

He looked down at her empty plate. "You can eat."

In her defense, "I been in a dark room all day and night. I'm starved, and I had no service to order something."

"I'll make sure y'all have catering tomorrow."

Jazmine wasn't his artist, so he wasn't obligated to do that. "I'm good, no special treatment needed." Yara didn't like handouts.

"I treat those who are special to me."

"The fact that I don't know if you do this with everyone bothers me, if I'm allowed to be honest."

They had been at the diner for about two hours discussing his fame, the music industry and what could be a successful career for her as a songwriter, producer or A & R, whatever she chose.

Yara soaked up every gem he dropped. Quentin was educated, she could tell from the way he spoke and articulated his words like an Ivy League graduate, which he was. And the plus was, he made eye contact and didn't have to speak with his hands. Kadeem spoke with his hands, and now she was convinced that all liars used their hands to communicate.

"What do you want to know? I'm single, and I don't date because I don't have time for games."

And she let him know, "Me neither, so let's not waste each other's time."

He held his hand out to shake on what she proposed. They had a deal. No bullshit and no games.

His watch sparkled so bright, she couldn't help but admire the piece. "I miss my Rolex," she blurted out.

"This is an Audemar, but I like Rolexes too." He didn't say it in a bragging way. Quentin was rich as fuck, Yara knew that from the house in Miami. The car they drove in tonight wasn't even out yet. He worked hard and deserved the fruits of his labor, and she couldn't wait to cash in on hers.

"It's a few things I definitely want if the song takes off," she told him. Quentin was curious, so he asked her what was on her list. "I want a truck. I'm little, but I really want like a nice ass truck, tinted windows, black rims, panoramic sunroof." She was on the video shoot for Nash's next release, and the Bentley truck they had on set had her pussy wet it was so nice.

"What else?"

She chewed on her bottom lip, unaware of how much she was turning him on with that one motion. "A watch like yours," she giggled. "And I don't know, maybe some earrings, things I had before I… yeah, that's it," she ended the conversation, not wanting to go into her time in prison.

"How was that? If you don't mind me asking."

She had an idea that he knew, and he had just confirmed her guess by asking her that question.

"How was *your* time in jail?" she redirected the question back to him.

Quentin smiled at her and rubbed his hands together. "You did your research."

She shrugged her shoulders. "Not really, office chatter."

"Is that another way of saying gossip?" He wasn't sure.

Yara redirected the conversation back to what they were supposed to be discussing. "So, how was it? Were you on Rikers?"

He shook his head. "I did white-collar crimes, baby."

"Neat and professional, huh? I got my hands dirty," she said and took a deep breath.

From what he was told, it didn't match her personality or her looks. And that's normally the ones he stayed away from. Behind a pretty face and a fat ass could sometimes be your worst nightmare.

"For your husband though, right?" he pressed. She sat back, chewing that bottom lip again. "Stop doing that," he warned her.

"What do you know about me?" she asked.

He sat forward and put his elbows on the now cleared table since the waitress came and picked up the fifty-dollar tip along with the dirty dishes.
"Do you really want to know?"

She nodded her head, he could either be right or wrong. She probably wouldn't confirm anything he told her anyway, so it didn't matter. Yara never incriminated herself, and she thought she did a good job at controlling her emotions but didn't. At least not in the presence of Quentin Brooks.

"Yara Moreland, granddaughter of the great Evangelist, Stephan Hagan. Your aunt is Prophetess Marilyn, known as the scammer, but your grandparents still ain't put two and two together. Your mother married Minister Jordan, you hated him and ran away from home at fourteen, met a bad boy from the block, your now husband. He went to jail for a year, and you had your first child alone. He came home and swore to you that he had the million-dollar plan, and you followed him. So, from there y'all started robbing on the west coast, taking whatever you could get your hands on and selling on the east coast until it caught up to y'all. And that's when you were facing what, fifty years? But you knew a secret about the Judge's son and got it down to ten. You sacrificed for your husband, and when I heard that shit, I asked myself what man would let his wife-"

"Stop it." She couldn't hear anymore. Yara's face was red. She was angry.

He had read her ass like a book.

"Your husband is a pussy, and I can't wait till you divorce that nigga. Okay, I'm done."

The car ride to the W Hotel where she was staying during her time in California was extremely uncomfortable. She didn't even bother wiping her tears. They wouldn't stop coming, so there was no point.

His music was on low, so he didn't hear her sniffling and shit. "Yara," he said her name as he placed the car in park and turned to her.

"Save it, Quentin." She didn't want to hear anything he had to say. He had said it all.

"I don't care about your past." And he didn't want her to be concerned about his.

"You'll never look at me in a good light, so I'm not even about to go there with you. You can't build something with no trust, and in your eyes, I'm a bitch that played for the wrong team." She already knew what was up. Yara had been in the game for a long time.

"You're wrong. I look at you as a woman, not a bitch, and you were loyal. How can I fault you for being loyal to your man?"

"How did you know about my family?" That was really her concern.

He shrugged his shoulders. "I remember faces, my peoples know them."

"Fuck all of them! They're all hypocrites." She now had snot running out of her nose.

Quentin wiped it. He didn't care how disgusting it was, being that he was a germaphobe. "Everybody that's saved ain't a saint and vice versa, you can't let them keep you from God."

She didn't want to hear that. She took her seatbelt off. "Don't come to the studio tomorrow because I don't want to see your skinny ass." She was serious too.

He ignored her because he would do what he wanted to do, and he had an early flight in the morning anyway. "Come here." He tried to pull her close to him, but she jerked away.

"I'm not a bitch that need saving. I don't need you to rescue me or show me what I'm missing, none of that. I've lived life better than you ever could, whether or not it was illegal." She wanted to let him know that she was not a charity case. Kadeem didn't put a gun to her head, well once, but that was when she threatened to take the kids.

"I want you to stop calling yourself a bitch, that shit is bugging me," he said and scratched the side of his head.

"Bitch, bitch, bitch, dumb ass bitch, bitch, scamming ass bitch, jailbird bitch, slut ass bitch-"

Quentin hushed the verbal abuse she was inflicting upon herself with a swift kiss to her lips. He tongued her down and dried her tears as he slid his tongue into her mouth, and she put hers into his. They danced for a few minutes until he pulled away and stared at her.

"When you let that hurt go, give me a call." She was right, and he was grateful that she had let him know. He had heard her loud and clear.

Yara didn't need him to save, rescue or deliver her from what she had been through. She needed to do that for herself.

Chapter Thirteen
"The first time I say no, it's like I never said yes." – Beyoncé

"Yo, you getting stingy with the head," Kadeem let his love know. He wasn't joking either.

Kamala almost choked on her cinnamon raisin bagel. "What?" she shrieked. He came behind her in the kitchen and fixed a cup of orange juice. "Kadeem Moreland!" When she called out his government name, she wanted a response.

"I'm saying, like you'll be down there for ten seconds and then plopping your ass on my lap." He wanted more, expected more, especially when he gave her all of him.

She couldn't believe they were even discussing sex. All the fucking they did, he shouldn't dare complain.

"First of all, I have to get to work-"

"Your ass in here eating a whole breakfast, save the excuses, baby." He wasn't even trying to hear it.

She rolled her eyes, this argument was so juvenile. "So, to be clear, how many minutes would you like your head to be so I can set a timer on my watch?" She was being sarcastic, and he knew that.

"Have a good day," he told her. Kadeem had shit to do, and he left the house without giving her a kiss or a hug.

She asked herself was she tripping, but the quickie he initiated this morning caught her off guard. Kamala gathered her laptop, work bag and purse. After she had all her things in the back seat, she set the alarm to "away" and hopped in her whip so she could beat traffic.

At the red light, she texted her fiancé, *I don't know what's up with you, but you're acting like you always get the two-minute treatment. I don't wake up every morning wanting dick down my throat. Have a good day.*

Thankfully, the coast to work was clear, so she got there with twenty minutes to spare before her first scheduled appointment. Kadeem didn't respond to her text message, and she couldn't dwell on his salty attitude. She knew how to make it up to him and would do so tonight. She applied a coat of rose pink YSL lipstick as the elevator opened.

"Good morning," she greeted the receptionist with a smile. Whatever she was dealing with at home never affected her performance at work.

"You have a visitor."

Kamala stopped in her tracks. "Busy day today, who is it?"

The receptionist pointed behind her and whispered, "Same lady from last time."

And there was Yara, looking like she had just hopped off a plane. Her skin glowed without the use of highlighter, bronzer or concealer. Yara smiled at Kamala and then waved.

"Can I help you with something?" She wasn't in the mood for the bullshit today.

Yara reached into the book bag she had at her feet. Kamala thought it was childish for women of her age to carry book bags, but to each its own.

"Got those papers you sent over."

Kamala checked her watch, time was limited. "Follow me to my office," she told Yara. Yara stood to her feet with her things in hand. "Be on standby with security," Kamala whispered to her receptionist. She would not have Yara destroying her office or causing a scene.

Yara heard her and told the woman, "Security isn't needed, I won't be here long." Kamala eyes got big, and Yara told her, "I have just as much to lose as you do, without the degree."

She admired all the cute ass pictures of her and Kadeem on her desk and some on her wall. They did things together, things that she and him never did. She could tell that Kamala controlled their relationship, it was in how she carried herself.

Yara was a submissive woman. She listened more than she spoke, and that's how she was raised. That's how she saw the women around her act. She was only doing what she was taught. Her grandmother followed behind her grandfather, and her mother did the same with her step-father. She wasn't sure of how she acted with her biological dad, he was a distant memory.

"You guys make a really nice couple," she told Kamala.

Kamala was sure she was being sarcastic, so she got straight to the point. "Did you sign the papers?" She had prayed for this day to come, and now she could finally get started with the wedding plans. God was showing out on this Monday morning. She would hold the news off until tonight over dinner to share with Kadeem if Yara didn't beat her to it.

"Not yet." Yara took a seat in the chair. Kamala was cute. She really was, and she could sort of see what Kadeem saw in her but knew there was more to the story. And that's why she was here.

"What's the holdup?"

"I want to know the exact discrepancy that resulted in Kadeem's early release, and who was the witness that testified against me."

"Yara-"

She didn't want to hear any bullshit. She interrupted her, "I'm not playing with you. You want your husband and your fairytale wedding, tell me what I want to know, and I'll sign them right now." For her to have peace, she needed to know who was behind those ten years.

"I have a meeting, it will take me like an hour to find the file," she said to her, and that was the truth.

Yara pointed to her book bag. "That's why I brought my laptop, so I'll work in here until your meeting is over. I have nothing to do other than signing those papers." Kamala wanted to oblige. "It's you and him that want the divorce, not me," Yara added.

"Why are you doing this?" Yara was too calm, and that gave her the impression she had ulterior motives.

"If you spent ten years in jail and came home to *your* man engaged to one of the lawyers assigned to your case, what would you do? How would you feel?" For goodness sake, she couldn't be serious right now. Yara had questions, and she wanted answers.

"I have a meeting. You can sit in the lobby and wait if you want to." She didn't trust her in her office while she wasn't present.

Yara was cool with that, so she posted up in the lobby with her headphones on while checking off her to-do list.

Kamala didn't come back to the lobby until one in the afternoon, which totaled up to four and a half hours that she had been waiting.

When they were back in her office, Kamala closed the door and handed Yara the file. "Here is what you requested. Don't ask me no questions because I have no answers for you. You can read the information and draw from it what you need, and whatever you do with the information is on you. I don't care if you go back to jail or not," she gave her a disclosure.

Yara opened it and read the paperwork. She read it carefully, over and over again. And then she closed the folder and placed it on Kamala's desk along with the divorce papers. She said nothing to her at all.

"That's it?" Kamala questioned.

"Congrats on the engagement," Yara told her and then exited her office.

Kamala tried calling Kadeem to warn him if there was anything in the paperwork that may have alarmed Yara, but his phone was going to voicemail. She prayed she hadn't made a mistake by letting her see the files, especially when it came to her man's safety. Yara was a woman scorned, so there was no telling what she would or could do.

η

Growing up, it was said that she would become the next Vickie Winans, Joyce Myers and even marry a pastor and follow in the footsteps of First Lady Serita Jakes, but Yara didn't want that life.

Her grandfather was a good man. It wasn't him she hated and despised, it was them other church folk. When she left home, she never looked back and had no desire to ever return. She turned her phone off and slid black gloves on her hands.

Yara didn't want to go back down that dark path again, but they left her no choice. Her freedom? It was the one thing that someone could take away from you, and they didn't just take it, they snatched it. She was taken from her children, her husband, her life, and she couldn't click her heels three times and get that time back. A knock on her window petrified the shit out of her.

"What are you doing?" Kadeem's voice always carried a bass, even when he didn't raise his voice.

"Go home," she told him when he tried to open her car door. "This ain't got nothing to do with you."

"If you don't open this door, I'm going to bust the window out," he threatened. She took a long, hard deep breath and clicked the locks. "You want to go back to jail, huh? You want to miss Yanna graduation? You gon' let these bitches send you back over some old shit?" He was all in her face. He was hoping he could talk her out of doing something she would regret. She came here to kill. He knew her, he could smell the urgency of murder all over her body.

"I never did nothing to no one." Tears fell down her face. She was so tired of mother fuckers trying her.

"Yara, I never wanted you to know this," he told her the truth.

He was full of shit too. "And yet… they're still living, all of them." She glanced his way, wondering why he didn't take care of the situation when she asked him to.

He stepped back and looked at her. "I couldn't, all eyes were on me."

"I don't give a fuck!" Ten years… my nigga, you couldn't get ten years back. Kadeem was continuously showing her that he wasn't for her. He didn't ride for her how she rode for him, and why she hadn't noticed before was seriously fucking with her.

"Yara, people that do evil shit like that, it always comes back to them. That's called karma, baby," he tried to school her.

All this crying was making her head hurt, and she was tired of wiping tears. She hadn't cried this much in years.

"Yeah, and I can't wait until karma come and visit your ass," she sneered before closing her door and speeding off.

Kadeem watched her leave, and in his peripheral, he saw someone close the blinds at the house she was parked in front of. He got in his car and headed to the hood, he needed to smoke.

Kamala was dead wrong for making that move without checking with him first. There was no way she could spin it to get him to see her reason other than she was thirsty to get married.

He was cool with wifing her. She was worthy of his last name and deserved it for staying down with him until he came back up. But still, the way she was going about becoming Mrs. Moreland wasn't right. She didn't know the can of worms she had opened by showing Yara that file. Kamala thought she knew her, but she really didn't. No one knew the shit Yara was capable of.

Kamala kept saying that she warned Yara about going back to jail, and that Yara ignored her. And yeah, she ain't say shit back for two reasons; she wouldn't dare incriminate herself, and second, she knew that she could kill the bitch and possibly get away with it. Even with her bare hands or no hands at all, Yara would watch her take her last breath. They were trained well at what they did. And that's how they got away with it for so long. He had to tell Meme to keep a close eye on their mama.

"Damn, who died?" his partner asked him, seeing the sad and down look his face.

He sat down in the green lawn chair. "Yara almost shot up the whole block on some old shit, she still a hot head." Every time he thought things were coming together or slowing down and peace would soon be on the horizon, some shit popped off.

"I never took her as a hot head. She didn't play the radio, that's all."

Riq agreed, "Yo, you ain't never lied. I only seen her yell like twice. She could kill you with one look and a slice to your neck," he motioned with his hands.

"Nobody colder than shorty," John chimed in.

Kadeem looked at his peoples. "Damn, I'm glad I trust y'all niggas…" He was speaking of how they were praising her like she was their bitch or something.

"Shit, you got a whole new wife. Yara ass is fine as a mother fucker, always has been."

Steeno had crossed the mother fucking line. And everyone in their circle knew it. Drunk or not, he was about to get his issue.

Riq moved out of the way, wanting no parts of what was about to go down, and John stood up once he saw Kadeem stand to his feet. He was needed to cease the fire before it blazed.

"He drunk, we been posted for a lil' minute drinking," he said to Kadeem, placing his hand on his chest which he knocked off.

"Fuck you say, nigga?" On his mama, if the nigga had enough balls to repeat himself, he was going to light his ass up.

"Man, you wasn't stunting that girl until she got out of prison, fuck outta here. She fine, and she single," Steeno fanned him away. Before he could pick up his can of beer, Kadeem had shot him in the chest.

POW!

POW!

"Whoaaaa!" Riq was not expecting him to kill Steeno, they all were like uncles to him. Steeno taught him how to dump a body. This shit was unreal.

He couldn't dwell on it, he had to dip before twelve hit the block.

Kadeem didn't blink until he realized what had just happened.

"Bro, let's go. Fuck is you doing?" John yelled at him. Right or wrong, he was riding with him until the wheels fell off and the casket closed.

Kadeem's gun was still smoking. Steeno died with a smirk on his face. He wanted to spit on him but didn't because then his DNA would be on the body.

They hopped in their cars and sped off. They were now at Steeno's house in his backyard, and he lived alone.

Kadeem told John, "It was disrespect, he disrespected me." He was trying to find a reason to justify his actions.

John still hadn't spoken. They had grown up together, all of them. He couldn't believe Kadeem had killed him. Kadeem was just tripping out on how he had just talked Yara out of not killing someone, only for him to turn around and shoot a mother fucker not even less than fifteen minutes later. Was this the karma she spoke of?

"You think it was any witnesses?" Kadeem asked.

John shook his head. "Nah."

He still was about to get low, to be sure.

Kamala came home early, and when she saw them in her living room looking down and out, she questioned, "Damn, what y'all do today? Kill somebody?"

Although it was merely a joke, the comment caused shit to land in Kadeem's boxers. He couldn't go back to jail. All he could do is run to the toilet and pray that this was swept under the rug.

η

Yara was in a cloud for the rest of the week. Although she hated Kadeem, if he hadn't pulled up when he did, she would be back in a cell. She wasn't thinking straight and vowed to herself that it would never happen again.

A knock on her office door came from her good friend, she then peeked her head in the door. "Are you okay?" Miko asked, noticing that she had little to say during the meeting.

Yara nodded her head. "No complaints." Mentally, she wasn't available right now.

Miko closed the door and stepped in, taking a seat and looking at her friend.

"You don't have to tell me what's going on, I'm not here to pry. When I first came home, it took me a while to step back into what was considered familiar territory. And maybe you should see a therapist because being in jail for all those years and dealing with what you've dealt with on top of coming home, and..." She didn't want to state the obvious. "I saw a therapist because I saw some traces of PTSD."

Yara had never heard of that before. "What's that?" She closed her laptop and gave Miko all her attention.

"Post-traumatic stress disorder. Have you heard of the Kaleif Browder story? I don't care what no one says, he killed himself because of PTSD."

Yara made a mental note to research on PTSD. "I'm fine," she lied.

Miko shook her head. "No, you're not, and that's okay. I'll text you the therapist's number."

"Why did you stop seeing her?"

"Huh?"

Yara then said, "You said went too? You don't go anymore?"

"No, I'm good now. She helped me accept a lot of things. I still practice some of the exercises she gave me to help with anxiety."

Yara wasn't into talking to somebody about her business. "I'll think about it."

"And that's all I ask, and you know I'm here if you need me."

Yara had baggage. She didn't consider herself bitter, though she had every right to be, but she wasn't. It took a lot out of her to accept that Kadeem wasn't perfect and to let go of the hurt he caused her before and after her incarceration. The name in that file took her back to a place she hadn't visited in a very long time.

Once she got home, she took a pizza out of the freezer and placed it into the oven. There was no way she was cooking tonight. Ever since she returned from Cali, she had been back in the office and was thankful that things had slowed down. She needed a break. She ate, showered and got in bed with the *Love Languages* book she had been reading.

Yanise knocked on her door. "Hey, Mama."

Yara sat up. "Did you have fun at Marsha's house with Shanti?" Her daughter came and sat on the edge of the bed, and Yara told her, "Come give me a hug."

This new generation, they'd rather hop in an Uber than get picked up. Normally, Yara would get her, but today she was tired. She didn't want to get comfortable putting her child in an Uber because people were crazy these days.

"Yeah, Shanti and me are cool. But mama, that daddy… something ain't right with him." She wagged her finger and balled her face up.

Her daughter was wise beyond her years. "Girl, if you don't look like your daddy," she laughed.

"I'm so for real, Ma! He is creepy, and he be tripping. I think they all scared of him." Her eyes got big.

Yara's mind went back to a conversation she had with Marsha one day over lunch when she was saying how she wanted to get away from him.

"Do you feel safe over there?" Yanise's safety and her feeling comfortable was a major concern.

"Oh, he better not even try it with me. One, my name is Yanise Moreland and two, my daddy is crazy." She wasn't afraid of anyone.

"Well, excuse me then."

Yanise told her, "Okay, I gotta call Charlie so we can catch up on our stories, you know she be acting funny when I don't call her."

"Tell her you'll be over this weekend."

"I can't make that promise to her, me and Shanti supposed to go to the movies."

Yara was surprised to hear that. "Are you asking or telling me?" She had to keep Yanise's ass in check.

"That was me asking."

"No, it wasn't. Try again tomorrow. It's pizza on the stove."

Yanise rolled her eyes. Her mama didn't see her do that because if she did, she would have taken her phone, and she just got it back.

Yara got comfortable again and turned the page of her book. Quentin had crossed her mind while reading the book, and she wondered did they have the same love language? She didn't feel good knowing he knew all her secrets, her past and probably her insecurities too. He had read her like a number one New York Times Bestseller, and she wasn't okay with being so exposed. Plus, he was right. She had some stuff to sort out mentally and didn't need to add him to the stinking pile.

If he was still around and available once she got her shit together, then maybe they were meant to be, and if not, she was cool. The whole falling in love again was the last thing on her mind right now.

η

"Babyyyyyy…" Meme came through the house happy as hell. Her mom had looked out for her and gave her the opportunity of her dreams. She had the chance to do hair for Fredo's first video, and she was so ecstatic.

Riq was on the couch with his head in his hands. The house was dark, and he wasn't smoking, and those two things told her that something was off.

Today was not a good day for him. He hated losing people. Yeah, it was a part of the game, he knew that, but family had killed family.

"What's wrong?" She still was mad at him but paused the madness to tell him her good news. He was her person; the first person she called whether her day was going good or bad. Before anything, before taking her virginity and giving her the first orgasm she ever experienced, they had been friends.

"Nothing." He didn't want to tell her.

She plopped down on the couch and rubbed his back with one hand and with the other she moved his hand from his face and saw that he was crying.

"Talk to me," she begged him.

"Steeno… gone." He still couldn't believe it. Riq wasn't an emotional person, and it had been a while since he shed tears. He didn't even cry when his children were born. Yeah, the nigga was out of order, but it wasn't reason to kill him. He had asked himself on the way home would he shoot one of his niggas if they were speaking crazy like that about Meme, and he wouldn't. Riq also didn't have a short temper either. He could appreciate that people knew his girl was bad, and that didn't bother him because Meme was all his, and he knew that without a doubt. He believed that Kadeem shot Steeno because he was speaking facts.

"Oh my God, I gotta check on my daddy." Steeno and her dad were thick as thieves, and back in the day, that statement was literal.

Riq didn't mean to grab her wrist as rough as he did when she picked up her cell phone. She looked at him as if he had lost his mind.

"My bad. Don't call him, he probably not going to answer the phone anyway."

She needed more than that. "What's going on, Riq?"

After he ran the story down to her, she was now in tears right with him. John and Steeno had looked out for her and her sisters when both of their parents were in jail. She remembered them dropping off toys, money and ice cream. Her whole life she knew them to be her uncles. Hell, Meme was closer to them than she was to her dad's real brother, who lived in Atlanta. He had married a billionaire, and she was cool, but they didn't really have a relationship with their uncle Kasim.

Riq seemed devastated over the death of one of his father figures, and he knew the streets would be hurt behind it. For her dad to kill Steeno off wordplay... only one question came to mind.

"Do you think he still loves my mama?"

η

Sex in your teenage years was a waste of time because neither you nor your partner knew what you are doing. Sex in your twenties is experimental, sex in your thirties is comfortable, sex in your forties is considered recreational, but sex in your fifties is life-changing.

She had been having sex with Kourtland since she was nineteen-years-old, and with age, he got better and better. She was sure he had other lovers in the past, but now that dick belonged to Charlie.

They had been at the rodeo for decades, and she seriously couldn't get enough of him. The way he tasted, the way he grunted and moaned when he reached his peak, even the way he bit his bottom lip when she told him that he was hitting that secret, sinful, sweet spot that he seemed to only find after they had wine and smoked.

She had a slight problem catching her breath, and he hurried to the kitchen to get some water. Her chest was tight as hell, and she held it, hoping that would ease the pain.

"Are you okay?" he asked her once she had downed the entire water bottle and now feeling better.

She nodded her head. "Yeah, you worked me today," she teased.

KK laughed, "Nah, you getting old, can't keep up like you used to." He reached over and kissed her lips, pulling her down against his chest.

They laid in bed, covered in sweat and sex, and neither was in a rush to get up.

Ayanna was hopefully sleeping because if not, she got an earful that she probably didn't want to hear. Grandparents across America were still having sex.

"Soooo, I was thinking," she said as she trailed the hair on his chest down to his belly button.

"Oh, Lawd." Charlie and her thoughts, he had no idea what she was about to say.

"It's actually a good thought," she laughed. She sat up so she could see his eyes to sense his reaction to what she was about to propose. "I love you."

He knew that even when she swore she didn't love him and that he was the worst person that God could have created, he knew that she loved him and always would.

"I'm listening, Charlie." The "I love you" stuff was fluff. He was expecting her to say that she wanted to take a trip or come to Atlanta for a while, but what came from her mouth totally threw him for a loop.

"You wanna get married?" she blurted out.

"For what?"

Charlie was floored by his response. "Are you serious? You've been asking me for years." He couldn't be for real right now.

"And I also stopped asking you two years ago because you kept telling me no," he retorted.

She got out of bed and grabbed the sheet with her, wrapping it around her body. She went to turn the light on over her bed because the lamp on her nightstand wasn't enough for this conversation. "Okay, and that's why I asked you this time."

He wasn't interested. KK shook his head. "Charlie, it's late, come back to bed." This conversation was over.

She was infuriated. "No, I'm not coming back to bed, KK. I want to know why you don't want to marry me? This is what you've always wanted," she reminded him.

"Yeah, you right. It's what I wanted, not you," he said and looked at her, knowing he was telling the truth. Something was up with Charlie.

"Well, now I do," she told him.

He rolled over and pulled the comforter over his body. They normally slept naked anyway, so he was good. "Night, baby."

"I feel rejected… you really told me no…" She was talking to herself more than him.

"Is this going to change us? Because if so, I'll fly out tomorrow." He didn't do confusion. It was nothing for him to go to Atlanta for weeks or even months.
Charlie would get in her feelings sometimes and need space, and he felt as if she needed that now.

"I don't know, you tell me," she said and left the bedroom, slamming the door behind her.

He didn't go after her, he was too tired to do so.

Ayanna crept into the kitchen and jumped when she turned the light on and saw her grandmother with a sheet tied around her body. "I'm not even going to ask where your clothes are? Yuck." She made a vomiting noise and held her nose.

Charlie ignored and continued sipping her tea. "Why are you still up?"

"I just woke up, and I'm starving," she said and pulled a bowl, cereal and milk out the fridge.

"Do you miss your sisters being here?" She needed to take her mind off KK's rejection, if only for a few minutes.

"No, not at all. The bathroom is always free, and it's cleaner around here. No makeup from Meme all in the sink, and no dishes in the sink from Yanise. They shoulda been gone." She loved having the bathroom and TV in the living room to herself. Her dad had installed thirty-two inches flat screens in all their rooms, but she preferred to watch Netflix in the living room.

"When you go to college, you gon' miss your sisters, mark my words." Sometimes, and especially tonight, she wished she had one real friend or even her sister to confide in. She had a few gardening buddies and women she played cards with, but not one person she could talk to about her feelings.

"Yeah, probably. I like spending time with them at mama house cus I get to come back here to my peace and quiet," she told her grandmother. She sat across from her grandmother at the table and noticed the sad look on her face. "What's wrong?" She had been asking her that all week.

Charlie shrugged her shoulders. "KK doesn't want to marry me." She was sad and had no one else to talk to.

Ayanna saw the tears welling in her grandmother's eyes. "Do you want to get married? Why now?" They had a weird relationship to her. She had never seen her grandmother with anyone else though, so he had to be her man.

"Y'all are getting older… I don't know. What if I get sick? I don't want to die alone."

"KK loves you with or without a ring." She didn't acknowledge the part about her dying because Lord knows she would lose it if she lost her Charlie.

Chapter Fourteen
"You the one I want on my side." – NBA Youngboy

"Do you have a charger in here? My phone is dead," Kamile asked her sister. Once a month, they went to visit the man that raised them as his own.

Kamala rolled her eyes at her sister and pointed to the middle console. "Girl, yes I have a charger."

"Look, I don't be knowing what you got, don't get no attitude with me, heffa." She connected her phone to the charger and sat back in the seat.

"You driving back too, so gon' and get you a nap in." Kamala worked as hard as her sister did, so she wasn't even trying to hear that excuse today.

"What was wrong with Kadeem this morning? He was a lil' salty," Kamile mentioned.

Kamala didn't know what was up with him, he had been hushed and distant all week. "Chile, who knows. I've asked him twice, and he keeps saying he's fine, but ever since she signed the papers, he's been acting funny." The weird thing is her women's intuition hadn't kicked in, so she didn't think it was another woman. Maybe he was going through a mid-life crisis, she wasn't sure.

"Men have periods too, I'm convinced," Kamile said and shook her head.

She wanted a relationship, and then on other days, she enjoyed being single and casually dating whenever she had free time. As focused and hardworking as she was right now, there wasn't even an open date on her calendar to be putting up with a nigga's attitude.

"I can't keep repeating myself. I told him I'm here for him if he needs to talk and left it at that. I'm about to enjoy my day with Unc." She wasn't letting his sour mood bother her. Their uncle now suffered from Alzheimer's, and one reason the girls worked so hard was because the facility he was in was very expensive.

In the trunk, they had new sheets, comforters and pillows for him along with fresh baked goods and groceries. The facility he lived in was residential style with twenty-four-hour nurses and doctors on staff. Their uncle liked the facility and told the girls they could only visit once a month now because he had a girlfriend.

"I want to look at dresses next week, what days are you off?"

Kamile shrugged her shoulders. "I don't know yet, I'll check the schedule. Are you sure you wanna start now?" Her sister was sensitive when it came to the dynamics of her and Kadeem's relationship.

"What you mean, start now? I've been waiting on them to get divorced so I could finally start," she said with a lot of attitude.

"And you act like you waited for months. The girl just came home, Kamala," she spat.

"What are you really trying to say?"

Kamile shook her head and said, "Nothing, don't worry about it." She reached forward and turned the music up. She wasn't going there with her sister today. At the end of the day, she would do what she wanted to do anyway.

Kamala didn't push her to say anything else, maybe because she already knew what she would say.

They rode in silence for the rest of the drive, and when they pulled up to the place and parked, she tapped her sister to wake her up.

Kamala left her Prada shades in the cup holder and hopped out of the vehicle. "I'm going to get a cart, we got too much stuff to carry."

It really wasn't that much, but Kamile knew her sister was extra as hell, so she didn't say anything.

After checking in and leaving their identification cards with the front desk, they went to their uncle's room, knocked on the door and walked in. He wasn't there, so they redecorated his bedroom, something they did every few months to keep his spirits up. And the old bedding and décor, they gave to the front desk because there were a lot of residents that had no family or friends to visit. Some people sent a check, and that was it.

Kamala and Kamile could never do that to their uncle. When their own parents didn't want them, he stepped up and raised them the best he could.

And a phenomenal job, he had done.

Uncle Raymond came waltzing into the room. "I know y'all lil' knuckleheads ain't snooping in my shit."

When they first noticed that something had changed, they were oblivious, chalking it up to him smoking weed. For about two years, they were in denial that their uncle had Alzheimer's. It wasn't until he went to sleep with the oven on and then left his car doors open did they take him to the doctor.

Kamala was surprised because their uncle was in good shape and healthy, he also wasn't on any medication. He worked hard, and as a man that's what he was supposed to do, so again, there weren't many factors they could use to contribute to him having early stages of Alzheimer's.

Over the years, it had gotten relatively worse, and they both feared for the day that they came to visit and he didn't recognize them. Thankfully, today was a good day because he knew exactly who they were and came over with hugs and kisses for them both.

Kamala handed him the Tupperware filled with Snickerdoodle cookies and brownies topped with nuts. Their uncle always had a sweet tooth and taught them how to bake once they could reach the cabinets that held the sugar and flour.

"Did you bring some caramel cake? My boo like caramel cake, and I told her my niece make a real good one." he asked.

Kamala looked at her sister. He didn't mention caramel cake when he called the other day. "No, I forgot, but I'll bring it on the next visit," she lied to pacify him, something they did a lot lately.

"Damn, Millie, all right then... hey, I like this comforter, this is playa," he said, smiling at the new navy-blue and green striped comforter on his bed.

"That's Lacoste, Unc," Kamala told him, she had picked it out herself.

He didn't care what it was. "Y'all treat me so good. Come on, let's go get something to eat."

They could finish decorating later. Normally, when they visited he had a whole day planned for the three of them. The facility did a great job at having daily activities and events for the residents and guests, especially on the weekends.

They spent the day eating, laughing and watching movies, and then finished with a walk around the lake, each with one arm looped around Unc's as he escorted them both on a nice, quiet and serene path.

"I come out here every night before I go to bed," he shared with them.

"By yourself? No, don't do that no more." Kamala didn't want him to get lost and wander off.

He shook his head. "It's guided. Me and my lady, that's how we walk off the dinner. Wasn't that food good? We got a new chef, and that nigga can cook," Unc said.

"Lunch was delicious."

He sighed, "Y'all make my day when y'all visit. Boy, do I wish I can be home cooking up some salmon cakes, grits, eggs, wheat toast, ooooh, and some coffee." He closed his eyes and daydreamed about the good ole days.

"Unc, I miss your breakfast," Kamile told him. They had fun together, he was the coolest uncle ever.

"Yeah, me too. You know I can get a visitation pass for the weekend, I'll love to cook for my babies again." His eyes lit up at the thought of being in his own kitchen again.

"What about for Fourth of July? Then you can meet Kamala's fiancé."

Kamala eyed her sister, that was something they should speak with the doctor about before getting Unc's hopes up. "Uh, we will see, no promises." She was always the rational one.

"Yeah, and my lady can come too, family dinner." He loved the sound of that.

They finished the walk, reminiscing about old times and when he first spanked them after getting caught in the house with boys. Unc was tired, and they helped him in bed and stayed until he was sleeping and snoring.

They left a check with the finance department and headed back home. The car was silent, both women lost in their own thoughts of their dark childhood before he rescued them and ultimately saved their lives. If it weren't for him, there's no telling how lost they would be.

"He's fine, Kamile."

Kamala knew how her sister was, beating herself up about him being there and not with them. She took a deep breath and grabbed her sister's hand. Unc was jovial, and that's all that mattered since they did what was best for him.

η

He hadn't slept since he shot and killed one of his best friends, and he regretted the impulsive move. He was wrapped up in his emotions about Yara willingly signing the divorce papers, finding out about the witness on the case and slowly but surely glowing the fuck up without him… and Steeno's words came at the wrong time. He wasn't thinking straight and shot him without thinking.

Kadeem had been shitting, crying and vomiting. He tapped out of society and hadn't left the house in a few days. He smoked all the weed he had and emptied out the liquor cabinet.

Today, he had to pull himself out of the drunken stupor that he crawled in because it was the weekend. Kamala wasn't busy with work, so he couldn't hide his vices. Thankfully, she wasn't around the house long because it was the day she went to visit her Uncle.

After she left, he called John to see what the block was saying and was told that Steeno's mama needed money for the funeral. He never understood how niggas could have so much money and ball out of control twenty-four seven but didn't take care of the woman who brought them to the world.

There was nothing his mother wanted that she didn't have. Charlie wasn't high maintenance or materialistic, so she rarely asked for anything other than pay for her to visit KK, or if she wanted to go on a vacation which was also rare.

Kadeem was guilty and told John that he would pay for the whole thing. So, he went into the guest room and opened the closet, moving some shit that Kamala's lazy ass stuffed on the shelves and grabbed four stacks that equaled to twenty-thousand dollars. That was enough to cover the funeral and put some money in Steeno's mother's pockets.

He showered and dressed in all black, which was becoming his signature color and headed to Steeno's mother's house. Everyone in the house was teary-eyed, and as soon as he handed his mom the money in a black plastic bag, she fell into his arms and thanked him repeatedly.

Riq couldn't deal with the dramatics and walked outside, followed by John and their other partner.

Kadeem patted her back and told her everything would be okay. He felt like a hypocrite.

"Are y'all going to find the man that did this to my baby?" she asked, hopeful they would avenge his death.

He nodded his head and told her that he would be back tomorrow, although he had no intentions of returning. Kadeem nodded to his peoples to come on down the sidewalk since their family members were on the porch.

"Shit is crazy."

They all looked at him, no one had any words.

"Yeah, his baby mama is distraught." Riq went over there yesterday and took her a stack of bills. He would pay her rent up for the year and pay her car off, that was the least he could do to take a burden off her.

"He don't got no damn kids." John shook his head, Riq didn't know what he was talking about.

Riq was the only person who knew about his newborn. "Shorty just had the kid about five months ago," he revealed to them.

"Why he ain't say nothing?" Nigel wondered.

They all were thinking the same thing. He wasn't one of many words and didn't have the same relationship with Steeno that they did with him, however, for everyone to use the word "brother" so freely, why would you not tell your "brothers" that you were having a child or had a child? Shit was weird to him.

Riq couldn't speak on that, he didn't know why he chose to keep it to himself.

"Shit, I need to take something over there too." Kadeem was guilty and wanted to do all he could to ease his own pain.

John had to skate, plus he had been over there all day. "I'll catch y'all later. Riq, let me know funeral details." He dapped everyone up before walking back up the block to his car.

Nigel needed to go as well. "Stay up, my nigga. Shit happens, don't stress yourself."

Shit happens? Don't stress yourself? Riq didn't like his comment. How do you tell someone not to stress when you shot your fucking brother in broad daylight over a comment about a woman you not even with no more?

They were the last two men, and Kadeem asked him where did his baby mama stay so he could take her the money.

He didn't plan on disclosing that information to him, so he suggested, "You can give it to me, and I'll drop it off."

"Yo, you got something you want to say to me?" Kadeem felt the tension, and the vibe damn sure was off. If there was an issue, the nigga needed to speak on it or keep it moving.

"Nah." Riq wasn't a lil' nigga no more, he could hold his own. He wasn't scared of Kadeem at all. However, he still respected him, but even that was to a certain extent.

"You know where to find me if you ever feel like you got something to say. I'll pull up on you tomorrow with that dough."

Riq watched him walk away and decided at that moment that he was falling back from being around him and the rest of them niggas too. They were all flaw in his eyes, and he was about to lie low. Riq was the youngest of their "crew" and had watched them carefully and learned from all their mistakes. Not saying he thought he was better than them, no, but he could now move differently based on their weaknesses. God worked in mysterious ways. For some time now, he'd been wanting to fly solo-dolo and didn't understand why. He was a humble dude and knew the OG's had laid the foundation for him, but Kadeem killing Steeno was an eye opener for him. It was now time for him to separate so he could elevate.

η

Post-Traumatic stress disorder is defined as a disorder in which a person has difficulty recovering after experiencing or witnessing a terrifying event.

Over three million people in the United States suffer from PTSD. Many people associate PTSD with being active in the military, but it is more than that. Not bouncing back or receiving proper treatment after experiencing tragedy, loss, or even defeat can result in PTSD.

Yara wasn't sure if she was suffering from PTSD. More often than she would like to admit, she woke up in cold sweats from having a nightmare about her time in prison.

Growing up, she was told that Jesus was the answer. Having a bad day? Call Jesus. Broke and in need of a financial blessing? Call Jesus. Miserable, depressed, heart and mind in shambles? Call Jesus. That was all she was taught and all she knew.

However, now at thirty-nine, she didn't technically believe that calling Him was always the only solution. True enough, she was fucking confused. Yara knew God for herself, she had experienced Him on a spiritual level and knew how to pray if need be. And during her time in jail, she had nothing else to do, so she studied other religions such as Islam, Buddhism, Hinduism and

Catholicism. She even got deep into African religions like *Winti, Umbanda, Kumina, Obeah...* all of them interested her.

She was now in between Muslim and Christianity and needed to pick one because she found herself sometimes saying, "Inshallah" and "Hallelujah" in the same sentence.

Starting life over in your late thirties was arguably one of the hardest things to do, and she never thought she would be sitting in a freaking therapist office, talking about her issues, issues she'd rather not admit to but knew she needed to discuss to heal.

Jay-Z said it best, *"You can't heal what you don't reveal."*

"Mrs... or is it Ms. Moreland?" the therapist asked before she sat down.

"My divorce isn't finalized yet, so I'll be Ms. soon." She had been married forever and didn't know how it would feel to *really* be single again.

"And will you be returning to your maiden name?"

She wanted to scream from the top of her lungs, *"Hell fuckin' no!"* but instead said, "No, I'll be keeping the same name as my daughters."

"How old are your kids?"

"Twenty-one, eighteen and fourteen." She was nervous as hell, and Miko reassured her that the woman was a great outlet to begin the healing process.

"How has motherhood been for you?"

Damn, she got right in it. Yara rubbed her sweaty palms against her tangerine colored tailored pants. She then turned her neck to the library in the corner of the woman's office and redirected her attention to the therapist. Yara Moreland was seeing a shrink. She wasn't ready for this.

"I think I made a mistake by coming here. I'm sorry for wasting your time." She stood up and threw her purse over her shoulder.

"Ms. Moreland, I can back up, and we can start slow. I'm sorry if I offended you with my question."

"I'm not offended... I haven't been in my kids' lives..." Those damn ten years.

"Because you were incarcerated, right?" she asked. Yara nodded her head, her arms frozen in place. "And you're home now, how has it been being reconnected with your daughters?"

She thought about it and then answered, "Well, we are making progress... it's my middle daughter who still seems to hate me."

Hate was such a strong word. "Why do you think she hates you?"

Yara slowly sat back down, but she didn't get comfortable. Her eyes were on the door in case she wanted to jet the fuck out of there. "Middle child syndrome, I guess. My older daughter has a relationship with me because she remembers me, and I think Yanna does too, but she acts like she doesn't, whereas my youngest, who was four when I was locked up, has clung to me. It's no love lost with her. I think she needs me, and Meme wants me and Yanna, couldn't care less."

She felt so much better saying that out loud. That was a load off her shoulder.

"Do you know how the relationship is with her father? Is it okay if I assume that he's her father?"

Yara saw her pen and pad ready to write down whatever she said. "All four of my kids have the same father," she stated.

The woman put the pen down and touched her chin with her red, manicured finger. "Four? You only mentioned three daughters. Am I missing something?"

"It's a boyyyyyy!"

The gender reveal was a success, she was the only person in her circle who did gender reveals with all her children. Everyone cheered, clapped and celebrated the couple. Kadeem finally got his boy.

"Knocked that mother fucker out the park," he whispered in her ear as he groped her ass and tongued her down.

They were madly in love, you could see that with your glasses off. Tears of joy streamed down her face. "I am so happy, Kadeem Jr."

"Baby KJ!" her oldest daughter clapped.

Yara loved that nickname. "Yes, yes, baby KJ!" She was elated.

"Okay, come on, let's cut the cake." Charlie knew it was a boy. She was the one that accompanied her to the doctor and received the note from the doctor to give to the baker.

"You finally got your boy," she winked at her son.

He loved all three of his precious baby girls, but with every pregnancy, he hoped that Yara carried a boy.

"Yeah, she getting them tubes tied, we are DONE." He was serious too. He didn't want any more children. Four was the final number.

Yara hadn't thought about her son in so long. She had pushed the memory to the back of her mind to ensure that she didn't slip back into that dark hole of depression.

She blamed herself. She hated Kadeem for what happened. And that's when their marriage went downhill, but on the outside looking in, they kept it tight. Everyone wondered how they could be so strong and still go out hustling and partying. It was all a facade. And then the FEDS came. Everything was a blur after that.

"Yara, did you hear me? You mentioned four children," the woman repeated herself.

"He's gone. I have three kids. My apologies, can we talk about something else? I want to stay… can we just, talk about something else?" she questioned the woman, as she wiped tears from her face. She desperately wanted to get a grip on her emotions. "Can you tell me what to do to stop crying so much? It's not like me." She desperately wanted to know was there a remedy to her dramatics.

The woman smiled at her, she was such a cute lil' thing. "Have you ever thought that maybe you're crying for all the years that you didn't?"

She was taken back by that. "No… I've been through so much, you could be right." Yara was holding so much inside; years of hurt, pain, betrayal, disgust, loss, and a broken fucking heart. "I want to get it all out, ma'am." She decided right then and there that she was done harboring all those ill feelings. "Can you help me?"

Before forty, she wanted to be in a new place, mentally. And she was prepared to go through the storm, to relive those nights that she forced herself to forget so her thoughts could be clearer. She wanted to smile and it not be fake, so that she could laugh, and it be genuine. And lastly, she wanted to be able to receive love again.

η

"Cheers to another successful week!" Marsha held up her goblet of wine to Yara and Miko.

They had formed a pact, and on Fridays before they went into mommy mode, a glass of wine was had along with accountability check-ins.

"Let's keep our fingers crossed that Nash hits number one." Miko was nervous as hell.

Yara thought it was cute how hard she went for her husband. His success was her success and vice versa. Although her life pretty much revolved around him, their child and his businesses, she pretty much oversaw all his ventures, and he didn't make any moves without her.

They were a power couple, and Yara still considered it a blessing how she and Miko were both from behind those walls and were now doing well. She toasted, "To us as black women doing the damn thing!" She was tipsy as shit.

Therapy was intense this week. Last week was light compared to her session yesterday. They were meeting once a week, and she was now on her third session. Every time they finished, she would look at the pile of tissues and cringe. Her therapist told her that crying was healthy, and it was needed for the soul to cleanse. She had even suggested bringing the girls in for a few sessions, but Yara told her no. That was one cup of worms she didn't want to open. She'd rather deal with it on her own.

Meme was doing well, Ayanna had finally chosen a school and Yanise was settling in school and making friends. Yara didn't want to mess that up.

"I am elated. Y'all give me something to look forward to every day," Marsha told them, and Yara couldn't help but wonder was that a loaded message that she should address or not.

Miko picked up her ringing phone, "Hold on, this is my honey."

Yara was the only single one in their trio, and that was okay. She was almost divorced and still wasn't eager to jump into the dating pool. She joked with her therapist yesterday that she didn't know where to even start when it came to dating.

Kadeem sort of told her that she was his girl, and she went for it. He didn't court her or do any cute, romantic shit to sweep her off her feet. There were so many things that she realized now that saddened her. Who could she blame other than herself? Was it her parents who didn't stick around long enough to teach her how to love herself and how to be treated? Yara didn't understand what a standard was until now. Kadeem was all she knew and all that ever really mattered to her. If he hadn't fucked her over, she would have come home and waltzed right back into his arms, ignoring all the wrongful things he had done over the years before they were incarcerated.

He had dropped the ball several years into their marriage, and she threatened to leave a few times but never did. What was her life without him?

She never thought she would see this day.

It was Friday afternoon, and she would be climbing into bed by herself tonight. On some days, she felt lonely, and then she reminded herself that she was healing and had to do it in solitude. No man wanted to repair a broken vessel, at least she didn't want them to have to.

"Okay, I have to go. He acts like we don't have a whole staff on stand-by." Miko rolled her eyes and fished in her purse for some loose bills to pay.

Yara told her, "I got it, girl go." Miko always treated her when they were out. She owed Miko for giving her this incredible opportunity. She was a hot commodity since Jazmine's song caught a buzz along with Fredo blowing up.

Yara was in the office throughout the day and in the studio at night. Miko managed her sessions as a producer, and she gave her a fifteen percent cut.

"He just got back in town, I'm about to go pick him up," she explained, feeling bad that she was always the first one to leave when they linked up.

"Chile, bye, see you later," Marsha waved her off. If her husband were as nice and sweet as Nash, she would have backflipped out of there. She was dreading going home to that monster and was already praying he had weekend plans or a business trip.

"What are you about to do?" she asked Yara.

"Girl, nothing. Go home and stare at the damn walls until I fall asleep. Yanise is with her dad this weekend." This was the first weekend she didn't have a session booked or had to fly out of town for business, and she thought she would be happy about being in the city, but now she was thinking she would bored out of her mind.

"Come on, get your stuff. I know where we going," Marsha said excitedly.

"Girl, where? It's traffic everywhere." She hated driving after five in Manhattan.

"Leave your car here, and Uber to work on Monday. I'll take you home," she suggested.

That sounded like a plan to Yara, especially since she had no plans this weekend and probably wouldn't leave back out until Monday anyway.

They left cash on the table and walked out of the establishment and down the street. Yara stopped in her tracks and looked to her left, knowing that her mind was playing tricks on her. It wasn't though. In Winnie Couture, front and center was Kamala trying on a dress that had to cost a pretty penny. It was beautiful, and she looked darling in it.

"What's wrong?" Marsha backpedaled and looked into the window where Yara's eyes seemed to be transfixed. "Is that… *her*?" She didn't say her name.

A tear fell down her face, and she quickly wiped it away. The divorce must have gone through, it had to be if she was trying on dresses. What pained her was that her daughters were there with Kamala, and none of them mentioned anything to her. Not even Yanise, who had asked could she spend the weekend with her dad.

Honestly, Yara didn't know what she expected from them. Did she want them to love her and hate him? Should they ignore the fact that their dad has a woman because mom is home? Yara was also human, and her feelings were hurt. She was left feeling as if she would never belong in her own circle of love. The bond she had created from her womb was a family… without her.

Chapter Fifteen
"We been through it all and we still living." – Justine Sky

Therapy had changed her, molded her, pushed her forward, kept her sane, centered her, revealed her, and it was all a process. Some sessions were easier than others, and she openly embraced each one knowing that eventually she could go in and talk about what wine she tried for the weekend and what movie she would see.

Her therapist shared with her that she had some patients that had dealt with their issues years ago but kept their standing appointment simply because therapy didn't have to always be associated with tragedy. Some people enjoyed a listening ear. Miko had addressed what she felt like she needed to face and then ended the sessions. Miko was also cheap, which was something that Yara noticed from spending a lot of time with her and Marsha outside of the office.

She was in better spirits these days and knew that it had a lot to do with her building friendships. Her therapist told her not to bring up the wedding dress in the window to her daughters. If the girls wanted her to know, they would have told her. She also believed that they didn't mention it because they weren't sure of her mental state when it came to their father.

The children were in the middle of a quarrel that had nothing to do with them. They loved their parents and shouldn't have to choose who to be loyal to.

Yara remained cool, although she wanted to react like a crazy woman. How could they dare have them in their wedding?

But, she listened to her therapist. She never brought it up, and when Yanise would tell her that her dad was coming to get her, she made sure she wasn't at the house. She hadn't seen Kadeem and had no desire to lay her pretty brown eyes on his conniving ass.

The only embarrassing thing she needed to deal with was that she couldn't stop playing with her pussy. That one night she allowed him to enter her was the dumbest, yet mind-blowing, thing she had done. And sadly, it was the only action she had experienced since being a free woman. It was the only thing she could use to get her rocks off.

Literally, before and after work, in the shower and right before, she prayed, she would repent for the sin committed. She was tearing her vagina up with the sex toys she purchased online. Life had truly changed. With one click on her phone, all kinds of items and packages would arrive in her mailbox via a service called Amazon.

"You don't think that's... weird?" she asked her therapist. Today, they were only meeting for thirty minutes because she had a flight to catch. Yara was appreciative that the woman was flexible. She told her that she had officially made her VIP list. And maybe that was because she paid for her sessions in cash and up front. They didn't always meet in her office, especially after she shared with her that being confined for so long made her eerie. She preferred to be outside or where there was lots of windows and sunlight. She would never take the simple things for granted again.

"No, I don't. I think masturbation is healthy," she said and shrugged her shoulders.

Yara rolled her eyes. Let her tell it, everything was fucking healthy.

Crying, drinking wine, writing all night until your fingers hurt, traveling as much as she did, taking on more projects than she could wrap her mind around, everything was healthy for Yara.

"I think I need to remove him off my mind... for good."

Her therapist sipped her coffee and then crossed her legs. She looked at Yara and gave her a warm smile. Yara was a beautiful woman, and she could tell from their first session that she had no clue of her beauty. Even her impeccable style and her hustle made her sexy. And still, she was oblivious.

For instance, today, although she had told her she was leaving the coffee shop and going straight to the airport for a turn-around trip to Los Angeles, she wore a cheetah jumpsuit and a red jacket. Without effort she was fly. But to her, it was always, "I threw this junk on." She downplayed everything about herself.

"Let me ask you this, if Kadeem and the woman broke up right now, and he came back to you on his knees, pledging his love and loyalty to you all over again, what would your response be?"

She didn't have to think twice or ponder the question, it was an automatic, "Kiss my ass." Yara glanced at her phone. "I have to get going, I'll see you when I get back."

"Safe travels. And, sweetheart?" Yara already had her shades on and was calling Uber. "Please enjoy yourself, you deserve it."

Everyone had been telling her that all week. When Miko called screaming into the phone, she could barely hear what she was saying, and then Marsha knocking on the door with a bouquet of white roses from Quentin congratulating her on her first number one hit, she fell to her knees and wept. Still not knowing which God to thank, she remained silent on the praise and worship, so she cried tears of joy instead. She had turned that pain into a check.

The record label that Jazmine was signed to was throwing her a soiree, and Yara was invited since she was the songwriter. The girls wanted to turn-up in Cali, but Yara told them that there was no need for them to roll with her. She was such a homebody and being that she had no other business to tend to while on the west coast, she was returning the next day.

As soon as she landed, she caught an Uber to the hotel and took a shower before laying down. Since tonight was considered an accomplishment, she was getting her make-up done and splurging on an outfit for the event. She was wearing an almost two-thousand-dollar dress designed by Oscar De La Rent and lucked up by finding a pair of Prada pumps on the sales rack.

After the artist left, and she stood in the mirror trying to decide how she would do her hair, she wished she still had her old jewelry. Her wrist and neck were bare, she needed diamonds.

"Ugh!" She was annoyed.

Yara stuck her head under the shower head, trying her hardest not to get her makeup wet. She needed her hair to curl up, although Meme had pressed her hair the day before. If her hair were big and wild, it would take the attention from her bare neck. The makeup didn't look the same because of the heat from the shower, so she said, "Fuck it" and removed all the makeup. She didn't need it anyway, natural was always her favorite way to be.

Once she was somewhat satisfied with her appearance, she noticed that she was now forty minutes late and ran out of the hotel, hoping that an Uber was circling the block. She didn't even know where she was going, the invitation wasn't loading on her phone, and the Uber driver kept saying, "I brought you to the address you put in."

Thankfully, the engineer on the project was late as hell too. "Damn, you look good. Yara, right?" He was high and his memory foggy, but he couldn't forget her hips or ass and was sure that she was Yara.

"Yep, that's me. Do you know where we're going?" she asked him.

He pointed to the red door. "We here," he laughed coolly.

She followed him up the steps to the elevator where they stepped on.

"What other projects are you working on right now?" he asked her as he scrolled through his social media, hoping to get an idea of who would be in the building tonight.

"Few things, mainly indie artists though." She wasn't much of a talker, and she didn't like the way he was eye-fucking her. The elevator was moving as slow as a turtle, and when it finally dinged and the doors opened, she was so relieved.

"Good seeing you," he said as she stepped off in a hurry.

She tossed a sorry "goodbye" over her shoulder and then went straight to the open bar.

The event was held at a posh lounge in downtown Los Angeles. Yara loved the weather in Cali, but she could never live here permanently, she was a New York girl until the day she died.

She ordered a martini and asked the bartender for a cherry. "Thank you." She twisted it with her tongue and then placed it on a napkin. Someone's eyes were on her. Years of being in the streets made her very aware of her surroundings. No matter if she was in the room full of industry execs or thugs, Yara was always ready and trained for whatever.

She looked over her shoulder, scanning the venue for any familiar faces and besides the people who approved the track and Jazmine, she didn't know anyone else. She played it safe and stayed at the bar, looking at pictures in her phone until Jazmine took the stage to welcome the guests, sing the track and then hopefully that would be the end of the night so she could go back to the hotel.

The plus-size brown skinned singer looked dazzling in an all-white dress and clear, mid-knee boots.

"Thank y'all so much for coming out tonight," was the first thing she said after being handed the mic. Jazmine looked out into the crowd, searching for someone and then asked, "Yara promised me she was coming, is she here?"

Yara turned around quickly, not wanting the lights, camera or attention to be on her. She was merely the songwriter, not the artist, nor did she want to be.
Jazmine gave up looking and thankfully, the creepy engineer didn't yell out that Yara was in the building.

"I'm sure she's here, so real quick before I get into this bomb ass song. This cute, small Indian looking lady was in the studio, and y'all know the GOAT, Mr. Quentin Brooks, who blessed us with his presence tonight," she said and bowed towards the top of the room where he sat. He nodded to her and waved to the crowd.

Yara quickly looked up and peeked at him. He was dressed up, and she wished she could see his eyes. He wore the darkest shades known to man, and she hated people that wore shades inside of buildings. It was stupid to her.

Jazmine continued, "When Quentin called and told me that he had a song for me I was like nah, I'm good. My album was almost done, and I wasn't as satisfied with it, if I can be honest with y'all... and then he asked me to hear it, and I heard it and was like, let's do this!"

She took a deep breath and then sipped from a glass of lemon water. "I want to thank the label, Quentin Brooks and Yara. We gotta get her a cool nickname. She wrote this song, and little did she know that everything she said in that studio resonated with me. Sometimes we can be blind to love. We as women are foolish for the man we think is for us, and then it's not until it's too late to realize how much time we have wasted. DJ Moon Pie, drop the beat," she said as she sat the water on the bar stool behind her and rocked to the slow beat, snapping her fingers and bobbing her head.

Everyone loved the song already. It was a fucking hit; number one across the board. Everyone was jamming to the song and it was on heavy rotation on all the radio stations along with iTunes and Tidal.

Jazmine needed this number one to get her name back popping. She had begun to play the background by writing successful hits for everyone else, and now she was ready to get her career back on track.

Yara loved the song. She wrote it from such a transparent place and was glad that there were millions of people that could relate to how she felt when you gave a pussy ass nigga everything you had, including your heart, mind and soul, last name and kids too.

Kadeem was broken, and she had fixed him. She put him together and told him that he could do whatever he put his mind to, even if that was taking from other people to come up.

She was the "yes man" in his corner, the coach in the boxing ring, the cheerleader on the field, she was that person for him. And what did he do? Turn around and love the next bitch better than he loved her.

At night, when she laid in bed filled with resentment, she remembered those pictures in Kamala's office. He loved her. From the way he hugged her from behind, the off-guard candids and the holding hands, everything was different. He did shit with her that they never did together. And no, she's not saying he didn't love her because she was sure he did, however, their love was on contingency.

He loved her because she had no one else to love her. He loved her because she gave him three children. He loved her because she was a shooter and arguably the most realest person in his circle. He loved her because he knew her ass wasn't going anywhere.

Yara had nothing going on. Oh, but now, her worth went up after being released. Yara used to tell him all the time that robbing and shit wasn't the quality time she was speaking of when she said she wanted more from him. Yeah, they got money together, and that was all fine and dandy, but she needed her husband.

Yara downed the last of her drink. Before she got deep in her feelings again, she decided that it was time for her to go. The song was giving her the blues. Because it was late, she decided to eat at the venue before going home.

After seeing Quentin walk down the glass spiral staircase toward the elevator, she noticed that he wasn't as social as people thought he was. He seemed to be introverted, much like herself.

She left a twenty-dollar bill on the table and grabbed her clutch. It had been a minute since she'd seen him, and she wanted to personally thank him for the roses he sent when Jazmine hit number one.

She put a lil pep in her step, not wanting anyone to notice her there because she wasn't in the mood to take any pictures or answer questions about her schedule. She couldn't be paid to write a song, it had to flow from her, and then she could sell it.

Yara didn't want to sit in a studio listening to beats trying her hardest to put some shit together. Her creative juices couldn't be controlled or put on a time frame. That's not how she worked or would work.

She placed her clutch in between the elevator doors to keep it from closing. He looked up from his phone and saw her. He smiled, and she returned the gesture.

"Hello," she spoke. Yara didn't expect to be nervous.

"How are you?" he asked.

She told him, "I'm fine."

The elevator tried to close again, and he stepped forward, extending his arm.

"Getting on?"

She nodded her head and stepped onto the elevator. What was she supposed to say next? She then remembered. "Thank you for the roses, they were beautiful."

He scanned her from her head to her toes. "You deserved them." Quentin wouldn't dare deny his attraction to Yara. Once they made it to the main level, he asked her, "Where are you staying? Let me make sure you get home safe."

"You know I'm Queen Uber."

It was late and dark outside. "I'll sleep better knowing I got you back to your room safe."

"I'm a big girl, I'll be fine," she smiled at him.

He nodded his head and gave a pink ticket to valet. "Cool."

Yara pursed her lips together and heard her therapist's soft and serene voice telling her to drop the guard and have fun. *Stop thinking so much, you're still young. Enjoy life.*

"Facts... Quentin." She didn't mean to call him by his street name, that life was supposedly behind him.

"I'm ready."

"Ready for what?" His Phantom arrived, and he was about to head home. It would have been easy for him to assume what she was speaking of, but he wanted her to say it.

"I'm ready... to do whatever we should be doing." She felt like a high school girl trying to find the courage to ask someone to prom.

"And what is that?"

"I don't know!" Her palms were now clammy and sweaty. She fanned her face, not wanting any sweat to form.

"You ain't ready. You ain't healed. I'm not a doctor, I don't fix broken hearts," he kept it gully with her. He was a grown ass man, his days of trying to figure out what a woman really wanted with him were over.

"I thought there wasn't a time limit?" she asked him.

He smiled at her slick ass. "Those were yours words, baby, not mine." He had no time to play games with her.

"Well, I'm ready," she put her hands on her hips and told him straight up. Now, if he rejected her then she would never talk to him again. Yara didn't kiss ass.

"Doubt it. Get home safe," he said and handed a ten-dollar bill to the valet attendant, who had been extremely patient.

"Quentin!" she called his name.

"What, man?" She had some balls tonight, and he knew it was because she had three drinks. He watched her the whole night, wishing she was right beside him instead of the groupies that thought they would get lucky and leave with him.

"I said I was ready, and I meant it."

η

"Why do you have so many books? I thought I read a lot," she asked him, as he gave her a tour of his home.

Quentin attempted to be a gentleman and take her back to her hotel, and she told him that she didn't want to be alone tonight. He had a good feeling about Yara and trusted that he wouldn't wake up and not have shit left in his crib. So, here they were, in his house on the West Coast that he cashed out with the first forty-million dollar check he received.

"Knowledge is wealth," he tapped his temple. Quentin was texting on his phone, and she noticed that he always had a phone in his hand.

"Is that work?" she asked.

He shook his head. "Nah, business though… in a sense," he mumbled.

She turned around and admired the shelves he had in his library, they were floor to ceiling, and every shelf was filled with books from different genres.

"Yo," he answered his phone and then walked off, leaving her alone to wander.

His home in Cali was ranch-style with a small attic upstairs that he told her he turned into a meditation room when he needed to clear his head. For him to be a bachelor, he had a lot of food in the fridge, and the place had a homey, cozy feel.

She removed her heels and walked barefoot through the rest of the house, peeking in three of the bedrooms but not touching his Master bedroom door. His voice got louder, and that's how she found him in the back of the house on the balcony, smoking a blunt.

She was on papers and didn't smoke nearly as much as she used to. Yara tip-toed out there and slid in front of him, taking the blunt from his hands and leaning against the grey wood.

His eyes left the trees and landed on her. She winked at him playfully and then took a toke of the blunt and held it in her lungs, wanting all the smoke she could get to catch a quick buzz. She reclined her head and blew the smoke out of her nose.

He didn't even know a woman could look so fucking sexy smoking weed.

Quentin wasn't a big smoker and really only smoked at night before bed because it helped him relax. He had so much going on that even when he was trying to chill, he really couldn't. His phone never stopped ringing, vibrating and dinging from emails. Everyone wanted him to be in a million places at once.

For instance, he only attended Jazmine's event because he knew Yara would be there. Whenever people got wind of him being in their city, they wanted him to come out, knowing that he brought a crowd out whenever his name was mentioned.

"What am I here for if you on the phone?" she asked him.

He smirked. "Keiter, let me hit you back, I have company. Yeah, I know. Shit, me too," he laughed. "I'll be there on Tuesday, got a meeting tomorrow then I'm flying back," he told his cousin. After they ended the call, he slipped his phone into his pocket.

"You smoke?" he asked.

She looked at the blunt and then at him. "Uh, yeah… what does it look like I'm doing?" she giggled, covering her mouth as the smoke seeped through her thin fingers.

"Give that back, you been drinking too." He took the blunt from her and then grabbed her hand. It was chilly outside, so he led her back inside the house.

"I love your place," she told him before she forgot. Quentin locked the door and then asked her was she hungry. She shook her head. "No, I'm fine."

"What are you ready for? And what makes you think you've had enough time to deal with your... situation?" he wanted to know.

"Divorce is final. And I'm in therapy, sir."

That was a fast ass divorce, he thought to himself.

She seemed to have read his mind. "His fiancé is a lawyer."

"Fiancé?"

"Yep, he's engaged, and I couldn't care less. Can we go sit down or something?" They were standing in the dark.

"If you care, that's okay." He didn't want her to feel as if she had to be a hard ass around him.

"But I don't."

Her tone was serious, so he let it go, her voice was full of confidence. Quentin was hungry even if she wasn't, so they went into the kitchen where he heated up leftovers from earlier.

"I feel like you know me, and I don't know you," she admitted.

That could be true. "I'm single, no children, I'm from the same place you're from, and I work seven days a week," he told her in short.

"What's your dream?"

He was about to place a lamb meatball in his mouth before she asked him that. "What is my dream?" The question surprised him because he had never been asked that before. To everyone, it would look as if he were living out his dream. He was rich as fuck and one of the most handsome men that had graced the planet. Wasn't that a dream of many? To be wealthy, successful and good looking?

"What makes you think I'm not living out my dream?" He wanted to know that first.

"Are you?" She crossed her legs in the chair that she sat in and looked at him.

The way she asked him questions sounded so sincere and genuine. Not in an interview way or "I want to get you talking to know all your business and leak it to the press." There was a calmness that surrounded her.

"No," he finally answered.

She smiled at him. "So again, what is your dream, Mr. Brooks?"

He shook his head and resumed eating. "Can't even tell you because I don't really know. Five years ago, I would have said to be a free man."

She could relate to that.

"Ten years ago, it would have been to become a professor or some smart ass that got paid for their opinion..." he continued.

"And today, it's what?" she questioned.

"Peace of mind, and to wake up and not have a million fucking things to do or pay for." He closed his eyes and then opened them.

A thought ran through his mind, she saw it clear as day. "And what else?"

He shook his head. "I'll tell you if you stick around long enough." Quentin was a strong man, with a lot of self-control. Many women had bagged him in the past, but none in the last year or so. Yara would have to prove herself worthy of his time, secrets, and so much more than that. He didn't really have a wall up. If she said the right things and her vibe remained how it was, then it would be nothing for him to grow with her.

After he finished eating, he washed his hands. "So, how does it feel to have a number one hit?"

She shrugged her shoulders. "Good, I guess. I don't know." Nothing made her super-duper happy anymore. "I don't want to talk about business though," she was sort of asking.

He understood that. "No industry talk then. Come on."

They settled in the living room, and he put a movie on. She stayed on one side of the couch and him on the other.

Quentin didn't know what they were doing and didn't know the last time he was able to chill in the crib. He hated the club and didn't really enjoy making it rain, although his social media would tell you otherwise.

"Can I come over there?"

He was smoking a blunt while they watched Chris Rock's latest comedy special on Netflix. "Yeah, baby."

She loved the way he said *baby* as if she were already his. Yara wasn't nervous anymore, and maybe it was the liquor and the weed. Who knows… She wanted to be up under him. It had been so long since she craved affection. After coming home and finding out about Kadeem, she developed a relationship with her toy and became content with the vibrated love. Being around Quentin tonight, paired with the courage from the martinis, she wanted to be right where he was.

Her cute ass crawled to him and laid her head on his chest. He wrapped his arm around her waist, and they kicked it all night. Yara fell asleep before him, and when he grew tired, he laid her down on the couch and then draped a brown mink blanket over her body. Quentin went to take a shower and crashed right after.

The next morning, she was wide awake on his balcony with a glass of orange juice and one of his books.

He tapped the window and motioned for her to come into the house. "What time is your flight?" He had slept through his alarm. Last night they agreed on him taking her to the hotel so she could grab her things and then dropping her off at the airport.

"I missed it." She wasn't tripping though.

"Damn, I'm sorry. I can't believe I slept that long." It was almost twelve in the afternoon.

"It's cool. I need to brush my teeth and stuff." She was speaking with her mouth covered.

"I have all of that, no clothes for you though. You want to go to your hotel?"

"Yes, and then maybe we can get some breakfast. What are your plans for today?" She would book a flight after he told her what was up.

"You."

Yara blushed and lowered her head, staring at her toes. "I meant what I said. I'm ready," she finally looked up and told him.

It was time for her to live and enjoy life. She had established a career, and things were coming together with her children, who would always remain her first priority. Yara had big girls, and eventually Yanise would be out on her own. Then what about her? She didn't want to be ashamed to admit that she wanted a companion.

He prayed that she was serious. "I am too."

The beginning stage would be full of questions and late-night conversations that he was eager to have with her. He had done his research on her, but something told him that there was so much more about Yara Moreland that he or no one else knew.

"I'm going to shower, and then we can go."

She watched him walk down the hallway. He was fine, and she was waiting to get a weird vibe, but one never came. He was patient and kind. When she woke up this morning, she was pleased that her clothes were still on and she wasn't in his bed. Yara would love some dick right now but believed in timing. There was nothing wrong when getting things on and popping, and in due time she knew they would take it there. For now, she would keep calm and see how things unfolded.

About forty minutes later, he reappeared. "Ready?"

"Yes."

"I want you to fly with me to Atlanta tonight, and then I'll make sure you get back to New York in time for Nash's listening party."

"What's in Atlanta?"

"New opportunities, baby." He had a lot of connections all over the place, and the South was killing it right now in the music industry. Yara had worked with a few people on the West and East coast, but now she needed to bless the south with her gift. If she got a hit from the dirty South, then she was well on her way to planting firm feet as a producer/songwriter.

He saw more in her than a pretty face and someone he could settle down with. She was talented, and on the business side, he wanted to do his part in making sure she got to the top. It felt good to have someone on his side that had the same hustle as he did. He loved that they were in the industry together, even if they were on different levels.

Models, actresses and even the Instagram famous chicks didn't understand his schedule or his creative process. Sometimes he didn't feel like talking, texting or Facetiming, he was trying to get shit done, and that required solace and no communication.

Yara understood that because she was the same way, he had watched her readjust her mental and fall into a deep zone to get the job done. So, in a few ways they were one in the same. And that was another plus in his book.

She was the one… he knew that shit.

Chapter Sixteen
"Ain't tryna flatter you, but baby you a star." – Kodak Black

"I didn't like the song," she blurted out. Hopefully, her honesty didn't ruin their first date. He had picked her up from her apartment and told her that he had been working crazy hours with one of the legends in the game.

Dinner was pleasant. The food was finger-licking good, and now they were headed to a lounge that was invitation only and of course, Quentin Brooks' name was at the top of the list.

As they waited for their drinks to come from the bar, she told him again, "I don't like the song."

He looked at her and smiled. "That was two hours ago, it's been on your mind?"

This was their first official date according to her. She wasn't counting the time they spent in Los Angeles, or the almost twenty-four hours they shared in Atlanta, or the impromptu trip she joined him on to Arizona. He even had his cousin switch her probation officer to someone they knew so that she could travel freely.

Yara was too talented. She had entirely too much going on and too much to look forward to, to be confined to staying in the city. Ever since Jazmine's song blew up on top of the height of

Fredo's newfound and heavily anticipated success, she was considered a hot commodity right now.

She shared with him that she couldn't desert her kids. He texted her yesterday asking to get away from the madness of work, but she told him that her daughter had something to do this weekend, and she had to be there. Yara was all for living her life, she deserved to do that, but not at the expense of abandoning her kids. Her therapist told her that she was thinking too hard, but no one knew her kids better than she did.

"Are you mad?" She squinted her eyes together, hoping she didn't piss him off. Their night was pleasant, and she was looking forward to spending tomorrow and Sunday with him.

He promised that he would be around her way this weekend for whenever she was available and had time for him. He appreciated that she didn't drop what she was doing whenever he called. He was doing the chasing and didn't mind it at all. She was worthy of his time.

Ayanna wanted to look for a graduation and prom dress tomorrow and surprisingly, she invited her to tag along with her sisters. There was no way she would turn that down. She had been trying desperately to make amends with her child and finally, they were making progress.

"No, you're entitled to your opinion. If it was your song, what would you do differently?" He was curious.

Yara moved closer to him and wrapped her arms around his neck. She pulled his ear to her mouth and sang a different melody to him than the one he played for her in his Maybach.

Quentin closed his eyes and bobbed to the tunes of Yara. He loved when she sang, but she told him that he would never get her on a track.

"I need you to lay that for me," he said and rubbed her thigh. Their drinks arrived, and he proposed a toast, "To my talented ass shorty."

"Shorty? Damn, I feel so official." She winked her eye as their glasses clinked. They were taking things slow, so a peck on the cheek here and there she was okay with, everything with Quentin was delectable.

A few known faces came to show love and respect to Quentin. She loved seeing him out in his element, although he swore he would rather be home watching Netflix with her thick ass between his legs.

"Before I leave, you gotta give me a session." He was serious about getting her behind the microphone.

They were on their third or fourth round of drinks, the lounge was dimly lit, and the vibe was right.

"At your house or the studio?" she teased him, knowing he prided himself on keeping his cool.

He leaned in and kissed her lips. "Whatever makes you happy, baby."

She was ready to go, and he had given her the green light. "Come on, this was fun," she said and stood up and pulled her skirt down. It wasn't on the short side, but she had to pull it down every few seconds.

"I love this on you." He came behind her and wrapped his arms around her waist, planting drunk kisses on her neck. His song was now playing, and he loved the tunes of Prince. They swayed to the beat, and he whispered in her ear, "What you gon' let me do to you?"

He couldn't wait until she really let her guard down, and it was more than the physical constraints. When he called her, he could detect the joy in her voice and didn't understand why it was hard for her to text and call him. They had a few subjects to discuss. The opportunity hadn't presented itself yet, and that was because every time they were in each other's presence, they were more focused on enjoying each other. However, for them to grow and build together, they had to tackle the difficult things. There was a lot more to Yara, and he wanted to know it all.

In the car ride home, he turned the music down and asked her, "What made you randomly tell me that?"

"I don't want to lie to you… ever." She couldn't enjoy the night knowing she hyped him up, and it wasn't genuine.

"And I don't want you to lie to me either."

She nodded her head. "Vice versa, I've been lied to enough."

He remained silent as they headed to her house. "You're staying with me?" she asked. She really wanted him to.

"Is your daughter here?"

"Heck no, I would've gone home with you." Yanise was at Marsha's house and would return tomorrow afternoon so they could go look at dresses for Ayanna.

"I don't know where I'ma park my car." He was scrolling her parking lot to see where his car would fit.

"Damn, I didn't think about that." Her complex was big, still there was hardly any parking.

"I'ma fuck around and cop you a house," he said casually.

She looked at him and smiled. "I'm fine with that. Gated, marble floors, master on the main and a pool," she told him what she wanted.

He nodded his head. "Noted, baby."

They agreed to go to his penthouse in Manhattan because he wasn't comfortable parking his half a million-dollar car on the outside of her complex on the curb, and she didn't want to feel bad if something happened to his whip overnight. Although she stayed in a nice area, a Maybach was a sight for sore eyes.

"I've been to your Miami mansion, your LA ranch, your Atlanta condo and now a penthouse. How much do you pay a month in rent?" Quentin had a lot of expenses, she no longer questioned why he worked so hard.

"No rent, I purchase cash. I hate mortgages." The only recurring bills he had were the ones that were infinite; like cable, phone, insurance, light, water, gas, etc. Anything that he could pay in full, he always did. That was something he learned from his parents. They had no debt, loans or outstanding balances. His father taught him at an early age to borrow nothing you can't afford to pay back, and that credit was worth more than the money you had in the bank. But, too much credit would make you greedy, so stay away from credits. And most importantly, for every million dollars he made, to acquire a piece of land and never sell it. Real estate was an investment you could always cash out if times got hard.

Quentin had more real estate than he had houses, cars and studios combined. He was more than what he posted on Instagram, although it was no secret that he came from a good, strong Christian upbringing and loved to read. He kept a few of his hobbies and interests to himself. In the name of Quentin Brooks, there was beauty in the eye of the beholder.

"Wow." Yara removed her heels and left them by the door which was an elevator.

"You want something to drink or you good?" He was a lil' faded and was done for the night, but he was still about to blaze.

"I'll take a glass of wine. You and that damn Crown apple got my legs wobbly." She ran her fingers across his textured walls, red suede covered the apartment from the floor to the ceiling. "You have all these places, and you live alone. Do you get lonely?"

She always was asking him questions. Tonight, he would ask some of his own. "Nah, I'm used to it. Can't miss something you never had."

"So, you've never been in a relationship?" He was fine as hell, she didn't believe that at all.

He pulled a Ziploc bag of weed out of one drawer in the kitchen. "Nah, I didn't say that. However, I will say I haven't been with someone I actually missed once they left, not to where I would say I'm lonely."

She could understand that.

"Besides your ex, have you been with anyone else?" he asked her.

She ran her hands through her tresses. "Physically or relationship wise?"

He cocked his head. "Both." She was bolder when she was drunk, and he loved it.

"I wasn't a saint when I met him, however, all of that... was forced. He was my first and only love." She spoke in a tone he didn't recognize.

"You were molested?" He was straight-forward.

She pursed her lips together, downed the wine he fixed for her and then poured another glass, this time more than a swallow.

"That's a bottle of-" He wanted to warn her that the bottle of Gen she was drinking was 17% alcohol.

"I'm good, and yeah, long time ago, nothing to be talking about tonight," she deaded the conversation. "Back to you, Mr. Brooks. So, you don't get lonely, you don't press for pussy-"

He interrupted her with a laugh and held his stomach as he chuckled loudly. "Excuse me, fuck that mean, yo?"

She sipped her wine. "You heard what I said."

"I'm going to act like you're not implying that I am a gay man. I'm far from that."

She looked at him over the glass of wine. "Not gay... you clearly have a lot of self-control over your body."

"When we act like gentlemen, we're considered gay. If I would've tried to fuck on the first night, then you would have called me a savage," he said and shook his head. Women were difficult.

"I'm not even saying on the first night. Here we are on our what... seventh sleepover?" She counted on her fingers.

"Sleepover? We are getting to know each other. I know you ain't ready, trust me." He lit the blunt and passed it to her.

She wasn't smoking tonight. The alcohol was enough, so she declined, and he inhaled and exhaled.

"What am I not ready for?" Yara was so tired of toying with her pussy. She wanted the real thing and had enough confidence that they would be more than a one-night stand. Even when he wasn't in New York, they talked daily and for hours. And it wasn't about work either. She appreciated the invisible line of separation they had somehow created to keep their business and personal separate.

He only discussed business via email, using words like, "To Whom It May Concern" And calling her Ms. Moreland instead of "bae, baby, and boo."

He cared about how her day went, asked about her kids, and she sent pictures of her dinner wishing he was there. Although she had been out of the game for a long time, she wasn't stupid. She knew when a nigga was feeling her, and Quentin was smitten. The feelings were mutual.

"Me," he finally answered.

She smirked at him. "Shoot your shot, you may score." She put her glass down and backpedaled out of the kitchen, removing her skirt as she walked.

Quentin leaned against the marble granite counter, smoking his blunt and sipping his drink while watching her drunk ass attempt to turn him on. "You had too much to drink, your ass better not-" And before he could get the "fall" out, she tripped over a suitcase and plopped on her ass.

"Ouch!" she yipped out.

Quentin couldn't help but laugh because that's what her drunk ass got for trying to seduce him when he didn't need seducing. She didn't have to do any of that, he was naturally turned on by her.

He padded over and extended an arm. "Come on, clumsy." Her nipple stared upright at him, and he licked his lips.

She tilted her head and told him, "Lay with me."

He shook his head. "Not on the floor, get up." He pulled her hand, and she huffed as she sat up and then stood to her feet.

"I'm horny. Okay, I said it," she finally admitted, tired of playing this stupid ass game with him.

Quentin kissed her forehead. "You don't think I know that?" He could smell her sex arising in the car ride to his crib.

"It's been forever."

They were on the same page. "I'm sure my forever and your forever is the same."

"Two months?" She raised an eyebrow.

Quentin looked at her funny. "You had sex when you came home?" That disappointed him. A few days ago, he jacked off to the thought of fucking her ten-year tight pussy.

"Once, and it was a big mistake." She had said too much. Quentin walked away from her, and she followed behind him. "Don't act like you're not fucking bitches, I saw you at Jazmine's event surrounded by women," she admitted.

He spun around and looked at her from her head to her pedicured toes. "And the whole time wishing you were the one I was with. "Goodnight," he told her and disappeared right before her eyes.

She sat in the living room, staring out at the almost perfect view of the city.

What did she do wrong? They weren't official. As far as she was concerned, they were kicking it and getting to know each other. She was going home.

Yara went looking for him and didn't know which door belonged to his bedroom, so she knocked on them all until she heard the television.

"Yeah?"

"Hey, I'm going to catch an Uber home."

He said nothing back, so she took that as a hint to leave. Yara was back in the living room putting her heels back on when he returned and told her, "I haven't had sex in almost two years. The next woman I sleep with will be my wife."

She processed what he said before asking, "You're celibate?" That was disappointing as fuck.

"Call it what you want, I'm not having pointless sex anymore."

"And I'm not getting married again."

He didn't like the sound of that. "Why? Cus you married a fuck nigga? That's not fair to-"

"It's fair to me, and that's all that matters," she shot back.

"Women like you-"

"Women like me, Quentin? You don't fucking know me!" She stood up, one foot in a five-inch pump and the other bare. "Don't judge me, stop trying to figure me out cus you'll never be able to. I'm not a puzzle, and you damn sure aren't my missing piece."

He nodded his head. "Like I said before, you're not ready for a man like me."

And that was that.

η

Mentorship is defined as the guidance provided by a mentor, especially an experienced person in a company or educational institution. It's also defined as a period of time during which a person receives guidance from a mentor.

Yara was never in denial about her shortcomings, flaws or her limitations. The new school that Yanise attended had a lot to offer the students, primarily those interested in STEM.

STEM stood for science, technology, engineering and mathematics, and her daughter had a strong interest in Math and Science, much like her big sister, Ayanna.

Yanise was so hyped about a program that the school started for females interested in STEM. They were linked with a mentor, a career professional who could provide information to the students along with life's experiences. Yanise was all smiles during the brunch when the advisor suggested each mentor have a meeting with the parents of the mentee. She was comfortable leaving early and turning her baby over to the safety of her mentor. The woman had a full day planned with Yanise, so she headed to work.

Yara was late to the studio session she had with Fredo, who was thirsty to drop new heat, although she felt as if he should ride the wave of the first mixtape.

However, she was paid by the hour, so she would do her job and keep her mouth shut.

"I'm sorry, I had to meet my daughter's mentor," she apologized as she rushed inside the studio. She threw her purse on the couch and told them, "Let's do it."

Everyone in the studio was high and chilling. Fredo said, "Damn, I never seen you so dressed up." Yara was fine as shit.

She looked down at the black skirt she wore with a fishtail hem and the rose pink sheer blouse she wore tucked in the skirt. Her hair was in a high bun with a few loose waves in the front, along with a pair of oversized, hot pink Prada frames that she wore as glasses and pearls around her neck and in her ears. She was fulfilling all their fantasies, looking like their science teacher.

"Boy, come on. We got work to do." She checked the time on her watch. He booked a six-hour session claiming that she performed miracles when she was on a deadline.

Yara sat down and listened to what he already had as she chewed on her bottom lip. "Hmmm, I mean it's okay, but they will want the same vibe from the last EP, if not better," she gave him her honest opinion. He played her a few more songs, and her feedback was the same. "Listen, what if we do a remix of one of the songs and then the acapella or acoustic version of the most popular songs?" she suggested.

Fredo loved that idea. "So, it's basically a volume two?"

"Yeah, and then you can have a two-minute prelude as the last track, and that can be a snippet of one of these songs to let them know you are working on new heat."

His peoples in the studio all nodded their head. "Shit will be popping."

She was happy that he heard her out and agreed. "Let's get started then." It was going on midnight when they wrapped up, and she told him "Two more non-stop sessions, and then you'll be done."

"What you doing tomorrow?" he asked her.

"Nothing that I know of, let's be back here early though." She wanted to be home at a decent hour to have time with her daughter.

They left the studio in one group, and she stayed behind to listen to the progress they made thus far.

"About to lock up," a voice startled her from behind. Quentin didn't expect to see Yara. "Oh, my bad, didn't know it was you," he apologized.

She swallowed her fear. "It's cool, I was leaving anyway."

They hadn't spoken since he pre-judged her from having sex *one* time, and he told her that he hadn't had sex in almost two years. Of course, she thought about him every single day and checked her phone every hour on the hour, wishing he would text her and apologize, or at least attempt to come to common ground with how they both felt. However, neither reached out. And she damn sure wouldn't be the woman to send a long text only to not get a response.

"I'll walk you to your car," he offered.

Yara pushed the rolling chair back a tad so she could stand up. "Been walking to my car alone for the past two weeks." That came out bitter as hell.

He heard the sadness in her voice. "Get your shit and let me walk you to your car."

"Again, I'm good. I don't need you to do nothing for me." She really wanted to curse him out.

Quentin stepped into the studio and folded his arms across his chest.
"You got something you wanna say to me? Cus I feel pent up pressure."

Yara chuckled. "Oh really? You ain't feel that shit the other night." She shook her head and bent down to grab her heels and purse, along with her phone that was plugged into a charger in the wall. When she lifted her head, he was even closer.

"So, this has nothing to do with us not speaking, this is about me not fucking you. That's all you wanted from me? To say you fucked Quentin Brooks? Damn, Yara, I took you for more than a groupie."

She didn't think she would slap him. However, the illness of his tone, his hurtful words and the way he looked at her with filth in his eyes etched her spirit. Yara could smell the alcohol in his voice and the weed on his clothes. Still, that wasn't an excuse.

"Don't you ever talk to me like that in your life! A groupie? You think I care if people ever see me with you? You're a regular nigga just like the rest of these mother fuckers out here." She took a deep breath, ignoring the hard daggers he was shooting her way. "I am a woman who has been through hell and high water, okay? I don't take being talked down to lightly! I will-"

He rushed her with a kiss; a long, nasty, throaty, full of tongue, passionate kiss. The kiss she wanted the first time she laid eyes on him, the kiss she dreamed about after being in his house in Miami, laying in his bed in Atlanta, in between his legs in LA, and on his floor in his penthouse two weeks ago. He had been playing a cat-and-mouse game with her since they started talking and apparently, it had been worth the confusion.

"Don't ever slap me again, never put your hands on me again," he warned her.

She nodded her head, adhering to his command. Quentin walked away, and she was wound up all over again. They were really done, and that saddened her because deep down she knew he was the one for her. But when she heard the door lock, her eyes found him. He didn't leave, he was simply giving them privacy.

The studio should have emptied by now and in case it wasn't, he wouldn't dare allow anyone to be privy to what was about to go down. Yara was a work of art, and he wanted no one's eyes on her other than his.

"Was your ex who you gave yourself to?" That question had raked his brain numerous times in the past two weeks.

She blew a breath of frustration out of her mouth. "Quentin," she sighed, not believing that was any of his business.

He was so fucking turned on right now it was ridiculous. His dick sprang to attention, and it hurt so bad. He touched her skirt and told her to turn around. "I like this on you, it's tight though," he shared with her as he yanked it down past her hips and knees. "Answer my question, Yara." He then reached for her panties and pulled them down too.

"Yes." She felt his temperature rising.

Quentin hated Kadeem and didn't even know him. However, he knew niggas like him. Those entitled mother fuckers who get a good wholesome girl, give them good dick and then fill them up with lies and nonsense.

"After I enter you, that's it," he warned her. Yara held her breath, hearing the unzipping of his jeans and the unclasping of his belt. "Nobody else baby, just me," he told her again. She had to become his, he wouldn't have it any other way.

"Okay," she submitted. He only arched her back a tad and then planted kisses from the nape of her neck to the crack of her ass, and she moaned.

"Loud, baby, this my shit, you can be as loud as you want." He wanted to hear his name being called.

Quentin feasted on her pussy from the back as she held on for strength by holding on to the chair before her. He pushed her cheeks so far apart and stuck his long, wet, meaty tongue all in her shit.

"Baby, yes, yes, yes!" she panted, trying to catch her breath.

She was the sweetest thing he had ever tasted, and boy had he eaten plenty of fine meals in the most exquisite places.

Yara found a rhythm of her own and bounced her ass against his lips and tongue. Her sweet cream filled his mouth, and he hungrily ate it up as if it were the first and last meal he would ever receive.

She told him, *"I have never been eaten like that before!"*

"It's more," he promised her as he kissed her mouth and ran his hands through her hair, snatching the bun down and causing her hair to cascade down her face. He took his time unbuttoning her blouse.

"I don't want you to break your vow." She was serious.

"Don't worry about that." They could discuss the formalities later. He bent and licked her nipple, looping his tongue around the caramel pebble.

She closed her eyes and enjoyed the foreplay he was delivering to every inch of her body.

Although the location wasn't as romantic as he would have wanted it to be, they still got it the fuck on. He picked her up and laid her on the couch where niggas had been smoking all day and then changed his mind and sat her right on his dick.

"I'm going to fall." She was scared.

"Nah you not, I ain't letting this pussy go," he said through clenched teeth.

He hadn't felt flesh in almost seven hundred days, and the fact that he was tipsy and horny as a mother fucker only heightened his desire to be inside of her.

"This dick feels so good, baby," she moaned and crooned.

He kissed her breasts as he lifted her up and down on his shaft. He was even grabbing and squeezing her ass, trying to get every single feel he could get.

Quentin didn't want to bust prematurely, but the way she was holding his penis hostage every time she went up and down, he knew he was about to nut.

"It's yours," she went on and told him, which secured the release.

As soon as he let her down and caught his breath, he told her, "Put your clothes on."

"Where are we going?" Yara was salivating and wanted more, her pussy never stopped pulsating or cumming.

"Second round at my house, in the shower."

Chapter Seventeen

"But you don't understand. It's way more... than fucking... when I fuck you." – Trey Songz

"Thank you for this. It's been so long since I've had a massage."

The next morning, she woke up to breakfast in bed prepared by a chef, a bouquet of white roses that he explained represented new beginnings and a drawn bath followed by a two-hour massage. She didn't realize how tight her back was until she groaned when the woman worked the knots out of her shoulders and lower back area.

Once her massage was over, she thanked the woman repeatedly and then went to find Mr. Brooks. Last night was mind-blowing. It was exquisite, so exquisite that she woke up with two songs on her mind and couldn't wait until she had some quiet time to write them out.

"You need to get them on the regular, being bent over on-" He was about to tell her that being in the studio for long hours could cause wear and tear on the body, but her horny ass seemed flushed when he used the words bent and over.
He laughed at her as she fanned herself playfully.

"I'm having flashbacks already."

He had to tell her, "No need for flashbacks," as he pulled her from where she sat to his lap on the couch.

The masseuse said, "I'll email you, Mr. Brooks," as she headed toward the elevator.

"Thanks, Brandi." He would have his assistant tip her graciously.

Yara kissed his lips, and he kissed her back, slipping his tongue inside of her mouth.

"I'm sorry for slapping you," she apologized to him for the millionth time.

He wasn't tripping because he punished her last night with the wrath of the thing between his legs. He made sure that she knew to never put her hands on him again in a harmful way. And she got the hint.

"Water under the bridge, baby. What your daughter say?" He had asked for her time before her studio session.

"I didn't text her. I'm heading home anyway." She didn't want to make a habit out of spending more time with him than Yanise. Her mother made that mistake with her step-father, and in return, she resented her and eventually moved out and in with her aunt who turned out to be the nightmare from hell.

"Cool with me." They would figure out a schedule for each other. He knew beforehand that she was a mother, which added more on her plate. Quentin would get in where he fit in.

"If it makes you feel any better, I don't want to leave," she said and stuck her juicy bottom lip out and pouted. He leaned forward and pulled her lip in with his teeth. "Hmmm."

How he went two years without having sex was crazy because he was now feening for her. "Hmmm what?" he whispered.

"I think one more round before I go would be perfect" she suggested, removing the white robe that the masseuse left on the bed for her.

"Whatever you want from me, you can get." And that was real shit. Her being magical in bed was the cherry on top of a perfect sundae. Her personality pulled him to her even more, and he was now officially smitten. He didn't want her to leave but knew she had to fulfill her motherly duties, and he didn't want to get in the way of that.

"Mr. Brooks, what is that poking out?" she teased him as she got comfortable in his lap.

He smooched her lips and wrapped his arms around her waist. "If this could be forever, I think I'll finally be the happiest man in the world."

Quentin was full of sweet little nothings. "Tell me anything," she murmured.

Actions spoke louder than words, so he quieted and kissed her again and again and again until she released a siren that alarmed everything in him.

"Your skin is like satin…" his voice trailed as he ran his fingertips in between her small breasts.

"I want my boobs done," she confided in him.

He thought she was perfect how she was, but if she wanted work done, it wouldn't hinder her beauty. "You want a lil lift? No filler, I love them this size." He kissed each of her areolas and then squeezed them.

She nodded her head and lifted her breasts in her hand. "See, I want em' right here, not down there," she pouted.

Quentin didn't care about her saggy titties, that's what they made bras for.
"We can fix it, baby." He would do whatever to make her happy.

Yara kissed his neck and then grinded in his lap, making his already semi-hard dick even longer and stronger.

"You must wanna ride?" Since last night, he had been in charge, placing her in positions he had been dreaming about since he laid eyes on her.

"I want to do whatever you want me to dooooo." Her voice was quick, and her hormones raged.

Quentin stretched his legs out and lifted his arms behind his head. "Get to work then." He had a lazy smirk on his face, and his eyelids were low from his morning wake and bake session.

She lifted up and planted herself on him, and he helped her by pulling his shorts and boxers down.

"Oh yeah, I'm coming back later," she shared with him.

He laughed as she slid down on his dick and then rested to allow herself a chance to adjust to his girth and width. "Damn!" He blew a breath of relief and satisfaction out of his mouth.

"Hmmm-hmmm, damn is right." She leaned forward and kissed him passionately.

He tapped her lightly on the butt, and she somehow got into character and rode him as if she had nothing else to do on this beautiful Sunday. Her pussy had a mind of its own. The home was quiet and still minus the early morning rush of traffic that could be slightly heard at the top of the building where he lived.

"Ooh, she wet for me," he grunted as he slid his fingers between her legs and toyed with her clit. He had a thing for that cute little juicy meat and apparently, every time he massaged that spot, she got even wetter.

Yara was a squirter. And once he discovered her G-Spot on their third or fourth round, he had hit the jackpot.

She reclined her head back, and her breasts stared directly at him, so he left her clit alone and pulled firmly on her nipples, squeezing each one to get more out of her. The moans she made and the expressions on her face were priceless. He gave her stroke for stroke, and every time she rocked, he rolled. Yara had him feeling some type of way.

"I am about to cum," she said each word with hope, as if her cumming was quite impossible to do. If she could ride him until the night fell, she would. However, she had shit to do today, so they had to wrap this couch session up.

"Cum then, make that mother fucker rain." He wanted her to squirt again. He had to taste her one more time before she left. Matter fact, he said, "Fuck that," and pulled her swiftly from his penis and placed her pussy on his mouth.

For him to be a not so muscular man, he sure had enough strength to do what he wanted when it came to satisfying her.

"Quentinnnnn!" she screamed out as his wet lips lathered her essence.
Not even a minute later, she was raining down on him and out of the tip of his penis came hot cum. The thrill of her climaxing made him release as well.

"How did you go so long without this?" she asked him after a shower.

He knew that it was worth the sacrifice. "Cus then I can savor every moment with you, for a time like this… it was worth every declined invitation," he answered and kissed her forehead and saw her to the door.

After he walked her out and made sure car service knew to take her car home as well, he cleaned up his house and took a nap. He was tired as hell. Yara was older than him, but that didn't mean shit. She had an intense amount of stamina and energy.

And once she made it home, she was in a daze the entire day and a goofy smile stayed plastered on her face. She couldn't wait to share with her therapist. Yara was moving on and damn, it felt good.

η

He was born and raised in New York and loved his city. However, any chance that he could fly out, he was pretty much gone. Yara didn't have that kind of leeway, so he had his assistant adjust his schedule around, not too much where he was upsetting people, but enough to make her happy and him as well.

"How do you do it?" she asked him once they were snuggled on his couch, after a very tasty dinner prepared by them both. She knew that he was wealthy, she got it, but she didn't feel the need to be swept off her feet by Prince Charming or impressed.

He was good how he was and once she told him that a few days after they shared each other for the first time, he smiled, nodded his head and kissed her lips.

Yara was laid back as fuck. The chef bringing her food, private dinners at the most exclusive restaurants, masseuses ready to work her body out as soon as she stepped out of the tub, even closing Gucci and Prada so she could shop in peace at his expense with her daughters in tow was all too much for her.

She hadn't formally introduced him to her children yet but did share that she was friends with a *celebrity*.

Meme was hype as fuck, especially when Quentin started throwing opps her way and hadn't even met her yet. For the past few weeks, every time Yara was jetting out of the door for a date or her phone rang, Meme would joke, "Tell my step-daddy I said hey."

Yanise liked him too and didn't even know him. Being able to get whatever she wanted out of a store was fun, and she had been asking when was the next shopping spree.

Yara had all the bags and shit, and she was appreciative, she really was, however, she told him over dinner, "Buy me a house, let me get some stock, that will make a grown woman like me really happy." She was joking when she said that, but Quentin had made a mental note.

He wasn't one of those men that felt the need to use his money to buy his love, that wasn't the case. He didn't know what else to do with and for her. For goodness sake, how many more times were they supposed to go out to eat? He was constantly asking her to create a bucket list, and Yara was good with just chilling. She was joyful with them in the crib in their pajamas. And here they were.

"Don't get tired of what? Making money? No, I make money in my sleep, I call them sleep coins."

She shook her head. "No, I know that. I'm saying the travel, the interviews… all of it seems so overwhelming." She shied away from the limelight and told him that she didn't need or want to be posted on his social media. They were low-key as fuck with this newfound relationship, and she wanted it to stay that way.

Yara was a convicted felon, and she had wronged many people back in the day. Out of fear of her troubled past coming back to haunt her and sabotage what her and Quentin were building, she'd rather keep it concealed. Plus, they were still in the beginning stages of this thing they were calling love, and she wanted to savor their peace for as long as she could.

"Is that why you won't do any interviews or make an Instagram?" he questioned.

She looked at him and rolled her eyes. "What would I possibly talk about in an interview? The meals in jail? I'm nobody important." She waved her arm up and down to signify that she was a regular chick from New York.

"You are someone important, do you know where we're going tomorrow?" he asked her.

"Quentin, this stuff excites you, not me," she told him for the millionth time.

They were opposites, and yet, he was so fucking attracted to her.

"What makes you happy then, baby?"

If she knew, she would tell him. "I don't know yet, that's why I'm in therapy."

"There are a few questions I want to ask you-"

She shook her head and tried to free herself from the comfort of his arms.

"No sir, not tonight." She was in a good mood; her week had been productive. She finished two songs, and her daughter found out she would be the Valedictorian of her class.

Yara wasn't going down memory lane because he wanted to know her better, digging up her past wasn't the way to do it.

"Relax." He kissed the side of her neck, he wasn't letting her go.

"Quentin, you know everything-"

"That's not true. If I did, I wouldn't keep trying to slide in these slick ass questions," he kept it real with her.

Yara took a deep breath. "You get three. One, two, three questions, and that's it." She was so serious.

"Okay, well you sit right here, and I will sit right… here." He moved around and sat on the edge of the couch so they could share eye contact. "First question… tell me about your mom."

She rolled her eyes. "Out of all the things you could've asked…. Okay, well, I don't talk to her, and she doesn't talk to me, and I'm okay with that."

"You ran away at fourteen?"

"I moved in with my grandparents. My grandmother was ill, so she didn't leave her room or talk much. My papa was always gone, you know that though, right?" She was being sarcastic. He remained quiet, wanting her to continue. "My aunt stole. She was a scammer, all in the church stealing them folks' money. When I found out, she threatened me, and I left."

"Why didn't you tell someone?"

"Well, after my daughter was born, I wanted my family around. I was alone, and Kadeem was locked up."

"I can't believe this!"

It was so hard for her to really be happy about becoming a mother or even look at Meme. She swore she was suffering from post-partum, and Charlie had told her to shut the hell up.

"Yara, you gotta get it together, baby girl. Here, try to breastfeed again." She got up with Meme in her hands and tried to give her to Yara again, but she turned her head.

She wished Kadeem was there. Pregnancy was hard, and she was hot and depressed the whole time, and Charlie drove her crazy. She hated living in her house and was so angry at Kadeem for getting caught up in some bullshit. He was sentenced to a year in jail and missed the birth of his first child.

"You're not even trying," Charlie told her the truth. Motherhood was a blessing and a job, you had to work at it. Yara attempted to breastfeed once and gave up. Meme wasn't latching, but it took time. She had so much to learn about being a mother. It wasn't easy and didn't always come naturally.

Meme was now three-days-old, and Charlie was more acquainted with the baby than she was. She whined for Kadeem throughout labor, and Charlie wanted to slap her.

"What do you want me to do? I'm a single mother!" she cried. This wasn't supposed to be her life. She had dreams, goals and plans. Stupidly, when Kadeem told her he wanted a baby, she got off birth control and gave him his heart's desires. But where was he now?

Charlie's patience was running thin with Yara. "You act like he got life, girl. Take this baby, I need a cigarette." She was two seconds from saying to hell with Yara and her unnecessary dramatics.

Yara took Amina from her and stared at her big round eyes. She looked like her mother. "I wish your grandmother would come meet you," she cried.

Yara had reached out to her mom and was unsuccessful. She wanted her family around. Charlie was a blessing, and she was thankful for her, although she never told her that but still, she wanted her mom there. Yara had never felt so alone in her life.

She hated going back there. They had more positive memories than bad, and she was on this path to righteousness, so talking about that day wasn't good for her.

"I'm sorry," he apologized once he realized her entire mood had shifted.

"It's cool, next question." She wanted to get this over with. Clearly, he needed to know for whatever reason.

"There is a book I want you to read, and when you're done, we can discuss."

"That's not a question."

He loved her smart-ass mouth. "I know I wanted to tell you that before I forgot."

"What's the book, Quentin?" she yawned. The bed was calling her name, she was sleepy as hell.

"The 5 Love Languages."

Yara was so surprised. *"Wow!"* She couldn't believe this.

"What? You read it?"

She nodded her head. "And loved every single page. What's your love language?" This was something she was interested in discussing.

Quentin got comfortable, seeing that she was slowly losing the attitude she had a few minutes ago. "I want to know what yours is first."

She had a thing for cowering to make herself appear small, and that was something he had to break her out of. Yara alluded strength and courage, she had to begin exemplifying all the wonderful qualities that made her the woman she was today.

"I'm words of affirmation. That's my love language, Quentin." She now wanted to know what his was.

"Acts of service."

In the book, Gary Chapman delves deep into the five love languages, which are words of affirmation, quality time, receiving gifts, physical touch and acts of service.

Yara's love language expressed that she'd rather have a supportive partner who acknowledges her beauty, hard work and worth.

Quentin's love language showed that he feels loved when his partner goes out of their way to make his life easier or to put a smile on his face.

"Explains you perfectly," she had to admit.

"Yeah, I work a lot every single day, so little things to make shit easy for me makes me happy."

"I will remember that going forward." Their relationship wouldn't be one-sided, she would make sure of that. Yara wanted them to be equally yoked.

"Your love language leads me to question number two."

She playfully hid behind one of the sofa pillows. "You are killing me," she laughed. Never in life had she met a man who actually cared about all the shit he seemed interested in.

Why couldn't they just kick it and have good sex? Quentin Brooks was his own type of man and when he told her months ago that she wasn't ready for him, he was not lying. She was thankful that she took a while to herself. Although it wasn't long, it was what she needed to process her thoughts and unpeel a few layers of herself during therapy. She was still a work in progress.

"Chill, chill, one more after this, then I'm going to put your ass to sleep cus' I gotta slide through this thing." He looked at the time on his watch.

"What thing?" They had been together all night, and not once did he mention that he had plans.

"I won't be there long, and I know you won't want to go."

Yara remained silent because she had a lil' trick up her sleeve. His ass wasn't going anywhere either. She knew how to put him right to sleep, like a baby.

"Tell me what your relationship was like before you went away?"

He had crossed the line for real this time. "How is that relevant to what we have going on in the present day?" Attitude was evident in her voice, and she wasn't even trying to downplay how the question made her feel. She was sure that Kadeem wasn't discussing her, and she didn't want to talk about his ass either. He was a non-motherfucking factor.

"You gave me three questions," he reminded her. Yara crossed her arms, she didn't even part her lips. "I'll go first then." He didn't mind opening up to her, although she had never asked him to. "So, about three years ago, I was on the road to marriage, well I thought I was. We were doing good, I was happy as hell, a free man coming back to a fortunate situation, and she was the first woman I linked up with and so yeah, long story short; she was pregnant. We went all out. My family was hype, and hers was excited. We did it all, the big gender reveal on social media, the whole nine. So, fast forward, my son is born and a few weeks go by, and his ears are getting darker and darker, so I'm wondering what the hell going on. My mom pulled me to the side and asked me did I have any reservations about him being my child. I took a DNA test, and he wasn't mine."

Yara couldn't even imagine being betrayed in that way. "Where is she now?"

He shrugged his shoulders. "Who knows, that's not important to me."

"Do you have trust issues?"

Surprisingly, he didn't. "Not at all. If I did, you wouldn't be here," he told her the truth.

"And you haven't dated since?"

He shook his head. "No."

"I met Kadeem when I was fifteen… he really is all I ever knew. Well now you, but he was my world. If he told me to jump, I jumped. If he said shoot, I shot. He said kill 'em, I killed..." She took a long pregnant pause, refusing to cry. "And when the FEDS snatched my kids out of their beds and arrested us, and he told me don't tell them anything after they had begged me to turn on him… I…" She couldn't get another word out.

"KADEEM, WAKE THE FUCK UP!"

She was high, but damn, she wasn't that high. She heard someone banging on the door downstairs, and before she could hop up and grab her gun, her kids' screams pierced her soul. Her biggest fear had been confirmed. And it wasn't anyone that they had robbed, it was the mother fucking FEDS.

He was on his side of the bed, naked as the day he was born and high as hell. They drank and smoked the entire night, eating fried chicken and French fries while listening to old school music and counting almost two-million in cash.

"Kadeem, wake your ass up!" she hollered at him.

Yara tried to hurry to their closet and hide the money from the last heist they did. They were so tired from partying downstairs that they had sex and went straight to sleep without putting the money in the safe.

If they were about to go to jail, she needed to hide the money and then tell Charlie to hurry and come get it. She almost died getting that money and would be damned if the FEDS took it.

He finally got up and said, "SHIT!" once he peeked out the window. Their driveway was full of marked and unmarked cars.

Yara tried to lock their bedroom door but was too late. They came in with their guns up, and she hurriedly raised her hands, not wanting them to shoot her.

"I need to put some clothes on," she asked kindly. She was naked as hell, and so was Kadeem.

Kadeem got mad. "Man, stop looking at my wife," he barked at the FEDS.

"Get back, nigga, get back," the captain told him. He was trying to give Yara a shirt that was on the floor by the bed. She covered her breasts the best she could.

"Let her put some clothes on please," he was now begging.

One hour later, they were handcuffed in two separate cars, and she ended up turning her head, unable to stomach seeing her kids come out of the house crying for their mama.

Kadeem couldn't believe they got knocked. He was pissed, and all he was thinking about was that last two million.

Yara hadn't dealt with that night yet, she hadn't accepted that he had turned his back on her and left her in a cell to rot. And if he really couldn't do anything about it, the least he could have done was told her. But instead, he lied, he held her sanity captive while he embraced a new woman.

"Quentin, all I ever had I gave it to him. He barely loved me back," she admitted. Ooh, a gust of strong wind somehow swept over her, and she wept.

He rushed to her and pulled her into his arms. "Lesson learned, baby. Look where you at now," he whispered in her ear.

She cried and cried and cried. Why it took her ten years of solitude to realize that he never loved her enough was mind-boggling. Kadeem loved her out of convenience, sadly. She believed she was nothing more than another soldier on his team. And, although she was way smarter and way harder, in his silly mind he had done her a favor by taking her in and loving her.

"You have no idea what I went through in jail. I was raped, stabbed, beaten." She choked on her words as she finally told someone other than Miko what she had gone through. And for Kadeem to not once ask her how she was or what she went through hurt her to her core. He didn't care, he never fucking cared.

What "boss" let his wife go to jail? Surely, anyone else would have taken the charge. Selfishly, he believed that if he was going down, she was too. Quentin was street. The crimes were behind him, but he had no problem getting his hands dirty in the name of justice. He was boiling hot thinking of someone invading his precious Yara.

"If I could take it from you, every nightmare, every fear, doubt and worry, baby, I promise I would," he swore to her. How that fuck nigga slept peacefully at night, Quentin would never understand.

She wiped her face with the back of her arm. "I'm seeing better days," she told him. Quentin wanted to pray. He took her hand and bowed his head, and she asked him, "What are you doing?" She didn't believe prayer would solve anything.

"We need to pray," he said to her as if she should already know what he was about to do. He was a 'God-fearing, Bible-toting, by the blood of the lamb and by His stripes we are healed' kind of dude, and she knew this.

Quentin didn't downplay or shy away from being a Christian. He never said he was perfect either, he had his flaws. He sinned. He fell short every single day.
And in times like this, he also knew what to do and how to call on the Heavens so that the angels could come forth. And baby girl needed Jesus.

Yara shook her head as her lip trembled. "I told you-"

"Told me what? Because you sounded confused last time we talked about God." He didn't mean to sound so harsh.

She snatched her hand away from his. "Call it what you want."

"Yara." One thing he didn't lack was patience. He had tons of it, but that stubborn, rebellious shit out of a grown woman was something he wouldn't tolerate.

"I'm not praying with you." She tried to get up and walk past him but he snatched her ass right back down.

"I don't know no other way to say this, baby girl," he said through clenched teeth as he spoke. She looked at him with attitude all over her face, and he couldn't care less. "I'm not asking you to join the choir or give your whole check to the church, but I'm a religious man, and I'm not dating an atheist or whatever you call yourself." Who she worshipped was a deal breaker, and he loved God.

"What are you saying?"

He didn't blink his eyes or bat an eyelash. "You need to get with the program, or this won't work."

Quentin wasn't forcing anything on her. She knew the Lord, she knew the Word was pure and true. He could feel that in her spirit. Yara wanted to blame someone for what happened to her, but she was pointing the finger at the wrong person. Her slimy ex was who she needed to blame, not God. God never failed us. He was always on-time. And Quentin hated to be the one to say, "You had to go to jail" or "You needed to do them ten years" but he believed that wholeheartedly.

Sometimes, God had to sit us down to get our attention. He must wreck our plans for us to get focused. When we take our eyes off Him, He will remind us who He is. God had a plan for her life way before she left her grandparent's house and way before she ran into the path of Kadeem Moreland. He knew that she was going to cry and suffer, and look at how he gave her joy for all those tears she cried. For those nights she spent in jail, He had blessed her tremendously.

"Pray then," she spat. Yara liked him too much to leave.

He bowed his head and asked God for forgiveness, peace, love, joy and most importantly, discernment.

Yara needed to open her heart up to receive Him once again because that's all it really took, a clear and contrite heart, and God would do the rest. That was in His word.

Quentin didn't do the most when he prayed, he barely raised his voice. "In Jesus name I pray, amen," he ended the prayer.

And she said after him, "Amen. Where do your parents go to church?"

"I'm adopted."

She didn't expect him to say that. Confusion was etched across her face. "Why are you just now saying something?" she wanted to know.

"Because it's something I don't share openly, and I wanted you to feel comfortable opening up to me."

She didn't notice at first, but for every question he asked her, he told her something about him. "Where are your real parents?"

"In the church, mega pastor, well my dad is. My mom is married, lives in uh… North Carolina. She had no more children. If I told you who my dad was, you'd be shocked."

She wasn't expecting that tidbit either. "Are you for real?"

He nodded his head. "Dad had an affair, and you know how that go, send the bastard child off." He could joke about it now, and that was because of prayer.

"And… you still love and believe in God?"

How could he not? "Can't blame God for someone else's mistakes."

"Have you said anything? Do they know you're famous?" She had tons of questions.

He smiled at her and kissed her forehead. "I'm a member of the church, I tithe faithfully and all of that. It eats my mother up every time I step in there, so I only go like four times a year." Quentin didn't know if his dad knew he was in attendance, he didn't have their last name.

"How could his wife do that? Why did your mom give you up?" There were some cruel people out here.

"They gave her a check, and that shut her up. You know how that goes."

"Gave her a check to not raise her child? Do you like your adopted parents?"

"I do. My mother is an angel, you'll meet her soon." He wasn't easy to raise, she had her work cut out for her. And that's why now he gave her everything she ever wanted and loved her to the fullest. She was the best mother a broken child like him could have ever desired.

The relaxed look on his face told her that he was at peace with everything that had come his way. "You are amazing." She wanted to hold him, love him, be there for him.

Quentin blushed on the low. "I feel the same way about you, babe."

She kissed his lips. "Thank you for praying for me." She needed it more than he would ever know.

"Yara, together we can accomplish so much." Deep down, he believed that.

She nodded her head, accepting what he said.

"Now what?" Tonight had gone in a totally different direction than she thought it would.

He pulled her back to his chest and rested his head on hers. "We meditate."

Sex was cool, and hers was addicting, but what they shared was in a realm of its own. In his quiet time or while she slept and he laid wide awake, he would try to compare their sex to another and failed. She was in a league of her own. And tonight didn't call for physical interaction because they had connected on a whole different level.

Yara was enjoying the time they spent, whether she was screaming his name or drawing closer to him in ways she wouldn't dare be able to imagine.

"This is perfect." The moment they were sharing was extraordinary.

He said to her, "Just like you."

And she wondered at that second if he ever really found out her secrets and all she had once done would he still call her perfect and see her as a woman who deserved to be praised...

Chapter Eighteen
"You don't need nobody else." – Bryson Tiller

Ninety Days Later…

Charlie had an attitude, and it was obvious. Everyone around the dinner table felt her weird ass energy, but no one said anything. Kamala looked at Kadeem, and he shrugged his shoulders. She didn't slave over a stove all day to have a silent dinner. In celebration of Ayanna graduating this weekend, Kasim, Kadeem's brother, and his family were in town, so Kamala thought it was the perfect opportunity for everyone to gather.

Ayanna was very proud of herself, as she should be. Graduating as Valedictorian wasn't an easy task, and she also scored over 1.2 million dollars in scholarships, which left her parents with nothing to pay for.

Kamala cleared her throat as she sat her goblet of wine that her future sister-in-law bought for her. "I'm so happy that everyone could make dinner tonight," she said with a bright smile on her face.

Her and Kadeem were matching, and while they thought it was cute, Ayanna, Yanise and Meme were in their group message rolling their eyes at the corny shit.

"You can cook, so we came," Meme kept it real with her. If she couldn't throw down in the kitchen, they would have declined the invitation.

"Well, I know your mom has had you guys all over the world lately, so I was thrilled that y'all had some spare time for your father," Kamala shot back.

KK looked at Kadeem, who seemed slightly amused at his fiancé's boldness.

"Hey, mama glowed up, can't be mad at that." Meme wasn't going to let this trick throw her mother under the bus. For goodness sake, what did they expect her to do, sit around and bask in her misery? The misery that Kadeem created. Meme was proud of her mother and her accomplishments, and because of her mother's climb to the top, she was putting her on every chance she got.

She hadn't told her dad yet, but she wasn't going back to school next semester. The set life was exciting, and if she didn't have so much on her plate which was mainly school, she could obtain more opportunities and build her name as a stylist. Her passion was hair, not nursing.

"Meme, cut it out," Charlie warned her to play nice. Tonight was about Ayanna, not Kamala speaking up for Kadeem. He was a grown ass man, and if he felt some type of way about the girls spending more time with Yara than him, then he should have said something. Now was not the time nor the place.

Giselle shook her head and continued eating. She minded her business, and so did her husband. Thankfully, she was able to nip the little drama Kasim had with his baby mother many years ago. Niyla knew not to even play with Kasim anymore.

"I'm happy to be here. Thank you, Kamala, for this lovely spread," Ayanna chimed in.

Simultaneously, Yanise and Meme rolled their eyes. Their sister took a special liking to Kamala for some odd reason.

"Ma, you not hungry?" Kadeem asked his mother.

KK looked at her to see if she would answer, and she nodded her head. "Yes, I am, don't you see me eating?"

Yanise laughed out loud, "Charlie ain't here for y'all tonight." She knew her grandmother well.

"Would you like some wine?" Kamala offered.

Charlie told her, "No thank you."

KK pushed his chair back. "Sweetheart, this was a beautiful dinner. I'm going to head out now."

"Pops!" Kasim called out to his dad to see why he was leaving so soon.

Kadeem shook his head. "Y'all arguing?" he asked his mom, and all she did was roll her eyes and pop a tomato in her mouth.

"It's been this way between them for like a month."

Yanise corrected Ayanna, "Nah, baby, more than that, like three months."

"Mind y'all business," Meme told them.

Both men stood from the table and followed their father out. Kasim was the tall vanilla version of KK, and Kadeem was his chocolate twin. They were pretty much the same height and possessed all their father characteristics. However, they were completely different.

Kasim hadn't viewed his brother in the same light since things went down with him and Yara but would never say anything to him.

"What's going on?"

KK lit a cigar and puffed on it as hard as he could. They were standing in the front of the house. It was a little chilly, but no one complained about the weather.

"She asked me to marry her, and I said no, and she's been that way ever since," he confided in his two sons.

"That's why you ain't been up here?" Kadeem asked his Pops, who only came to town for Ayanna's graduation.

"She's so set in her ways." He seemed saddened by her pushing him away.

Kasim remained silent as always. Charlie wasn't his mother. He lived with them during his last three years of high school, and she was mean; mean as shit. However, her silent treatment was nothing compared to the hell he lived in while staying with his birth mother, so he dealt with it. It wasn't until Kasim grew older that he and Charlie developed a relationship. He loved her, not unconditionally, but if something were to happen to her, he would mourn. Mourn more for Kadeem who was a mama's boy and for his father, who he knew never loved anyone else other than her.

"Why did you say no?" he finally posed the question.

KK shrugged his shoulders. "Not interested." He was older now, old as fuck, and if they didn't marry all those years ago, why now? KK knew that something was up with Charlie, and he wouldn't be marrying out of convenience. Marriage was suitable for her now, but now they were no longer on the same page.

Kadeem wanted to know how would they bounce back from him rejecting her proposal. "So now what?"

KK put the light out of the cigar. "Don't know, son. And to be honest right now, I really don't care."

η

After dinner ended quite awkwardly, the girls left in one car, and Charlie bided her farewell. Giselle sent the kids to their home in New York with security and now the two couples were prepared for a mini turn-up at a lounge that Kamala had recently visited with her girlfriends.

"I haven't been out in so long," Giselle said. She returned to work a few years ago, and it wasn't at *Gen*. She was now a private consultant for start-up companies and overseeing a clothing line for women with physical impairments and disabilities. Her new mantra was, "nothing is a limitation" and that's now how she lived her life.

"This is nice," Kadeem complimented the extended Escalade they were being driven around in.

Kasim wasn't as fancy as his wife. "She don't drive much," he tried to downplay the luxuries he now had access to.

Giselle's eyes met his and smiled. "And you do? Don't listen to your brother, Kasim ain't drove in years." She was too tickled at his coolness.

"I was just down there, and we went to get weed," Kadeem remembered.

"Rare occasion, I promise you."

Kamala still couldn't believe that in a few months she would be a part of their family. "Giselle, I don't know if you got my text about being in the wedding or at least coming to the festivities, my sister has so much planned." And that was the truth. Kamile and April were in charge of her parties, and she wasn't just having a regular old bridal shower. No, Kamala was having a pajama party followed by an all-white brunch and then the real turn-up would commence a week before the wedding in Punta Cana, Dominican Republic, where everyone was ready to slay.

Kadeem was still being indecisive about nailing down a date but luckily, one of her clients was letting her use one of his properties out in the Hamptons. Yes, Kamala Crawford, a poor black girl now hot-shot attorney, was getting married in the Hamptons. She couldn't wait.

"I believe I got the message. If I show you my inbox, you would be surprised." She had three phones and only used the one that no one had the number to other than her husband, father, assistant, pastor and Teka. So, there was no telling which number Kamala had been texting.

"I understand, we are both busy women."

"Yeah, so we will be at the wedding, but I think I will pass on being in the wedding party. I'm not much fun." She tried to say it as nice as she could.

Kamala didn't beg or kiss ass, so she told her, "No worries, let's turn-up." She turned to her fiancé, who was already high from smoking two blunts with his brother.

She kissed his face. "You good, babe?"

He nodded his head. "Yep, I'm better with you. Dinner was splendid tonight," he used one of her words and winked his eye. She knew that he was being funny too.

The couples filed out of the truck and into the front of the line where Kadeem handed the security guard a nice hefty tip and then moved out of the way so Giselle, who was still considered a celebrity, could hurry into the lounge.

"This is a nice section," Kasim said once they were escorted to the top floor, where the top-dollar patrons were seated.

"I told the waitress to bring four bottles of champagne, is that cool?" Everyone nodded their head. "We got an early start tomorrow," Kamala added.

Ayanna's graduation started at eight, and she knew they wouldn't probably leave until twelve or one. After the ceremony, they were going to dinner and then the next day she was having a brunch that Kamala also put together. She was hoping that Yara came.

A bottle girl appeared in shimmery clothing and gold accessories. "Here y'all go," she said, dancing and moving her thick thighs from the left to the right while waving a sparkler in the air.

Giselle recorded a quick video to send to her good friend Teka, who promised to fly in for a day to see her godchildren.

After the glasses were filled, Kamala raised her glass. "A toast." Everyone followed suit, and she said, *"To family!"*

No one thought much of the toast, no one other than Giselle, who was extremely uncomfortable around Kamala for some reason. She could tell that Kadeem was happy, and that was good. Everyone deserved love. Even if you had to fuck over some people to get it, she still wanted what was best for her brother-in-law.

Yara stayed on her mind often, though she had never had an actual conversation with her. However, they had built a relationship while she was imprisoned. Giselle sent books often, letters of encouragement and kept money on her books. It was Giselle who became a bright light in her life through her husband, who seemed heavily affected by her arrest.

"To family," she toasted and then took a large gulp of the bubbly.

η

"Why did we stay out so late?" Yara tried her hardest to stifle a yawn as they walked through the double doors that led them to the auditorium where Ayanna's graduation was being held.

Meme and Riq shook their head at her. Yara thought she was young and could hang with them, but clearly, she couldn't.

"I need coffee," she yawned loudly.

Riq told his boo for the third time, "You look so good, baby." He loved when she put that fly shit on.

Meme was normally dressed in all-black being that she was either at school or doing hair. However, she took off this weekend to celebrate her lil sis's graduation. And baby, Ayanna wasn't just graduating, she was the valedictorian of her class. Everyone was so proud of her.

Kamala did the most and ordered life-size cut-outs of Ayanna's head and all kinds of other corny stuff that Ayanna shed a tear for when she saw it.

"Thanks, baby." She hurried up and kissed his lips in case her father, uncle or grandfather was lurking around the corner.

It took Yara forever to come downstairs, since she asked them to pick her up. She was the reason they were late, and Meme told her grandmother that, who was mean mugging them once they joined the section they had locked down for everyone.

"Ma was moving slow."

Charlie ignored her and handed her a few programs to pass down to the family.

Yara knew it was nothing but good therapy and her praying boyfriend because there was no way in hell she ever thought she would see the day where she could sit behind her ex-husband and his new thing. Surprisingly, she wasn't bothered at all.

Yara had upgraded in a major way and even more important than that, she had healed. She was no longer trying to act like her and Kadeem's marriage didn't exist, nor was she trying to replace his memory with people or her career.

They were married, he hurt her, lied, cheated and had used and betrayed her. All of that was her reality, and that was okay. She accepted all of that and even forgave him, although he never issued a sincere apology.

Shortly after they arrived, Giselle and Kasim were coming up the steps. Yara hadn't seen her brother-in-law since he came to visit her while she was in prison.

Her face lit up and so did his. "Yara in the building!" he barked, not caring that they weren't the only people in the place.

KK loved to see his family all together, even if Charlie was still being a bitch. He ended up getting a hotel room last night, not even wanting to be around her.

Kasim told him that he could have stayed with them and so did Kadeem, but their father enjoyed his space.

"Shhh," Yanise told her uncle.

Giselle smiled and kissed her nieces on their heads, and then Meme introduced Riq to her, and Kadeem finally peeped how close they were sitting.

It wasn't weird that he was here because all his peoples were in the building, what bothered him was that he didn't speak.

"Yo, son."

They all turned and looked at him, well, everyone except Yara. That nigga knew to never speak to her again.

"No love?" He extended his arms out.

Riq nodded his head. "What up, OG." He didn't mean that at all. Kadeem wasn't shit in his eyes and damn sure wasn't an original gangster.

"All good, thanks for being here today... family supporting family." He never took his eyes off Riq, even after Riq had turned around and mumbled something to Meme.

Yara was too tickled, and she was glad that none of them could see her face.
She barely spoke when she sat down. She also made sure to smell her best. The Dolce and Gabbana perfume she wore was a random "I love you" gift from her good girlfriend Marsha, and the white linen suit was cute, comfortable and casual. The pants were Capri-styled and wide-legged, stopping at her ankle, along with a pair of hot pink gladiator sandals from Target and a knit blazer with a few Chanel pins on the collar.

Kasim spoke to his brother and Kamala, and then pulled Yara in for a big hug. "Man, did you age backwards?" he asked her, seriously. Yara's skin looked better than it did before she went in.

She was blushing at his praise. "I wish." She hugged him back and then waved to his wife. "Good to see y'all holding on," she said and smiled. Love looked beautiful on Kasim, and she was genuinely happy for him. "Where are the kids?" she asked him.

"They didn't want to come to the graduation, but you'll see them before you leave, you know me and Giselle had twins and a son," he bragged, pulling his phone out to show her pictures.

"They're big now though," Giselle told her.

"It's been ten years, I bet they are."

Kamala sat behind the trio, and they barely acknowledged her. She told Giselle, "We had fun last night, girl. Gotta do it again tonight."

Kadeem shook his head. "Hell nah, I'm getting old." He barely got up in time for the graduation.

Yara handed Kasim his phone back. "Beautiful family, K." She was the only person that ever called him that. She looked over him and grabbed Giselle's hand and looked into her eyes. "Thank you."

They shared a moment, and no one knew why or what Yara thanked them for, other than the two people that needed to know.

Kamile, Kamala's sister, was sitting next to Yara and turned around and looked at her sister with a confused expression on her face, and Kamala shrugged her shoulders.

Kadeem wanted to know what that thank you was for as well.

"And now we will have a speech from our Valedictorian, Ayanna Moreland." They all stood to their feet, whistling, clapping and hooting.

"Not yet, not yet," Charlie tried to tell them to chill out. Her grand baby had been telling her all week that she didn't want them acting all loud and ghetto at her graduation. She was adamant about them being reserved and chill. Black people didn't know how to act at graduations, and Charlie tried to warn her that she wouldn't be able to keep them cool.

Yara sat back down and threw her ponytail over her shoulder, almost hitting Kamala who was bent over scratching her foot.

"My bad," she said and then gave her attention to her daughter.

Ayanna's speech had moved half of the auditorium to tears. No one would have ever known that she felt the way she felt, and she was viewing today's accomplishment as another stepping stone into a new future. She was ready to go to college and start what she was calling "life" for once and for all.

Kasim tossed his arm over Yara's shoulder. "You good, sis?"

Sis? *He didn't call me sis last night,* Kamala thought to herself. She didn't want to be jealous, Lord knows that wasn't her, but she couldn't help but to feel as if everyone's focus was on Yara.

After the speech was over, they immediately began talking and stuff, not caring about anything other than Ayanna.

"Yeah, I'm good, my baby graduating, two down one more to go." Yara glanced at Yanise who was taking selfies with Giselle and Meme. "Let me get in one," she said and moved down the aisle and playfully plopped in Giselle's lap and posed for the pictures. They took tons of cute photos. "Send me the last one," she told her daughter.

Her phone vibrated, and it was a Facetime call from Quentin, who was supposed to be flying in tonight because he missed her oh so much.

"Hey, babe," she greeted him with a big ass smile on her face. Kadeem and Kamala were both being nosey as shit.

"Y'all still at the graduation?"

She laughed, "Now you know graduations be like six hours."

"I just hopped on the jet, I'll be there about time you leave."

"Jet?" Kadeem blurted out loud, unknowingly.

Yara turned around and rolled her eyes. "Call me when you land," she told Quentin.

They ended the call quickly, and Kasim asked, "New boo, sis?" with a big playful smirk on his face.

"Yep, and that's all I'm telling you." She wasn't going into details in front of Kadeem. He would see him in due time, and that could be soon.

Giselle needed to use the restroom and asked, "Yara, come with me to the ladies' room?" Yara got up and followed her down the steps.

Kamala asked Kasim, "When did they get close? Y'all weren't married before she went to jail."

Charlie shook her head, that girl needed to mind her own damn business.

Kadeem would have checked her, but he wanted to know as well.

"I think she sent her books and stuff, I don't know." He really didn't.

"Well, how she get her address if you don't know?"

KK told all of them, "We are in public, family." The shit they were talking about was irrelevant.

As they bypassed all the people asking Giselle for a picture, Yara asked her, "Does that get on your nerves sometimes?"

"Only when I'm trying to spend time with my kids. It's like, back up a lil bit."

Yara understood that.

"How are you doing? I'm happy you're home, I wish we could have visited sooner."

Yara thanked her, "I really appreciate you making sure my head stayed above the water, you didn't have to do that at all." She was forever grateful.

Yara and Kasim had always been close, and Kadeem used to accuse Yara of flirting with him, but they were family. She would never do no trifling shit like that.

And when she went to prison, he told her repeatedly that he would hold her down, and him and his wife really did that.

Every holiday, she received a card and something to make her smile on her birthday, and that kind of encouragement and support went a long way when you were behind those bars. And for Yara, it seemed as if the packages always came when she needed them the most.

"We women gotta stick together. My husband was so pissed about you being arrested and him being free, he could barely sleep some nights," she shared with her.

And boy, no one had a clue. She had it terrible in there. "I'm so glad to be home, that chapter of my life is behind me," she told her with a warm smile on her face. She was happy to be with her family, seeing her baby graduate. She missed Meme's graduation but she wouldn't miss her college graduation, whenever she finished, nor would she miss Yanise's high school graduation or any more of her daughter's accomplishments.

When they returned, Yara seemed in an even better mood, and she could tell it was bothering two people in particular.

Meme wanted Kamala to stop worrying about her mother so much. She kept her cool though, knowing that this wasn't the time or the place for her to act up.

The graduation ended in another hour, and they remained where they were knowing it would be easier for Ayanna to find them versus them searching for her.

She then called and told them to come outside, and it took them twenty minutes to find her.

"Congrats," they all screamed in unison.

Kadeem scooped her up in the air and spun her around, he was so proud of his baby.

Charlie wanted tons of pics. "Okay, Meme and Yanise get in there." She pushed them toward Kadeem and Ayanna.

Everyone took pictures of them and then KK said, "Yara, can we get one family photo please? The girls are big now, I've never seen this before." He was getting teary-eyed.

She wanted to tell him no, but the talk she had with Giselle gave her even more peace than she already had. "Sure." She walked over to them and stood behind Yanise and next to Ayanna, Kadeem was on the side of Meme.

"Oh my, I thought I'd never see the day." Charlie was so happy to snap that picture. No matter the status of the parents, they were able to come together for the kids.

"What time is the brunch tomorrow?" she asked Charlie.

"Two o'clock, and I'm cooking tonight if you want to come," she offered an invitation.

Ayanna said, "I won't be there." She already had plans.

"Girl, you coming for at least an hour, all that food I went and bought," Charlie told her.

"That's the point of tomorrow," Ayanna reminded her.

Charlie didn't want to hear that. "Again, tonight, I, your grandmother who raised you, is having a fish fry at the house, and you will be there. My friends are coming."

Meme asked her, "What friends you got, Charlie?"

Everyone busted out laughing, even KK.

"My new boyfriend, now stop playing with me. I'll see y'all at seven."

KK no longer found anything funny. "If you know like I know, you won't dare have another man in that house."

Everyone stood still. Charlie put her hands on her hips and told him, "You wasn't invited no way." She wasn't playing with his ass and was done with him.
She felt like a fool for even asking him to marry her.

"I'll see y'all tomorrow. Giselle, call me if you wanna get out," she told her and then kissed her girls goodbye.

"Tell Quentin I said hey," Yanise told her mama, she already knew who was in the back of the Maybach. Sometimes he drove, and sometimes he had car service. Today, he was feeling like a boss.

"Come tell him yourself."

Kasim nudged his brother. "Oh yeah, sis. I see ya." He was happy to see that she had upgraded in a major way and not with another nigga like his brother.

Yara didn't want all the attention to be on her, today was about Ayanna.

"Call me if you need anything, baby," she told her daughter.

Yanise walked with her mom to the car and when she returned, her dad asked, "Who is that?" He kept his tone neutral so his fiancé wouldn't trip.

"Who Quentin? That's mama boyfriend," she said it so casually.

Meme wanted to be messy and say, "That ain't no regular nigga in that Bach, that was Quentin Brooks," but she remained silent.

The look on her dad's face was priceless as the vehicle rolled away.

η

"Are you nervous?" he asked her as they rode the elevator to the third floor.

She snorted, "Uh, no I am not, are you? Was this a good idea? Are you ready to do this?"

Yesterday, he met Yanise on a whim, and she seemed cool with meeting her mama's man, and he did too.

Were they moving too fast? she suddenly asked herself.

Quentin chuckled, "If I wasn't ready, it's too late now, princess," he said to her as the elevator dinged, and he stepped out and then extended his hand to escort her into where the brunch was being held.

"You can leave if you want, and I'll catch up with you later." She didn't really think this thing through. They hadn't been dating for a long time, and maybe he wasn't interested in doing the family thing, especially with her ex being there.

"I'm good, I do this every day."

"This is personal, Quentin, not business," she reminded him. Meeting her children wasn't another task on his never-ending to-do list. She was nervous, and that's why she was being snappy with him.

"Come here, babe." He pulled her into a corner since the lobby of the place was a tad bit crowded with people coming in for Ayanna's soiree. "When you invited me, I instantly said yes, right? I want to be here. Okay?" He pulled her in for a warm hug and planted a light kiss on her lips.

She nodded her head. "Let's get this over with." Yara wasn't as bothered as she probably should be being that Kamala took over *her* daughter's graduation. Yara would be a good sport, and that's another reason she invited Quentin, so she wouldn't feel like an outsider at the child she birthed graduation brunch. She noticed that Ayanna took a liking to Kamala and vice versa, and maybe it was because she lived the life that Ayanna wanted.

Kamala was college-educated and polished, plus she was a Greek and knew a lot of important people. In Ayanna's eyes, Yara was probably nothing more than a housewife turned jailbird.

She shook those evil thoughts out of her head and answered Quentin's hand as they walked into the brunch, and it seemed as if the world stopped as the millennials and even a few old heads, mainly Kadeem's friends from the block, recognized who Quentin was.

"Whoa, can I get a picture?"

"Aye, do you got time to hear my cousin mixtape, it's a banger."

"Oh my God, I made you my #MCM last week, did you see the post?"

Yara gave Quentin an apologetic look, and he brushed it off. "It's all cool baby, go hug your peoples. I'm going to grab a drink." He was fine. He spoke to everyone who spoke to him, he was the perfect gentleman.

"Whoa, you showing out today," KK teased as she walked toward what was the head table.

There was one spot empty at the end, and she asked, "Is that supposed to be my seat?"

Kamile nodded her head. "Yeah, my sister wanted to make sure you had somewhere to sit, near the family."

Kamile used the word *family* as if Yara weren't a part of it, or if she wasn't the reason there was a family today. Yara gave her a forced and tight smile, begging herself to not go the fuck off on this hoe. "I think I'll sit with the common folks. Where are the girls?" she turned and asked KK.

"They're making a grand entrance," he said casually as he sipped his mimosa.

"This is beautiful." She had to give Kamala her props. Kamala had rented what had to be the largest room the place had since there was a mimosa station, full bar, DJ and about twelve round tables with white linen and the cutest, personalized table toppers.

Yara noticed that each table had a picture of Ayanna throughout the years, so she went to each table to get a good look at her daughter, who had grown into a beautiful woman. And Yara had missed it all.

Quentin graced her back with his hand. "You good?" he asked, wanting to make sure his lady was fine.

She nodded her head. "Let's take our seats, it's about to start."

The DJ announced that the "family" was in the building, so she turned around and watched Kamala, Kadeem, Meme, Charlie and Yanise walk in to Jay-Z's popular song, "Family Feud."

It was a cute thing to do, but she couldn't ignore the panging in her heart of feeling left out.

The DJ then asked everyone to stand to their feet to welcome Ayanna, and she came in Diddy Bopping with her cap and gown on. Once she got to the front of the room, she removed her gown and revealed what school she was attending by wearing the shirt with their name and logo on it.

Everyone rooted, while her dad seemed distraught that his baby girl was going across the coast all the way to California to attend UCLA. There was a quick prayer by someone who said he was a friend of the family and had been in Ayanna's life since she was a little girl, but the man wasn't familiar to Yara.

And then a slideshow appeared on the projection.

Yara took a deep breath, praying that whoever put it together thought to include her, and she then told herself that if she wasn't in the slideshow to not take it personal. She wasn't around. She was in prison.

Four minutes into the slideshow, and she was barely holding her tears back.

Quentin felt her legs trembling under the table and asked her again, "You sure you good?"

She nodded her head. "Hhmm-hmm," she lied straight through her teeth.

Once the slideshow was over, everyone was wiping tears from their face. It was a beautiful collection of Ayanna's life up until now. And she wished that her tears were of joy, but they weren't. When Yara saw Ayanna hug Kamala and tell her thank you, she knew it was time for her to go.

She told Quentin, "I need to leave… *now*."

"Babeee." He didn't think it was a good idea for them to leave. He felt bad and was pissed that they didn't include Yara in the slideshow, but if they left, then whoever did the spiteful shit would know that they got to her, and he couldn't have that.

"I will leave you in here," she told him straight up.

He took a deep breath and pushed his chair out, and she stood up leaving Quentin to catch up with her.

Meme saw her mom leaving and hopped out of her seat to follow her. Yanise did as well. "Ma!" they called her name right before the elevator closed.

"I'm good, have a good day with your family."

Chapter Nineteen

"Start off with the mind, and end up with your heart." – French
Montana

Yara was surprised when Marsha told her that there was a Giselle Braxton-Moreland requesting to see her. There was only one Giselle Braxton-Moreland.

Yara applied a fresh coat of lipstick and told Marsha to send her in. The weekend started off so beautiful, but yesterday was completely fucked-up. Thankfully, Quentin got the hint of her needing space and ended up catching up with a few of his comrades. When he made it back to his place, she was in bed soaking in her tears.

He tried his hardest to love the pain away, but sex was temporary. Only for a select time was his penis able to soothe her. As soon as she climaxed, and he released his seeds, the ill feeling of never being accepted by her daughter came back.

Yara was never happy to see Quentin leave, but this was one weekend where she counted down until she heard him say he had a meeting or something more important than her. It finally came.

He left this morning and when he texted to check on her, she didn't respond. Yara was always an introverted person, but Kadeem never cared enough to notice. He and Quentin were two completely different people.

"Giselle, what are you doing here?" she really wanted to know, which is why she asked the way she did. They weren't friends, nor could they be considered family members being that she was no longer married to Kadeem. She should be trying to make friends with Little Miss Kamala.

Yara was thankful for the nice sweet notes and things she sent. Although she never said they were from her and not Kasim, she knew Kasim better than he knew himself, and he wasn't sending her no books or Christmas cards.

"We are heading out soon, and I wanted to say goodbye and exchange numbers," she told her in a pleasant tone, one that didn't match Yara's.

Marsha looked at her with a scrunched up look on her face, silently begging her to be nice. This was got damn Giselle Braxton-Moreland. Yara was tripping.

"Follow me back here," Yara told her and turned on her heels.

Once they were in her office, she tried to be nice and offered her coffee or tea, and Giselle told her, "No, I won't be here long. Do you mind sitting?"

She did mind. "I rather stand." She was nervous, and not knowing the purpose of her being there made her uncomfortable.

"You left the brunch so fast, I didn't get a chance to give you my number."

"Would you have stayed?" The question wasn't rhetorical. She really wanted to know what she would have done if she were in her shoes.

"Probably not. However, I understand why you did, and I don't blame you one bit."

"Giselle, I'm not perfect, and I've done a lot of awful things, but one thing I've always done right, the one thing I didn't get wrong, was becoming a mother and being a mother," she said with so much firmness. She didn't have a good example of what a mom was supposed to do, be or act, and that didn't halt her from being the best mother she could be. Yara loved her children and when she took that plea, she had to convince herself that ten years was a long time but not long to where she couldn't come home and resume the role of mother. Yara wanted everyone to know that and hoped Giselle would relay the message.

"I remember you," Giselle told her. Maybe Yara couldn't recall meeting her, but Giselle remembered her vividly. "You walked around that club like you owned it. I was like wow, whoever that is has so much confidence," she admitted.

Yara shook her head, not able to recall. "Really?"

Giselle nodded her head. "Yes, honey. You used to run Kadeem, my husband has told me several stories."

"Yeah, on rare occasions I could get him to listen to me. I'm fine, and I appreciate you coming to check on me, it means more to me than I'm probably showing." She had a guard up. There was a wall that sadly, couldn't be knocked down right now.

"And I want to thank you for being a positive light in my kids' lives, they speak very highly of you," she added.

Giselle stood up. "There's so much more I wish I could say, but I understand how you feel. I have spent many nights praying for you, and I am ecstatic to see you smiling and glowing up," she told her and went for the door.

Yara didn't respond to what she said. Giselle was the first person to tell her that she was full of joy for her. When she first came home, she wondered if her old friends even knew she was home, because no one ever reached out. No one stopped by the hair salon or came by Charlie's house, and she realized that they weren't her friends to begin with.

When they lost everything after the FEDS busted their home and businesses, people ran from them, treated them like they were the plague. Many nights she cried to Kadeem wondering how her friends could turn on her in a blink of an eye. And ever since then, she was hard.

Yara somehow allowed Miko in, and now she was like a sister to her. She had built a bond with Marsha as well. Yara had to realize that everyone wasn't out to hate you or wish you the worst.

She jogged to the lobby area to catch up with Giselle. "Why did you send me those books and stuff?" she asked her. She had asked her in the bathroom during Ayanna's graduation, and she never told her why.

Giselle took a deep breath. "For some reason, my husband has a soft spot in his heart for you, and whoever he loves I love because he's the head of my home. So, when you went away and I saw how he was taking it, I had someone get me your information," she explained.

And she was right, Kasim always protected her. He would be her brother forever, no matter what went down between her and Kadeem, and she knew in her heart that he didn't agree with how Kadeem moved. It always showed on his face.

She hugged her, long and hard. Marsha stood behind her desk, smiling.
Yara needed that.

"Those books... kept me on some nights."

Giselle had sent her tons of devotionals, some were simple morning affirmations to keep her sane. Giselle rubbed her back and told her, "We are family... for real."

η

"Soooo we're going to have dinner and not say nothing to each other, really nigga?" Kamala couldn't take it anymore.

It was a Wednesday night, three days since the graduation brunch, and he had barely said two words to her. When the check came after the brunch, she expected him to pay for it being that it was his damn daughter who had graduated, but he left right after Ayanna said her speech, leaving Kamala to settle an almost four-thousand-dollar tab. She was pissed and still hadn't brought it up because he was in a sour mood.

He took a shot of Hennessy and continued to eat the food she cooked. On top of going to the gym, being in two meetings and being in court until six o'clock, she was tired.

"Kadeem Moreland."

"You saying my whole name don't do shit," he let her know.

She was not his damn mama. "Why are you acting like this?" her voice shrieked.

Did she really not have a clue, or was she playing mind games with him?

"My investor pulled out today." That was fifty percent of why he was in such a sour mood.

"Okay, and what was your problem yesterday and on Monday?" She wasn't buying that excuse.

He looked at her like she had two heads. "Oh, so me losing out on fifty thousand means nothing to you?" He was banking on this man's check to secure this building that he planned on turning into a family entertainment center. It was guaranteed to bring in about a million dollars a year after expenses and construction.

"I'm sure you have a backup plan, so tell me what's really going on." She looked at him and crossed her arms. Kamala hated when they weren't talking. The energy in their home was off, and she could barely sleep when he didn't touch or cuddle with her until she closed her eyes. He had been giving her the cold shoulder.

"Kamala, I shouldn't even have to tell you," he said and took a deep breath and dropped his fork.

"But you do, cus if I knew I wouldn't be asking or sitting up here looking stupid."

He went on and told her since she was begging for it, "The slideshow."

"Okay? It was beautiful, everyone was crying." She was lost.

"Everyone except Yara, Ayanna's mother."

Was he serious right now? He couldn't be. "Uhhhh, what pictures did I have of her? She's been fucking locked up. That's why you're not talking to me?" She was in disbelief.

"Did you not see her leave?" He knew that she did.

"Actually, I didn't. I know you think I play with my pussy to her mug shot every night, but I don't. She doesn't cross my mind."

He held his tongue on that comment. "It was rude not to include her, that's all I'm saying."

She snaked her head. "And all I'm saying is, I didn't have any pictures of her." She wasn't apologizing for shit. She did nothing wrong.

"Why couldn't you use the picture we took at the graduation? I'm not saying make it about her, but you have to understand how she felt."

Kamala didn't understand or care. She went to jail on her own and should have considered her decisions beforehand.

"And my friends were there, my colleagues… did you really think I would put that picture of y'all looking like the damn Cosby Show without me?" Was he drunk and high?

"She's their mother, Kamala, and everyone knows we are engaged," he reminded her.

"Which brings me to my next question, when are we getting married?"

He looked at her and got up from the table. She didn't care about anything he was saying, and it was vice versa.

The last thing on his mind right now was getting married… again.

η

After the graduation, it seemed as if everyone got busy. The group message wasn't popping, they said good morning and have a good day, and that was about it. Yara was all over the map traveling with work. Yanise was spending the first six weeks of the summer at STEM camp, and Ayanna left the first weekend after graduating from high school. She was getting a jumpstart on her courses and was taking twelve hours in summer school.

Yara was happy that she wanted her to help move her into her dorm, so she stayed in California for a few days to make sure baby girl had everything she needed, and then she flew to Atlanta to help Yanise get settled. Yara didn't know that Kadeem had already told Ayanna that she was taking her and not Kamala. At first Ayanna was pissed, but she ended up having a good time with her mom. That was their first outing together without Meme and

Yanise, and she really saw her mom in a different light. And Yara felt they had made some progress while she was in Cali. Being a mom was a full-time job, even after your kids finished high school.

That was two weeks ago, and she had barely heard from those two and now Meme was on the roll as well. Quentin had been plugging her with as many people as he could, and she was on the set of a photo shoot for Essence when she got a call that wrecked her whole day.

The model whose hair she was wand-curling saw the tears forming in the corners of her eyes. "Are you okay, girl?"

Meme had been upbeat all day, but since she returned from the bathroom where she took the call, she hadn't said two words.

"Yeah, I'm good," she lied. She was now counting down until the shoot wrapped up so she could Uber back to her hotel and cry her eyes out.

Fibroids. Her test results were back and showed that Meme had fibroids, and it could be the reason she couldn't carry a baby full-term. She hurriedly sent Riq a text message with a sad face.

He wasn't feeling her new life or busy schedule because it didn't really include him, and he was used to having her waiting for him when he was out in the streets getting money. Now things had turned around. Riq never had to chase a female or be on someone's else's times, and he was trying his hardest to adjust to their new routine.

Thankfully, the shoot wrapped up less than an hour later, and she packed her things quickly and called an Uber.

Riq answered her call on the second ring. "Been buzzing you all day," he told her with an attitude.

"Sorry, we're just now finishing." She was on the brink of more tears.

"What's up?"

Meme took a deep breath. "Basically, the doctor thinks I have fibroids," she told him.

"What is that? Cancer?"

Why did black people link cancer to anything wrong with the body? "Oh my God, no. Not cancer, nigga, don't say that."

He was running out of patience and wished she would tell him what was going on with her body. "What is it then? I ain't never heard of that shit, Meme."

"Normally, it's no symptoms, but the fact that my back and legs are always hurting, plus my heavy cycles and how long they be is what raised the red flag with my Doctor. And they're affecting my tissue growing on the uterus. I need lining for a successful pregnancy."

"What did she say you need to do differently?"

"Eat better and watch them close. She said they rarely turn into tumors, but it is possible."

He heard the pain and sadness in her voice. "And you gotta stop stressing, baby."

Riq was right about that, all she did was worry and try to figure out her next move. "I know." The Uber had arrived at the hotel she was staying in while in California. "I'm about to shower and take a nap, I'll hit you when I wake up."

He wanted to talk to her some more but he didn't even trip. "Cool."

Meme took a deep breath, her doctor seemed hopeful about her being able to become a mother. She kept asking herself was a baby what she wanted right now, being that she was finally making strides as a stylist. Half of her still wanted to be a mom, and then the other half of her was saying, "Girl, stay focused and get your money."

Her savings was sitting pretty, and she could do what she wanted without having to ask anybody for nothing, and that felt damn good. She would do some research on fibroids after she woke up from her nap.

After she got out of the shower, she dried off, tied her weave up, and then sent Riq a message, *"Love you baby, can't wait to get home to you."* She missed him so much and wished he could be out there with her living in the hills.

Riq texted her back immediately, *"Needed to hear that more than you know ma."*

She had to do a better job with making time for him because she knew that all these trips were something he wasn't used to. Meme was grinding and only had eyes for his fine ass. Riq had nothing to worry about. She knew who she belonged to.

η

This getting "out of your shell" thing wasn't that bad. Her therapist was going to leap for joy during their next session when she told her about all the social things she did that normal people found fun but were difficult for her. Being in an all-women's prison was hard as hell, especially when you were fair skinned, clearly mixed as hell and had long beautiful hair. The women in there hated her for no reason. Yara had been in countless fights simply because she wasn't about to be nobody's bitch or human sex toy.

She told Quentin the other night, and she was extremely honest with him, which she vowed to always do. It was taking her a second to get comfortable being hit from the back. Although it felt good as shit, she was raped twice in prison by women. One stuck a broomstick so far up her ass that she was constipated for two weeks. Yara was then taken off kitchen duty. She was tormented, abused and damn near beaten to death. Although she didn't snitch, one of the guards caught the women in the act.

Quentin grew angry every time she shared a story with him, but her therapist told her that she needed to talk about it more. And tonight, she was being a cute little social butterfly by attending Miko's dinner party at her house to celebrate her birthday.

Miko shared with about eight of her closest girlfriends and two of her gay friends that she didn't want to do too much this year, something intimate where everyone could be comfortable to share and laugh. There would be no cameras, since her and Nash were doing a reality show, and she told them that she regretted it already.

"This is really, really good," Yara told Marsha. She was on her third cup of shrimp and grits. Miko had tons of appetizers before the actual dinner started, and Yara was tearing the food up.

"Are you pregnant?" Marsha had to ask because lil' mama hadn't stopped eating since they arrived.

Yara almost choked on a piece of okra. "Girl, hellll no! I'll be forty this year," she reminded her.

Miko's friend chimed in, although they weren't talking to her, "That don't mean nothing, I had my daughter when I was of age."

"How did she turn out?" Yara asked.

Lauren laughed, "She's healthy and grown as hell."

She knew she wasn't pregnant though. "I'm not carrying a child. I'm just hungry, I had a long day," she announced.

Miko was still upstairs getting her hair and makeup done. She told everyone to come causal and thankfully, they all knew Miko well enough to still come looking good. Her definition of casual didn't match everyone's else's, and Yara learned that early on.

She wore a brown satin dress that stopped above her knee and a pair of open toe Sam Edelmen heels and no makeup, feeling that the "Smoked Purple" lipstick by Mac that she applied to her lips did the trick to make her look "fancy."

"I'm Lauren," the woman introduced herself to the only two women that were standing around the kitchen, Marsha and Yara.

"Marsha."

Yara knew who Lauren was. She and Miko had plenty of free time in jail, and she learned all about the infamous Underworld and her relationship with each member. Miko deeply regretted how her and Lauren's friendship played out, and she was happy to see her at Miko's gathering tonight. That alone told her that they were making strides to reconnect.

"I'm Yara,"

"The roommate, right?" Lauren was familiar with her as well.

Yara smiled. "Thank you so much for not saying cell mate." She cringed at that word.

Lauren understand how she felt. "I did three years. I know it's not as long as most people, but I totally get you."

Yara wouldn't allow her to downplay her time because the shit wasn't easy whether she did three days, thirty days or thirty years. Jail was jail. "You did your time, so hey, cheers to us free women."

Although Marsha had never been arrested or convicted of anything, she felt as if she were living in a cell at home, serving life. So, she toasted right along with them and took another shot after that.

There was something about Yara that drew people to her, and Lauren found herself stealing glances at her while she hungrily snacked on everything that was out in the open.

"Girl, don't eat all this shit up," Miko hissed as she walked into the kitchen with a phone to her ear, still in her robe.

"Umm, missy, we been here for an hour, what time does dinner start?" Marsha asked because she couldn't be out late.

"In another hour," Miko laughed as she popped a grape in her mouth.

Yara had nothing to do or anywhere to be. Her kids all had lives outside of her, and her man was in Miami for the weekend. "Girl, let me get this wine." Yara grabbed a bottle of whatever was in a bucket and parlayed to the den. They fell into a conversation about black girl magic and the recent Oscars.

Marsha tried to act cool, calm and collected, but her eyes kept looking at the clock. She'd rather leave now than interrupt the dinner party. "Ladiesss, I have a family emergency, so I need to get going," she said and stood up with her purse in hand.

"Is everything okay?" Yara was now alarmed.

"Yes, yes, girl, I will see you at work on Monday, tell Miko for me." She was out like a light.

Lauren looked at Yara, who did nothing but shrug her shoulders and sip on her wine. "I'm sure she's good." Yara crossed her legs and draped a mink blanket over her lap. "I'm excited for tonight," she admitted to Lauren.

"Me too. Miko is good at these. We used to have dinner once a week at our friend... MJ's house." It was so hard for her to accept her friend's death, and she fought tooth and nail to get her some kind of justice.

"Miko spoke about her a lot, sorry to hear about your loss."

"Thank you. It's been a few years, I'm in a better place now, ya know?"

Yara did. She had experienced loss before. "I definitely do."

"How does it feel to be free? Have people asked you that a million times? If so, I'm sorry," she apologized in advance if she was getting all in her business.

"Actually, they haven't. I used to wish someone did, but I'm in therapy now, so she's paid to listen and to care."

Lauren and therapy weren't a good match. She'd rather go to God. "Church is my therapy," she shared with her.

That was still something Yara was still coming to terms with and thankfully, her man had been patient.

"You don't believe in God?" Lauren asked, seeing the look of disconnect on her face.

"I did... I do," she cleared it up.

"But?" There had to be something else.

Yara took a deep breath, knowing that Lo was a PK kid much like herself to a certain extent. "I'm sure you've had church hurt, how did you not let that affect your relationship with Christ?" Yara seriously wanted to know.

Lauren took a deep breath and sat her wine down because she wouldn't dare talk about her precious Lord and sip wine at the same time. And Yara did the same. "The key word to what you just asked me was *your*. It's *your* relationship, so no matter who hurt you, you still have *your* relationship with God. He didn't hurt or betray you," she told her straight up.

Yara closed her eyes. "It's so much easier said than done."

"It's not if you don't want it to be. I've been alone, I've been low, extremely low, so low that I had to crawl to God, girl." She was so thankful that those days were behind her now.

"I have too." Yara had been there.

And Lauren shook her head to tell her, "You couldn't be because if you were, you wouldn't be questioning Him."

Yara wasn't thirsty for God's presence in her life, and that's why she was suffering. She moved on to her next question because she knew that Lauren was right, and that was something she needed to address during her quiet time.

"What happened between you and Nasir, the boss?"

Lauren laughed at, "the boss" reference. She had known him way before he had ten dollars in his pocket. And now Nasir King was spoken of in such a regal way. It still amazed her.

"Life," Lauren kept it short.

"And how did you forgive him, like truly in your heart forgive him so that you could move on?" she asked Lauren. Yara hadn't realized how much she needed this tonight. And even though the party hadn't started, she was having a good time right here on this couch with Lauren.

"I had to because his apology never reached my soul. He said it a million times, but I never felt like he truly meant it. So, it wasn't until I realized that I could never love my husband or even myself for that matter until I truly forgave him and moved on."

She hated Kadeem, with everything in her. However, she wasn't bitter, nor was she sitting around miserable. Sometimes she would wake up in cold sweats when vivid memories and sometimes nightmares of all the things she had done with him and for him came to haunt her. And she recently told her therapist that she was resentful towards him and still felt heavily affected by their relationship. To be clear, she didn't love him. She was over him, she just couldn't seem to get over how he treated her and how his actions led to her being arrested… for ten years. That was Yara's hang up.

"Girl, you just gave me life." Yara held up her hands as if she were worshipping.

Lauren had been where she was. "It doesn't happen overnight. Take every day as a new step into the right direction, which is a life of pure joy, peace and most importantly, contentment." She could only speak from experience. Lauren had been broken for many years and in her solitude, those three years of prison was sadly, what she needed. She didn't stop going, she was always fulfilling something for someone. While in prison, she was able to really process everything she had been through. It wasn't until she came home did she realize that she hated herself.

It took her a while to look in the mirror and be content with what she saw, and it had nothing to do with her physical appearance. Her soul was ugly, her heart was torn, and she was spiritually and mentally a mess. Therapy was good for some, but for her… all she needed was a serious fast and some time at the altar. That did the trick for her.

Yara had another question, and then the doorbell rang.

"I'm the host, let me grab that," Lauren told her before getting up and going to let Miko's guests in. Clearly, Miko wanted her closest friends here before everyone else arrived.

Ten minutes after, the living room was full, and Yara was in the kitchen helping Lauren bring trays out.

"Thank you… before tonight gets hectic," she told Lauren.

Lauren winked her eye at her. "Anytime." She was only a vessel.

Yara now knew what Miko meant when she would tell her during their late-night conversations when she crooned, "Everyone needs a Lauren Howard in their life."

That girl could get you together like no other. Yara was going to seriously invest in herself, she had to if she really wanted to move forward in life. It was time to put the past behind her.

Chapter Twenty
"Do you know what it feels like to fall in love?" – Stwo

"So, meeting his family, does this make you want to reach out to your parents, grandparents, your aunt who you seem to hate, or perhaps your estranged ex-husband?" She was on a roll today.

Yara was feeling attacked. "Are you in a bad mood?"

"No, are you?"

Yara stood up and paced the floor. "I was feeling good until I came here, to be honest. I was super happy to tell you about the girls' night and me meeting Quentin's mother. I felt like I took a few steps forward, and now you're pushing me back."

"I'm pushing you back to the things that you are running from? Okay, I'll admit to that."

Yara didn't agree. "What am I running from?"

"Your family, your truth, your heritage. Do you really think you can be around your children and not have a conversation with Kadeem ever again?" Yara was tripping.

"Actually, I can. I did it at the graduation and will do it again at Yanise's birthday and whatever else that I have to go to." She didn't want to talk, and why did she have to?

"Aside from him, how does it really feel to not have spoken to your mother since your daughter was born? Be for real, Yara." Her therapist believed that she had brainwashed herself to thinking that she didn't need or want her family, but that was far from the truth.

"It really feels like nothing. I don't think about them at all." She was serious. Her family wasn't her concern, and it had been that way for years.

She had accepted whatever happened with them.

Her therapist shook her head and removed her glasses. "I think we are done for today." She was irritated. Yara looked at the time on the watch, and the woman told her, "If you want a refund for the remaining thirty minutes left in this session, get it from the front desk. I am done for today."

"Why?" she wanted to know.

"Because you are wasting my time, and I don't have the patience today. There's the truth," she said and slapped her glasses on her desk and looked at her.

Yara was confused. Wasn't this considered unethical or professionally incorrect? Could her therapist tell her that she didn't have time for her today? "Did I miss something?"

"You miss a lot of things, darling, and normally I can play this game with you, but today I can't." She was tired and weary. They had been at a standstill for a month.

"Well, bye!" Yara wasn't about to beg her to talk. She grabbed her things and left.

When she got in her car, she cried like a baby. Was she really in denial?

What if she didn't want to talk to Kadeem, why did he have to be a part of her healing process? Little did she know that soon, and very soon, she wouldn't have a choice but to talk to him.

She was quiet during dinner with Yanise, and her daughter picked up on her mood. "Good day today, or nah?"

Yara blew a breath of frustration out of her mouth. "It was okay, what about you?"

"Good, I'm ready to go back to school. Is that weird?" Ever since she took an interest in STEM and had finished a program that her mentor was able to get her in, she was eager to return to school. That turned Yara's very shitty day around. The Fall would be here soon.

"Not much longer to go," Yara told her. These new generation kids were different because she used to love the summer. You couldn't force her in the house before the street lights came on.

"Back to you though. What's wrong, Mama?" she asked, scooping a heaping of string beans into her mouth.

She didn't plan on discussing her therapy session with anyone, but since her baby asked, "Have you ever wondered where my parents were? Like, why you only have Charlie and KK?"

Yanise thought about the question before she hurriedly answered, "Uh, a long time ago, but not really because Charlie and KK are like hippie grandparents."

"Yeah, but you've never met my mom or dad," she reminded her.

"Have you?"

Was she kidding? "Girl, yes. Yanise, I have a mom, a dad, aunts, uncles, cousins, a sister on my dad's side," she went on and on.

"Okay, where are they at? I'll meet them."

If only it were that simple. "I don't talk to them, I was just asking."

Yanise looked at her mom and told her, "You got us, Mama, you don't need them," giving her some reassurance in case she felt as if she had no one.

Yara smiled at her daughter. "Thanks, baby."

She was looking forward to making memories with her kids as the years went by, something her parents never tried to do with her. The first argument that Yara and her step-dad had, her mom kicked her out. She never reached out, not once. And the thing was, her mom was an okay woman. She wasn't the mother of the year, nor did she try to be.

"I'm going to lay down and start over tomorrow." Her mind was incredibly heavy.

Yanise gave her the best smile she could. "Okay, love you."

"Love you too."

The next morning when she arrived to work, she was trying her hardest to pep up, and even the coffee that Marsha specially made for her every morning wasn't doing the trick.

"What's wrong, mamacita?" Marsha saw her pacing the floor back and forth.

"I think I'm going to pop up at my mom's house," she declared.

Marsha stopped typing. "Okayyyy, want me to go with you?"

She was on probation and didn't know how she would react to seeing her mother for the first time in so long. "You would do that?"

Marsha smiled and nodded her head. "Yes."

Yara was now happy as shit. "Okay, let's do some work till noon, then we can go." She was pretty sure her mom lived in the same house since it was owned by the family and there was no mortgage.

Why did Yara know all of that at such a young age? Because they made her an adult at ten. Yara knew everything, all the family business, which led her to be a runaway. It was all too much to bare at only fourteen-years-old.

She dialed Quentin on the drive to her mother's house, and he ignored her call and then followed up with a text, *"Meeting, baby."* He was such a busy man.

"My heart is beating so fast," she told Marsha.

"That's your nerves, you'll be fine."

They continued the drive in silence until she spotted the red house on the end of the street. Nothing had changed other than maybe a new roof, and there was a nice car in the driveway.

"That's it right there." She jumped in her seat. She couldn't believe she was actually doing this right now.

"Want me to come in with you?" Marsha questioned.

Yara shook her head. "No, be on standby though. If I send you a gun emoji, come in and get me." Her anger and temper was still a work in progress.

Yara got out the car and walked up the long driveway, feeling sort of optimistic about possibly repairing their broken and strange relationship. She could see it now, her mom coming over for dinner and going to awards stuff with her.

She knocked on the door twice, and then she heard footsteps growing closer.
It was her mother's footsteps. Her heart was thumping loudly.

"Who is it?" asked a man's voice.

"Yara…"

What a surprise. The door unlocked and then opened, and her step-father who had aged a billion years stepped out.

"Yara?"

"Hey, is my mom here?" She wasn't here for him, so she didn't feel the need to make small talk with him.

"Wow, how long has it been?" He couldn't believe how beautiful she had grown up to be.

"Twenty-four years. Can you get my mom? Or do I need to come back?" Her tone held so much urgency.

His face was solemn. "She's not here."

Yara nodded her head. "Cool, I'll come back. Don't tell her… please. I want to surprise-"

"Your mother passed about eight years ago, in her sleep."

Marsha asked her a million times what did the man say, and she remained silent. When they returned to work, she grabbed her things and left in a daze.

She stayed home for the rest of the week, sending Yanise to Charlie's or Kadeem's She honestly didn't know where Yanise was but was sure she was safe.

Her phone was turned off, and she had tapped out from the world. Someone banged on her door and demanded her to open it before they knocked it down.

And that someone was her boyfriend, who was about to lose his mind if he didn't lay eyes on her. He hadn't spoken to her in three days and when he called the office yesterday to see was she tied up in the studio and Marsha confided in him, Quentin stopped everything he was doing and touched down in New York.

When she opened the door and saw the look on his face, she remembered that she hadn't washed her body or brushed her teeth in days.

"My mother died… I never got a chance to tell her-" He rushed into her and grabbed her in a bear hug, closing the door behind him. "Quentin, I have nobody, no mama…" she cried loudly from the depths of her soul.

"I'm here, and I'm not leaving you," he promised her.

η

He wasn't perfect. Kadeem never admitted to being the man your mama prayed for you to be with and luckily, he quickly won over Kamile and the uncle that raised Kamala.

Things between him and his lady hadn't been good, and he would partially blame himself, but she had to admit that she had done some wrong as well. However, Kamala was an amazing woman, and he didn't take her for granted. When he was getting his shit together, she was patient and held him down. He had been giving her the run around with setting a wedding date, which was their recent argument, and all he wanted was to spend the weekend with the one who had his heart on lock.

"I wasn't expecting you to do all of this," she admitted to him.

In traffic, leaving court and heading home, she already had her mind on a bottle of wine and catching up on her shows. She was sure that Kadeem would come home right before he knew he would get cursed out for coming in too late and go straight to sleep.

Work was a pleasant distraction for her, and once the weekend arrived, she was forced to deal with her dilemma. And being mean to Kadeem wasn't any fun, she'd rather be laid up with him and giggling, which was what she was used to doing.

"Gotta get you back smiling." He reached over and kissed her lips.

Kamala came home to a few fresh bouquets of roses and a small teal bag from her favorite store, Tiffany's. No matter the size of the bag, it was quality inside and plus, what girl didn't love new diamonds from Tiffany's? She was looking forward to whatever he had planned for her and when he told her to dress up like she used to, Kamala went upstairs with a mission to have his jaws on the marble floor when she returned. And that she did.

He wanted to eat her ass up right on the island, but she told him that it had been way too long since they had date night, and she wanted to be wined and dined.

So, here they were, leaving their first stop which was him getting a haircut while she stayed in the car, and then a mini pre-game at a bar across the street from where he had made dinner reservations for eight followed by a movie. She was super happy to be spending time with him and had been stuck to his side like glue since they left the crib.

"I love you," she told him with lust and admiration in her eyes. When she first met him, the day she was assigned to work with one of the most influential partners they had at the firm, she couldn't believe the man was so damn fine. But her career was on the line. And, he was married. Not to mention, he was rarely seen without Yara. All those years ago Kamala visibly saw the love she had for him and the loyalty, and she pitied that woman. Although Yara was many years older than her, she deemed her to be so stupid and dumb. She often wondered was she now... Yara. Did she love him to the point of stupidity? Would she jump over a bridge for him? Lie for him? Kill for him?

Kamala knew about his past life, she knew what he had done and what he plead innocent to, although he was guilty as fuck. She had seen him at his worst, with tears in his eyes promising his kids that they would see him again. Kamala was present.

And when she glanced at him again, telling him, "I really, really fucking love you," she wanted him to know that for a fact.

Kadeem never had to wonder or ponder on if this was real. She wasn't Yara though. She wouldn't bend over backwards or put her own freedom on the line, but she seriously loved him and all that came with him, including the baggage.

He loved her more and had to do a better job at showing it. "Love you too baby, you up? You good?" he asked her as he backed out of the parking lot and headed to their final destination.

She was tired as shit and her feet were staring to hurt in the new red bottoms she wore tonight, but because she was really enjoying herself, she would suffer and stay home all day tomorrow.

"Yep, where to next, baby?"

η

Fragile is defined as easily broken or damaged, flimsy or insubstantial or easily destroyed. In relations to a person, fragile is defined as not strong or sturdy, delicate and vulnerable.

Quentin would describe his Queen's mental state right now as fragile. She could accept that she hadn't spoken to her mother in x amount of years, she could accept that she was quite sure the woman knew she went to jail and still hadn't tried to reach out, she could also swallow the fact that her mother possibly knew she had three daughters and a husband at the time and never thought to make amends to be a grandmother to her grandchildren, but as long as she knew where her mother lived and that she was actually still living, the discord didn't bother her.

Her mother was a mere memory that occasionally when triggered, made her miss something she never really had. Because truth be told, she didn't have much of a mother to begin with. She never really had anyone. Everyone was too busy "churching" to notice her. And that was her issue with church folks, something that she eventually had to deal with and let go, but they spent so much time, years in fact, preaching how to love and teaching on the fruits of the spirit and living right and doing the Godly thing like forgiving people, not casting the first stone, or judging your neighbor, and what did they do? All of that and then some.

Her family was so focused on looking good for the members of the church that they were suffering internally, especially her.

"Hungry?" he asked her once she appeared in the kitchen, looking at him with a tilted head, trying to read his mind while he tried to read hers.

"My mom is dead." She could process not talking to her mother, but to know that she was dead, and that they would never have another conversation again, even if it was one-sided, even if the woman never wanted to speak to her again or even see her, hurt her to the core. Yara had so much to say. She had so many harbored emotions and feelings that she had tucked deep in her heart many years ago, and the other day, she was prepared to lay it all out on the coffee table and move on. However, that wasn't possible now. Her mother…. had died.

Quentin sat his phone down on the counter along with his iPad and notepad. "Yes, I know. Do you want to eat?" He wanted her to put some food on her stomach. The wine paired with her emotions wasn't a meal.

She shook her head and crossed her arms across her belly. "I was happy to meet your parents." Her eyes met his again. She needed a reaction from him for her to feel comfortable.

"They felt the same way, and they love you already."

She took a deep breath. "I want that… I wish I had that with my parents," she admitted. She thought to herself, *or anyone that wasn't associated with my ex-husband.* She got fatherly vibes from KK, but he was Kadeem's father and before the lies, Charlie was a motherly figure to her.

Quentin reminded her that she wasn't alone. "And as much as I love my parents, it would make me feel good if you were meeting my biological parents."

Yara came a little closer into the kitchen, hers wasn't nearly as big as his. "Thank you for being here. I know your schedule is probably all messed up right now." She didn't want him to put his life on hold for her.

"Don't sweat it, I'm where I want and need to be," he said and he meant every word.

She closed her eyes, thanking whoever was above listening to her. Hopefully, it was God. "I think I am hungry."

Quentin smiled at her and then stepped forward to pull her in for a hug. "Give me a hug." He wanted her in the worst way right now but knew that sex was most likely the last thing on her mind. He wasn't a selfish man.

To his surprise, she was hungry for him, and not just food.

"Did you say hungry or horny," he whispered as she stuck her hands into his pants and squeezed that hard thing that had been driving her up a wall for a little while now.

She smirked at him and told him, "Both" as she dropped to her knees, pulling his pants and boxers down as she went to the floor. With his dick in her mouth, she mumbled, "What would I do without you?" She began to suck him harder than the last of the meat on a turkey wing.

"Shit, baby, I feel the same way," he grunted as he tilted his head back and bit into his bottom lip to keep from screaming out like a bitch.

Yara had told him on several occasions that she loved to hear him say her name, even if he was whispering it for only her to hear.

He told her he only did that when she was doing something to make him say her name, and so every time they were active, that was her mission. She wanted to hear her name come from his lips when she was sucking his dick or riding him like a ride at the fair.

"Hmmmm…" Giving him fellatio made her pussy wet. Pleasing him did her justice because she knew once she finished up he was going to plummet into her as if his life insurance policy depended on every stroke. Quentin's love making was splendid. He had her mind so gone, and she was trying her hardest to stay cool and calm about how good he made her feel.

"I want you," he told her. The head was good as fuck, but he wanted to be inside of her warm and wet pussy. He knew her juicy ass was dripping all over her kitchen floor, and he was ready to take a deep dive into her pool. Yara kept sucking, pulling him further into her mouth with every lick. Her eyes landed on his, and he smiled at her. "Shit, you sexy," he said and pulled her up, unable to take it anymore. He had to have her.

She took her clothes off and asked him, "How you want it?" Whatever he wanted, however he desired to have her, whatever position crossed his mind, he could have her in. Yara would do anything to bring him to his climax.

He looked at the kitchen table and then the counters, and then his eyes found the handle to the oven, and he grabbed her up and sat her on the small and barely-there counter and pushed her legs apart.

"I need this," he told her. Work was sometimes stressful and traveling wasn't always fun, but being inside of her gave him peace and being around her became his refuge.

"Me too."

They kissed for a few minutes, rubbing and gyrating into each other. She was horny as hell, and his dick was harder than the last final you take before graduation.

"Quentin, fuck me!" She couldn't take any more of the foreplay and shit, Yara wanted that dick.

He slid into her as fast as he could and exhaled loudly as he grew comfortable inside of her. To drive her even crazier, he moved his dick around in her pussy, from left to right, touching every wall she had and as she got louder, he slowed his pace and stroked her nice and slow.

"Right there? That's your spot, ain't it?" he asked her as he nibbled on her neck and earlobe. She nodded her head, holding her breath as her pussy pulsated.
"Let me get that nut, ma," he begged her, knowing that she was as stressed as he was.

Quentin didn't have the remedy to her problems, and if he could carry her baggage he would gladly put that shit on his back, but he couldn't. And yeah, this session in the kitchen would only be a temporary move to get her mind off what she was dealing with.

"Quentin! Shit baby, yes daddy, hmmmm, Papi." She called him all the pet names she had crafted for him. Yara's head was hitting the top cabinets as she fucked him back. Quentin was thrusting into her with so much force and passion, trying to get that

same feeling she was having since she announced that she was cumming.

The one look he took at her dripping on his dick made his toes curl. His ass cheeks tightened as he felt a big bust coming. He hurriedly pulled his dick out and spilled his seeds all over her belly button. You never know how bad you needed to cum, until you came. His heart was beating loudly, and he had sweat all over his forehead.

Yara was still glowing and blushing. "Damn!" She was drained and was starving for real. He kissed her forehead and backed up to catch his breath.

She told him, "Baby, order UberEats," as she limped to the shower.

Quentin did as she told him and then joined her under the hot water. "We got twenty minutes before the Thai food arrives." He wanted to slide inside her once more before he got high, ate and fell back to sleep.

Yara was on the same page as he was. Instead of responding to him, she dropped the washcloth and tongued him down.

η

"And you hadn't heard from the victim… in how long?" The investigator was trying to make sense of what the parents were saying, or were trying to say. The word "victim" was making her skin itch.

"Please… do not call her a victim, okay? Her name is Ayanna. Ayanna Moreland. And she is a freshman at UCLA, and she was raped. Do not refer to her as a mother fucking-"

Kadeem pulled her back. "Officer, please give us a second," he asked him kindly and walked her down the hall of the hospital.

She was emotional, her head space was fucked up. How could someone do this to her baby? "You gon' let them keep talking about her like she lied or something? She was a *virgin*. Who lies about being raped? It's pretty obvious she was-"

The words barely escaped her mouth good before she lost it again. Yara didn't expect to allow Kadeem to comfort and console her. But here they were, coming together for the sake of their daughter.

Meme had been blowing Yara's phone up, and she answered as soon as she saw the slew of missed calls. Meme asked had she spoken to Ayanna because she was back in California for two days and wanted to take her lil' sister to lunch.

Yara told her that she was probably sleeping, that her summer schedule was hectic. And Ayanna was recently saying that she put too much on her plate and needed to get out and enjoy the city.

It was Yara's first day back in the studio since learning of her mother's death, so she was deep in the zone, writing a new song about taking losses and winning at the same damn time. She told her daughter to call her again and to let her know if she got in touch with her.

A day later, still nothing from Ayanna, so Meme went up to the school, only to be told by the resident assistant that Ayanna hadn't checked in to her dorm in two days. And that's when Yara had no choice but to unblock Kadeem and tell him that she was heading to California to check on her baby and see what the fuck was going on.

Meme was on a hunt for her lil' sister, and when they discovered Ayanna battered, bruised and out of her mind in the bathroom of a hotel where she attended a party with a few classmates, Meme's first instinct was to go fight the bitches who left her sister alone, but she knew that Ayanna and she were two different kind of females.

Ayanna wasn't hood or gutter like she and Yanise. She was clueless when it came to watching those around you and checking your surroundings. She didn't know about snakes in the grass and bitches hating on you because you were beautiful. She'd had the same group of friends since she was a little girl, and this was her first time being around new people. And her little sister was gorgeous, she was often mistaken to be an Instagram model.

Ayanna was oblivious to her thick thighs, voluptuous breasts and daring smile. She didn't think she was ugly, to her she was just another chick in the hood with a lil swag. Which was another reason she was so anxious to move so far away from New York.

"I'm going to kill them bitches, know that!" Kadeem was enraged. Whoever violated his daughter wouldn't see the light of day for much longer. Ayanna didn't know their names, all she knew was they were on the football team. And it wasn't just one. They ran a train on her, *repeatedly.* She had to get stiches on her vagina and ass.

They didn't bruise her physically. There were no major visible scars, however, mentally she was ruined. How would she ever recover or bounce back from this tragedy? She told her parents that she wanted to leave. She didn't even want to return to her dorm to get her things. So, Meme handled it for her, and she also went to the registrar's office to let them know that as of now, Ayanna wouldn't be starting her freshmen year at UCLA.

Yara wanted to go to the President's office and demand justice. The officer and investigator didn't seem concerned at all, and Meme peeped that one of the men had a UCLA key chain, and that's when she knew that they were protecting their football players.

"Ma, we gotta get a lawyer," Meme told Yara after they returned to Ayanna's room. "Kamala has some contacts here."

Yara said nothing, she had tuned them out. She watched her baby sleep, high off meds. She grabbed her hand and said a silent prayer of a speedy recovery. Yara knew how it felt to be violated, and rape wasn't fair to anyone. She was devastated by the news and the phone call.

"She came here to get an education, they gotta suffer," she cried into her hands. If she were still that old bitch she used to be, them boys' dicks would be cut off and shoved up their mama's asses. However, she couldn't move like that anymore. One, she was a new person and two, she was on probation. Yara had to pray and leave this situation with God, although her trigger finger was itching.

She would never forget her first kill. It was sweet and sinful, and she got the revenge she needed to sleep better at night. Kadeem was right at her side, groping her ass and yearning to fuck her. He was so proud of her.

"I'm gon' lick you all night."

She was still high from the kickback of the shot, and her adrenaline was rushing. "Are they dead?" She wanted to make sure she killed all four of them. They had wreaked havoc on her life, and she wanted them GONE.

"Yep, you got good aim, baby," he said and kissed her again.

Yara was in a daze, she wasn't stunting him touching all over her. She had killed the men who fondled her at church in her grandfather's office while he preached and prophesied while her aunt looked on.

Kadeem didn't know that he had awakened the beast that lived deep down inside of her.

Chapter Twenty-One
"Show too much of your heart, I promise they'll confiscate it." –

Wale

"I'm sorry, baby." Her bottom lip poked out as she watched him throw around the few things he brought to California to enjoy some quality time with his boo. However, Meme had been working like crazy, and all they did was have a morning quickie… two days ago.

Riq was stuck in her hotel room by himself and other than sleep and smoke, he did nothing. She texted him every few hours promising that she was wrapping up and would be there soon so they could do brunch, go shopping or any of the things they used to do.

He told her, "It's good, baby. This is the life you always dreamed of." And he meant that sincerely.

Things had changed between them. He knew it, and so did she. She wanted to hold on, and he wanted to let her be free. Meme was young, she had goals and shit. He was a street nigga with two kids and two baby mothers, and he wasn't leaving New York.

"The life I've dreamed for *us* together, Riq," she corrected him. He was the only man she ever knew, he made her a woman. His voice held so much uncertainty, and she worried that he was slipping away from her all because she was across the map grinding. "I'm going to be home soon, Charlie has surgery. She don't think we know, but KK told us."

And while she was home, if she wasn't with her family, she wanted to be up under him, like old times. Meme loved California, and if there weren't any soul ties back home, she would move to California for good. However, Riq owned her heart and home was the heart was, and in her case, that mattered. She didn't want to gain all the riches in the world if she didn't have the man she loved by her side.

"Cool, just hit me when you get out there."

Meme put her lipstick down. While he was preparing to head to the airport, she would be going to work. A new reality show was being filmed, and she was one of the stylists. Every day she thanked God for her mama because if it weren't for her, she wouldn't have any of these opportunities.

Quentin was always showing love. He was in L.A. about two weeks ago and took her for lunch, something her father never did. And surprisingly, Meme found herself asking him questions and soaking up any advice he had to offer. He told her that she was young and should spend this time of her life making as many memories as she can.

She texted her mom after he dropped her off and told her that she was so happy for her and Quentin was the man for her. Yara, being who she was simply texted back and said, "He all right" but deep down, she knew her daughter was telling the truth.

"Why are you saying it as if we not going to talk before then?"

He chuckled, "Are we? I doubt it. Either you gon' be busy, sleep or my new favorite one, your phone is dead." His voice held so much sarcasm that Meme honestly didn't know what to say back to retort what he said. "It's good, shorty. I'm a grown man, my feelings don't get hurt," he played it off. A blind woman could see that he wasn't okay with how things were between them.

She dropped her head and took a long deep breath, wishing the words would flow from her mouth, something to make him see that she wanted him and her dreams too. She could have both. A few miles apart and a couple missed calls shouldn't be the reason for their demise.

"Riq, you've always respected and loved me because I was a go-getter," she reminded him.

And she was right. "Yeah, and I still do… that's why I'm letting you do you." He would still be around.

"I love you, I don't want to stop loving you or you to stop loving me."

He walked over to her and kissed her lips. "How can I not love you?"

She was beautiful, his favorite sight in the morning and before bed. He was a nigga who had fell in love unexpectedly and now she wasn't available. Riq loved her, that wouldn't stop, but he was damn sure about to fall back. Meme was gorgeous, and he knew she stuck out in California. Not only did she have her own flavor, but she was from New York, so she had that northern charm that niggas loved when they were from somewhere else, and she was pushing her mother's boyfriend's whip; one of plenty that he had at his California home.

Temptation was a mother fucker, and Riq refused to be at home being faithful while she was out here. He came to Cali with good intentions and left with doubt. Long distance relationships weren't his thing. He had never been in one before but knew that it wasn't for him. This weekend proved that to be true.

η

The bags under her eyes were only a glimpse of what she was going through. On the outside she was trying to hold it together, but she was suffering.

Charlie knocked on her bedroom door, startling her. Ayanna dropped the mug of Chamomile tea and screamed, terrifying her sick grandmother.

"I didn't mean to scare you," Charlie apologized. She was walking on egg shells around Ayanna. Ever since she returned home from school and the rape, her grandchild had not been the same.

Ayanna pounded on her with awful words as tears streamed down her face, "*What do you want?*"

Every little thing petrified her. Every night when she closed her eyes, horrid memories of them climbing on top of her would force her pupils open. She'd rather stay awake. Ayanna was suffering from insomnia. How would she ever be normal again? She didn't know.

Yara suggested a few sessions with her therapist to help her recover, but she refused, and the fact that her father didn't agree with therapy and was vocal about his opinion didn't help either. Sometimes, she wished they would have killed her. She would rather be dead.

"Nothing baby… nothing." The sparkle in both of their eyes was gone.

Charlie wasn't so sure about having surgery to have a pacemaker put in. She felt good on the inside, but her doctor told her that her heart was weak, and she still didn't understand why.

Ayanna was brutally raped, simply for being a pretty girl who was naïve.
She hated herself so much for allowing her "friends" to talk her into hanging with the football team. She didn't even know them, and they had her number. Not one person reached out to her since the incident.

Ayanna deleted all her social media apps, and none of her friends back home even knew that she was home. She mentally tapped out of life. Her family was attempting to be supportive, but everyone still had their everyday lives. She needed someone to hold her and let her get it all out. And not one person was available for her to reveal and release, and so, those feelings were boiling deep down in her spirit, creating a monster in her young body. She was only nineteen-years-old and felt as if life was over. That was no way to think, feel or live.

Charlie closed her door and went into her room and cried. She was failing everyone. Yanise had an abortion, Ayanna was raped, Kadeem was a maniac and the one person who had loved her unconditionally was now a stranger in her own home.

KK arrived in town two days ago for her surgery but had barely said two words to her. He slept on the couch and spent the last two days away from her house. They hadn't said much since she proposed, and neither of the two initiated a conversation about what was going on between them and how to move forward. If it were that easy for KK to discard his feelings, then Charlie didn't want him anymore.

She pulled it together and took a shower. Her doctor's appointment today was the last one she would have before surgery tomorrow.

KK stood up when she made it to the living room. "Ready?" He seemed so unconcerned or interested in her, and it bothered her so much.

She nodded her head. "Yes, let me tell Ayanna that we are leaving." As she turned on her heels, she opted out and decided to text her instead, not wanting to scare her again.

Charlie told Kadeem last night that she was fearful of leaving Ayanna at home by herself, she wasn't confident that she wouldn't self-inflict if left alone.

The girl had been raped, she no longer trusted anyone. Charlie heard her cry at night, and she couldn't remember the last time she saw her eat.

KK was waiting in the car on her and when she got in, he turned the radio up. Charlie got the hint, so she remained quiet, wrapped in her own thoughts.

The appointment was a quick one, but still, something about going under frightened her. She told KK once they made it back home, "If something happens to me, can you move here? Kadeem will need you."

Charlie was convinced that she wouldn't make it out of her surgery. It was as if she vividly saw her death, funeral and all. Her concern was how her son would take losing her, for so many years she had been all he had. She spoiled him and even raised his kids when he was perfectly capable of doing so. What would Kadeem do without his mama?

KK shook his head. "You will be fine, Charlie, and Kadeem is a grown man." He didn't baby him the way she did, and he wouldn't hold his hand through life. That wasn't his job as a father. He raised his sons better than his father did him, and both of his kids went the street route and were now legit men. That made him proud. He didn't agree with everything Kasim and Kadeem did and rarely voiced his opinion, he only served as a listening ear, a sounding board. In life, it was important to make your own decisions not based on what others thought you should do. There is nothing wrong with taking advice and seeking counsel, but at the end of the day, you must do what's best for you. And KK always told his boys that. He did nothing he didn't want to do, nor did he worry about making everyone else happy while he struggled with his own joy. He was his only priority these days. And after Charlie's surgery, he would be moving on to the next chapter of his life.

η

Few people knew of Quentin and Yara being a couple. Those who knew were most likely close friends and their inner circle, which didn't consist of many people. She didn't care who knew, and he didn't either. And thankfully, when they were out people didn't ask they just smiled and kept it moving.

In the studio, Yara had built a team, a power squad of her, the same young girl who recorded her first song, an engineer and a pianist. She loved the sound of the piano, and most of the songs she had written and produced had a melody that included the keys, either in the intro, the bridge or the end after the beat fades.

She loved her job because Marsha was one of her best friends and she made work fun. Her side-hustle was writing songs and producing when she had time. The only person she would stop whatever for was her kids and Quentin, her boyfriend.

He flew her out to Miami to get her advice on an album for one of his artists. She asked him why couldn't he email it to her and then he lowered his head between her thighs and showed her in that way. Now, here they were an hour later.

Yara was glowing after that beat down he put on her kitty, and he was faded.

Quentin sat on the couch, in the back of the studio and out of the way. And she was at the soundboards, nodding her head, adding her extra touch on a few songs.

He couldn't take her eyes off her ample ass and got up and came behind her, wrapping his arms around her waist, not caring that the studio wasn't just the two of them.

She froze up and then relaxed once she got a whiff of his cologne. "What are you doing?" she whispered to him.

He didn't care who the fuck was looking. "I miss you, I'm ready to go." They hadn't been there long, but he needed another round with her.

She turned around and kissed his lips. "One more hour, let's perfect this. Business first." She then gave him a serious look and got back to work.

Quentin could do nothing but respect it. He patted her butt and then went to sit back down, impatiently waiting for his shorty to finish.

One hour became seven and when they left, Yara was in the passenger seat with her head against the window. She was sleepy and lightly snoring. His hand rested on her thigh, and the weather in Miami was perfect. He loved when it was cool and slightly windy.

Once they made it to his place he woke her up, and she smiled at him. "We got here fast."

He was speeding actually. "You are so beautiful." He was always showering her with words of admiration. She blushed every single time.

"Thanks, baby." Yara saw something in his eyes and asked, "What's wrong?" She didn't compare him to her ex-husband, nor did she assume he was fucking around when he didn't answer. Or when they were together, and he was on his phone while they were chilling, her mind didn't jump to him messaging a chick. And if they didn't have sex for a few days, she didn't assume that he had fucked someone else. That took a lot out of her to not do or think that way, but he made it easy for her. He was kind, attentive and most importantly, consistent. Yara now believed that what was for her, was for her, and when it wasn't, then it was a lesson. She was giving love a second chance, and you couldn't do that fairly and hold on to your past and be bitter at the same time.

"Do you trust me?"

Had Quentin read her thoughts? She didn't hesitate as she answered him, "Yep, with everything in me." He strummed his hands across the steering wheel, contemplating his next sentence. "Talk to me," she told him, not wanting any secrets between them. Her last marriage was full of conversations they never had because they were trying to protect each other's feelings.

"I'm starting my own label, I want you to come on as my VP," he blurted out. Did she hear him correctly? He continued, "Nash is my brother, it's no ill feelings. I just want to do my own thing, and I want to do that with you."

Quentin had made great strides with Nash, and it was all love. But, he was moving in a different direction than him. His vision was to expand and take over the industry, and Nash was growing tired. He was rich as fuck already and wasn't grinding how Quentin was. Some people yearned for wealth and then got it, and that was it. They worked to get where they wanted to be and then paused. That wasn't Quentin Brooks. He loved what he did, whether a dollar was attached to it or not.

"Vice president," she more so repeated it to herself for confirmation. Who would have ever thought this would be her life?

He told her, "Let's do this power couple shit all these chicks be talking about on Instagram. We can do that for real, baby." He had so many ideas. Quentin knew the office space he wanted, logo, name and everything. It wouldn't be right if Yara wasn't by his side. She was the Bonnie to his Clyde, and she grinded how he did, so why not get some real money with her?

Yara was speechless. She was so fucking excited, but she had to talk to Miko about it to make sure they were good on the personal side. "Have you told him that you wanted me to do this with you? I do work for them, they gave me a chance…" She didn't want to seem disloyal or ungrateful because she truly was.

Quentin shook his head. "I had to talk to you first, but let me handle that."

She still needed to reach out to her friend, it was the right thing to do.

"Is that a yes?" he was anxious to know her answer.

Yara took that damn seatbelt off and crossed over the car to his side, and kissed him in his mouth. *"It's a hell yes."*

η

"Charlieeeeeee…"

She heard someone's voice, but it sounded so far away.

"Move, Yanise, give her some space," Meme chastised and pulled her back.

Ayanna was there, in the corner dressed in slouchy clothes. She barely said two words to her sisters when they picked her up to go check on their grandmother who had surgery.

"Mama?" Kadeem touched her hand. The nurse told them that she would be a little drowsy after surgery.

Charlie heard them talking, and her eyes fluttered open. They all smiled.

KK was in the lobby reading a book and having a coffee with Kamala, who he was understanding a little better. Charlie never gave the poor girl a chance, and because of the circumstances, he understood. However, Yara and Kadeem were now divorced, and both had moved on.

Charlie squeezed Kadeem's hand. It wasn't a strong grip but enough for him to have some peace about his mother's surgery.

She wondered how they knew. That damn KK. How could she expect him to not tell her own son and grandchildren? They would have been so hurt.

"She look good to me. Can she eat?" Yanise asked the nurse. The lady shook her head.

"Ayanna, come say hey to Charlie."

Ayanna didn't move. "For what? I live with her, I'll be there when all of y'all leave," she mumbled under her breath.

Meme gave her sister a sympathetic look. "I'll be here for two weeks, sis. You won't be taking care of her by yourself. If you want to link up with your friends, you can," she suggested. If she could get away with killing those fuck boys that raped her sister she would, and she expressed it to her daddy more than once. For her sisters, Meme would do anything. Those were her hearts.

"I'm good." She didn't want to see anyone. Ayanna was supposed to be enjoying her freshmen year, not back home in the fucking hood. She didn't work her ass off for nothing.

"When are you going back to school?" Yanise asked, quite frankly sick of her sister's attitude. Yanise was pregnant and had an abortion not even a week later. She got over it, and in her opinion, her sister needed to do the same.

However, it was not that easy, and she didn't understand that nor did she ask. Yanise was sexually active, Ayanna wasn't. Yanise was a willing participant in what happened to her, which resulted in being pregnant. Ayanna was a proud virgin and had no burning desire to even have sex. And not just one person, but several scarred her by snatching her innocence from her without her permission. Yanise had no idea how that felt.

"Never," Ayanna finally answered.

Kadeem spun around. "What you mean never?" Surely, they all expected her to return next semester. They understood taking this semester off, but never?

"Exactly what I said."

His daughters had smart ass mouths that they must have gotten from their grandmother and sadly, he had grown accustomed to it.

"Sis, you gotta go back to school, you worked so hard," Meme told her. The voice she now used when she talked to Ayanna was so annoying to Yanise. She was not a baby, and they were treating her like one.

"Oh, and when are you going back, Meme?" Yanise asked her since she was out here pressing Ayanna.

Kadeem shook his head, "Y'all gotta get it together."

They then looked at him, wondering when was he going to get his own shit together. No one said anything.

"Let's let her get some rest," Meme suggested because they weren't even focused on her, the subject had been changed twice. Before they filed out of the hospital room, they kissed her gently.

KK stood once they made it back to the lobby. "Is she up?" He was such a calm man. They all were worked up about the surgery but not him. He heard everything the doctors said and was confident that everything would be fine. And it was.

Kamala looked at her fiancé to make sure he was okay, mentally. He seemed fine.

"What are you doing here?" Kadeem was so fucking tired of Riq popping up at all the family functions and shit. He didn't really fuck with him like that no more, and it was vice versa.

Riq pointed to Meme and then handed her a bouquet of flowers that put a sure smile on her face.

KK was amused at the young boy's courage to do so.

Yanise and Ayanna were saying in their heads, *finally, nigga!*

And Meme was praying that this didn't become a big deal.

"Checking on Ms. Charlie," he told him coolly. Kadeem didn't pump fear in his heart. He was a fuck nigga in his eyes, and he had absolutely no respect for him.

Kamala was now holding and squeezing his hand to keep him calm and rational.

"You need to leave, and I don't want to see you no more." He meant every single word.

Meme spoke up, "Why, Daddy? Look, me and Riq are together. There, I said it," she exhaled. She had been holding that secret for so many years.

Kadeem shrugged his shoulders. "Was together, you single now. Bye, nigga," he told Riq. He would lay him out in this hospital. Riq wasn't his lil' homey no more, which was sad because he had raised him like a son and gave him all the tools to succeed and get the money he was getting now. Oh, how quickly did mother fuckers forget?

Riq thought he was funny, and he was feeling real bold today. He stepped to Kadeem close enough so only he could hear him and said, "How you feel knowing I made your daughter my gutter bitch?"

Everyone gasped as Riq landed on the floor. Kadeem knocked him the fuck out. He was tired of people taking advantage of his daughters. Was it too late for him to step up to the plate and be a father?

η

Therapy was a hit and miss for her. Sometimes when she left, she was good and would tell herself she could have gotten her nails done instead of sitting with her therapist talking about past episodes of Housewives of Atlanta and then other sessions, she couldn't get out of bed the next day. And because she had been having the same nightmare for the past few days, something told her that this was the session she had been avoiding. And it was finally here.

Everything in her life was going so good, and then she got the call about Charlie having surgery from KK, who thought she should know.

"Yara, you keep zoning out. What's going on?" She picked up the mug of tea and sipped it then sat back.

"Did I tell you my mother-in-law had heart surgery?" Yara started off. Her therapist shook her head, and so she continued, "Yeah, she's doing okay, it was last week."

The comment was random and had nothing to do with what they were discussing, so her therapist asked her, "How do you feel about her having surgery? Does it affect you?" Clearly, there was an underlying issue here.

She took a deep breath. "My mother died."

From her notes and past sessions, Yara had never said anything about her mother dying. "When was this?" She got up to look through her notes because she knew that it wasn't previously mentioned.

"It's not in your notes, I just found out. She died a few years ago, and I don't know how to feel."

Her therapist pondered over her own thoughts before saying, "Does this have something to do with your mother-in-law having surgery? If it's okay, let me ask how you would feel if she didn't make it out of surgery?"

Instantly, the dam broke. Tears flooded her eyes and slid down her face.

Her bottom lip trembled. "I don't know," she wept.

The therapist rushed to her side and patted her back. "Okay, let's unpack this." She always used that phrase whenever she saw Yara opening up.

"She was the only mother I ever had, and I'm so mean to her. I give her my ass to kiss every time I see her now. And had she died, I don't know what I would do. My real mama is dead, and I never cared to reach out to her because I always had Charlie," she sobbed uncontrollably.

"And have you visited her?"

Yara shook her head. "No."

She stayed away, feeling that Charlie now had Kamala, who Yanise told her had been over there a lot lately seeing about Ayanna and Charlie. She knew that Ayanna and Kamala had a relationship, but she had taken Charlie from her too.

"I think you should see her, I'm sure she misses you."

Yara was so fucking stubborn, she had always been that way. "My mother is dead, we never got to talk. There was so much to say," she admitted out loud.

"What would you tell her if she were here right now?"

Yara closed her eyes shut. Forgotten memories of her childhood resurfaced, and conversations she had tuned out replayed in her mind. Her own problems, past and demons then began to play like a movie in her head.

Yara opened her eyes. "I lost my son, and I needed her. I wanted no one else but her." *Whew.* That's the one load she couldn't seem to drop from her back; the loss of her son, her child. He came from her.

"Why did you need your mother? Didn't you have Charlie?"

Yara looked at her with bloodshot eyes. Her therapist questioned her own mind state today being that she could now clearly see Yara's slumped shoulders and absent smile, and she wasn't super fly today. Her hair was messy, she wore no makeup and her clothes didn't match, nor were they ironed. She seemed out of it.

Whatever this was that she had been dealing with was affecting her heavily.

Her hard truth was everyone not loving you how you love them. The one pill that took her forever to swallow was being lied to. It pained her something serious. When she was released from prison and learned of everything that had transpired behind her back, several emotions went through her body.

Regarding Charlie, it was nothing other than betrayal. Their trust was gone. She trusted her with her life and her children's lives. Charlie was her person. They didn't always get along, and when they disagreed it was because Charlie was such a strong person and would tell her to stop letting Kadeem run over her.

Many times in relationships, a man's mama was never on your side. No matter what their son did, he was still righteous in his mama's eyes. Not Charlie.

She called Kadeem out on his shit and told Yara on several occasions that she shouldn't be running the streets with him, risking her freedom *and* dealing with his flaws.

That was all too much, and Kadeem used to get so mad at Charlie for not minding her business. Over time, he got it together, but by then the damage had been done.

Her therapist asked her again, "Yara, tell me why you're so emotional right now. Why do you feel so bad about not being there for your mother-in-law, who's not really your mother-in-law anymore? You are divorced," she reminded her.

Yara shook her head; this woman didn't understand. Her relationship with Charlie had nothing to do with Kadeem. They met because of him, but he didn't play a part in the bond they built.

"Charlie is the only mother I ever really had."

Chapter Twenty-Two
"We gotta make it up out the hood someday, some way." – Jay-Z

Now and then she would go real hood on him to remind him of who she was, and she was not the one to fucking play with. The curse words were flying out of her mouth so fast he could barely keep up with what she was saying. And not only was she calling him every mother fucker and black nigga in the book, but homegirl had the finger nail in his face, poking his long, pointed nose, and her eyes were rolling and neck snaking.

"Man, get back," he finally yelled at her. She had been screaming at him for the past thirty hours, non-stop. "Damn!" He wiped the beads of sweat that formed on his forehead. He was frustrated as fuck, and her constant bitching was getting on his nerves.

"Kadeem, I already sent the save-the-dates, so whatever you're going through, nip that shit in the bud." That was the last thing she had to say to him.

"I feel like you're making-"

"I'm making you what, Kadeem?" She crossed her arms over her chest and stared at him, silently daring him to piss her off even more so she could have an excuse to go upside his head.

"How do you secure a date without asking me? What if I had plans that weekend?"

She rolled her eyes again. "What plans you got without me, nigga? I book your flights. Where you trying to go?" Right now, the only thing he needed to have on his schedule was the wedding. *Point, blank, period.*

"A wedding is two people. You don't plan the wedding by yourself, Kamala. Shit like the date, you were supposed to come to me with. I don't care about all that other shit, but the date? Come on now, man." She didn't get it, and she rarely attempted to hear him out.

"What is so wrong with the fucking date?" she snarled at him. There was something he wasn't telling her, she could feel it.

He was done with this conversation. "Nothing, don't worry about it. Is there anything else?" Mentally and physically, he was drained. She was supposed to be his calm after the storm, but hell, lately it seemed as if she was the tornado after a lil' rain.

"Do you still want to get married? Do you even still want me?" she had to ask him because lately, they weren't connecting. Ever since Ayanna's rape and Charlie's surgery, he hadn't been home much, which is why she started going over to her future mother-in-law's home more often.

"Yes, why do you keep asking me that?" He was so tired of her questioning him about his love and loyalty to her.

"Act like it then!" Tears sprang from her eyes. This wasn't what she wanted. They used to be so happy, but all his baggage was stressing her out.

Kamala used the wedding to stay positive. It was the only thing she had to look forward to, and it was the one thing she felt like his family couldn't taint with their problems.

Thankfully, Yara had moved on and was doing her own thing. She didn't expect her to be so peaceful, but there was no baby mama drama between them, and she was thankful.

Kamala was even more infuriated because she assumed that Yara would be the reason they didn't wed so soon but no, it was Kadeem all on his own. He was holding them up.

"My daughter was raped... she was violated. Do you know how that feels? No, because you are not a parent."

She peered at him and shook her head. "Dating a man with kids is not easy, and I thought that because you had daughters who didn't technically have their mom around would be easy breezy for me but Kadeem, it has not. Okay, so don't fucking come at me with that bullshit." She loved his daughters, although they were extremely wishy-washy. Some days they spoke, some days they didn't. Sometimes they called and texted and on others, she was merely the woman who broke their family apart. But was Kamala really to blame? Was she the reason their parents are divorced now? No, she was not. Kamala wanted him to say something back. "You don't have nothing to say?"

He was seriously tired. "Change the date." That wasn't up for debate, he was not getting married on the day she told everyone. He didn't care that the save-the-dates had been sent, venue booked, things arranged and scheduled for that date. He refused to get married on that day. It was bad luck.

She gasped, "Why, Kadeem? You don't resend save-the-dates, people don't do that." He didn't get it. She loved the way date looked on the paper stock before her and her sister stuffed them into envelopes and sealed with them with a gold "M" for Moreland, her future last name.

He ran his hands over his hair and down his face. "Kamala, why can't you just do what I said?" He wasn't going to tell her. She wouldn't understand and instead of her hearing his pain, she would only ask why that wasn't in the files and why had it remained a secret.

She was a great person, he would tell her that all day. But emotionally supportive? She was not. Kamala was raised a lot different than him. He grew up with love around him, she did not. So, she wasn't necessarily the most understanding person.

"Whatever it is, will you at least tell me one day?" she asked. She had been with him for quite some time now and couldn't relate any significance to that date, so what was it?

He slumped his shoulders. "Yeah," he answered and walked away with his head down.

She watched him wondering, *did she really know the man she was set to wed in only a few months?*

η

"Hmmm, is that a, 'congrats, I'm so happy for you and Quentin' or 'congrats but in your head, you're regretting telling me he's a good person because I just told you that I quit?" Yara was straightforward; always had been, always would be. Yara could be an asshole if she had to.

Miko was her friend, and she was extremely grateful for everything she had done, not only on the business side, but being a listening ear and a good friend. She loved her so much and hoped they could end things on a good note business wise and remain close.

She didn't want things to change between them because of her decision.

She was riding with Quentin for sure and was excited about the new business venture and partnership. Working with your lover was something she had been used to her entire life, but now it was legitimate, and they were about to make a lot of money.

Lauren Howard accompanied them to dinner at La Grata, an Italian restaurant in South Bronx. Marsha was also invited but flaked at the last minute.

Lauren was surprised to hear Yara bark back on Miko but understood why she asked the question, because Miko's congrats was dry as hell, and her face held no emotion or expression.

Yara sipped her champagne and sat back in her seat.

Miko took a deep breath and rolled her eyes. "I am happy for you, let me say that-"

"But?" She knew there was something else she had to say, and it would be nothing Yara wanted to hear. However, she wanted Miko to come on out with it.

"Nash was hurt behind the move, it came out of nowhere. Totally unexpected, and now you're leaving too. Yara, you've become our golden girl."

"And now she has to support her man, and he's making her the VP. Now, if she were going over there to be the receptionist, I'd be giving her the side eye," Lauren gave her unwarranted two cents. Her opinion wasn't popular in the eyes of Miko's, but she couldn't care less. Miko knew that Lauren would keep it real.

"What about us though? We are building a legacy," Miko added.

Yara asked, "You don't think I would want to do that as well, build an empire… a legacy for my kids? You got kids, and I do too."

Miko told her, "This has been my life for quite some time, Nash has been in the industry for years."

Yara wasn't sure if that came out right, and when Miko didn't rush to take it back or clean it up, she knew that Miko meant exactly what the fuck she said.

"I see. I guess I'm copying off you?"

Miko shook her head. "Did I say that?"

There was some tension at the table, and Yara thought it was best if she left before things got crazy between them. "I will see you around. Good catching up with you, Lauren." She patted the table and grabbed her classic Chanel bag and slung it over her shoulders.

Miko didn't even say goodbye, she picked up her cell phone and started texting.

Lauren smiled at her, wishing she could school Yara on a few things. They weren't far apart in age, but she had been through life more than once. Yara was money, it was coming to her. Lauren wasn't a prophetess or anything, but she saw it all over her. Yara was going places, with or without Quentin or hell, even Miko.

Quentin hadn't gifted her much after they shared their love languages with each other, he learned that material things didn't cause her to leap for joy.

Yara heard her name being called from behind her. "Wasup?" she asked Lauren, who came outside where the valet stand was.

"I'm proud of you, and keep me posted on everything. I will be there to support," she said and reached for a hug. It caught Yara off guard. The way Miko carried on in the restaurant really proved her theory to be accurate. "People will love and support you until you start doing better than them or getting close to them."

And that wasn't cool at all. Yara was done with the whole "friend" thing.

Lauren smiled at her. "I get it, you weren't expecting that from her. She's in her feelings, she'll come around."

"She don't have to, I'm fine," Yara told her. Miko didn't get to pick and choose a date to support her. That's not how Yara worked.

"I would have done the same thing, and she would have too, so don't let all of that back there fool you. Miko has chosen Nash over everybody, a few times at that," she shared with her.

Yara knew all about her selfish ways. That was one thing she could say Miko was upfront about, the struggle with balancing her relationships and her friendships. Yara didn't have that problem. And Lauren didn't either.

"I appreciate you." That was the least Yara could tell her because since they met, Lauren had been one hundred.

"Back in the day, everyone already knew which way I was rolling. They didn't even ask me," Lauren laughed, thinking of the good ole days. If Nas said they were going to Africa for one day, she wouldn't dare ask him why they were only going for a day when the flight took fucking forever.

"And what way was that?" Yara asked. She was curious.

It was chilly outside, so Lauren backpedaled toward the door to return to dinner with Miko.

"Whichever way Nasir King was going, baby." She winked her eye and then told her she would see her around.

η

Every kiss he planted on her bourbon skin sent shivers down her spine and every time he touched her, she floated toward heaven. He was gentle, so light with his movements… things had never been this way.

She had been sexing him for a few years now, so she was familiar with his routine, but every time wasn't the same.

However, the way his eyes met hers, the way he tickled her belly button, inhaled her sweet fragrance and stroked her like it would be his last time coming home, she knew they were done.

When she told him that she thought it was best for her to move to California permanently, he hung up in her face and blocked his number. She had just returned to L.A. once she saw that Charlie was doing okay. So, here she was, in the city once again to pack her things and wrap up loose ends, including things with him, which is what it seemed like. Her family was having something for her tomorrow, and it be would be farewell Meme.

Quentin told her that she could stay at a place he owned and had never slept in, free of charge. Love was growing in his heart for Yara's daughters, mainly Yanise and Meme, who he had spent a lot of time with over the past few months.

Meme was excited to start this new chapter of life but didn't want to leave behind the one who had her heart. He was fucking her with so much passion, as if he was trying to prove a point.

"Wait, wait, wait," she panted, trying to push him away. The head was too damn good tonight. She could barely wrap her head around at what he had been doing to her over the past four hours. There was barely a break or a time to catch her breath. He had the energy and stamina of a horse. Riq lifted his head, and his eyes landed on hers once again. A frown plastered his face, and she asked, "What's wrong? I just need a second."

"Why the fuck is you leaving?" He wanted and needed a better answer than "better opportunities" because wasn't shit wrong with living in New York. People moved to NYC to make their dreams come true, so what made her different? Had she met someone else? Was she tired of him?

When Kadeem knocked him out, his first thought was to kill his bitch ass but decided not to. He knew he had Meme's heart and his intentions were pure, that's all that mattered to him.

Meme rolled her eyes and pushed him away from between her legs. He sat up and gave her his back.

"I don't want you to leave," he exhaled.

He had no choice in the matter. "Come with me then," she offered.

"My kids are here, I'm not leaving my kids." He would never do that shit. Was she crazy?

She bit down on her bottom lip, holding her comment to herself because what she wanted to say was, "Your issue, not mine. I don't have no damn kids."

"I don't see why you can't keep going back and forth. What was wrong with that?"

She shook her head, she was tired of doing that. "Riq…"

He didn't want to hear her simple ass excuse. "Yo, just get the fuck out," he snapped, reaching over toward his dresser for the half-smoked joint and his lighter.

"Are you serious?" She couldn't believe him right now. They were enjoying their night, and it was damn near four in the morning.

"You heard what I said shorty, get dressed and scat." He was enraged. Riq had shitted on his baby mother for her and cut all his hoes off, and this is how she did him? He would never love and trust another. Meme didn't consider him when she moved.

"You told me you understood, Riq." Meme was now on the verge of tears. She didn't understand where this was coming from. After she popped up at his crib demanding him to answer the door and his phone, they had a long talk, and that's how they ended up in his bed making love.

"Nah, I changed my mind. I'm good on you. I wish you the best, Amina."
He tilted his head back and blew smoke out of his nose. The clouds disappeared before they could hit the ceiling.

Tears ran down her face as she stared at his tattooed, chiseled back.

He turned around about three minutes later. "You still here?"

She shook her head and snatched the covers back from covering her bare bottom and stomped into the bathroom to wash up quickly and put her clothes back on. When she returned to his room, she finished getting dressed. He remained silent, lost in his own thoughts.

He felt played, in all honesty. "You know, now that I'm thinking about it, maybe this why your ass couldn't keep none of my babies. We was never meant," he chuckled sarcastically.

And before she knew it, she had tackled his ass to the floor and was pounding him with her fists. *"Don't you dare say that shit again,"* she cried hard.

Riq grabbed hold of her hands. *"It's the truth! You don't give a fuck about me!"*

She couldn't believe this was the man she would have run in traffic for.

All she could hear in that moment was her mother's words, *"Never settle, baby. And never love him more than you love yourself."*

She didn't understand what Yara was saying then, but she did now. Meme now had the confirmation she needed. She had made the right choice by moving to California.

She got up and walked out of the room, stopping in the kitchen to leave his key. Meme would never step foot in his place again. Riq was officially a distant memory.

η

Quentin was kind enough to let Yara use the event space in the building of his penthouse. For residents, it was free of charge if you reserved it fourteen days in advance.

The room had a panoramic view of the city, floor to ceiling windows, marble floors and enough space to hold an intimate group of about fifty people. Tonight, the room was full of only family and friends who genuinely wanted the best for Meme, so it was only sixteen people, give or take.

Yara had a chef make a few dishes of shrimp and grits, chicken and waffles, scallops and black bean cakes since everyone was claiming to be vegan these days, and a sangria. Her going away cake was the shape of California, and people even brought gifts.

Meme wasn't expecting to receive so much love tonight, and she really needed it after breaking up with Riq. It took Meme an hour to pull out of his driveway, she was overly emotional and couldn't believe that he tore through her with his words.

"This food is so good," Ayanna whispered to her sisters.

"Girl, nah, try the sangria."

Yara heard her youngest daughter talking about the adult beverage and turned around. "Give me that damn cup." Her lil ass was pushing it.

She laughed, "You act like I got a car and gotta drive home." She didn't understand why her mom didn't let her drink. She had been sipping the last of Charlie's wine since she was little.

"Your mentor is here, what would she think if you were drinking?" she hissed. Her baby girl had done a 180, but they still had some ways to go.

Ayanna fanned her mother away. "You are soooo dramatic!"

Yara wasn't stunting her. She pulled Meme out of the huddle she was in and made her dance and move her hips to Drake's newest release, "Signs." It was one of her favorite songs.

"You drunk?" Meme asked her mother. She had never seen her so… happy. And, she was glowing.

Yara had a weave in, and it was long too, the tresses stopped at her butt crack. She wore tan boho pants and a white bralette with an oversized jean jacket, and her face and feet were bare, per usual. She loved being free.

She sang and waved her arms in the air, *"You wanna dance like Trini."* This was her jam right here.

"Mama, you been drinking?" Meme questioned her again.

She shook her head and told her, "I'm on top of the world, baby. Ain't no drink or no smoke can give me this feeling." She was joyful. Everything in her life was working itself out.

She was thankful for her kids, her man, her passion and her mother fucking therapist. Slowly but surely, Ayanna was getting out more, and Yara knew it was because she went to see someone. It wasn't her therapist, but she didn't care as long as she spoke to someone. Kamala's best friend was a licensed therapist, and Ayanna was comfortable with her.

"I wish I felt like you did right now," Meme pouted. She didn't want to keep thinking about Riq, but she couldn't help it. And his childish ass had blocked her on social media, which made it worse.

"You will, let whatever ain't making you better go." She grabbed her chin and looked her deep into her eyes. She then kissed her on the nose and danced away.

Meme went back to sitting with her sisters. "What are y'all staring at?" she asked them, sounding irritated.

"Girllll, Daddy followed Quentin in that room. Who you think gon' win?" Yanise asked.

Ayanna shook her head. "Daddy." She had her money on her Pops.

"Quentin is skinny, but he from the hood too, so I don't know," Yanise told her.

Meme shook her head and went to inform her mother and Kamala, who hadn't said two words the whole night. She and her sister sat on the couch, looking very ready to go.

"Ma, daddy and Quentin are in the kitchen by themselves." Yara was still dancing and crooning to the song. She jerked Yara's arm. "Did you hear me?" She didn't want anything bad to happen.

Yara shrugged her shoulders. "Quentin is the most peaceful man I know, they all right." She couldn't care less. If they were going to scrap, it would have happened so long ago, and if anything they discussed were of any importance, he would tell her when they laid down tonight.

In the corner of her eye, she saw Kamala staring at her, and she smiled. She had no beef. There was no comparison when it came to her past and her present. Kamala didn't return the smile, and that was fine. Yara had made her own peace, Kamala needed to do the same.

Her and Kadeem still hadn't really talked about everything and if they never did, she was okay with that. There was no explanation to appease her anyway. He was better off letting her think what she thought.

For a split second, she wondered should she check on Kadeem and Quentin but left it alone, low key hoping he punched Kadeem in the mouth if he got out of pocket, which he was known to do.

"We haven't formally met. Kadeem."

That wasn't the first thing he said though, and that's why when he stuck his hand out for a handshake Quentin smirked at him and said, "I'm good, what's up?" He wanted to know why he followed him into the kitchen. He came in here to get a napkin and turned around because someone said, "I don't need you trying to buy my daughters, they got a daddy." And then, he backed it up with the informal introduction.

"This... shindig is nice. We could have had this at my mama house though," Kadeem said and shrugged his shoulders.

Charlie was home recovering and couldn't make it. Meme spent the day with her in bed, silently crying over Riq.

"Yara didn't think it was appropriate to crowd your mother's house with people being that she's recovering from heart surgery," he informed him. He chose to not speak on the latter of him "buying" Yara's children. That was some lame shit to do, and it wasn't his style.

"What are you doing with Yara? I'm curious. She's hood, and you are-"

Quentin wasn't a pussy by far. "I'm what?" He was from the hood, so what was Kadeem trying to imply? And what did that have to do with anything? In his eyes, he saw nothing but hate for him, and love for her. This trifling nigga still loved Yara.

"Not her type," Kadeem belted out.

His mind shifted to her tongue wrapped around his balls and how she screamed his name repeatedly, not even ten minutes before the guests arrived... Oh yeah, he was her type all right. Shorty was sprung, and he was too. And even if he wasn't her type, that had nothing to do with him.

"I could be mistaken, but aren't you engaged?"

Kadeem couldn't stand this wanna-be P. Diddy mother fucker. Pulling up in his flashy ass car, giving Meme jobs and places to stay, upgrading Yara, making Yanise think he was the coolest nigga on the planet, and then he had the nerve to come in the party late with gifts and shit.

He said that he was handling something at his penthouse, but really, he was washing Yara off his top lip. That was nobody's business though.

"My nigga...." He grew closer to him.

"I made Yara who the fuck she is, so everything she doing for you, please know I taught her that shit. We used to rob and kill mother fuckers like you," he snarled.

The good thing about Quentin was that he wasn't easily fazed by what someone else had to say. He and Yara had talked about her past. And so, he wasn't surprised by anything Kadeem thought he was revealing to him.

"Is this the part where I tell her to get out and stay away from me? Am I supposed to call my accountant and check my accounts?" he scoffed. Quentin was going to show this nigga how to treat a real bitch because he obviously didn't know how. "You know, I've been trying to stay modest being with her, knowing that she don't care about gifts and shit. But my nigga, going forward every time you see her, she gon' blind you." He was about to boss Yara the fuck up just to prove a point.
She was *his*.

"It ain't nothing you can do she ain't already had. I took care of mine, *well*." Yara had traveled, shopped and been wined and dined. That's why she wasn't easily impressed. Kadeem did a good job of making sure of that.

"Yeah, I've heard, but wasn't none of that in her name now, was it?" Deeds and pink slips only, that's how Quentin Brooks rolled. "And shit, let's not mention loyalty. She ain't never have that from you, did she?" He shook his head and walked out of the kitchen. Kadeem was a joke.

Yara was dancing with her daughters when he rejoined the party. He tapped the photographer that he hired and told him to capture the photo. She was always telling him that she didn't care for pictures, and now she loved them.

He bought her a Nikon about a month ago, and she was so happy. He loved seeing the smile on her face, and he knew that she was the happiest when she was with her kids, working and with him. Quentin would do whatever to keep her cheesing like that. Kadeem came out of the kitchen and walked past him, telling Kamala they would be leaving soon.

Once the party wrapped up, Meme said a small speech thanking everyone for coming, and then had the nerve to say, "Never thought I would have two sets of parents, but I do, and I know I don't say it probably ever, but each of y'all have planted something in me whether or not you know it, and I'm grateful. I'm taking all of those gems to Californiaaaa, baby!" she sang from the top of her lungs and then started bopping. Her sisters joined her, and everyone laughed and clapped. The night was perfect.

Yanise left with Marsha and her daughter, who was now her best friend. Some girls from the shop wanted to take Meme out tonight, and her sad ass needed a turn-up, so she was looking forward to enjoying her night.

Ayanna was staying the night with her dad, and she kissed her mom and hugged Quentin goodbye.

Yara waved everyone out and didn't say two words to Kamala, her sister or Kadeem.

Once they were alone, she asked Quentin, "Everything good?"

He nodded his head and pulled her in for a kiss. "I love you. Don't worry about saying it back, I want you to know though."

She looked at him and then told him, "I love you too."

Quentin would keep the conversation he had with Kadeem to himself.

On the ride home, everyone seemed to be in their own thoughts until Ayanna said, "Daddy, I think I'm ready to go back to school."

Kamala was delighted to hear that but asked her, "Are you sure? It's kind of soon."

She was certain. "Yeah, I don't want to see them... ever again. Maybe I'll go to NYU." She would think about it some more.

"Baby, you ain't gon' never see them niggas again, I promise you that." His hands clenched at the steering wheel as the thought of them violating his daughter made him angry all over again.

Ayanna wished he could guarantee that.

Kamala looked at her fiancé, wanting to ask him so bad what he really meant by that.

Kadeem was growing tired of people taking advantage of the people he loved...

Chapter Twenty-Three
"Let's focus on communication." – Khalid
A Few Months Later…

Charlie was all right. One day at a time… She wasn't smiling as much as she used to, and that was okay. She accepted that everything didn't always result in a fairytale ending. The house was empty now, and that's probably why she felt so lonely. Ayanna returned to school, not in California, thankfully. She stayed close to home this time. Meme was living in Los Angeles and enjoying her new career. She was slowly making a name for herself. And her precious Yanise was excelling in school. She made the Honor Roll and recently went to Cuba for seven days with the STEM program at her school. Yanise spent the weekends with Charlie being that Yara worked a lot, and it required her to travel.

Kamala stopped reaching out to her, giving up on ever having a relationship with her future mother-in-law, and Charlie was relieved. It was something about that girl that she couldn't get with, and she told Kadeem that Kamala didn't really love him. She believed wholeheartedly that if something better came along, Kamala would leave him with no hesitation.

In the back of his head, he thought the same thing. Kadeem had to become a better man and step up to the plate before he lost her.

Charlie shook the thoughts of her people out of her mind and went back to tending to her garden. Now that her heart was functioning properly, she could return to the things she loved, which was mainly her garden. It wasn't big or anything, but it was hers.

Gardening for Charlie was therapeutic. She loved the whole process of digging up the soil and preparing it for planting, watering and fertilizing and eliminating weeds. It was something she enjoyed doing, and it kept her mind off *him,* the love of her life, her baby father and what used to be her best friend. Now, they were nothing, not even associates.

As soon as he saw that she was walking around and getting back to herself, he was out of her house with a wack excuse of needing to check on one of his investment properties in Texas.

Charlie had been down this road before with him, so she knew what was happening. He was pushing back and moving on. What bothered the fuck out of her was that he had been chasing her tail for years. Literally, he would call and ask her what did he have to do for her to become his again. He fucked up terribly in the past, and she never forgave him. He always had access to her bed, but her heart was on an "as needed" basis. When she needed love, affection and attention, he was available. Once she was finally prepared to live her life and do that with him, he recanted his feelings and closed his heart.

They hadn't been intimate in God knows when and when he came up for her surgery, he slept on the couch or in Meme's bed. Charlie and KK were tip toeing around each other as if they were strangers and not friends and lovers for the past forty-something years. The crazy thing was, she really didn't want him to leave but when he did, she realized how long she had been holding her breath around him. She could exhale once he closed her front door.

The house phone rang, and she rolled her eyes wondering who was calling her and why didn't they text. Although she was getting older, she was thankful that she was living to see technology change and improve. Every time she sent or received a text message, she cringed at all the phone calls she had to have back in the day because text messages weren't a thing or answering the phone and asking who was it because caller ID hadn't been created yet. The world was evolving.

Charlie removed her sun hat and glasses and marched up the steps in her backyard and ran to the phone. She breathed loudly into the phone, "Hello."

"Charlie?"

He knew good and damn well it was her, who else would it be. She lived by herself now, he left her alone. "Yeah KK, what's up?"

This was her first time talking to him since he left, but it wasn't the first time he had called. She could tell that he had told Kadeem to check on her more often because three or four times a week now he was stopping by, and it didn't feel genuine.

Her son was dealing with some demons, and all she could do was pray for him and leave him with God. She was done telling Kadeem to do the right thing.

 Her grama used to tell her you could lead a horse to water, but you can't make them drink, and that rang true for her stubborn son.

"Not much, caught you at a bad time?"

She wasn't doing shit, when was she ever? Them girls were her whole life. "Gardening." She was dry and really wanted to know what he wanted.

"Oh okay, weather is nice to start your garden back up."

This conversation was dragging. The days of sitting on the phone all day were over. "KK, can I help you with something?"

"Well, I moved… to Arizona. This is my new number in case of emergency."

She laughed, he had some nerve. "In case of emergency? I didn't need your number," she told him straight up.

"Charlie, I still care about you, and since the surgery that's heightened."

The comment he made didn't even sound sympathetic. He could have kept that shit. "And you know what? I would've rather died on that table than to live with a broken heart. Take care, KK." She slammed the phone down and then put her hands on her hips, refusing to cry. Today was a good day, and that wouldn't change just because he had started his life over without her.

She went back outside and returned to her gardening, telling herself that everything happened for a reason.

"Fire workssss," she hummed the lyrics to the dope ass song she wrote and had given to their very first artist signed to YQ Recordings. When Quentin told her the name, she jumped in his lap and rode that nigga until the sun came up. She had a Charlie horse, and he was limping for two days, that's how much love they made to commemorate their new beginnings and partnership.

Yara was working like crazy and trying to be the best mother she could be at the same damn time. Her therapist suggested they do their sessions over the computer since her schedule rapidly became hectic, and that was working for her.

"Shoulda did everythinggg... See, you hear that? Cut the beat," she told her producer.

Yara's focus was the music while Quentin's focus was marketing and artist development. They planned on staffing people for travel, bookings, artist management and social media branding. Everything was a process, and they were taking their time. Well, Yara was. Quentin barely slept. He had so much faith in the vision of YQ Recordings that he was putting in overtime to get them up and running.

Yara's fingers danced in the air as she hummed the song and bobbed her shoulders. "See, feel that vibe, feel it and let the beat control you, don't control the beat," she instructed her.

Their first artist was a younger girl from Detroit, and she had a lil swag to her. She was a tomboy with a pretty ass face, and Yara loved working with her so far. Her voice was light and melodic, plus she played the guitar. They had a whole vision for her. Quentin told Yara to get a number one hit and not to call him until they got it.

This was day three of no sleep, and they were hibernating in the studio. Yara searched her journal and found a song she wrote a few months ago, and it was perfect. Now here they were at three in the morning trying to lay the vocals.

"You feel me?" She wanted to make sure the girl understood what she was saying.

The girl nodded her head. "Yep, let's do this," she said, attempting to stifle a yawn.

Yara was sleepy too, but she had grown used to being up all night in the studio, yearning for a hit. Whenever they left she would check in with her kids, shower and crash. Her sleeping pattern was off, but it was okay with her. If she were sitting around not doing shit, then she would be mad at herself. Yara was grinding like crazy right now.

Her phone lit up on the table, and she frowned when she saw Miko's name pop up along with a picture of her and Marsha at a basketball game.

"Damn, y'all not cool no more?" one engineer asked, being nosey.

She ignored him and told them she would be right back. In the industry, Yara's name had a little buzz. Well, according to her it was little, but to others, Yara was the mother fucking truth. She was a musical genius.

When the news hit that duo Nash and Quentin Brooks were splitting up, all kinds of stories came out, and Miko nor Nash denied none of the allegations. They could have easily released a statement but never did.

People were accusing Quentin of stealing the money, fucking Miko and getting caught by their nanny. It was literally the sorriest stories, and Quentin had no other choice but to clear his name and tell them that it wasn't a personal decision, more like a business one.

Thankfully, no one knew that Yara was his partner or serving as Vice President, yet. On the blogs, they were questioning what the Y stood for in YQ Recordings.

Quentin posted a picture of the logo of their record label with a caption that read, "It's grind time." In less than five minutes, the picture had about 700,000 likes, and the comments were mixed.

Some people were saying, "bout time" and how Nash was old and washed up and needed to retire, and that Quentin was the brains behind the label and some were saluting him.

Yara hadn't spoken to Miko in so long, but before she could get outside to answer the call, Miko had hung up and sent her a text message. *"Have you heard from Marsha? Worried about her... she hasn't been to work in a few days."*

Marsha... She had been so busy she hadn't spoken to her in a few weeks. The last time they talked the conversation was rushed, and Marsha told her that she loved and was proud of her.

She made a mental note to call her tomorrow morning and to check in with Yanise to see what's been going on over there. If Miko had reached out, it had to be important. Plus, Marsha loved her job, it wasn't like her to miss work.

Yanise was always coming home with stories about how weird Marsha's husband was. Quentin told her to stop letting her go over there, so Yanise cut back a tad but they kept in touch.

She texted Miko back, *"Hey, how are you? No, I haven't but will call her first thing in the morning. I'm sure she's good."*

Miko responded with a *"K."*

And Yara hated how petty she was, especially when she didn't have to be. She genuinely loved Miko and was thankful for everything she did for her. There was no need to be at odds. She was a grown ass woman and needed to grow the fuck up.

Yara never thought in a million years that Miko would be kicking shit this way, but again, she probably never expected her to come up in the world either. And the sad part was, she was only getting started. There was so much more in store for Yara Moreland, the sky was the limit.

η

Lil mama lost a lil weight, her edges had grown back, and no one could deny that she was looking like money and walking like it too. Meme was happy, on top of the fucking world and stacking her money to the ceiling because she had no bills in California. Life was bliss.

Every morning she woke up and did what she loved to do. She was thinking about opening a hair salon in Compton but was waiting on Quentin to have some time to talk to her and let her know if that was a good idea. In her eyes, he was a business guru and a real-life mogul. If she trusted anyone's opinion on making real money moves, it was his.

Meme was doing hair one day out of the week out in L.A. since the other days she was jam packed doing hair on sets for television shows, photo shoots, movies and videos. That one day out of the week she would do hair from five in the morning to the next night. She couldn't believe she was becoming a celebrity hair-stylist. Meme now had loyal clients who wouldn't let anyone touch their hair but her. God had blessed her hands.

She was in New York for a few days to check on her grandmother, spend some time with her sisters and to meet with a graphic designer that Quentin put her in contact with to do a logo for her brand.

Meme didn't have much free time to do anything else when she came to New York, her weekend would already be mapped out. When her friends called saying they missed her and wanted to catch up, her first response was she was tired, but she couldn't remember the last time she went out. And with her recent weight loss, she hadn't shopped for new clothes. On set she wore black to stay professional, so she rarely had anything on other than all black attire.

When they stepped into Starlet's, niggas from all over was pulling her arm trying to get her attention, but that was not the way to go about getting her to stop walking and holler at you.

"Yo, ma."

"Aye, shorty."

"Damn you thick."

They were all in her face, and her best friend told her, "Yes, bitch, stiff on all these niggas, I love it!"

And it wasn't even like that, she was just focused right now. Riq crossed her mind every blue moon, but for the most part, she was doing better these days.

"How is the dick in LA?" another one of her homegirls asked.

Meme shrugged her shoulders and flagged a waitress down, she wanted to order a bottle of Crown Apple and some wings. They moved so slow in the strip club that about time the food came, she would have smoked her blunt and would have an appetite.

"I wouldn't know," she yelled to them.

They all looked at each other and then at her. "You haven't had no dick since Riq?"

Meme's eyes bucked. "Let the whole club know, damn!" She wasn't pressed for sex. Meme worked so much that when she made it home after she ate and showered, she was going straight to sleep. Her parents were always saying they never heard from her other than a text message, and it wasn't intentional.

"Girl, you need to move on."

She did. "I have moved on. I'm not dating right now, but I'm not hung up on his ass either. That's facts. " She was serious too.

Her song came on the radio, and she bobbed her head. "Yesss!" her friends hyped her up. Meme looked good as hell, and they were happy that she was bossing up. She was the one that really got out of the hood and was living her life.
She pulled her skirt down, not wanting her goodies on display. Meme was a classy lady.

Tonight, she wore a red latex skirt, black booties that came up to her ankles and a black bra. Her hair was cut in a blunt bob with a blonde streak on the left side. She did her own makeup and had a fresh set of lashes. All eyes were on her as she lit her blunt. Most niggas liked girls that smoked, she honestly didn't give a damn whether it was a turn on or off for whoever, she smoked because she wanted to. That was the one habit she picked up and didn't put down after she and Riq broke up.

"Riq baby mama need to take her ugly, pregnant ass home," her friend said, rolling her eyes in disgust.

She knew she heard her wrong, so she asked, "Pregnant?"

"Yeah, I sent the screenshot in the group message. You didn't see it?"

She shook her head, she was barely on her phone these days. "No, how far along is she?"

"Girl, too damn far to be in the club," another of her friends chimed in.

Meme looked at the thot and shook her head. Moving to California was the best thing she could have ever done. Lord knows how far gone she would be over Riq if she had stayed. And the fact that the same bitch he swore he cut off was now pregnant or had been pregnant the whole time, made her glad she chose herself and her career over his ass.

"Let's enjoy our night, ladies. I wish them nothing but the best." And she meant that wholeheartedly.

Meme was an upgrade. Riq would never find her again in another woman. Girls like Meme weren't walking around New York. Loyal girls who were pretty, hard-working and independent were rare, and Meme was one of a kind.

η

"I love it. How do you feel?" Kamala asked Kadeem, who looked uninterested in picking out wedding bands. He shrugged his shoulders and stared at the platinum ring on his left hand.

"Yeah, I guess." He was hungry and ready to get high.

She rolled her eyes and asked the jeweler, "Can he see that one right there?"

She was so happy that he had time for her today because he had been "oh so busy" and she really wanted to lock down his ring so she could knock this off her ever-growing to-do list.

Kamala had a good day today and refused to let his sour ass attitude ruin it. "Kadeem, try this one."

He took a deep breath and slid the ring off and put the next one on. She really wanted him to get a Cartier band but his attitude was horrible. He never wore his ring while married to Yara and didn't plan on wearing this one either.

"This is a waste of money," he finally told her. Things were real tight right now, and his money was funny. His investment properties weren't seeing the return he expected, and he had done an awful act and was barely sleeping. The sad part was that she hadn't even noticed. All she cared about was the fucking wedding. It was their only topic of conversation. She never asked him about his day or what was going on with him. Not that he didn't want to get married, he loved Kamala. He just wanted to slow down a tad. She was in a rush with everything.

"Picking out your wedding ring is a waste of money?" How could he even be for real right now? She was growing tired of his moody ways.

"I'm not going to wear it."

The jeweler looked at him, quite amused that he was so bold. Men came in the store all the time looking at wedding bands with no real interest in them but knew that a happy wife equated a happy life, so they bought it anyway.

"What the fuck do you mean?" Lately, her mouth had gotten trashier, and it was such a turn off.

"Me and Yara got tattoos, she didn't make me wear it," he said and shrugged his shoulders, his lazy eyes meeting her now red ones.

She turned to the jeweler. "I'll be back without him." She walked away from him and headed to the car.

Kadeem removed the ring, thanked the man and followed her out.

As soon as he got in the car, she said to him in a sharp and snide tone, "Do I look like a mother fucking Yara to you? Don't ever in your life say that shit again. Are you out of your mind?" In her eyes, comparing his first wedding to their upcoming one was an insult.

"That's not what I meant, and you know that," he said in his defense.

"Kadeem, you said what you said," she moved her hands as she spoke.

He exhaled and reclined his head on the seat. "My head is hurting."

She wanted to slap the hell out of him. "I don't give a fuck-"

"Yo, watch your mouth!" He was tired of her talking to him like he was some lame ass nigga.

"Watch yours!" she spat back.

He was hoping she started the engine so they could head home.

"Is this what you want, Kadeem?"

That question was growing old. "Ask yourself that," he muttered. The conversation was over on his end, he had nothing else to say.

She stared at him for a few seconds before shaking her head, blinking back tears and biting her tongue. There was so much more she wanted to say to him but didn't.

The up and down and unexpected attitude was getting on her last nerve.

She didn't understand what the issue was now. His mother was still alive and doing well, and every time they Facetimed Ayanna, she was smiling and bragging on passing another quiz or test. Meme was bossing up in L.A., and Yanise had recently returned from Cuba and was spending a lot more time at their house and building a relationship with them both since she never really looked at her father as "daddy."

So again, what was the fucking problem? He had nothing to complain or worry about and yet and still, he was down, sour and outright bitter. He hadn't made it to any of the scheduled appointments with the wedding planner. He had no input on the color schemes, songs, menu, DJ and when she asked about the honeymoon, he told her that Miami was cool with him. Kadeem wasn't even trying to put in any effort on making this day special for her.

She didn't care that he had been married before. It was her first time walking down the aisle, and she expected him to be more upbeat. It wasn't fair that she was doing this all by herself, and on the money side as well. Kamala was waiting for him to ask her how much did this or that cost, and it still hadn't fallen from his mouth.

Something was going on with him, and she didn't get paid to read minds, so she wasn't trying to figure it out. Kamala wanted her man back... the one she prayed for and fell in love with. The one that swept off her feet and erased any doubt of love from her mind. The one that did anything to make her smile. The Kadeem sitting next to her wasn't the man she had been dating all these years. He had changed. And ever since Yara came home, things hadn't been the same.

When they made it home, she pulled inside the garage and turned to him. "Don't you ever forget, you got on one knee, not the other way around."

η

She heard whispering from outside of the bedroom door and rolled over, wondering what the fuck was Quentin and them out there doing. He and Yanise acted like kids when they were together and normally she didn't mind, but they had touched down in New York not even seven hours ago. She was tired, her head hurt, her body was drained, and she needed three days of sleep to refuel.

Something fell, and that jolted her to get out of bed. She pushed the comforter to her feet and sat up, blowing steam out of her mouth as her toes met the carpet and she grabbed a robe to throw on her body since she slept naked.

"What in the world are y'all-" Her eyes lit up as they skirted across her not too big living room. How he got all these things in her home was something she would ask him later.

With Quentin Brooks, you never knew what to expect, and she loved it that way because him being unpredictable kept things exciting for her.

"Oh, my Lord," she said slowly as she clenched her heart.

Ayanna teased, "She gotta be happy, she mentioned God."

Quentin told them, "She doing better, leave her alone."

She wasn't stunting any of them, and tears welled in her eyes as she noticed the little things. Not the designer gifts, but the handwritten love notes on the corner of the table. They were all surprised that the first thing she picked up was the cards.

Yanise said, "Girl, it's like a million-dollars' worth of gifts in here, read them notes later." She was anxious to see what he bought her mother.

Yara held her breath as she read one of the notes from her lover,

Everything you ever told me was mentally being recorded for this special day.

Happy 40th Birthday to you, my love. Your first birthday with me and as a free woman, cheers to many more birthdays together. Love QB.

Yara walked up to him and hugged him for so long, whispering in his ear, "Love you, love you, love you." It didn't matter what he bought, she couldn't care less. She was with him because of the joy he brought into her life.

"Mamaaaaaa, open the gifts." Yanise just knew that he copped her mother some fly shit that she would end up taking out of her closet.

It took Yara almost two hours to go through all the boxes. Quentin really over did it, but nevertheless, she was grateful.

She had every bag in the Fall collection of Chanel, Gucci and Louis Vuitton. Not only did he get her new earrings, but she received a Rolex and Audemar that he told them was custom-made for Yara. She also received four Cartier bracelets. Literally, she had told him one day that she always wanted a stack of Cartier bracelets.

More than anything, the gifts she opened were all thoughtful, and she knew he didn't send one of his assistants in the mall to get them. Quentin Brooks copped these himself.

Yara had about ten bottles of Bond perfume, four pairs of red bottoms and the baddest fur any woman has ever seen.

He told her to throw something on because he had another surprise for her, and the girls were surprised as well. Quentin was the best man in the world in their eyes. They wanted someone just like him when the time came. It was so obvious that he loved their mama.

"What else you got her? This enough for all of us," Yanise told him.

Yara shook her head. "Quentin, no, I don't need anything else, baby." She held on to him.

He kissed her forehead. "Come on, baby."

She did as he told her and changed into a jogging suit, brushed her teeth and pulled her hair into a ponytail at the nape of her neck.

The car ride was full of the songs their artist was working on. Quentin wanted to know how Ayanna and Yanise felt about it, and they told him that the songs were hot.

"That's your mama, she the truth."

When they pulled up to a gate, and she snapped out of la-la land, she started jumping up and down in her seat.

"No, you did not! Oh my God! I can't believe this!" She was like a little girl on Christmas, and the smile on Quentin's face was big because those gifts back at her crib were nothing compared to this.

They made a left and then a right. The girls were in the back seat with their eyes glued to the window, wondering where they were going.

She screamed so loud, *"Quentin!"*

They pulled into a straight driveway, and before them was a four-level townhome with a single car garage.

He shushed her and turned around and told Yanise and Ayanna, "When I first met your mother, she told me if I ever wanted to impress her don't buy her a bag. She said, and these are her exact words, 'Buy me a townhouse and a Maybach or a nice ass truck, that's how you really impress me," he mocked her.

Yara was now sobbing. He heard her that day. She got out and stood in front of the house. "Blessings." God was real. Her prayers, the prayers she thought fell on deaf ears and made her turn to false Gods, they were answered.

He came behind her and wrapped his arms around her waist. "Happy birthday, here is your last gift."

He told Yanise, "Press it." She was holding the garage clicker in her hand.

Yara turned her head toward where the sound was coming from, and she almost fell out when she saw a white Lamborghini truck in the garage with a red bow on the top.

"Ain't no wayyyy!" Ayanna was in disbelief. They rode around in Quentin's nice ass cars all the time, but now her mama had one.

Yara's mouth was wide open. This man…. what did she do to deserve him? All she could do was hug him. There weren't enough words to express her gratitude.

Yanise told her sister, "Girl, I'm about to have a whole photo shoot in front of mama car. My Instagram is about to be lit baby, do ya hear me?"

Chapter Twenty-Four
"No one wins when the family feuds." – Jay-Z

"So, how are you feeling about attending church with him knowing how important religion is to him in your relationship?" Her therapist always came on too strong.

Yara gave her a coy smile. "No, how are you doing today? Did you enjoy your birthday?" she teased as she crossed and then uncrossed her long legs.

"Time is of the essence, my lady," she said and returned the same look to her.

Yara took a deep breath and pondered over the question before answering. "I'm going because he asked me. Am I prepared? No. I haven't been to church since I was fourteen."

"You didn't have a funeral for your son? Did you get married in a church?" she had a few questions for her.

Yara shook her head. Yeah, this session would be intense. She could feel her emotions arising already. "He didn't die, he was kidnapped." That was all she would get out of her today. And her wedding day was very different. "No church wedding, we both wanted something non-traditional."

"Do you plan on marrying again?"

She shrugged her shoulders. "I'm not much of a planner, but if he asks, will I say yes? Probably so." She would certainly marry Quentin Brooks. He's been consistent from the beginning and was everything she never thought about wanting or needing in a man. He was attentive, supportive, loving and hard working. Quentin kept her first. Together, they were focused on building an empire. She couldn't see herself not marrying him.

"If he wanted to get married in a church, what would you do?"

"Can we talk about this when and if he proposes?" To her, the conversation was pointless.

Her therapist removed her glasses and scooted forward to get as close to her as possible to make leveled eye contact. "Yara, your boyfriend, who you seem to be getting very serious with, is a devout Christian, the son of well-known Pastors, and his adopted parents are also religious. How do you plan on dealing with this?"

"I pray with him, we pray together." She was making progress, but no one could force her to do anything or believe in something she wasn't so sure about.
She acknowledged that there was a higher power in her life, and that higher power was God. Yara was dealing with church hurt, and no one could heal her of that but... well, she didn't know.

"Is that enough for him?"

She didn't care if it was or it wasn't. "One day at a time. I will never in my life do anything I don't want to do ever again." She spent her twenties doing that, following after her husband, making him happy, being a damn fool, turning a blind eye to what was right in front of her, chasing after dollar bills, living life in the fast lane and taking innocent lives for their own greed. Yara wasn't doing that anymore.

Her therapist got up and grabbed a larger notepad and a black marker. "I have an exercise for you. Write down every word that comes to mind when you think of church and the people that hurt you in the church."

This wasn't something she wanted to do, if she could be honest. "It all happened a very long time ago, I'm good. Just because I don't go to church-"

Her therapist shook her head. "Come on, boo, write it down."

"You write it, I'll throw the words out." She had to have her way, somehow. She closed her eyes, mentally traveling back to one of the darkest times of her life.

Hurt

Abused

Manipulated

Robbed

Chastised

Hypocrites

Liars

Scammers

Molesters

"Fa-" She choked on that last word, Family." When she opened her eyes, her therapist had scrambled the last word and turned the small pad around to her.

"Now, what if we scratch lines through these words, ball them up and throw them in the trash, will you let it go?"

If only everything in life were that easy. "I wish," she mumbled under her breath.

"What did your family do to you?"

That was an easy question that didn't require any thought. "They didn't protect me."

Her aunt was the damn devil. She made her life a living hell. She'll never forget the day she told her that Elder so and so was fondling her in the back of the church, and she called her a liar. Once, she actually caught the four men that had been messing with her for forever and instead of running to get her father, Yara's grandfather, she watched. In her sick mind, it turned her on to hear Yara whimpering and squirming. That woman was going to rot in hell, and Yara wished she would have died instead of her mother.

Her mama, she could have forgiven. She was young, dumb and in love. That could be looked over in Yara's eyes. And Yara never understood how could a grown woman hate a little girl so much.

"I want to challenge you to go to church with your boyfriend with an open mind and a clean heart. Spend the next few days meditating and reflecting on nothing but good things." She then added, "Sweetheart, you have so much to share with your boyfriend. Things that he deserves to know about you."

It was a lot that Yara hadn't discussed with her therapist, with anyone for that matter, and she wondered would her past ever come back to find her.

"He knows the gory details, he still loves me," she poked her chest out.

That's not what she was referring to. "Does he know about your son?"

η

She couldn't go another day without talking to her. Every weekend that she dropped Yanise off at the curb, Yara didn't even pull into her driveway. It pained her to admit that she hated Charlie, and hate was such a strong word, but that's how she felt when it came to her mother-in-law. Did anyone ever count the days in ten years, because it was a lot, a fucking lot.

How could they walk around and even smile, especially during the holidays or her birthday or Mother's Day? Or, what about their birthdays or the important days in their life like prom, middle school graduation, science fair, social studies projects, bad days, good days… all she wanted to know was did anyone ever stop and say, "Damn, Yara isn't here." Or did they think about telling her? Did anyone contemplate defying Kadeem?

Yara suffered in prison. She was beaten because she was pretty, and she had to fight because a woman recognized her as the chick that set her brother up. Shit in there wasn't peaches and cream. It wasn't a vacation, it was fucking hell. She cried until she couldn't cry anymore. Once she accepted that she wasn't going home until she finished her sentence, she grew tough skin. She stopped smiling and counting down until she came home. Ten years. Yara would never get those ten years back. They were fucking gone.

She took a deep breath and turned her truck off. She told Quentin via Facetime earlier that she was going to make amends with Charlie, and he was proud of her.

His comment was, "We being blessed, baby. Can't hold no grudges with people."

And he was absolutely right. If she never spoke to Kadeem again, she would be fine. He was nothing in her eyes. But Charlie... she had been a mother to the motherless, and Yara always thanked her for stepping up to the plate. It was Charlie who told her that women should be graceful and modest and kind and loving. She taught her how to cook and clean, how to care for her kids, how to budget and pay the bills, how to basically be a woman and a mother. She had never been married, but she knew how to love a man. Yara and Charlie needed to talk.

Charlie was surprised to see her on the doorstep when she opened the door.

"Hey, Yara... the girls okay?"

It was sad that the first thing she thought of was bad news when she saw her. They didn't use to be this way.

"Yeah, yeah, everything is fine. How are you? Can I come in?"

Charlie unlocked the screen door and moved aside so she could step in.

It had been a while since she had been inside of the house.

"Is KK here?"

Charlie rolled her eyes. "No, he moved to Arizona, with some young ass girl." She had been lurking his Facebook, and that man was living his best life with some girl twenty years younger than him.

"Say what now?" Yara wasn't expecting to hear that.

"Yeah, I don't care though. What brings you by? You look good. Happy belated birthday." She gave her a hug, and Yara held on to her for a long time.

They both said nothing as they hugged, eyes wide shut.

When they finally released, Yara told her, "I forgive you."

Unlike Kadeem, who only said he was sorry once, Charlie had expressed her guilt repeatedly, and she believed her. She always did, it just took her some time to accept it and let it go.

"Thank you, Yara." She had tears in her eyes.

"How are you really doing, Charlie?"

Heart surgery was no joke, and Charlie looked the same, but one thing she learned from going to therapy was that, that "How are you?" question goes a long way, and some people never ask people how they're really feeling.

People suffer in silence, and you would never know because you didn't stop and ask. When you pick up the phone, it takes one second before you jump into what you need and what you got going on, instead of asking the person on the receiving end how are they doing.

Charlie's bottom lip trembled, and she wanted to lie and act like it was all fine and dandy, but it was not. "I miss him so much." Before she knew it, she was crying hard. KK broke her heart. She was lonely, sad and downright miserable without him. He didn't just break it, he took it off the table while she was in surgery and ran off with it. How could he leave her? They weren't just lovers, he was her friend. She had her latter days planned out, and they were supposed to be spent with him.

Yara gave her another hug. "You still have your whole life though, Charlie, forget him. You not ugly, you can meet someone else."

She was stuck in her ways and all she ever knew was KK. Charlie wasn't interested in starting over. She would be alone until she died.

"Have you called him? Maybe that's all he wants." Yara knew their history, and he had been chasing after her for years.

Charlie was stubborn and prideful, which is where Kadeem got those traits from. KK was a sweetheart.

"I'm too old to be trying to convince someone to love me," she said and turned her nose up. KK knew how she was, and she knew him. Whoever this young chick was had to be important, and that was cool.

Yara sighed but kept her thoughts to herself. She rubbed Charlie's back and spent the rest of the day over there until she got a phone call from Yanise screaming into the phone. Her worst fear had been confirmed. Something was wrong with Marsha, and there was nothing Yara could do about it now.

Her husband had shot and killed her, and their daughter as well.

η

Sadly, death brought people together and in a middle row of the church sat Yara, her daughter, Quentin, Nash and Miko. Behind them sat the rest of their office staff and other label execs that had come into contact with Marsha over the years.

She was loved and so was her daughter. Yanise opted out on sitting with the girls that she had met through her friend. She needed her mother. Her baby girl had never experienced death before, had never lost anyone that she really loved and cared about. Yara rubbed her back while Quentin rubbed hers. She had failed her as a friend.

Lauren didn't attend funerals. She said ever since her husband's funeral she was scarred. She sent flowers and her love in her absence.

The choir was swaying the entire congregation, and there wasn't a dry eye in the room. Yara hadn't slept since Yanise had called her with the bad news. Did she really overlook the signs of abuse, neglect and domestic problems? Yara wondered was Marsha silently crying for help, and she was too busy to hear it.

She blamed herself and Miko did as well. Her whole life she considered herself a bad friend, and losing Marsha only made it truer. She sank into a deep hole of depression, and there was no one to pull her out of it, not even her husband.

Yara bent over and wrapped her hands around her neck. She didn't expect to be in church so soon, especially when she was planning on going in two days with Quentin.

Marsha was her first friend when she returned home. Her bubbly personality, charming smile, light laugh and daring style, Marsha was an amazing friend. She was so supportive, she could come to her about any and everything and whether her advice was what Yara wanted to hear, she would give it to her. The last time they spoke was brief, and she told her that she was so happy for her and Quentin. Yara would hold on to that conversation forever.

"Oh no, this can't be hotshot producer, Yara Moreland calling me? No, no it can't be. I'm in disbelief right now," she *teased as soon as Yara picked up.*

She had to do better with checking in with the ones that loved her. "It's been so crazy, charge it to my mind and not my heart," *she asked her kindly.*

"Girl, I'm teasing you, I think congrats are in order, missy. When was you going to tell me?" She was speaking of the new label.

"Happened so fast," she told her, and that was the truth.

"Well, I'm happy for you. I prayed for you to find love again, Yara, I really did."

She had to do better with nurturing her friendships and checking on people. Her friend was expressive about feeling stuck and being unhappy in her marriage, but she didn't think it was that deep. All she kept reflecting on was how many times Yanise told her that Marsha's husband was insane and creepy. Yanise was dramatic, so she never really knew to what extent did insane and creepy meant, but she also never asked either.

Everyone in the church, not just Miko and Yara, but Marsha's sisters, her mother, her cousins, line sisters… everyone was questioning themselves. After the murder, it was revealed that there were several reports of abuse from Marsha. Her neighbors also came forth on the news that the couple had arguments on their front lawn, which led them to call the police over the years. Of course, the mother fucker was in jail, and Yara prayed they threw the death penalty at his evil ass.

He killed them both and laid them in the bed together. Someone called the police, and he admitted to killing them for being disobedient. She wasn't sure if he had a mental illness or what, but he had taken two innocent lives.

Marsha looked so graceful in the casket, according to Quentin. Yanise and Yara both opted out on going up to view the body. She didn't accept death well and wanted only good images of Marsha, seeing her one last time wasn't necessary for her.

After the funeral, they all crowded in the parking lot, and Miko hugged Yanise. "It will get better, I promise you".

Yara gave her a weak smile, she appreciated her trying to give Yanise hope.

Nash dapped Quentin up. "Good seeing you." They hadn't talked much since the separation.

"Same, my *brother*." Quentin added so much emphasis on the word brother.
Nash's actions towards him came as a huge surprise. They were better than that.

He gave him a tight look but kept his mouth shut until Miko chimed in, "We aren't hating or anything, for the record."

Yara shook her head, that girl needed help. "What is it then?" she asked her.

"I don't understand why we couldn't all get money together, which is what we were doing, we were doing well," she sighed.

Nash stuffed his hands in his pants, he could have told Miko to come on but he really wanted to know as well.

"Our goals became different." And that was as simple as he could put it. Nash really wasn't grinding anymore. He was getting old and was more concerned with his wife and kids. And that was cool, really it was. However, Quentin was still getting that money like the rent was due. He didn't think it was fair to still break bread with a nigga that wasn't in the kitchen kneading the dough.

Yara grabbed Quentin's hand and told them, "Take care", before her, him and Yanise walked off to the car.

η

Yara was so fucking nervous it was ridiculous. She smoked a big blunt before Quentin told her that he was ready. She loved her new home and never slept in the apartment again after her birthday. She didn't have to worry about breaking her lease because the rent was paid up, so Meme would have somewhere to chill if she wanted space whenever she visited.

Yara and Yanise had a ball decorating, painting and furnishing the townhouse. Yara told her that once she started the eleventh or twelfth grade, that she could turn the basement into her little haven. But for now, she needed to keep a good look on her. Yanise had come a long way, but the way her snappy ass mouth was set up, she wanted to keep her close for as long as possible.

She painted the townhouse in different shades of grey with pale blue on a few of the walls, serving as an accent color. The furniture was modern yet comfortable, and Quentin turned one room into a recording studio for her to work in when she was home. She loved the house and barely wanted to leave these days.

"How you feeling?" he asked her as they watched the garage close.

"Church twice in one weekend, fantastic." She was full of sarcasm this morning.

He grabbed her hand. "This means a lot to me, baby. You have no idea."

She rolled her eyes and prayed that this was the fastest service in the world. They spent the car ride wrapped up in their own thoughts while Mali Music played on low. He was an independent artist who specialized in contemporary R & B and gospel. Quentin loved his songs, and Yara loved his voice.

Once they made it to church, she took a long, heavy, deep breath filled with a lot of nerves and weariness.

"Yara, I believe that this church service is going to bless you," he told her in all seriousness.

She said nothing back to him as she unbuckled her seat belt and slid her feet into the nude Pigalle's she wore with a simple navy dress that stopped past her knees. She was dressed for the church service, and Mr. Brooks definitely complimented her fly. He wore a navy suit and a white button-down with a red lapel. They had on their matching Audemar's and together looked like a lot of money as they walked into the church holding hands.

"Can we sit in the back?" she asked him.

He always sat near the door anyway. Today, his adopted parents were joining them for service, and they were going to brunch following service.

"Yeah, my parents are right there waiting on us." They had hit a bit of traffic, which is why they were running a few minutes behind.

Praise and worship were in full effect as they walked down the aisle saying, "Excuse me" as they scooted to where his peoples were. Quentin kissed his mother's cheek and shook his father's hand. Yara hugged them both and then sat down.

She agreed to come to church, she never said she was taking part in service. Thankfully, he didn't turn around and give her a funny look about it.

Quentin lifted his hands to give God praise. Yara was a grown woman, she could do what she wanted. When she was little, her mother would snatch her down the aisle and beat her tail in the bathroom if she thought she was about to sit down in church. She was forced to dance, praise and sing the whole service. But when the presence of God was in the building, there was nothing you could do to ignore it, no matter how hard you tried. God was a big God, He was powerful, He was mighty. And the words the choir was singing were largely displayed on monitors across the screen. Yara looked up and couldn't help but to sing along.

"This is my winning season," she moved her lips to sing, unsure of what was happening to her or why was she crying so hard and so fast.

The woman leading the song was prophesying to the congregation. *"I don't know who this is for, but God said you've been knocked down a million times, and He is telling you to get back up."*

The praise team sang behind her, *"It's your winning season..."*

"Come on church, the Lord is in here this morning." The praise singer tilted her head back and began to speak in a language that Yara was all too familiar with.

She hadn't spoken in tongues in years, though she was blessed with the gift at the age of eight. Her grandparents told her mom that she was a true vessel. And now, she thought otherwise.

She wiped her face, refusing to give in to the worship. "Nope, Yara," she told herself, but the tears kept coming.

"God is saying the battle is already won, give Him the GLORYYYYYY," the woman said.

She shook her head. Fighting with God was the wrong thing to do, but she couldn't help herself.

Quentin looked behind him to check on her and saw her eyes fluttering, lip trembling and her chin covered in tears. He pulled her up off the pew and held her hand.

Yara heard him pray, and it was so beautiful. She was being incredibly stubborn and still, this man was going to God on her behalf.

"Let Go and Let God" was the next song the praise team sang. And that's when she knew… she couldn't fight it anymore. Yara submitted to Him again. She begged for Him to forgive her of all her sins, and she wanted to be made anew in His eyes.

Quentin's mother stepped across her husband and moved Quentin out of the way. She began to pray for Yara and a few other women in the church came over and interceded for Yara.

She didn't know when she stopped crying or when she was sat down, but she was free. Every burden she had been carrying since the age of fourteen was lifted from her, and she had accepted God back into her life for good.

When church was over, she thanked Quentin's mom for praying for her when the words couldn't come to mind. She was truly grateful.

Quentin rented them a room at a popular Soul Food restaurant in Jersey, which was on the outskirts of New York and out of the way of the paparazzi.

Today was intimate. Yara had a real encounter with God, and he didn't want the peaceful aura that was surrounding them to be tainted by extra people, flashing lights and cameras. So, privacy was best for their gathering.

He ordered pretty much everything on the menu knowing that Yara loved to eat.

Platters of fish, fried chicken, roast beef and gravy, mac and cheese, dressing, collard greens, shrimp and grits, chicken and waffles and peach cobbler came out one by one.

Yara's fat ass lit up at all the food. "Hmmm, I'm definitely not cooking today."

"You cook? Quentin didn't tell me that, we will have to do dinner soon," his mother said.

Yara nodded her head. "I can cook. Not as much as I wish though, but I would love that."

"My son tells me that you have kids, how old are they?"

"Big girls," she laughed. "Fifteen, eighteen and twenty-two."

His parents were obviously shocked. "Girl, how old you are you? We were worried that you were barely over twenty-one," his mom admitted.

Quentin gave his mother a confused look. "Are y'all for real right now? She looks young, but she ain't!" he cleared that up.

Yara playfully nudged him in his side. "Chill, cus we ain't that far apart," she reminded him and winked her eye. Gosh, she couldn't wait to get home and suck him until the night fell.

Thankfully, Yanise went to Charlie's house after the funeral. They didn't get a chance to christen her house yet, and tonight they would be starting on the bathroom and bedroom before making their way to the kitchen. It was something about getting her pussy eaten with her back on the cold marble top of the kitchen island that did something to Yara.

"Well, however old you are with three big kids, you look amazing, honey," his mom said with a warm smile.

His father asked for everyone to join hands in prayer. "Father God, we thank you for this precious day. God, you showed up today in that service, and we thank you Lord for your grace and mercy. God, bless this food that we have received, bless the hands that prepared for it. God, we thank you for this angel that my son has found. Bless their union and stay in the midst of it, it's in your son's name that we pray, Amen." His dad had a loud and hearty voice, it held so much might. These weren't Quentin's biological parents, but he clearly had a lot of their ways.

"Amen," everyone said in unison.

They all dived in at once, and the conversation flowed with no awkward moments on the way home.

"Can I ask you a question?" she asked Quentin. He nodded his head, twirling his hand in hers as he drove to the crib. "Do you think it was weird for your parents to be in the same church that your dad pastors?"

He told her, "Nah, as long as I'm under the Word, that's all that matters to them." He had practical parents, and he had stressed them out so much growing up. They were very proud of the man he had become.

"Have you ever thought about talking to him?"

Quentin shook his head. "For what? I was raised by the best parents in the world. Most people go into foster care and be fucked up, that wasn't my case at all. That's a blessing, baby." He was right about that.

Once they got home, she kept hearing her therapist's raspy ass voice playing in the back of her mental. She took her church clothes off and slipped on a two-piece pink pajama set and went searching for her boyfriend.

"Babe?" She found him in the den smoking a blunt with a glass of wine at his feet, listening to his favorite album and singer.

"You looked relaxed." He smiled and patted the seat beside him.

Yara shook her head. "I need to talk to you, and I want you to hear me and don't interrupt me, please Quentin."

He told Siri, which was connected to the HomePod speaker that Apple had just dropped, "Pause, Prince."

Purple Rain ended abruptly, and he sat up, giving her all his attention. Quentin was chilling, sipping and reflecting on how cool today was. His parents loved Yara and wanted to meet the girls on their next outing, and he was happy. Now, Yara was before him with some shit.

"I'm listening," he told her once he saw that she wasn't prepared to talk.

She looked down and then up, giving him teary eyes. "I can't have no more kids. My tubes are gone, and I don't want no more kids, so if you want this perfect family, I'm not the woman you want," she laid it all out. His face didn't reveal how he accepted her news, and that boggled her mind. "My son was kidnapped, and I got angry and had my tubes burned. Quentin, I didn't feel worthy anymore because I failed my son, and I punished myself by burning my tubes." Snot was running out of her nose. She was emotional as fuck right now.

He already knew about her son being kidnapped, and he also knew that she didn't know that Kadeem had found her son, who was smuggled and left in an abandoned house. That was one secret that Kadeem would go to his grave with.

See, Quentin knew a lot of people who knew people, and when he did his research on Yara, he was sure to discover everything because he hated secrets and surprises.

He got up and ran his hands down her side. "We can break up, I know you want to," she told him, giving him the green light to move on.

"The good thing about this is, I never wanted kids, and your three daughters have individually fulfilled me. Yara, I take pride in the whole the step-daddy thing," he told her straight up.

He didn't think about being a father, he liked money. He wanted to work and would consider marriage sooner or later, but for the most part, he was good on that part.

"Are you just telling me that, Quentin?" She would hate for her to get comfortable with him and then he tells her that he wants kids and it's not working out.

"No, I'm dead ass." He hugged and kissed her. "You are the one, baby."

Chapter Twenty-Five

"You got everything you want, you got everything you need." –
Snoop Dogg

She wasn't interested in dating. Riq was the only guy she ever took seriously and gave her time to. And not just her time, but her energy, her attention, her body, her goals and her thoughts. All of her… was him. That relationship was more like a situationship, and it took her removing herself from the equation and going across the map to California to see that how he was treating her wasn't the best.

Meme was so thankful that she opened her eyes when she did. He did the bare minimum when it came to getting her and keeping her. After messing around with Riq, the price went up. She had new standards and refused to date anyone with children from now on. She didn't care if the baby mama lived in Timbuktu, she wasn't fooling with no more niggas with kids. It was the one thing she refused to compromise on.

Meme now knew that when you raised your standards, men either had to meet them or keep it moving. Never in a million years did she think she would be at Nobu with rookie player, Dresden Green. Not only was he a southern man, but he was fine as hell and the perfect gentlemen. They met a few weeks ago on set during a photo shoot for the popular skateboard apparel line, Supreme, and Meme was one of the hairstylists.

Dresden couldn't stop staring at her, and she wasn't paying him any mind until he walked right up to her and asked for her number. He was polite and called her during respectable hours. This was their first official date since he was always on the road with the Los Angeles Lakers. His first night back in the city, and he wanted to spend in with her.

Meme was nervous as hell but quickly warmed up and relaxed because he was the same person she texted and talked to throughout the day. The only difference was now they were in each other's presence.

Dresden didn't shy away from liking her, he was upfront that he didn't want to play around with her feelings. He was interested in her and told her that he wasn't like these other niggas in the league. She didn't tell him that she had heard it all before, but rather allow his actions to speak louder than his words.

"You look beautiful, Amina, did I tell you that already?"

He wasn't cheesy with his compliments either. Everything about him was smooth and laid back. Her body flushed with heat as he openly admired her. She had on a wavy wig, and he told her that his mom and sisters all wore wigs and as long as she had some hair when she took it off at night, then he was good. She reassured him with a selfie of her natural hair, which was mid-length to her shoulders. She admitted to him that that weave gave her an extra boost of confidence, and he swore that she was fine without it. Meme wasn't hearing that though, she loved her wigs.

"Thank you, this food is so good," she told him, taking his attention off her.

He knew what she was doing and wasn't tripping. He loved how modest and humble she was and prayed it wasn't an act. So many chicks played the radio to get his attention, and he was done with the frauds. Dresden wanted something real.

Her phone vibrated rapidly in her clutch, and she wasn't one of those chicks that sat on their phone during an entire date.

He told her, "Answer that, it may be an emergency."

She gave him an apologetic smile and pulled her phone out. It was her best friend from back home, and she had called three times.

Meme returned the call. "Yeah, wasup?"

Her friend hollered into the phone, "Girl, it was a big ass shoot-out on the block, Riq got arrested."

Meme could hear sirens and such in the background. However, they were done, so what did that have to do with her? She still was trying to come up with a nice way to tell her crew that she didn't live in New York anymore and didn't care about the happenings of the hood. Meme was on to better things. And it wasn't that she thought she was better than anyone, she had just moved on with her life.

"Oh, okay, prayers up," was all she could think to say. Riq knew the life he was living, and she was seriously over him.

"Damn girl, you must really don't care about him no more?" her friend asked.

Meme had to get back to her date. "I'll hit you tomorrow," She told her and ended the call. Thankfully, her friend could barely hear her so she hung the phone up and slid it back into her clutch. "Where were we?" she asked him, batting her long mink eyelashes.

He loved her lips, they were her greatest asset other than her hustle and cool ass personality. "Grabbing the check so we can go kick it before it gets too late."

That sounded like a plan to her. She was from the hood, and Nobu was nice or whatever, but it was too pompous for her. Meme wanted to hear some music and eat chicken wings. She smiled at him. "Yes, let's do that, Mr. Green."

Life was good. Actually, it was great. This time last year, doing hair and being outside of her zip code wasn't even a thought. It was crazy how things could change so fast.

η

"Baby, are you sleep over there?" Yara tossed a pillow in Quentin's direction. She was tired as hell, so she knew he had to be as well. They landed back in town and got straight to work. There was so much to do, and she was running on empty.

He wasn't asleep. The paperwork his lawyers sent were all over the place, and he was searching for the bottom line.

"Nah, I'm up. So how you feel about us doing this liquor?" he asked her. Jay-Z had Dusse, Puff had Ciroc, Jeezy was pushing

Avion and Rick Ross had Bellaire Rose... Quentin Brooks needed a liquor.

Her man was so ambitious, and she loved it, but they needed to lay a solid foundation, one business at a time.

"It's a dope idea for later."

He shook his head and stood up from the couch, stretching with every step he took. She couldn't help but to look at his dick jumping in his basketball shorts. If her body weren't still recovering from the beating he put on her pussy this morning, she would have taken him down.

"Nah, when we launch we can drop it all; label, apparel, liquor, everything baby. Real *big*." He used his hands to add emphasis to his statement.

"Or, we can focus on one thing at a time so that all of it won't crumble because we didn't plan properly," she responded. She wasn't into wasting money, and Quentin had so many ideas she wanted them to be actual profit projects, not just doing everything they saw everyone else doing.

He turned around and went to her, bending down so they could be eye level.

She was sleepy, he didn't see it in her face or hear it in her voice until now. "Do you trust me?"

He already knew the answer to his question, she was starting to think he got something out of hearing her say that she trusted him and loved him.

She rolled her eyes. "Come on now, Quentin. You know I do," she whined and yawned at the same time.

"If you trust me, you know that all these plans are beneficial to us." He had the biggest smile on his face.

"Do you sleep?" she asked him because she always fell asleep first and when she woke up, he would either be gone or downstairs on the phone.

"Yeah, here and there," he said it so casually.

Yara wanted to know what the hell did that mean. "Every day? For at least eight hours?"

He laughed at her, "Hell nah, girl. Come on, all that sleep is unhealthy." She was tripping, he could never sleep that long. His back would probably start hurting if he stayed in bed for eight hours. "Let me show you something," he said and pulled her up from the couch.

She kissed his lips. "I want you to come lay with me." She was serious. He would eventually crash if he kept it up.

"Yara, I haven't slept that long since I was locked up. I'm good, baby. I promise," he shushed her worries and concern and took her hands, leading her through his penthouse into one of the rooms he had turned into his office.

She stayed by the entryway and watched him walk behind his brown oak desk. He pulled the first drawer, closed it and then opened the second one. When he returned in front of her, he had a black journal in his hand with the word, *Vision* on it. "Second page, turn to it," he instructed. It was his goals.

Yara looked at him and said, "I need to do this."

"I got us covered until you do." His grind was for her. She was his motivation, his inspiration and his aspiration. Yara made him the happiest man in the world.

"The stuff we doing, the shit we working on… is it on the list?"

She scanned the list and then nodded her head. "Yes."

"You feel me? So, baby, all of this was already written down and prayed over, but now is the time. We gotta manifest our dreams."

She pursed her lips together and then asked him, "What if my only dream was to be free?" Yara enjoyed life with him, but his ambition was unmatched. She wanted to keep up with him. She was happy with her life and what they had. Quentin seemed to never be satisfied, so she supposed that was a good thing.

He smiled at his sunshine. "We got new dreams now, baby." He kissed her forehead and then he had to take the call that was now coming through on one of his many iPhones.

Yara watched him walk away with the phone to his ear. She went back to the living room and grabbed her phone and went to his bedroom. Quentin could stay up all day and night but she couldn't. Yara was human, and she needed sleep.

As soon as she dozed off and got comfortable, her phone rang. "Ughhhh!" she groaned. Who in the hell was calling her? She was sleepy as shit. She saw Kadeem's number flash on her phone.

The only reason she had his number saved was because Yanise was at their house a lot.

"Yeah?" She wouldn't jump to the conclusion of thinking that something was wrong with her baby.

"Hey, you was sleep?" he asked after hearing how groggy she sounded.

She said, "As if you care. Is Yanise okay?" she got straight to the point.

"Yeah, why you ask me that?"

She sat up in the bed. "Kadeem, if our daughter is okay then what do you want?" Was he drunk?

"Do you really not miss me? Are you over me for real, Yara?" he asked her. His tone was low, so she knew his ass was sneaking on the phone.

She wasn't doing this with him. "Goodnight," she told him.

She was about to hang up and then he begged her, "Was I a bad husband, Yara?" He had been in his feelings so much lately and contemplating everything.

"No." And that was the truth. He really wasn't. Kadeem had his flaws, issues, demons and things he needed to work on, but she had loved him unconditionally. And then he betrayed her. Now she hated his ass.

"Yara, I fucked up, I really, really fucked up." There was so much agony in his voice.

She closed her eyes. "I'm good." She didn't need this from him. He had ample time to have this talk with her.

"No, not you."

Why did she really think he was referring to her when he spoke of his mistakes. "Of course not."

"Are you happy?"

She was on top of the world. "Very."

"He seem like a cool dude, don't tell him I said that shit though."

Yara knew that Quentin couldn't care less what Kadeem thought of him.

"Kadeem, what do you want?" It was late, why was she even on his mind right now? He damn sure wasn't on hers.

"Missed you, missed your voice," he admitted.

She heard the regret in his voice, it was covered in pain. "Well, you know sometimes we make irrational decisions and then be looking stupid in the end." She wasn't protecting his feelings or pacifying him. Shit, nobody did that for her.

"Yeah, I know, right?" he snickered.

Quentin's voice was getting closer to the room. "Kiss my baby for me, I have to go." She was trying to end the conversation on a good note versus hanging up in his face.

Kadeem sighed loudly into the phone, "Okay, I know you got a life and a man and shit." Never did he think she would be happy without him.

"Yeah, I do, and you do too. You'll be married soon," she reminded him, since he seemed as if he forgot.

"She wanted to get married on Aiden's birthday," he confided in her.

Yara's heart stopped beating. That date held so much significance to her and him. "Really? Did you change it?" She prayed that he did, if he had a heart he would have.

"Hell fucking yeah. Come on now man, don't try me." He was offended.

Kadeem wasn't a monster, he loved his son and was so happy the day he was born.

"I'm sure she'll understand."

Kadeem didn't go into detail with Kamala about the date, she wouldn't understand and would have way too many fucking questions. It was the lawyer in her, she couldn't help herself.

"Yeah, hopefully." He didn't correct her and let her assume that Kamala already knew.

Quentin was calling for her, not knowing that she went into the room to sleep. "I gotta go," she told her ex-husband and hung up in his face.

When he entered the room, she was like a deer in headlights. "You good?" he asked her.

She was going to tell him yes and leave it at that but didn't want to start keeping anything from him. "Kadeem called me."

Quentin was shocked. "For real? What that nigga want?" He came to bed.

He knew he made his women happy, and when you were confident in yourself and your relationship, no one else mattered, not even her raggedy ass ex-husband.

"Nothing really, saying he missed me and a bunch of other pointless crap."

He crawled to her side of the bed and laid his head in her lap. "They never miss what they had until it's gone, he seeing that shit now."

She massaged her scalp. "Something sounds wrong with him."

Kadeem hadn't changed too much in the past ten years, so she knew when he had done something he wasn't supposed to. His voice was full of guilt and sadness. She didn't probe because she honestly didn't care.

Quentin yawned, "That nigga all right. He probably regretting what he did, but it's too late now, playboy." Yara wasn't going no damn where. He had his shit on lock. Every day he was putting a new fresh smile on her face. That's what you did when you appreciated what you had and never wanted to lose it.

On the other side of the city, after Yara hung up in his face, Kamala walked into the den, scaring the fuck out of him.

"Girl," he panicked, holding his heart. She couldn't be rolling up on him like that. He was already paranoid as hell.

"You miss her? And don't lie to me." She was enraged right now.

"What did you hear?" he wanted to know. Kamala's chest was heaving up and down, and she was two seconds from knocking him out. He sighed, he had no privacy anymore. She was on his ass like white on rice.

"What was I supposed to hear, Kadeem? Fuck is wrong with you?" She didn't even know him anymore.

He wasn't listening to shit she was saying. "Why aren't you sleeping?" he asked a question of his own.

Kamala had on one of his t-shirts and her hair tied up. If he didn't have so much on his mind and if she wasn't pissed, then he would slide right between her legs. They barely had sex these days and on the real, it had been the last thing on his mind.

She walked up on him with her fists balled up, ready to knock his ass out. "Our wedding is-"

There she goes again reminding him of this stupid ass wedding. "Kamala, I know, okay. I know when we're getting married. Stop fucking reminding me!" He was exhausted mentally more than anything.

"What is going on with you?" she asked him, desperately wanting to know.

He ran his hands down his face and exhaled loudly. "Why do you keep asking me that?"

Kamala shook her head, she was two seconds from calling the wedding off. She pointed her finger in his direction. "I'm going to ask you this one more time, Kadeem, one last fucking time."

He shrugged his shoulders. "I'm listening, baby." All he wanted was for her to take her ass back to sleep. And then he also wondered again what all she heard from his conversation with Yara.

"Are you one hundred percent sure that you want to marry me?" It was a simple question, and all she needed was a yes or a no. That was it. She refused to marry him and it be one-sided. Kamala didn't believe in divorce, she only wanted to marry once.

"Yes, baby, yes I do."

She looked him up and down and stared at him for a long time before she sighed, "Okay, I won't ask you again."

"You don't have to," he assured her.

When she left him alone, he couldn't believe he didn't tell her then and there.
Kadeem had been living a lie for so long, it wasn't even hard to keep the facade up, and that wasn't a good thing.

When she got upstairs, she held her heart as tears came down her face. He wasn't the same man she fell in love with, and she really didn't know if he was worth marrying anymore. She fell asleep with a heavy heart and mind.

η

A few days had passed, and Kadeem was trying to act as normal as possible, but Kamala wasn't a dummy.

Yanise was back at their house for the weekend, and she asked Kamala, "You do these Girls' Night in every month, and they never bring nothing. That don't bother you?"

Kamala laughed, "Uh no, I'm the hostess, they don't have to bring anything."

"Yeah, but still, they never even offer. No wine, not a trash bag, a plate, nothing." She wasn't with that and to her, Kamala's friends were free loaders.

"It's not like that, baby, I promise. Do you want to help me set up?"

Yanise shook her head. "My show is about to come on." She helped her put the groceries up, and that was it.

Kamala didn't have much time to decorate the table, cook dinner, make dessert and get dressed along with doing her makeup. Tonight's Girls' Night in wouldn't be the fanciest. She made fish and chips with salad and for dessert, they had brownies and tons of wine. The way she had been feeling lately, all she really wanted was the wine, to be honest. She hummed, "Ambitious Girl" by Wale under her breath as she got dressed.

"Kamala, your sister here," Yanise yelled up the steps.

She had just got out of the shower and only had a towel on as she lotioned up, brushed her teeth and did her makeup. However, it was her baby sister, she had seen her naked a million times.

"Millie, come up here," she hollered back.

When her sister appeared in her room, she complimented her, "You look so cute, damn I need to put some real clothes on," she said and rolled her eyes. Millie noticed the frumpy purple jumpsuit on the chaise in front of the bed. "Well, I hope you're not wearing that Miss Celie outfit." She turned her nose up.

Kamala was tired as shit. "Girl, I'm not in the mood tonight. The only reason I didn't cancel was because I didn't want to hear everybody mouth," she admitted.

"What's wrong?"

She sighed. Kamala didn't plan on telling anyone her good news, but this was her sister for goodness sake, her secret was safe with her.

"I'm up for partner."

This was what she worked hard for, so her sister didn't understand why she wasn't jumping up and down and crying tears of joy. And secondly, why was she just now hearing about it?

"And you're not happy becauseeee?" She was trying to figure things out.

She shrugged her shoulders. "I don't know, I want to be happy. But partner right now? I'm about to get married, and I'm ready to start having kids. Like, as soon as possible." She and Millie had always been different. She wanted love, of course. Who didn't? However, Kamile was chasing after success right now.

They were both still so young, Kamile didn't see why was she rushing. "And you can't have all of it?" she asked her.

Kamala wasn't sure. "I don't know, I feel like I have to choose." And she really didn't.

Her sister wanted to know, "Do you really want to get married?" In her opinion, Kamala wasn't on cloud nine anymore, and it had been more bad news and complaints than good news and smiles when it came to Kadeem and their upcoming wedding.

"Yes, I do. Why would you ask me that?" She didn't know what she wanted right now. Kamala worked hard as hell, and it was about time she was recognized, and she rightfully deserved to become partner.

"Just asking, sis. I think someone is pulling up. I'll make drinks until you get dressed." She hugged her and left the bedroom.

Kamala took a deep breath and plopped down on the edge of the bed. She had so much on her mind it was ridiculous. Twenty minutes later, she had pulled it together and when she emerged into her dining room, Kamile was in a deep conversation and stopped talking as soon as she saw her sister.

"Hey, friend," April greeted her first.

Kamala knew they were talking about her and rolled her eyes as hard as she could. "Let me get some wine before y'all piss me off." She knew her friends all too well and could smell the intervention in the air.

"Oh, bitch, we ain't even about to do all of that," Denise giggled, knowing that she could sometimes push her sweet friend there.

Sue, her other friend, kept it real with her. "And, honey, if you didn't feel like cooking we could have ordered Ruth Chris to go, cus don't nobody eat no damn fish and chips." They all laughed. No one had touched the food, only the wine.

Kamala told her, "First of all, I had a busy week. You want a sandwich?" She had options.

Sue shook her head. "I have plans after this anyway."

April hugged her from the side as Kamala took a seat next to her. "How are you?"

Kamala shot her sister a "What the fuck girl" look. Her sister couldn't keep her mouth shut for shit.

"Sooooo, boo, we need to talk. First, congrats on partner, they better had offered you a nice package. Second, let's talk about how you gon' get your refund on this wedding."

"The one time I invite you, this what happens," she said to her sister. She wasn't a sensitive person, but right now she felt ganged up on. They all had sympathetic eyes on her, and she was uncomfortable.

"Don't fuss at her. We are your friends, we love you. We gon' get through this with you," Denise said.

"Get through what? What am I getting through?" Yes, she was frustrated, and things hadn't been peaches and cream with her and Kadeem, but she still wasn't ready to throw the towel in.

"Okay, let me ask you this. In five years, where do you think y'all will be? I mean let's be real, Kamala, is he even making any money?" Sue's gold digging ass asked her.

"Yes, and why is that your business?" That was a good question because he hadn't pitched in much for the wedding. The bills were paid, but other than that, she hadn't received any gifts or shit from him lately. Was she missing any signs?

"I don't like him," April finally admitted.

Millie scratched her neck. "Uhhhh, me neither."

Kamala was shocked to hear her say that. "You are so full of shit, you love him!" She needed her sister to be on her side.

"I used to, he's weird as fuck now. I know you've noticed the change if I have and hell, I don't even live here."

"And, Kamala, you're about to become partner. Like, he's a felon."

She knew of his past before deciding to be with him, so they didn't need to do all that. Kamala held her hand up. "Okay, this is enough." She was done with this conversation. "Whatever decision I make needs to be because I want to. I don't like this feeling." They were attacking her. Everyone sipped their wine in silence while she was in deep thought.

"What do I tell people?" she croaked a little while later.

"Are you calling off the wedding?" Millie asked her, hoping so.

She shook her head and then moved it up and down. "Listen, I don't know, I don't know." She pushed her chair back and stood up, pacing the floor. "I love him, I really do." She was telling herself that more than them.

April rolled her eyes. "Chile, please."

Kamala needed space. "Can y'all go home? I will call in a few days… please?"

She couldn't think straight with all of them ogling her and adding their unwarranted two cents. It was too much for her.

They left, leaving the food where it was. Kamile stood at the door, not leaving as quickly as the others.

"You're my heart, I only want the best for you," she told her, praying that deep down she followed her first mind and trusted her gut with this decision.

"I know, sis, I know," she said and hugged her for a long time.

After she closed the door behind her, she slid down to the floor and said a prayer, *"God give me the strength to do this and the peace to accept what's to come."*
She didn't want to be miserable and unfocused because of this breakup. Kadeem had been a pivotal point in her life, had played a major role. From the beginning, she constantly asked him what he wanted with her and where he stood with Yara. She never wanted to be anyone's rebound or second in command, and he reassured her of that, until Yara was released. Their first date was so cute and intimate, and she was head over heels. Kamala was smitten with him, and everything about him turned her on.

"You know I have to address the elephant in the room," the words slowly left her mouth as they took a nice, quiet romantic walk through Central Park.

Kadeem had wined and dined her, and she was full. The night was beautiful, not to mention that every time he flashed his million-dollar smile at her a dollop of lust dropped in the centerfold of her panties.

He took a deep breath dropping his head back, already knowing where she was going. "Well, technically, we're in the middle of the park-"

She loved his sense of humor. "Stop it, Kadeem. No seriously... I have to ask." She stopped walking and faced him.

In law school, she was taught to study the faces of whoever was on the stand, and be able to identify any signs of a lie, confusion, nervousness, hesitation or a second thought. So, after years of experience, she believed she had mastered the art of knowing if someone was truthful. But little did Kamala know, she wasn't prepared to stand before Kadeem Moreland. He used to lie, steal and rob mother fuckers for a living.

"What's the deal with you and Yara? Are you holding her down?" she really wanted to know.

"Yo, baby, to be honest, me and her wasn't doing good before we got knocked, ya feel me? So, I mean, she's still my wife and the mother of my kids, but when she get out shit is a wrap," he lied through his teeth.

If Kamala were to go visit Yara today, she would tell him otherwise. Yeah, they weren't perfect, what couple was? And they also did business together, so keep that in mind. Sometimes the line crossed, and she would have to remind him that she was his wife first. The money didn't come before their love. Kadeem often forgot that.

"What happened to y'all?" she asked, because she had worked heavily on their case, and Yara was madly in love, head *over heels and sprung off Mr. Moreland. She pitied her for quite some time.*

Kadeem was done with the conversation. He had answered her question, and that would be that. He didn't want to spend the rest of the night discussing Yara and then have to go home and be up all night because she was on his mind and shit. He knew that he had fucked up tremendously by leaving her in there and not telling her. He also knew that being out crushing on a new shorty was the wrong thing to do, but for some reason, he always liked dancing on the wild side...

And no matter how much fun they had together, she was always asking about Yara and what would he do when she came home and did he really love her. Now, all she could think about was would he leave her if shit got rough or tough? How far did his loyalty go?

So, Kamala had to choose herself this time. She was in a position to make more money and to excel in her career. And truthfully, she was stressed out now, and they were only engaged. A marriage wouldn't make things any better. If she wasn't happy now, then certainly an "I do" and the change of her last name wouldn't make things turn around overnight. She was no longer in denial.

Kamala called her sister, "Hey, how far away are you?"

"Leaving out of the subdivision, what's wrong?"

She ran up the steps to grab her keys and was out of breath. "Nothing, come help me pack my stuff up before he gets home."

Kadeem was drunk. Kadeem was high. He was out of his mind, and it was nothing but God's sweet mercy and grace, oh, and the angels he had encamped around him, ensuring that he made it home safe.

When he walked into the kitchen, the first thing he did was turn the light on and remove his shirt and shoes. He needed water to sober up before he made it upstairs. It was about three in the morning, and he didn't even notice that Kamala's car wasn't there. He gulped a bottle of water down and belched loudly, unaware that he was loud as fuck and had woke his daughter up.

"Are you drunk?" Yanise asked him with a scowl on her face.

If she didn't look like her damn mama…. "What you doing up, baby girl?" his words slurred. Kadeem leaned against the counter top and took a deep breath. He was drunk as hell.

"Uh, you in here making a mess." She picked up the paper towels and mail that he knocked over.

"Where Kamala at? Baby! Wake that ass up!" he belted out. He wanted to kiss all over her and fuck until he crashed out.

She looked at him. "She didn't call you?" *Ooh, shit was about to get messy*, she thought to herself.

He looked at his daughter like she was crazy. "Call me for what?" She was always busy at work, so other than a few text messages they sent throughout the day, they normally talked at home. And yeah, he got here a lil' late… after hours. So, she probably was pissed at him.

Yanise picked up the ring and tried to hand it to her daddy. "She left, she told me she was going to call you." Why did she have to be the one to deliver the bad news? Her father looked horrified.

"What you mean she left? Did her uncle get sick?" he questioned as he paced the floor.

"Nah, she left. Like, she left you. The wedding is off."

He didn't believe that shit. "She probably got cold feet, I'm about to call her."

Yanise pursed her lips together. "Nah, Daddy… she packed her stuff up. Me and her sister helped her take it to the car."

His entire world came crashing down. How could she leave him? Kadeem turned to Yanise and asked, "Why?" He wanted to know why she left.

She shrugged her shoulders. "I don't know, Daddy. Do you think this is karma?"

Epilogue

"Talk to me different, let's come up together." - Wale

One Year Later…

Today was a very important day for Yara and Quentin, and she was wondering should she have pushed it back for the sake of her three children.

Kadeem was sentenced to forty years in prison a few days ago, and they weren't taking the news well.

However, she couldn't care less. She tried to care but really couldn't. The only thing she did to "support" him was pay for the lawyer. Quentin got him the best lawyer he could and still, they convicted him of murder. He didn't murder one person, but four.

The four players that raped Ayanna, their bodies were found floating in a river near the state line of California. When the girls told Yara what he said, her heart sort of went out to him but not really. He swore that he was so broken and hurt from seeing her struggle with being abused and taken advantage of, and he had to kill them.

Charlie packed up her place and moved to Florida right after the case. The girls promised to visit. And as far as Kamala, Yanise kept up with her on social media, and she was dating a well-known, prominent Judge. She moved on pretty fast, which made them question if she ever really loved their daddy.

Yara looked at Quentin and told him to give her two more minutes. Her makeup was flawless, and the black Oscar De La Renta custom-made dress she wore fit her frame perfectly.

She kneeled before her girls and made sure they all gave her eye contact. "I love y'all okay, and things happen for a reason. Your father is a grown man who has to pay for the crime that he committed," she told them.

Yanise wasn't as concerned as Ayanna was, she was downright blaming herself for her dad being in prison.

η

Lord Jesus, there was so much more she could say, so much more she wanted to say, but her visit with Kadeem was between, her, him, her therapist and the man above.

She had no intentions of visiting him, and in all honesty, she prayed he rotted in hell for the shit he took her through. However, her therapist suggested that she see him and bare her soul, for once and for all.

Yara made sure she looked thicker than a snicker. Her outfit was so fresh, she turned every head in the waiting room, and the perfume she wore tickled the nose of every person she walked past. It took all kinds of strings to be pulled for the visit to happen because she was a felon, and by no means were felons to visit jails. However, her therapist seemed to know people... who knew people.

Kadeem expected the conversation to go one way, but it went in a totally different direction.

"How did you sleep on your first night?" was the first thing she asked him.

He looked at her with confusion etched across his forehead. "Huh?"

She asked him again since he clearly didn't hear or understand her question. "Your first night, how did you sleep?" Kadeem didn't see a smile, a smirk or a look of humor on her face. She wasn't laughing at all.

He shrugged his shoulders. "Good, I guess. I was tired, it's been so long since I slept, to be honest," he told her.

"Oh, you actually closed your eyes and rested?" How could he?

Yara's first night, she pissed her pants and boo-booed on herself. She was frightened at the thought of having to spend the next ten years of her life in a cell.

"Yeah, I told you I was tired as fuck, why did you ask me that?"

She placed her elbows on the metal table, still in disbelief that she was back in jail. Kadeem had to be a fucking idiot to return to jail. She understood his reasoning, but there was nothing or no one she would go back to prison for. It was real behind those gray walls. She didn't wish that kind of solitude on anyone. Your mental health is extremely affected when you are forced to be behind bars. And yeah, she got it. *Do the crime pay the time,* but fuck that, jail was hard!

"Your daughters are hurting." She wanted him to know that she was the one wiping their tears and telling them that everything was happening for a reason, and that their daddy would be okay. Kadeem wasn't a punk, he would be okay. His eyes were weary, he was drained. She could see it clearly.

"I know, man, I know. My head was fucked up." He shook the thoughts off.

"Do you regret it?"

He told her, "Hell the fuck nah."

The parents of the boys who raped her daughter didn't miss a trial date, and from what the girls told her, they were hurting, but what about her daughter? Ayanna was abused. She was horrified, had nightmares for weeks, only God and therapy kept her mind.

"Kadeem, I'm not happy that you're here but it... I can't even explain it." She had this idea in her head that she would walk in here looking like the baddest bitch there was to remind him of his fuck ups and his mistakes, but when she looked into his eyes, she didn't see a demon staring back at her. She saw a man who truly regretted everything he had done.

And so, all she said to him was, "I'll make sure the girls make you proud, Kadeem." That was it.

She grabbed her purse to prepare her exit, and he reached out to touch her hand. "You were the best thing that ever happened to me." He wanted her to know that.

"Is she the reason? Like for real, is she the reason you did what you did? Why you left me in there to rot?" she asked him, with her tilted to the side, trying not to cry.

Kadeem knew she wouldn't believe him. "Yara, we met after I got out, that's on my son."

And she closed her eyes, blinking back tears. "I wish I believed you." She stood up. "Take care, Kadeem."

η

Meme complimented her mama, "You look so good, girl."

Yara winked her eye. "Thank you." She really had to hit the red carpet but didn't want to seem insensitive. "I'm going to handle this lil business, and then I'm coming right back," she promised.

Yanise stood up. "I'm going with you. I want TMZ to get my good side, we the black Kardashians."

Meme rolled her eyes. "Girl, no we are not, we are the Moreland's," she corrected her.

She was doing pretty good for herself these days, and her followers went from a few measly thousand to 2.5 million, and it was because of who her famous ass boyfriend was.

MTV and VH1 were constantly emailing her, they were interested in doing a reality show on her and Dresden's relationship, they were like the next Kobe and Vanessa minus the scandal. He was the best man ever, and Meme could have easily become a baller's girl but no, she stayed working. Not only did she open one salon in Los Angeles, but two, and was thinking about putting a salon on the same block she grew up on. Life had truly changed for her, and she was grateful.

"Moreland's ain't got Kardashian money, boo-boo," Meme reminded her.

Yara told her girls, "We on the way there." And that was the truth. She was making major moves, and no one could have ever told her that she would be a runaway, a wife and mother before twenty-two, go to jail for ten years and come home a convicted felon and then start her life over. She went from being an assistant, to an A & R turned songwriter and producer, and now she was the co-owner and Vice President of one of the largest independent labels, YQ Recordings.

And she was doing so much more. Yara had opened a group home in New York, and their liquor was scheduled to be in stores next Spring. Quentin was about to launch a music app and a film company... they were the real power couple.

Ayanna hugged her mom. "I'm proud of you, Mama." She was also seeing better days, recently pledging AKA and enjoying college. She asked her mom could she move off campus next year, and Yara told her, *hell no*. Ayanna needed to stay in her dorm where it was safe. She wasn't aware that Quentin had hired twenty-four-hour security to follow her around. She hadn't really talked to any boys, still fearful and lacking trust. Her therapist told her that it would take some time for her to feel comfortable around a guy, but it would happen.

Yara really wanted them to walk with her and Quentin down the red carpet. All her hard work was for her kids. Tonight wasn't just about her but them as well.

She made sure they were all prim and proper before meeting Quentin and the security at the elevator.

"Ready?" He wanted to make sure.

She nodded her head. As soon as they got off the elevator, they were escorted into a black Escalade.

He checked the time on his watch for the billionth time. "We won't be here long, we have to catch the flight in less than three hours."

She wondered what was he more excited about; their trip to Jamaica to get married, or YQ Recordings being nominated for their first Grammy.

Quentin got out first and helped Yanise, Meme and Ayanna out before Yara.

He looked at her and smiled. "Damn, you look good." He couldn't wait to eat her up. This was their first public appearance as a couple, killing all the rumors and speculation of, were they together or not?

The girls looked like fierce models as they took the red carpet. Everyone wanted to talk to Meme to see if she would crack on if Dresden was leaving the Lakers. Other photographers wanted to know who her sisters were and if they were also dating someone in the league. It wasn't a secret that she was the daughter of Yara, big-time producer, but her sisters, they were gorgeous and the press was eating it up, taking tons of pictures, loving their melanin. None of her kids had plastic surgery, nor were their faces full of makeup. Meme wore a wig, but Yanise and Ayanna were all-natural with their long hair cascading down their back.

Someone called Yara's name, a reporter, and she looked to Quentin to see what should she do.

He nodded his head. "Do your thing, ma. It's your time."

The End

Giselle Braxton and Kasim Moreland have their own love story, read Giselle: Crème De La Crème now!

If you enjoyed the story, please leave a **review**!

Authors love REVIEWS!

For more updates and sneak peeks into **upcoming** releases written by NAKO

Text NAKOEXPO to 22828

www.facebook.com/NAKO

Twitter: nakoexpo

Instagram: nakoexpo

NEWSLETTERS:

Single Ladies, will receive an email every Wednesday from NAKO.

Every Friday, The N List is delivered to your inbox with the top 5 things you should spend your weekend doing. Join today!

Join **NAKO'S READING GROUP** on Facebook…we're more than a reading group, join today and find out!

Join **NAKO'S READING GROUP** on Instagram…we're more than a reading group, join today and find out.

Join **SINGLEANDOK** on Facebook to unite with single women who are enjoying life and living it up to the fullest.

Text NAKOEXPO **to 22828** to join NAKO'S MAILING LIST and exclusive samples on **#samplesunday**

SUBSCRIBE TO NAKO'S YOUTUBE CHANNEL: NAKOEXPO

SUBSCRIBE TO THE PASSPORT PODCAST EPISODE II IS ON YARA!

BEHIND THE PEN IS A BTS LOOK INTO BOOKS WRITTEN BY NAKO!

ALSO, IF YOU'RE INTERESTED IN PURCHAING SIGNED PAPERBACKS AND APPAREL VISIT NAKOEXPOAPPAREL.COM

NAKOEXPO SUBSCRIPTION BOX!

Subscription Box will include:

Welcome Box:

Official NAKOEXPO shirt and pen

Bookmarks

Do Not Disturb I'm Reading Sign

Welcome Letter from NAKO

How does this work?

Every month you will receive a package from NAKO, a signed paperback of the month's release for the year of 2018.

To sign up email nakoexpo@gmail.com

If it's a book you don't want, you have the option to PASS. By passing on the booklet, you're able to shop at nakoexpoapparel.com for the valued amount, or GIFT the book to another reader or maybe a friend. Must notify info@nakoexpoapparel.com before box is shipped.

NAKOEXPO PRESENTS IS NOW ACCEPTING SUBMISSIONS. EMAIL NAKOEXPO@GMAIL.COM or publishing@nakoexpo.com. FOR MORE

INFORMATION, SEND THE FIRST THREE CHAPTERS OF YOUR MANUSCRIPT FOR CONSIDERATION.

Visit www.nakoexpo.com for **The Passport**, personal stamps written by women for women.

-

Nako's Catalog

The Connect's Wife 1-7

The Chanel Cavette Story

If We Ruled the World

Love in The Ghetto 1 & 2

The Connect 1 & 2

GIRL BOSS SERIES:

In Love With A Brooklyn Thug 1-3

GISELLE: Cr me De La Cr me (standalone)

The King and Queen of New York 1 & 2

Salvation: Saved By A Savage 1-3

COLLAB:

No Fairytales: The Love Story in collaboration with Jessica N. Watkins

The Underworld Series

Please Catch My Soul

Pointe of No Return

From His Rib

The Christ Family

Stranger In My Eyes

The Arraignment

Resentment

The Arraignment II

Redemption

Orange Moon

Before You Judge

The Arraignment III

The Sentencing

Made in the USA
Middletown, DE
03 November 2019